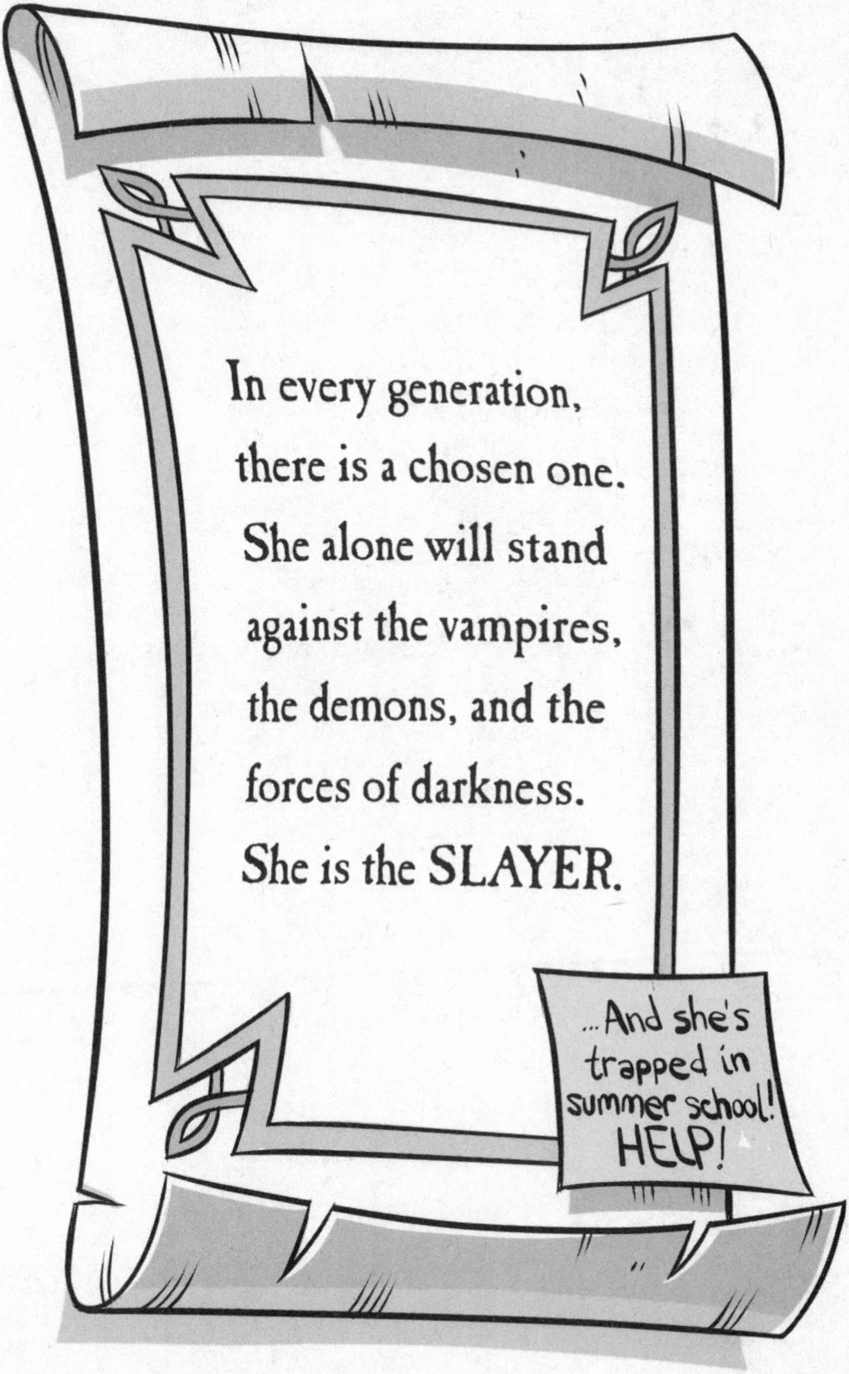
In every generation, there is a chosen one. She alone will stand against the vampires, the demons, and the forces of darkness. She is the SLAYER.
...And she's trapped in summer school! HELP!

Illustrations by Carolyn Nowak.

Cover design by Véronique L. Sweet & Christina Quintero.
Cover illustration by Carolyn Nowak.

Little, Brown and Company
Hachette Book Group
1290 Avenue of the Americas, New York, NY 10104
Visit us at LBYR.com

First Edition: September 2019

Little, Brown and Company is a division of Hachette Book Group, Inc. The Little, Brown name and logo are trademarks of Hachette Book Group, Inc.

The publisher is not responsible for websites (or their content) that are not owned by the publisher.

Library of Congress Control Number 2018962662

ISBNs: 978-0-316-48756-6 (paper over board), 978-0-316-48752-8 (ebook), 978-0-316-48754-2 (ebook), 978-0-316-48753-5 (ebook)

Printed in the United States of America

LSC-C

10 9 8 7 6 5 4 3 2 1

Buffy the Vampire Slayer

THE CURSED COVEN

Carolyn Nowak

LITTLE, BROWN AND COMPANY

New York Boston

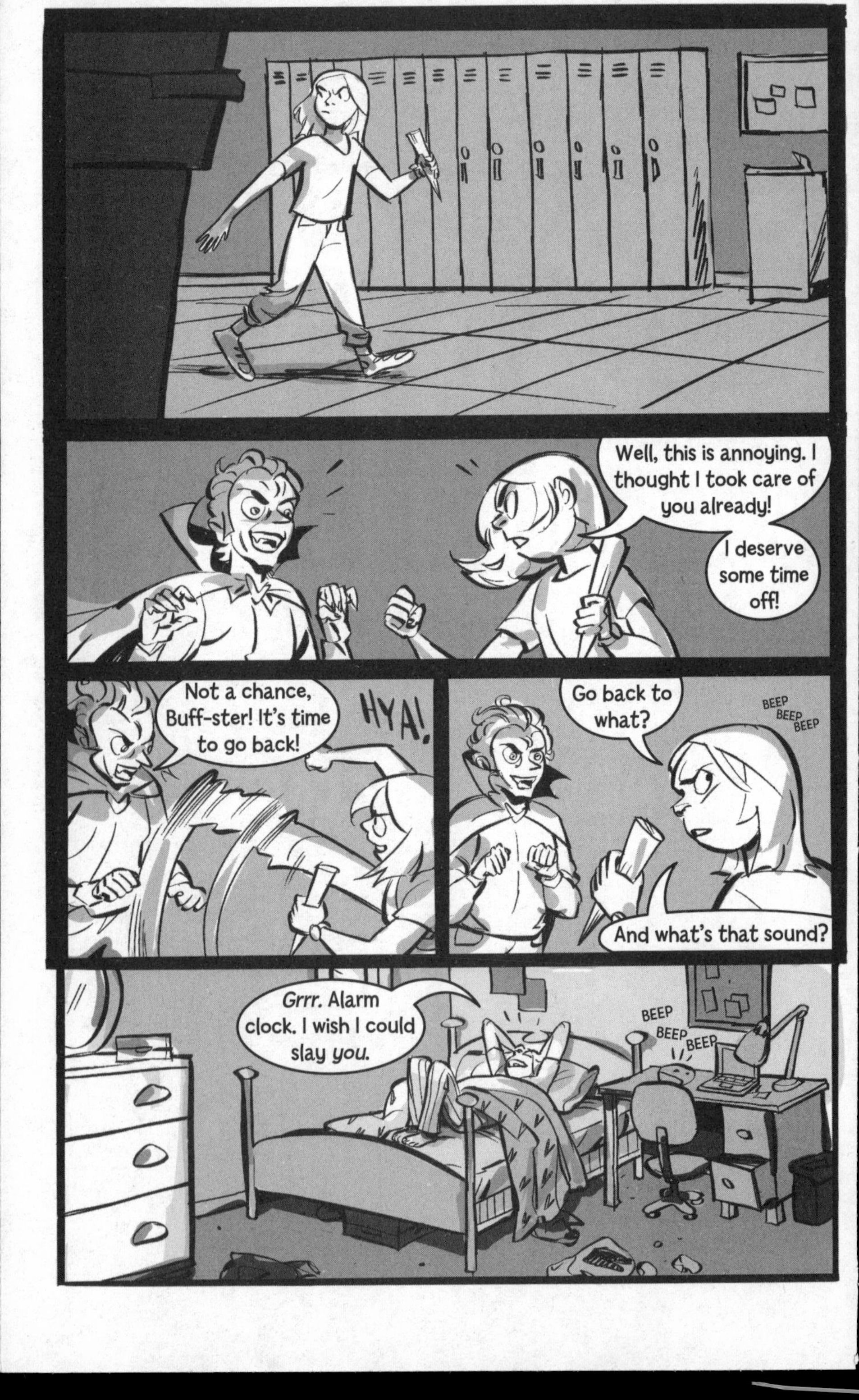

Well, this is annoying. I thought I took care of you already!
I deserve some time off!
Not a chance, Buff-ster! It's time to go back!
HYA!
Go back to what?
BEEP BEEP BEEP
And what's that sound?
Grrr. Alarm clock. I wish I could slay *you.*
BEEP BEEP BEEP

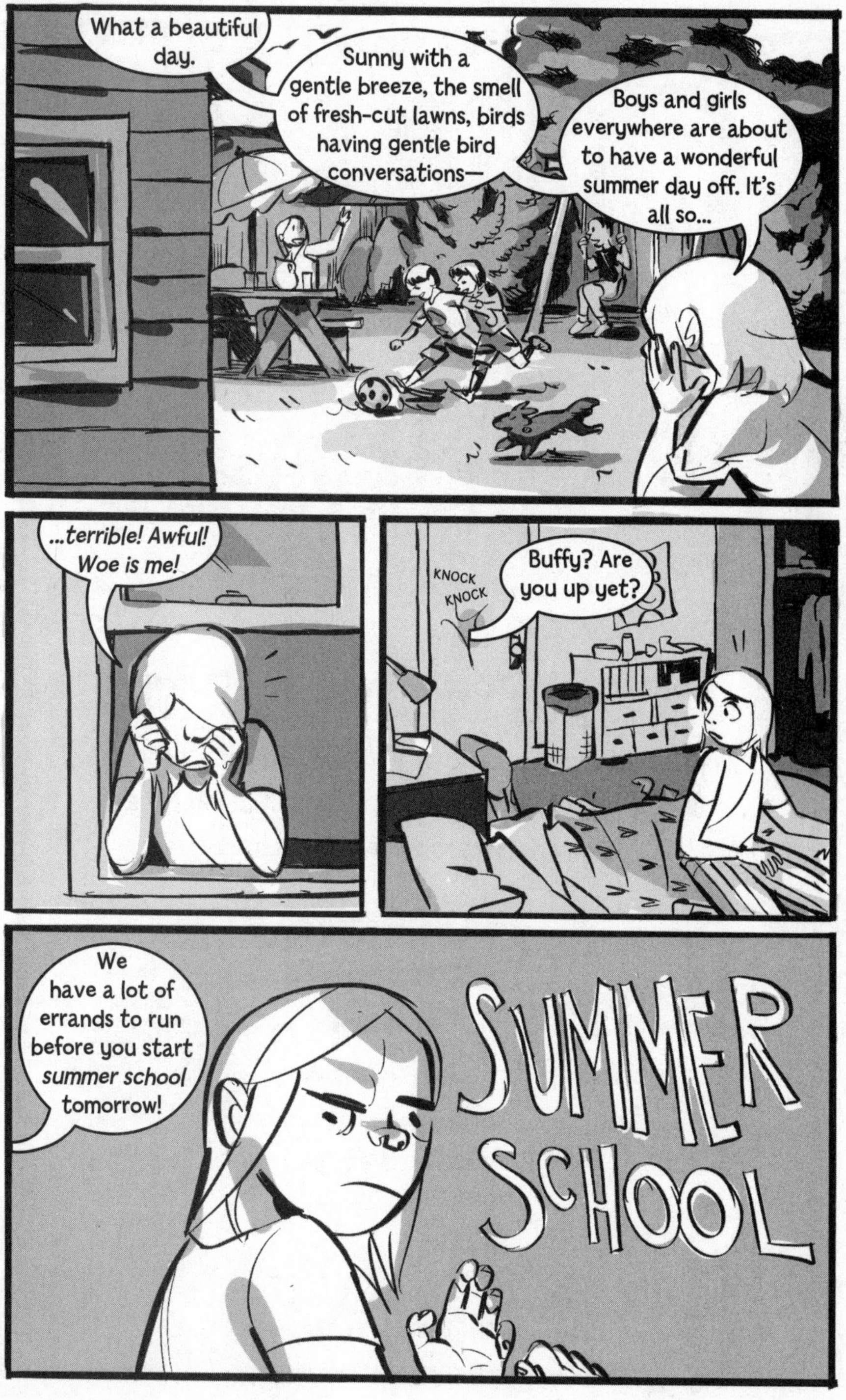
What a beautiful day.
Sunny with a gentle breeze, the smell of fresh-cut lawns, birds having gentle bird conversations—
Boys and girls everywhere are about to have a wonderful summer day off. It's all so...
...terrible! Awful! Woe is me!
KNOCK KNOCK
Buffy? Are you up yet?
We have a lot of errands to run before you start *summer school* tomorrow!
SUMMER SCHOOL

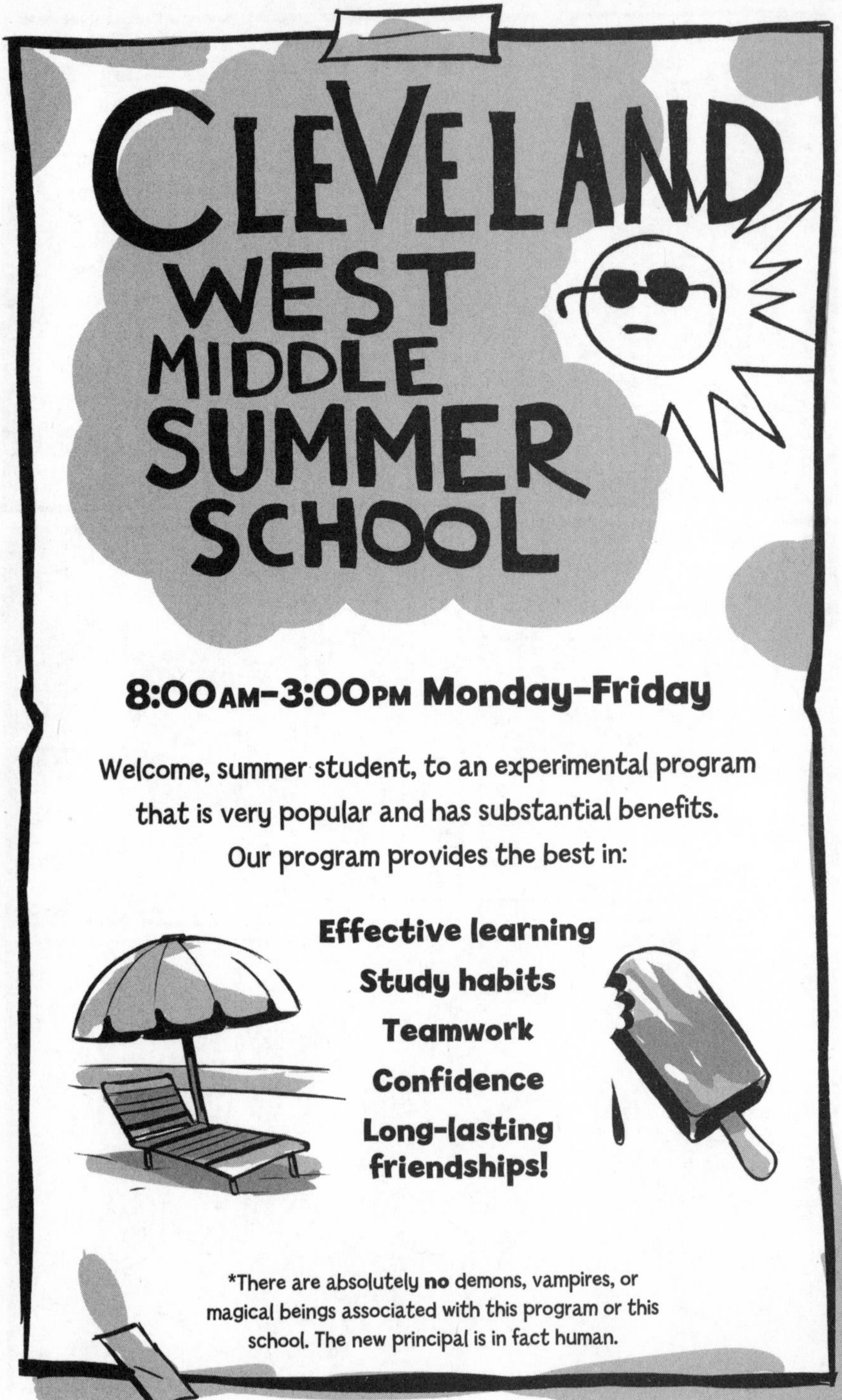

CLEVELAND WEST MIDDLE SUMMER SCHOOL
8:00AM–3:00PM Monday–Friday
Welcome, summer student, to an experimental program that is very popular and has substantial benefits. Our program provides the best in:
Effective learning
Study habits
Teamwork
Confidence
Long-lasting friendships!
*There are absolutely no demons, vampires, or magical beings associated with this program or this school. The new principal is in fact human.

Dear Diary,

Well, well, well! You're probably like, "Why is Buffy Summers writing in me during her summer vacation? Why isn't she throwing on her swimsuit and jumping through a sprinkler all day?" And you know what, Mr. or Mrs. (or Miss?) Diary, those are really good questions! Here's a better one: <u>WHY AM I GOING TO SCHOOL DURING SWEET, SWEET SUMMER?</u> I mean, my last name is Summers. I should be being all summery. Enjoying the sun and the ocean and the sand and—okay, so the only beach in Cleveland is on the edge of a kind of creepy lake, but you know what I mean.

I'll tell you why I'm in summer school:

<u>Reason numero uno:</u>

Cleveland is the site of a mystical Heckmouth, which equals lots of vampires. And I'm the <u>vampire Slayer.</u> That means it's my "destiny" (barf) to <u>slay vampires.</u>

Here's the problem: Vamps sleep during the day, so I gotta hunt those creepy creeps at night when they tiptoe around, looking for innocent folks to feed on. And that means I lost lots of sleep during the school year and had to make up for it with a few math-class-naps. And a few history-class-naps. Plus a couple of science-class-naps. Maybe an English-class-nap here and there. Okay, basically I slept in school all the time, which is why I kinda got a ton of bad grades. <u>But keeping this town safe is exhausting, and I shouldn't be punished for being a hero who, like, totally saved everybody!</u> (Right?)

<u>Reason number two:</u>

As the Slayer, I deal with all kinds of evil. But nothing quite as sinister as...(drumroll please) my mortal enemy, <u>MELANIE DUTCH</u>! My awful grades may have put me IN the doghouse with every teacher at school, but it was Mean Girl Melanie who KEPT me there all year. She made fun of me and got me in trouble, and even framed me for cheating! There's no way I'd be in summer school if it weren't for her plotting against me! At least Little Miss Perfect and Evil won't be in summer school. That'll be nice.

That's right....I'm a positive thinker. Hmm. What else good is happening in the life of me?

Well, Mom took me shopping. Sure, we got Buffy-torture-tools like pencils and paper and other school supplies, but I also got some cute new socks and a new backpack. Mom said the one I was using "smelled like an old pizzeria." Little does she know being a Slayer stinks—like, for real stinks!

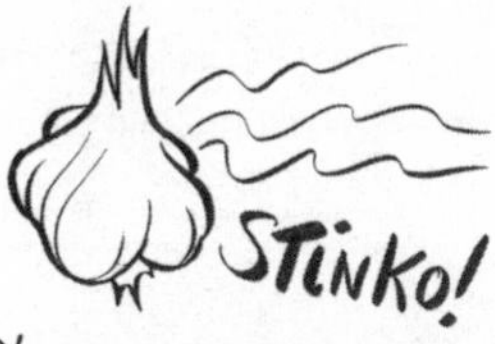
STINKO!

Buffy

Oh, and tonight I get to go on patrol for vamps with my best friends, Sarafina and Alvaro! My Watcher, Sparky, will be there, too. She said she has a surprise for me! Maybe she used some ancient librarian magic power to get my summer back?!

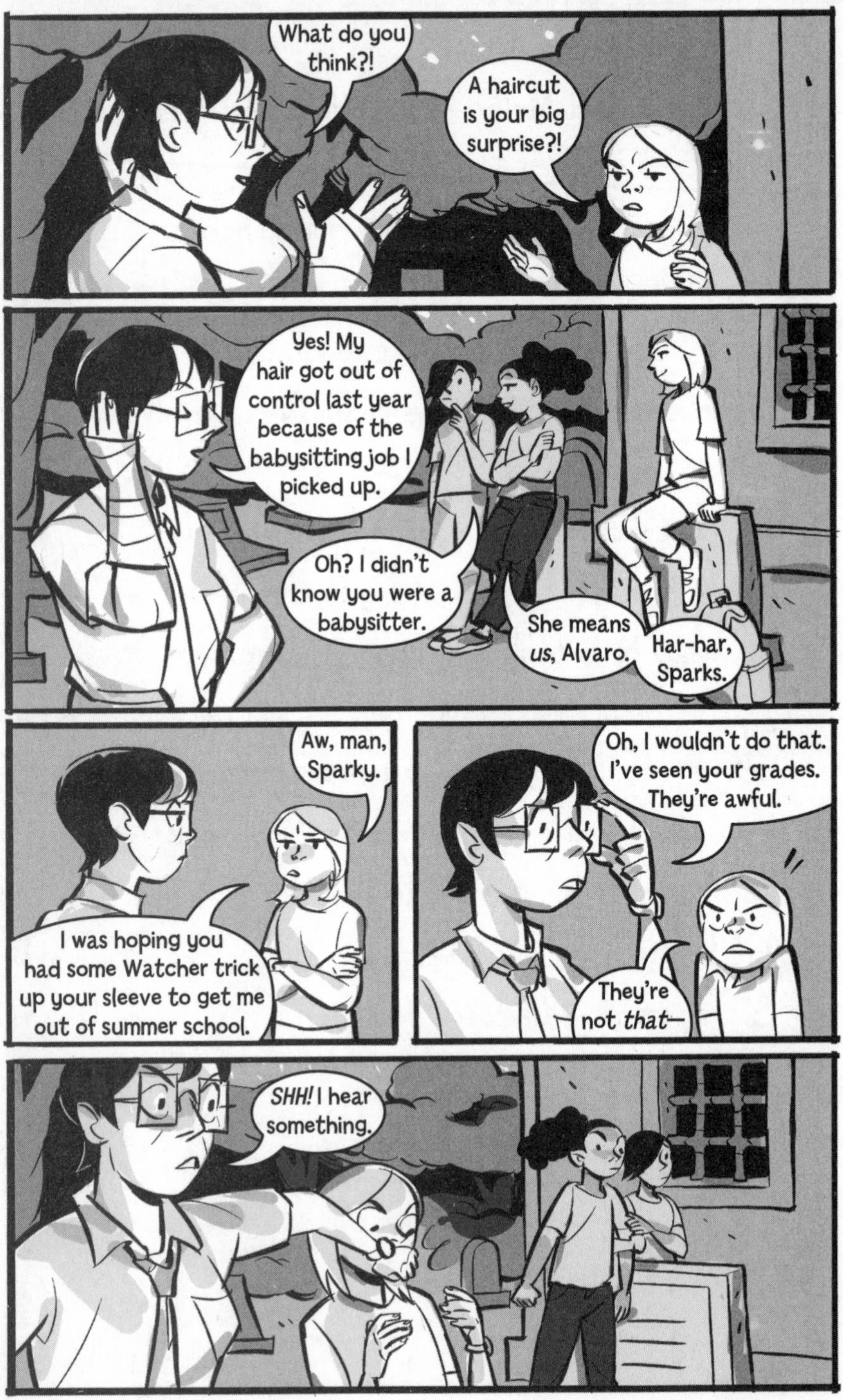
What do you think?!
A haircut is your big surprise?!
Yes! My hair got out of control last year because of the babysitting job I picked up.
Oh? I didn't know you were a babysitter.
She means *us*, Alvaro.
Har-har, Sparks.
Aw, man, Sparky.
I was hoping you had some Watcher trick up your sleeve to get me out of summer school.
Oh, I wouldn't do that. I've seen your grades. They're awful.
They're not *that*—
SHH! I hear something.

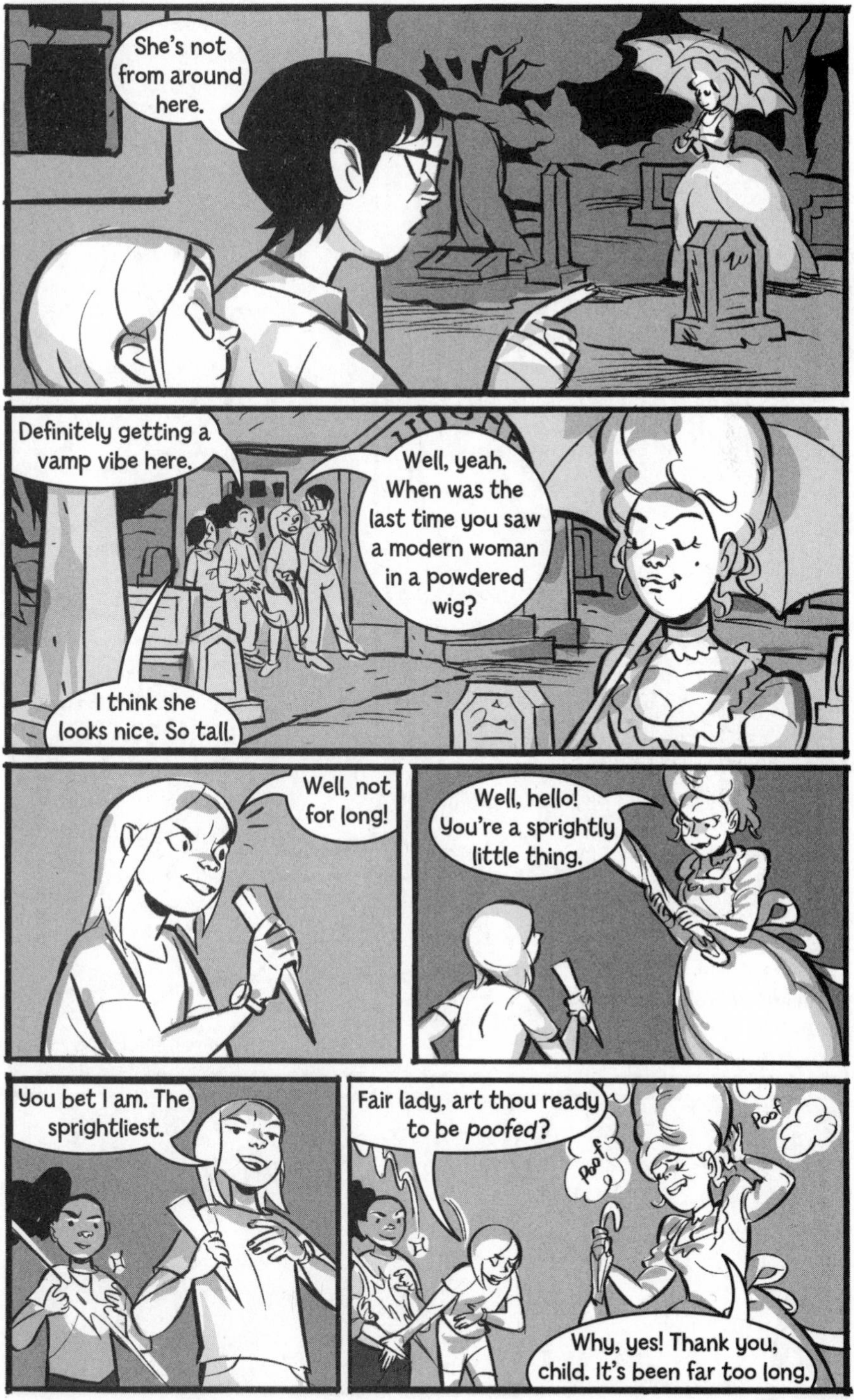

She's not from around here.
Definitely getting a vamp vibe here.
Well, yeah. When was the last time you saw a modern woman in a powdered wig?
I think she looks nice. So tall.
Well, not for long!
Well, hello! You're a sprightly little thing.
You bet I am. The sprightliest.
Fair lady, art thou ready to be *poofed*?
Poof
Poof
Why, yes! Thank you, child. It's been far too long.

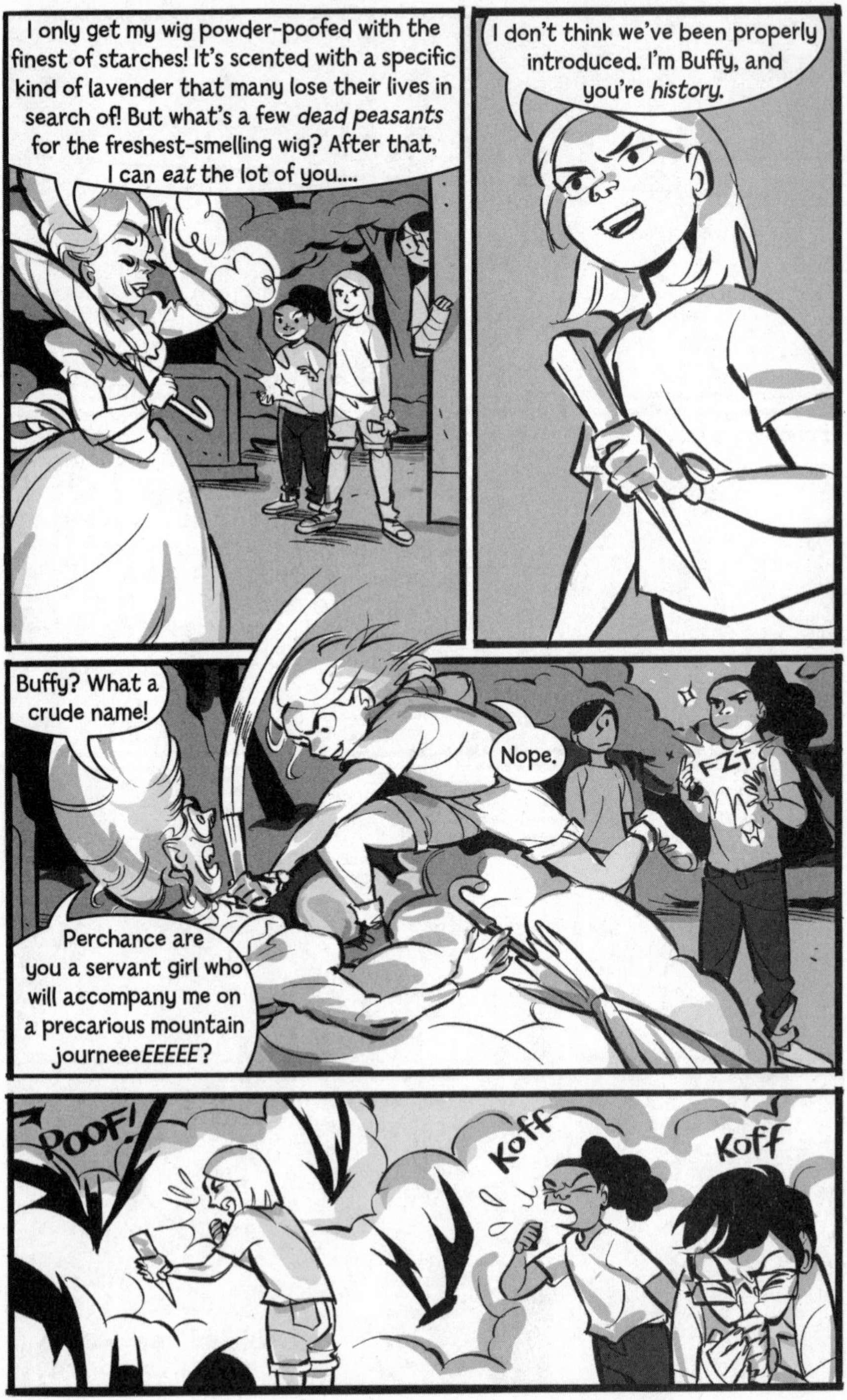

I only get my wig powder-poofed with the finest of starches! It's scented with a specific kind of lavender that many lose their lives in search of! But what's a few *dead peasants* for the freshest-smelling wig? After that, I can *eat* the lot of you....
I don't think we've been properly introduced. I'm Buffy, and you're *history.*
Buffy? What a crude name!
Nope.
FZT
Perchance are you a servant girl who will accompany me on a precarious mountain journeee*EEEEE*?
POOF!
KOFF
KOFF

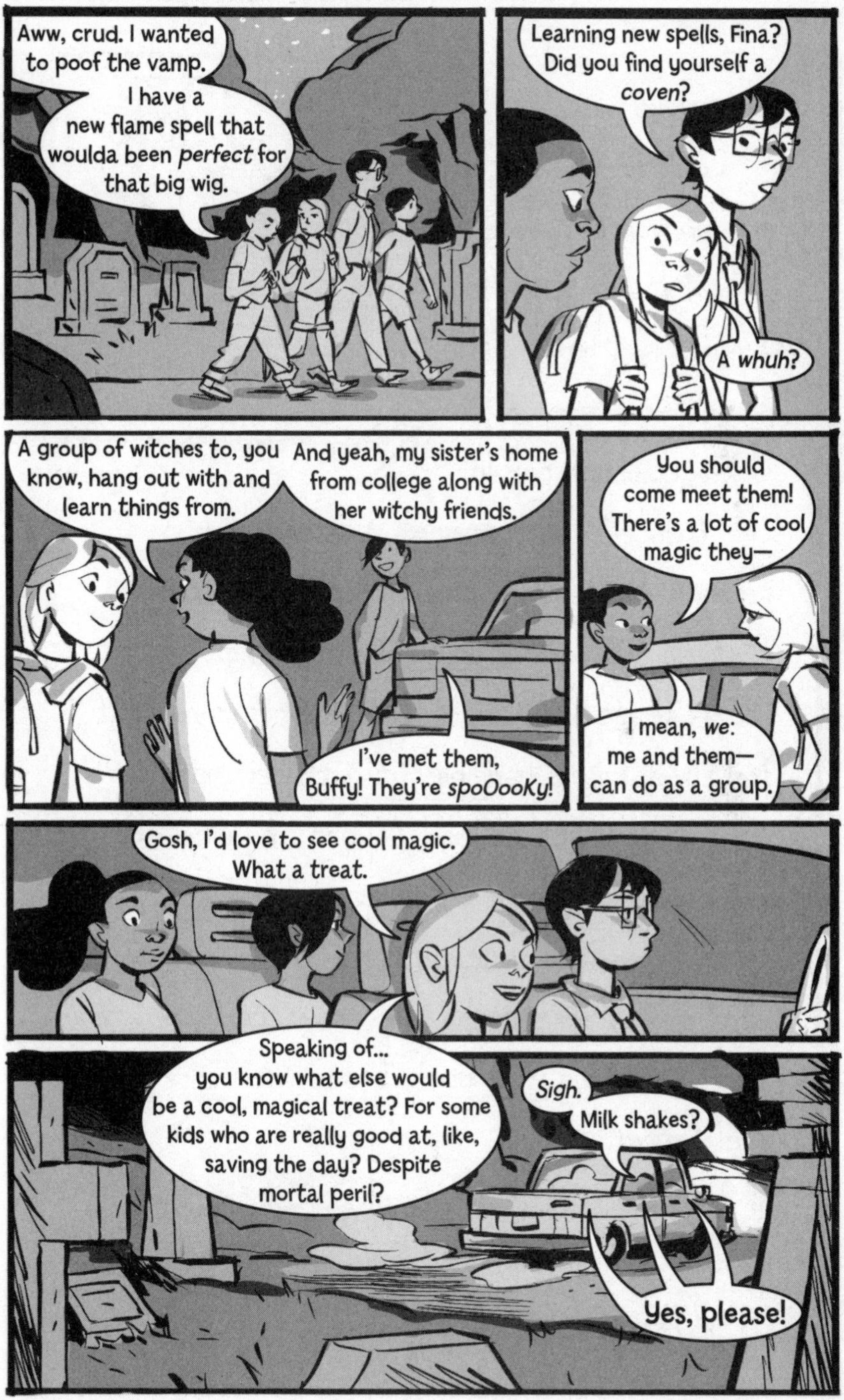

Aww, crud. I wanted to poof the vamp.
I have a new flame spell that woulda been *perfect* for that big wig.
Learning new spells, Fina? Did you find yourself a *coven*?
A *whuh*?
A group of witches to, you know, hang out with and learn things from.
And yeah, my sister's home from college along with her witchy friends.
I've met them, Buffy! They're *spoOooKy*!
You should come meet them! There's a lot of cool magic they—
I mean, *we*: me and them— can do as a group.
Gosh, I'd love to see cool magic. What a treat.
Speaking of... you know what else would be a cool, magical treat? For some kids who are really good at, like, saving the day? Despite mortal peril?
Sigh.
Milk shakes?
Yes, please!

Dear Diary,

Look at this photo of happy pre-summer-school Buffy with her friends and her frosty, sweet beverage. What will become of her in

SWEET, FROSTY VICTORY!

the trenches of...<u>learning</u>? Will she ever recover from having one of her few precious preteen summers <u>stolen</u> from her? Sigh.

At least my friends have their fun cut out for them. Fina's hanging out with her sister and some other witches, and Alvaro's headed off to art camp. He's nervous about it, but I keep telling him, "You faced a horde of vampires— what's a spider-filled camp toilet compared to that?" Strangely, it doesn't seem to make him feel better.

I should probably go to sleep. Since (and maybe I mentioned this?) <u>SUMMER SCHOOL STARTS TOMORROW</u>. Ugh.

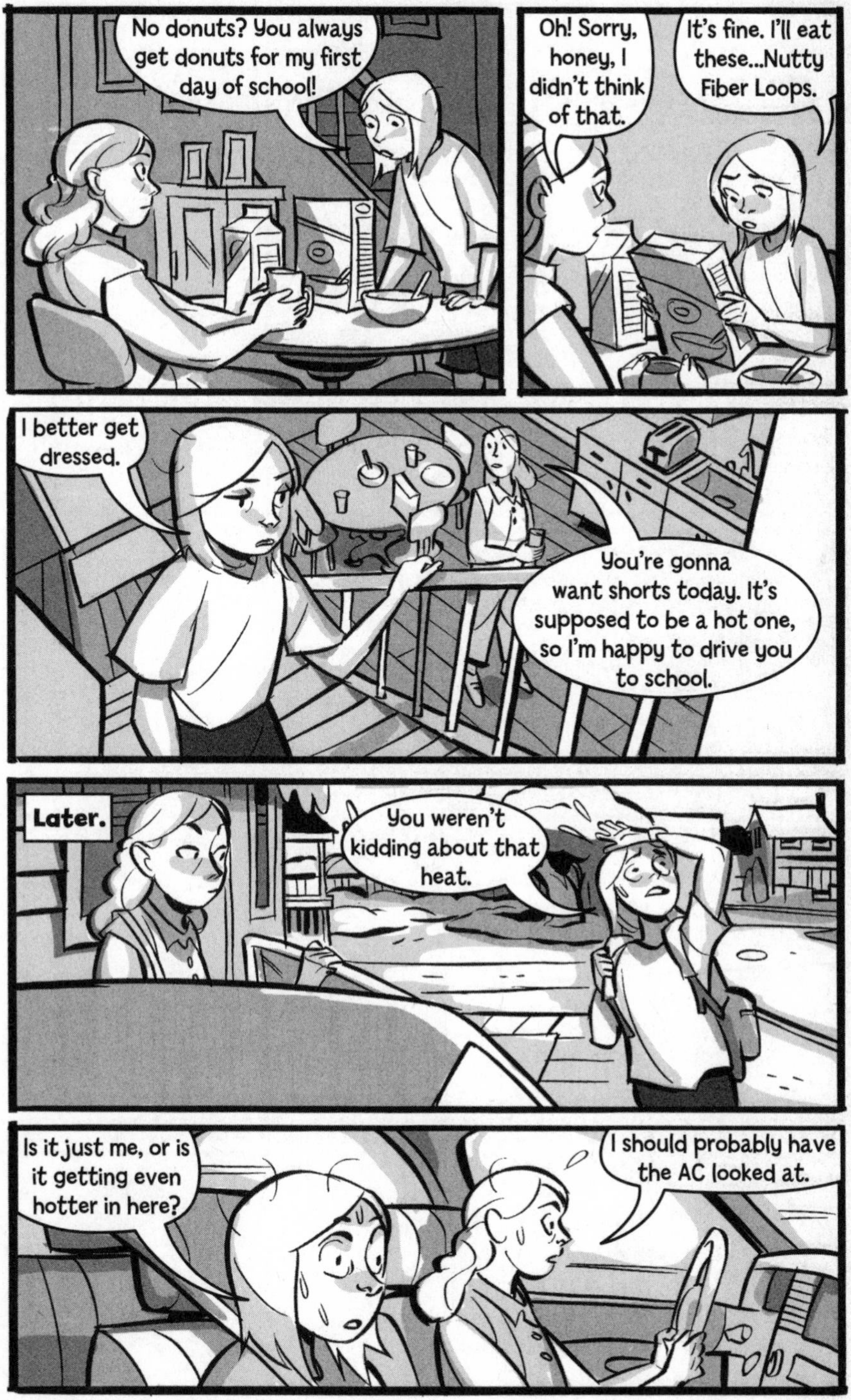
No donuts? You always get donuts for my first day of school!
Oh! Sorry, honey, I didn't think of that.
It's fine. I'll eat these...Nutty Fiber Loops.
I better get dressed.
You're gonna want shorts today. It's supposed to be a hot one, so I'm happy to drive you to school.
Later.
You weren't kidding about that heat.
Is it just me, or is it getting even hotter in here?
I should probably have the AC looked at.

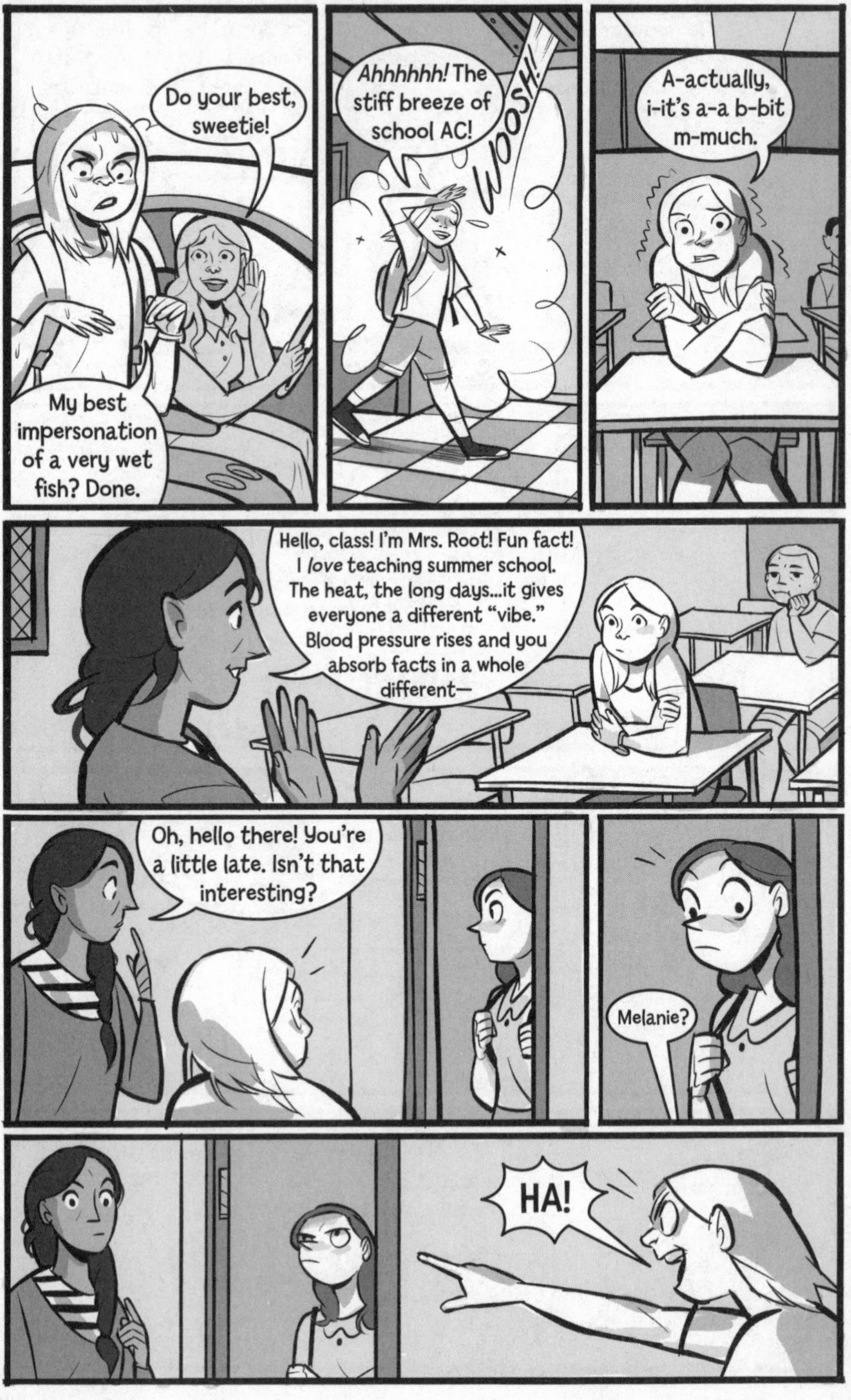
Do your best, sweetie!
My best impersonation of a very wet fish? Done.
Ahhhhhh! The stiff breeze of school AC!
WOOSH!
A-actually, i-it's a-a b-bit m-much.
Hello, class! I'm Mrs. Root! Fun fact! I love teaching summer school. The heat, the long days...it gives everyone a different "vibe." Blood pressure rises and you absorb facts in a whole different—
Oh, hello there! You're a little late. Isn't that interesting?
Melanie?
HA!

Official Scooby Gang Chat

GUYS! CRAZY NEWS!

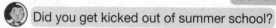

Did you get kicked out of summer school?

Did you prank 'em like I said? Shaving cream? Cocktail shrimp?

No. I didn't have the budget for all that. Plus, shrimp are weird.

Are we all in supernatural comas, communicating through a psychic dream link and being stalked by a bald guy with way too many cheese slices?

What? Um, no.

It's MELANIE! She's in SUMMER SCHOOL, TOO!

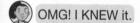

OMG! I KNEW it.

She skipped too many classes to go shopping with her mom.

And when she WAS in class, she was always on her phone.

I thought we were being nice to Melanie now?

PFF, that was until I found out I had SUMMER SCHOOL!

Which is totally HER fault!

...Okay, but don't you think it's partially YOUR fault for not studying harder?

Not my fault! Vampires! Remember?!

At least Melanie can't act like she's better than Buffy anymore.

That's right! Take that, Melanie!

You know what they say: Karma's a witch. Guess Mel had this coming....

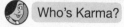

Who's Karma?

Dear Diary,

I should get an award for being RIGHT about stuff, cuz I was super right about summer school. It's bad, and it's boring. It's always either too cold or too hot—sometimes both at the same time. Also, the teachers are extra strange, and the learning is...well...learning.

Meanwhile, outside in the real world, days are getting longer, which means I <u>SHOULD</u> be chasing ice cream trucks and catching fireflies with my friends. Instead, I have to go to bed when the sun goes down and get up when the sun comes up, like some kind of <u>reverse vampire</u>! Or, I guess, a normal human being. I bet the vampires are having a good summer while I'm here practically wasting away. I bet <u>THEY</u> get to go out and catch fireflies.

Anyway, like Mom always says, there's a silver lining: The first week is finally over. <u>AND</u> my archnemesis, Melanie, is ALSO serving some well-deserved time in summer school. Watching her suffer slightly soothes my sun-deprived soul.

Oh, and just so we get all the bad news out in the open: I have DOUBLE HOMEWORK! Mrs. Root was like, "Summer semester is only <u>half</u> as long, so we have <u>twice</u> as much to do." That kind of summer math is evil. Pure evil.

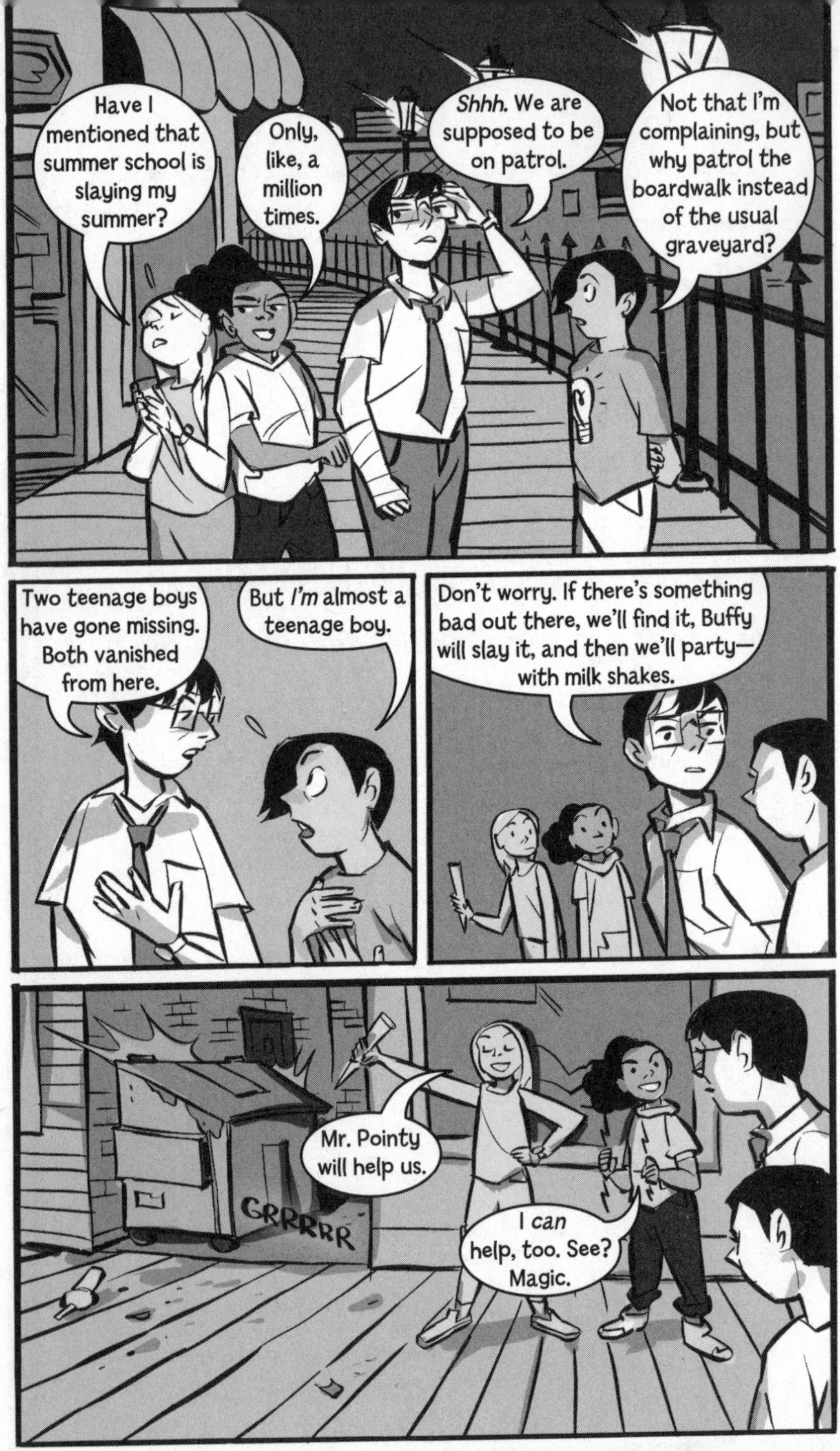

Have I mentioned that summer school is slaying my summer?
Only, like, a million times.
Shhh. We are supposed to be on patrol.
Not that I'm complaining, but why patrol the boardwalk instead of the usual graveyard?
Two teenage boys have gone missing. Both vanished from here.
But *I'm* almost a teenage boy.
Don't worry. If there's something bad out there, we'll find it, Buffy will slay it, and then we'll party—with milk shakes.
Mr. Pointy will help us.
GRRRRR
I *can* help, too. See? Magic.

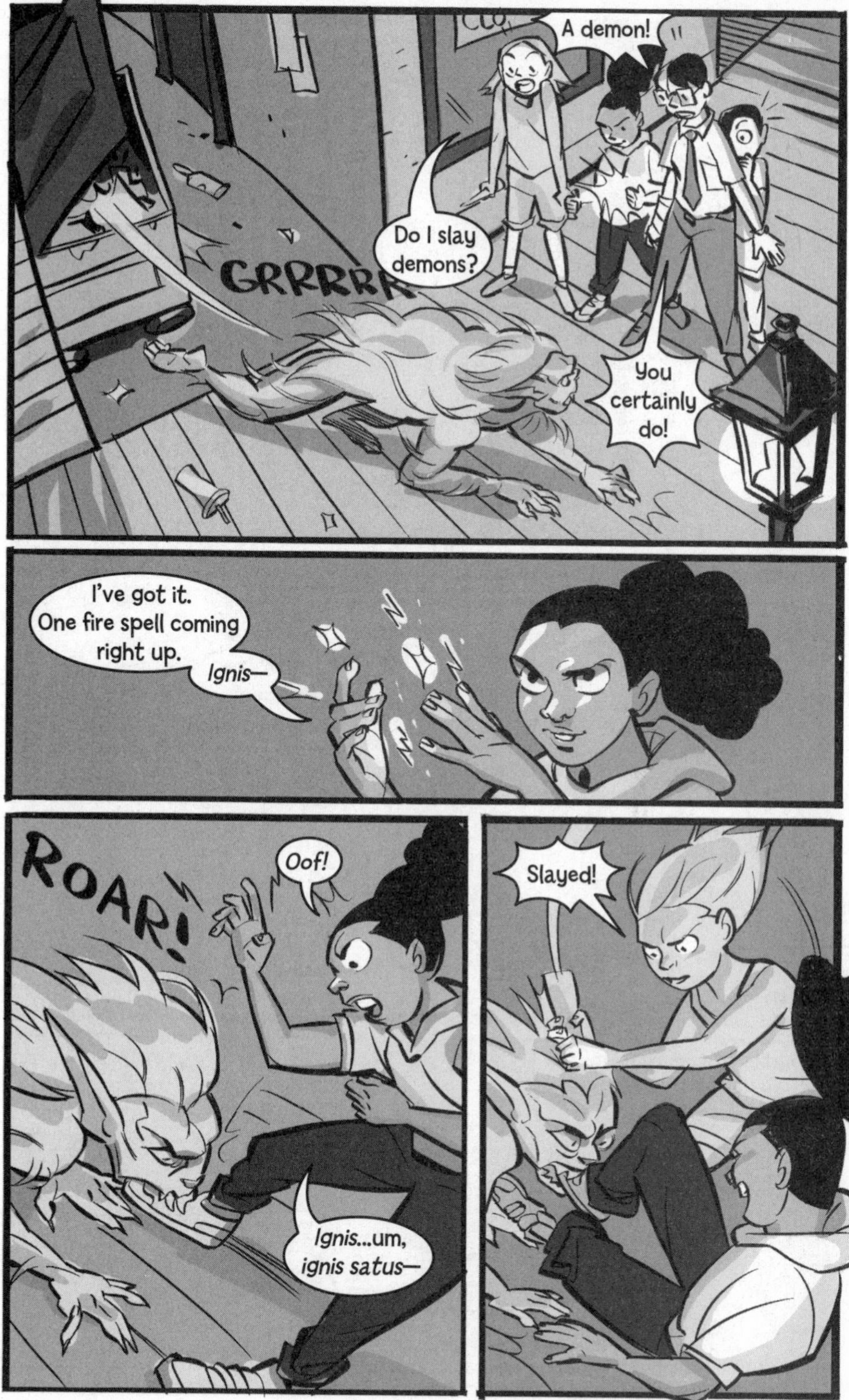
A demon!
Do I slay demons?
GRRRRR
You certainly do!
I've got it. One fire spell coming right up.
Ignis—
ROAR!
Oof!
Ignis...um, ignis satus—
Slayed!

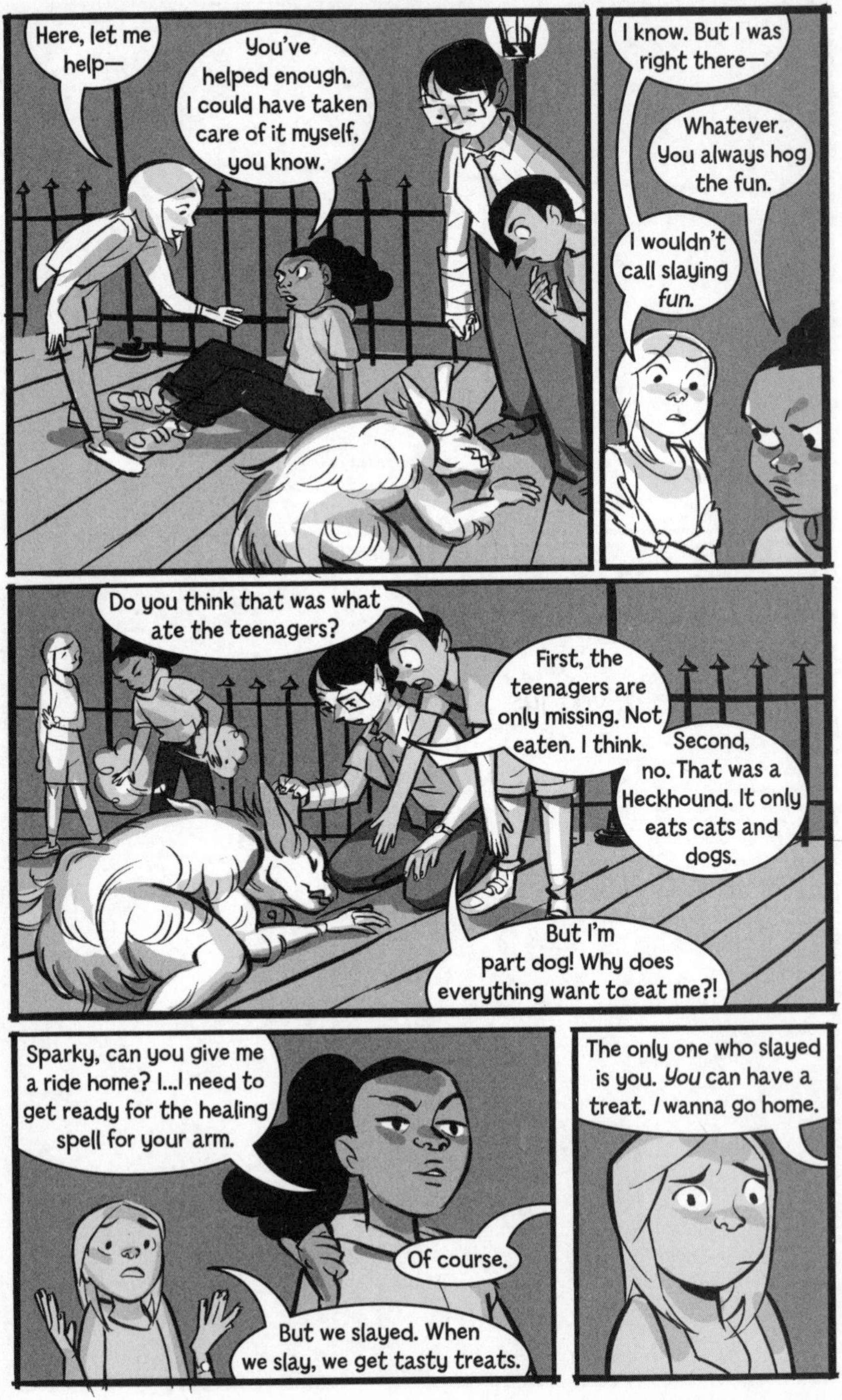

Here, let me help—
You've helped enough. I could have taken care of it myself, you know.
I know. But I was right there—
Whatever. You always hog the fun.
I wouldn't call slaying *fun*.
Do you think that was what ate the teenagers?
First, the teenagers are only missing. Not eaten. I think.
Second, no. That was a Heckhound. It only eats cats and dogs.
But I'm part dog! Why does everything want to eat me?!
Sparky, can you give me a ride home? I...I need to get ready for the healing spell for your arm.
Of course.
But we slayed. When we slay, we get tasty treats.
The only one who slayed is you. *You* can have a treat. *I* wanna go home.

Hey Diary,

Last night was <u>no</u> fun. Fina got upset with me, and I don't know why. We were on patrol, and this big, scary demon dog showed up. It was about to bite Fina's foot off, so I slayed it. Then she got all mad. The whole way home, she kept mumbling about not getting to use her magic and how I always take all the glory. But that's not true. If it were up to me, I wouldn't even <u>BE</u> the dumb Slayer. I'd much rather be a normal kid who just has to worry about her grades and her friends and not about a bunch of creepy monsters. I didn't <u>WANT</u> to save the whole school at the end of the year—I <u>HAD</u> to. I don't <u>WANT</u> to be thanked for it or whatever. It was just my <u>JOB</u>, and it was a part of my duty. Maybe I should have said that to Fina....

Anyway, you know how I'm called the <u>VAMPIRE</u> Slayer? Apparently, I don't just fight vampires. I'm also responsible for demons and other weird forces of darkness, too! So I asked Sparky, "Shouldn't my name be Buffy the Vampire-and-Demons-and-Forces-of-Darkness Slayer?" Sparky didn't find it as funny as I did. Instead, she gave me a long lecture about how I should have read the giant Slayer Handbook she gave me for Christmas. It only says VAMPYR on the cover, but apparently it covers all kinds of monsters and demons and supernatural stuff, like the Heckmouth in Cleveland.

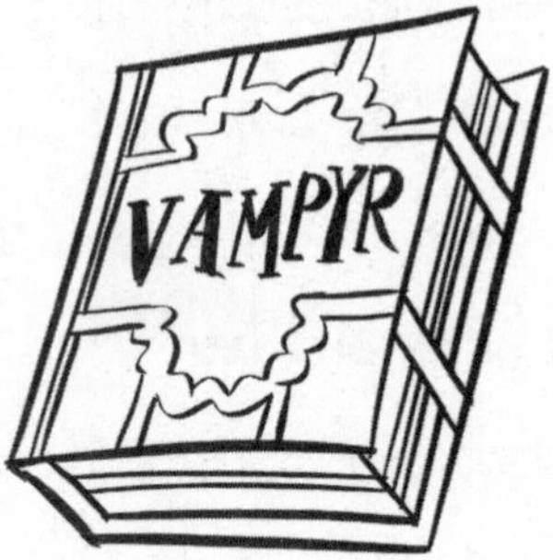
VAMPYR

I don't know how Sparky expects me to be a student AND a Slayer. Either one is a lot of work by itself—but together? I may never have a summer, a winter, or any kind of vacation ever again. I miss you, sunshine!

SLAYER STUFF

The Slayer Handbook is a sacred text given to Slayers by their Watchers to instruct them on the history and rules concerning magic and the supernatural world, and I expect you to read every single word of it....

HECKMOUTH

These are places where the walls between different dimensions are super thin. (Kind of like the walls of my house!) Because the walls are thin, doors can open up between our Earth dimension and other, crazier dimensions. (Kind of

like the door to my bedroom!) Magic flows pretty easily through the doors, which draws monsters and other supernatural stuff to the Heckmouth. (Like how my mom is drawn to my room when she hears me doing things other than homework.)

THE GENTLEMEN

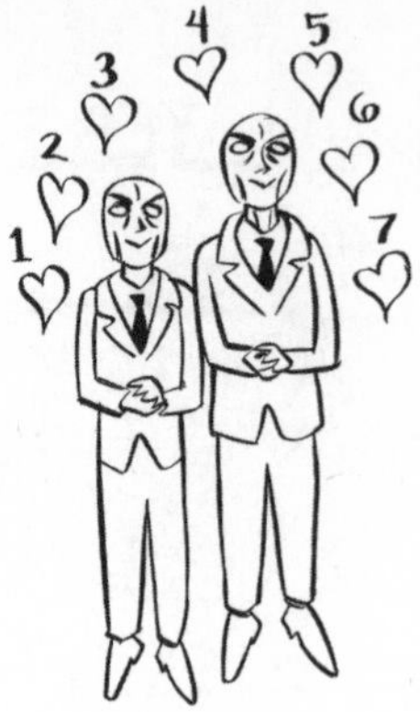
1
2
3
4
5
6
7

This is a group of demons who come from fairy tales! (That sounds pretty nice!) They can't talk, they wear suits, and they travel from town to town to take hearts out of seven people. (YIKES! That does NOT sound nice!)

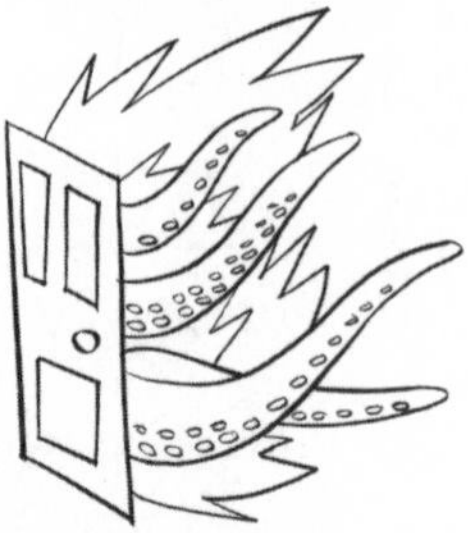

HECKMOUTH SPAWN

This is a huge, icky demon with tons of tentacles. It lives right on the other side of those dimension doors I mentioned.

GROXLAR

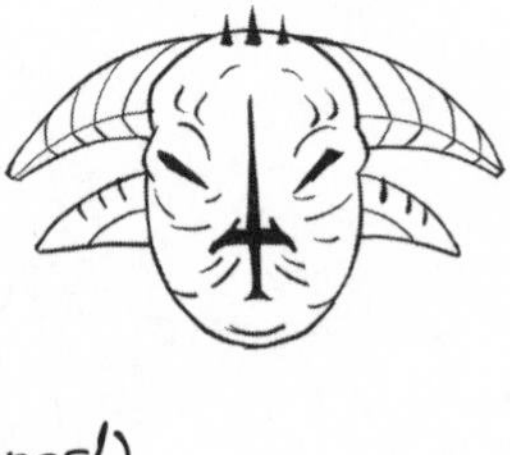

These guys are demons with horns coming out of their heads. They apparently bite the heads off babies. (Why is Sparky telling me this stuff?! I'm going to have nightmares!)

VENGEANCE DEMONS

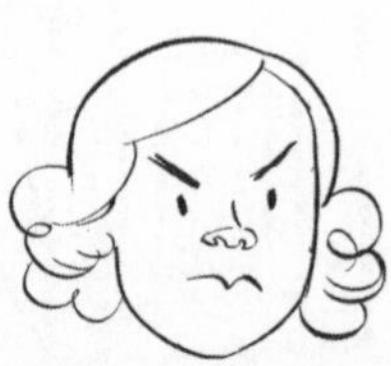

Sometimes called justice demons, these monsters grant wishes for people who are mad at other people. (I better hurry and apologize to Fina!)

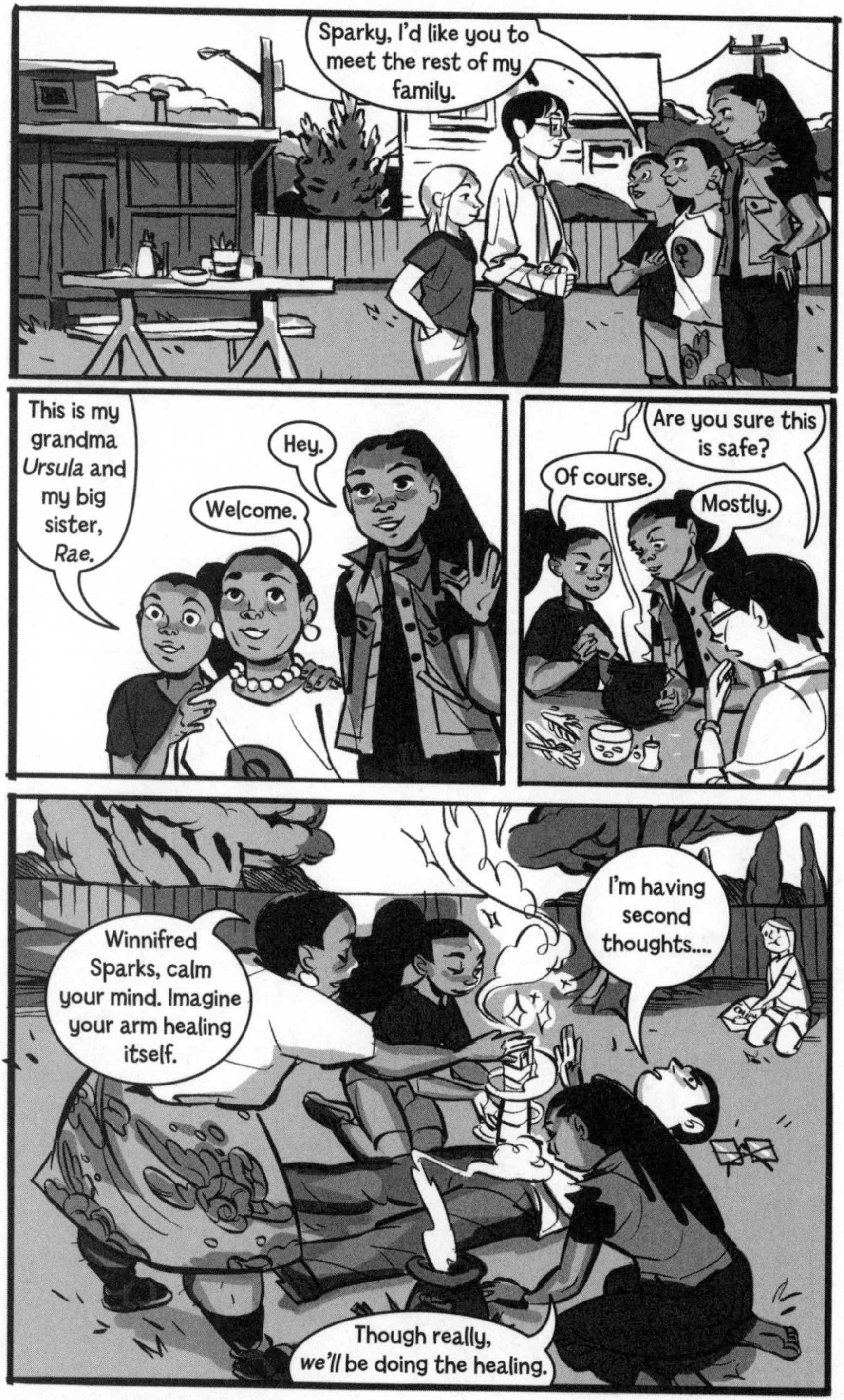

Sparky, I'd like you to meet the rest of my family.
This is my grandma *Ursula* and my big sister, *Rae*.
Welcome.
Hey.
Are you sure this is safe?
Of course.
Mostly.
Winnifred Sparks, calm your mind. Imagine your arm healing itself.
I'm having second thoughts....
Though really, *we'll* be doing the healing.

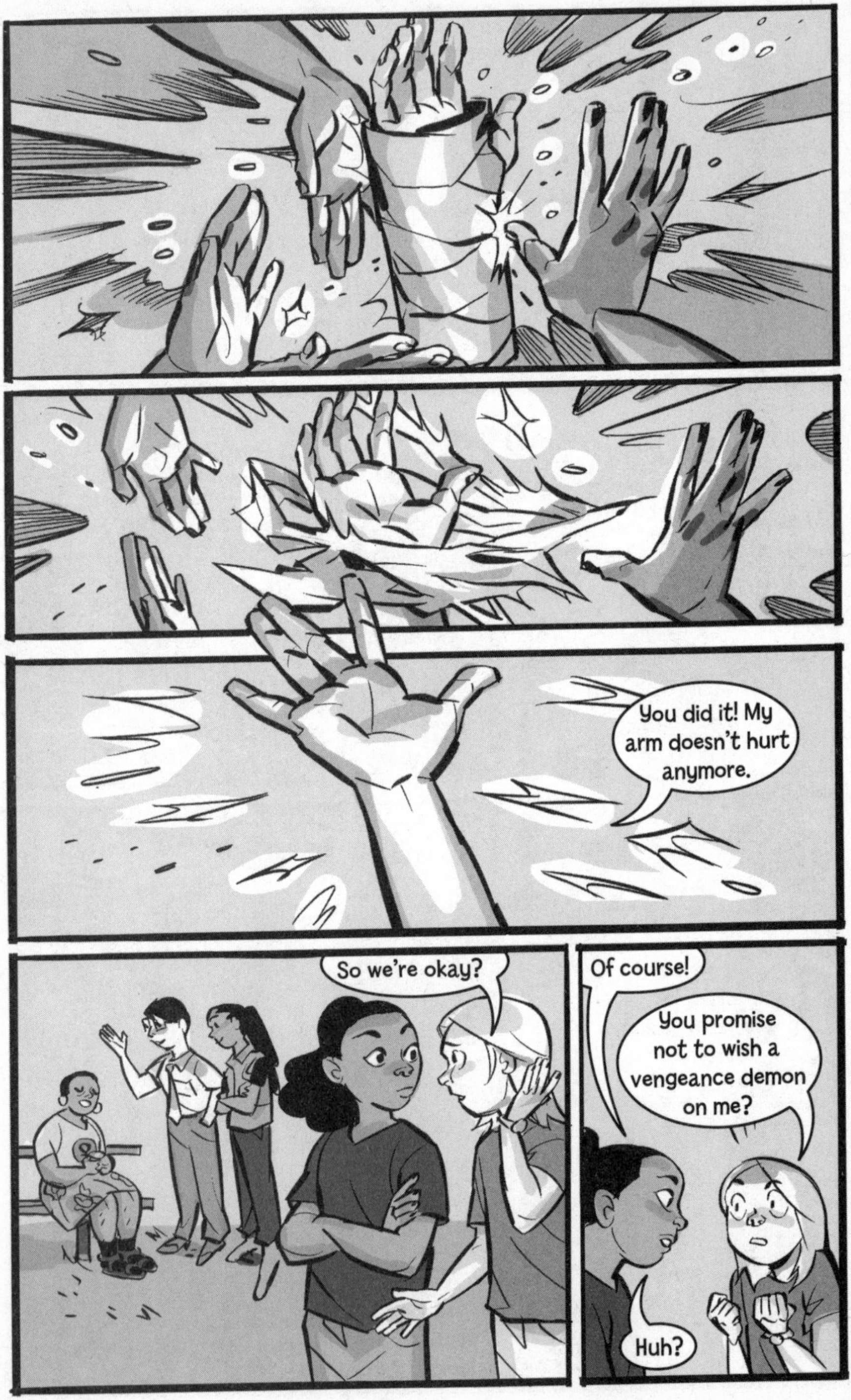
You did it! My arm doesn't hurt anymore.
So we're okay?
Of course!
You promise not to wish a vengeance demon on me?
Huh?

Official Scooby Gang Chat

Alvaro! Where are you? You just missed the most amazing incredible fantastic magical thing I've ever seen.

Yeah, it was pretty cool.

Fina and her grandma and her sister healed Sparky. They totally fixed her broken arm. It was amazing.

Next time we get Scooby gang bumps and bruises, we can skip the hospital.

We should start charging....

Do I get a friends and family discount?

Of course!

Where is Alvaro?

STOP TEXTING.

I lay down for like two seconds and my phone starts blowing up.

But did you read? You missed the coolest thing!

So you said.

Can I go back to my nap now?

Someone woke up on the wrong side of the PUPPY bed.

Yikes. Someone needs a juice box and a BONE.

Dog jokes for the werewolf boy. Hilarious.

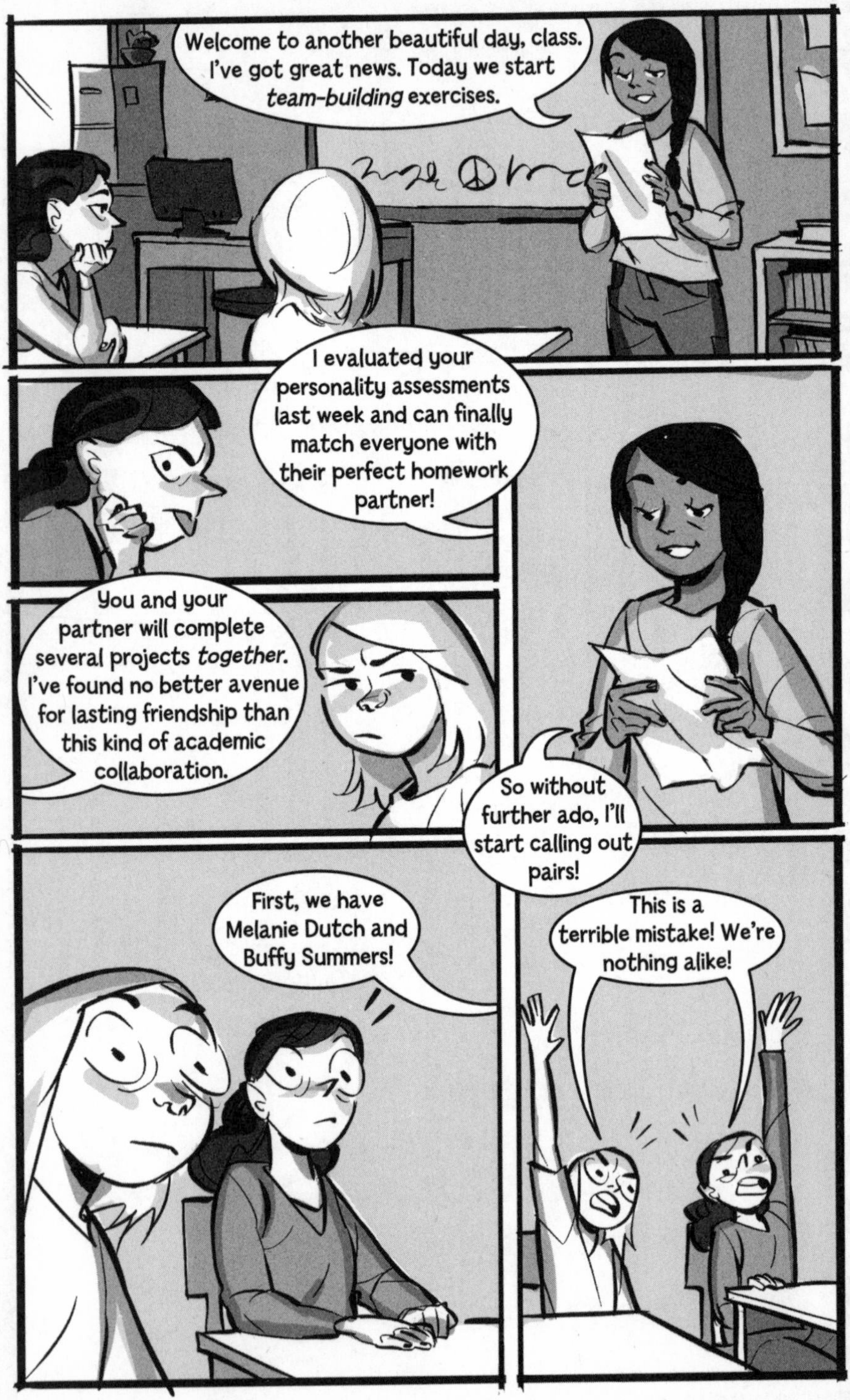
Welcome to another beautiful day, class. I've got great news. Today we start *team-building* exercises.
I evaluated your personality assessments last week and can finally match everyone with their perfect homework partner!
You and your partner will complete several projects *together*. I've found no better avenue for lasting friendship than this kind of academic collaboration.
So without further ado, I'll start calling out pairs!
First, we have Melanie Dutch and Buffy Summers!
This is a terrible mistake! We're nothing alike!

<u>Deer</u> Diary,

Okay, my summer school teacher is completely nuts! Me and Melanie begged and begged for a <u>whole hour</u> to get reassigned to different

homework buddies. Mrs. Root just shook her head and told us again and again that we were meant to work together this summer, that she simply felt something "cosmic" between us.

What am I gonna DO? Melanie's the worst! She's mean and bossy, and probably won't do her share of the homework. Then I'll fail. Wait, what happens if you don't pass summer school? Is there winter break school?! Why couldn't

You're even collaborating wonderfully right now, whining in tandem!

Mrs. Root have paired me with someone who LOVES doing homework instead??

UGH!! Well, at least I'm good and heated for patrol tonight....(Have I mentioned how <u>hot</u> it's been in Cleveland lately?) Sparky said teens in town have been vanishing left and right. She's thinks a lot of vamps stuck around to feed after we poofed Principal Big Bad. Now it's my job to clean up the whole mess. Slayer? More like vamp-cleaner-upper.

I can hear Mom doing her pre-bed yoga. She loves to hum. That means I need to do my

pre-patrol cheerleader-competition reality TV. It's the only thirty minutes of the day that are mine.

Stop feeding on unsuspecting adolescents and get out of here, you bad vamps!

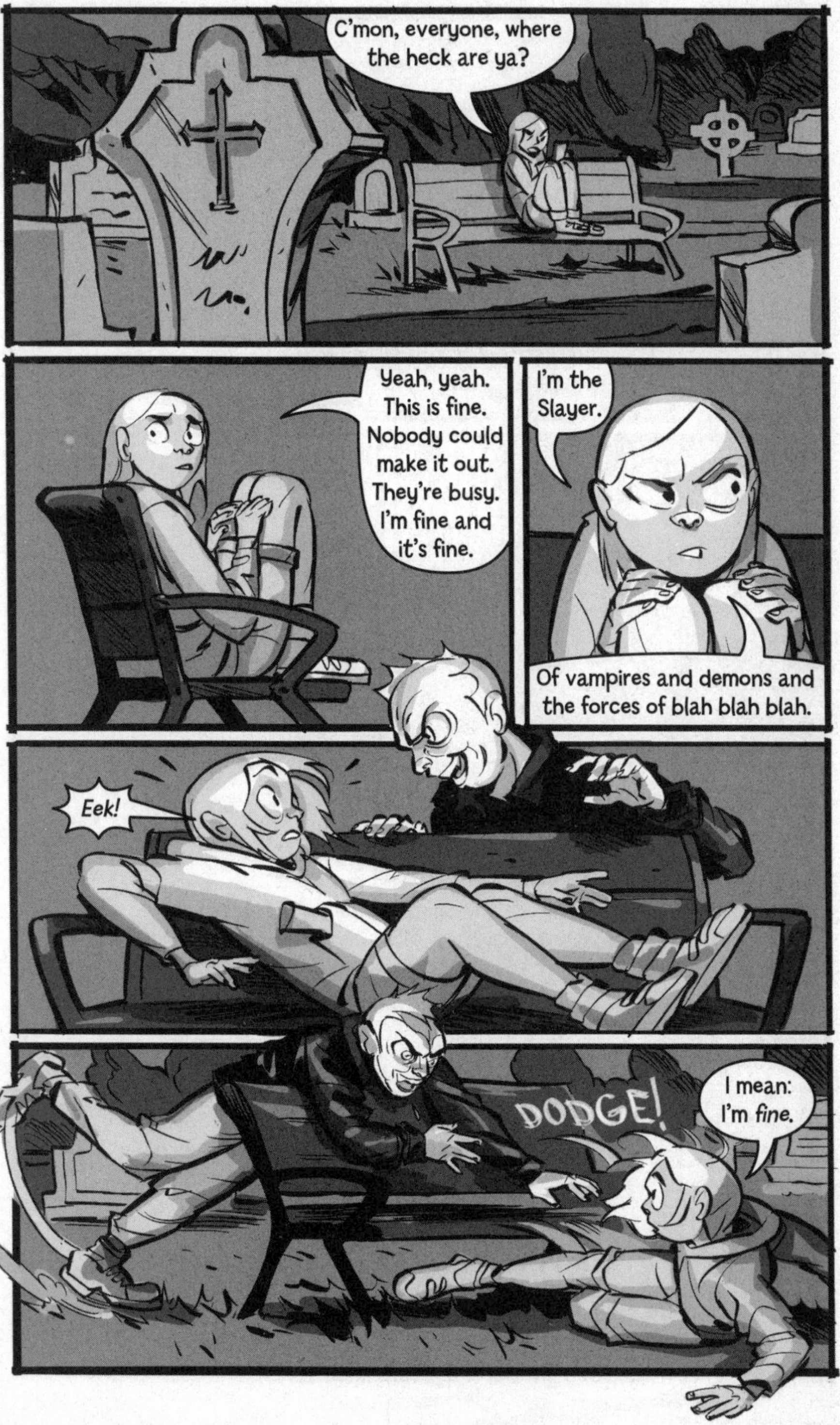

C'mon, everyone, where the heck are ya?
Yeah, yeah. This is fine. Nobody could make it out. They're busy. I'm fine and it's fine.
I'm the Slayer.
Of vampires and demons and the forces of blah blah blah.
Eek!
DODGE!
I mean: I'm *fine*.

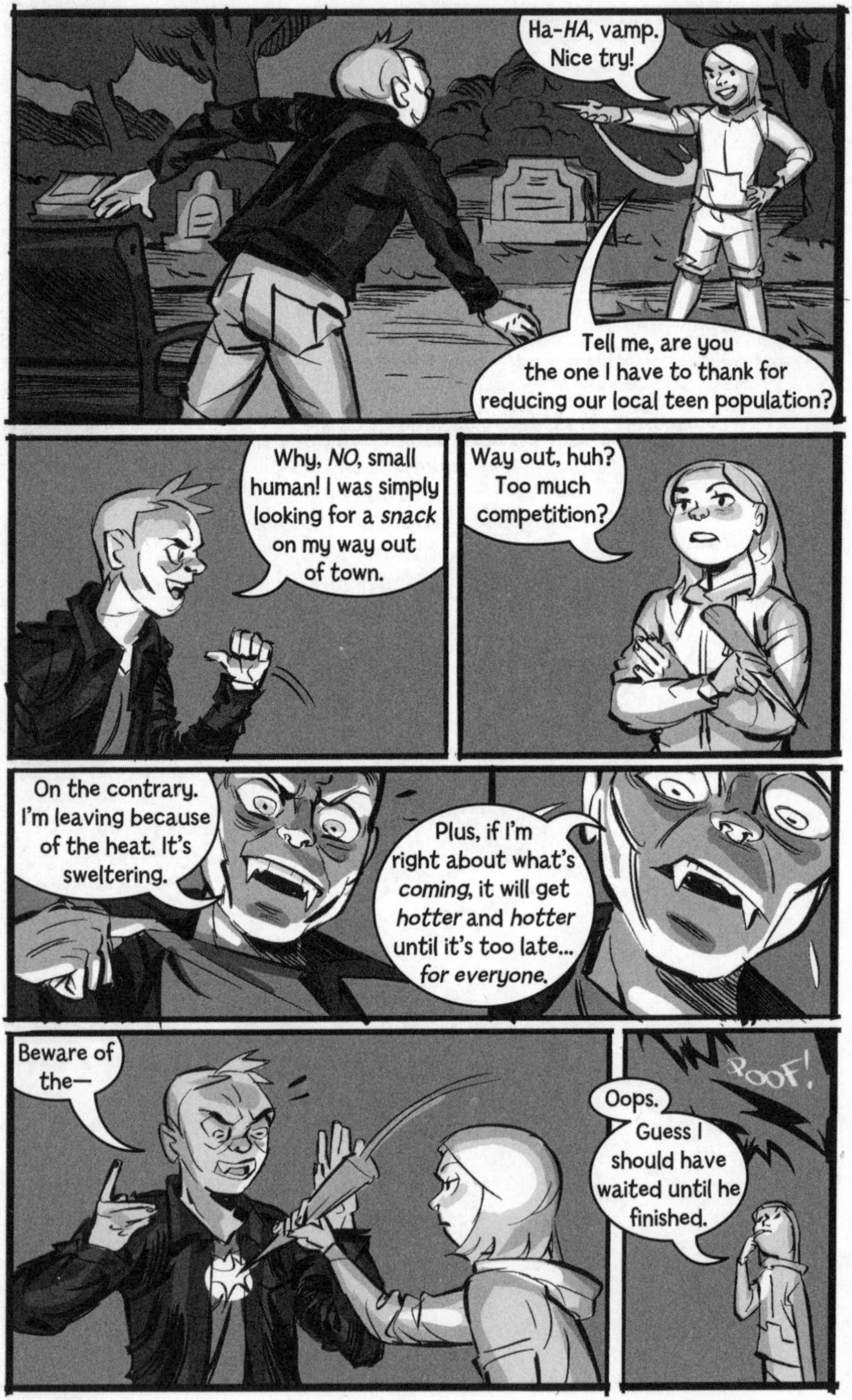
Ha-*HA*, vamp. Nice try!
Tell me, are you the one I have to thank for reducing our local teen population?
Why, *NO*, small human! I was simply looking for a *snack* on my way out of town.
Way out, huh? Too much competition?
On the contrary. I'm leaving because of the heat. It's sweltering.
Plus, if I'm right about what's *coming*, it will get *hotter* and *hotter* until it's too late... *for everyone*.
Beware of the—
POOF!
Oops.
Guess I should have waited until he finished.

HELLO?! ARE ANY OF YOU ALIVE?

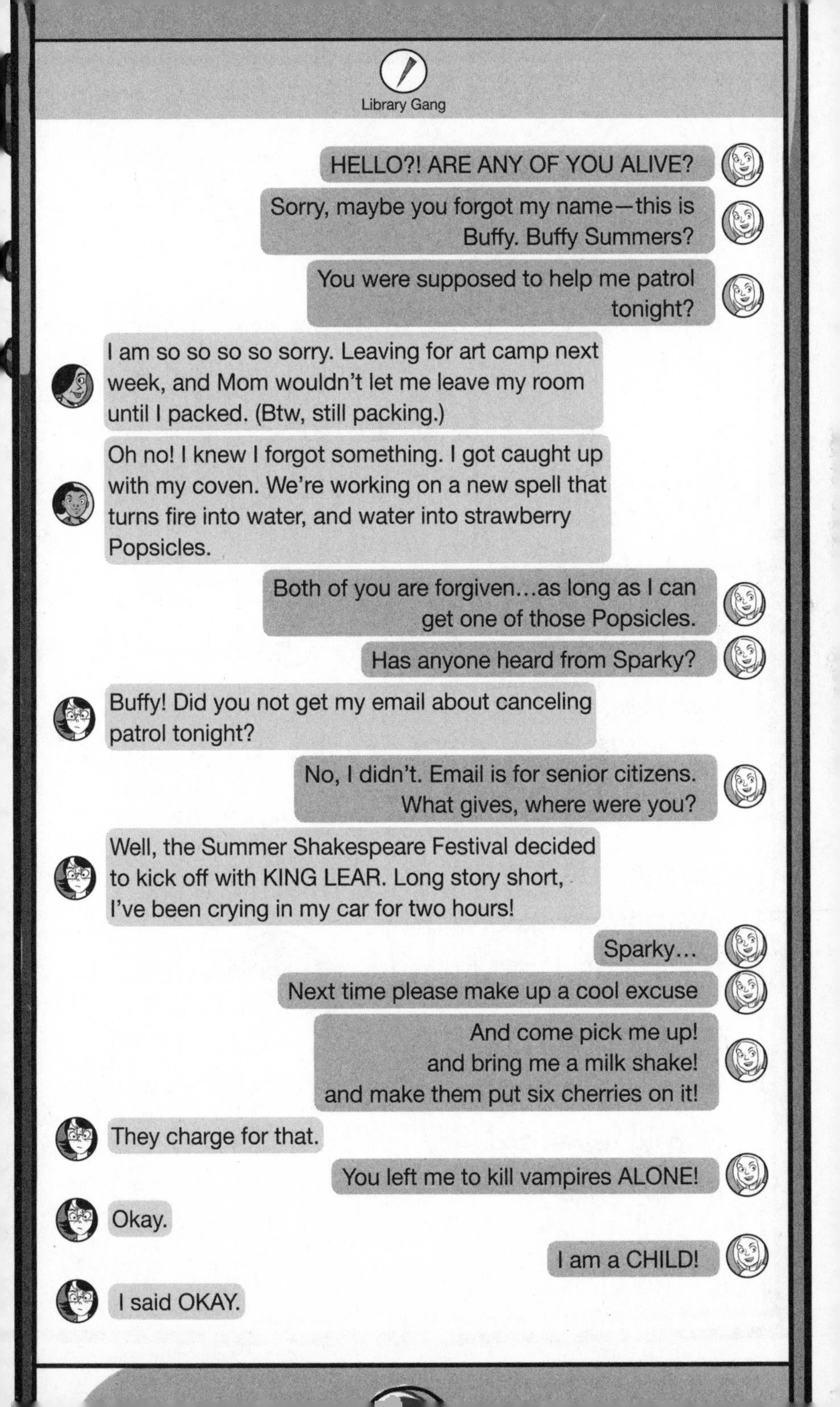

Sorry, maybe you forgot my name—this is Buffy. Buffy Summers?

You were supposed to help me patrol tonight?

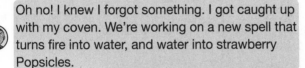 I am so so so so sorry. Leaving for art camp next week, and Mom wouldn't let me leave my room until I packed. (Btw, still packing.)

Oh no! I knew I forgot something. I got caught up with my coven. We're working on a new spell that turns fire into water, and water into strawberry Popsicles.

Both of you are forgiven…as long as I can get one of those Popsicles.

Has anyone heard from Sparky?

 Buffy! Did you not get my email about canceling patrol tonight?

No, I didn't. Email is for senior citizens. What gives, where were you?

Well, the Summer Shakespeare Festival decided to kick off with KING LEAR. Long story short, I've been crying in my car for two hours!

Sparky…

Next time please make up a cool excuse

And come pick me up! and bring me a milk shake! and make them put six cherries on it!

They charge for that.

You left me to kill vampires ALONE!

Okay.

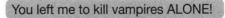 I am a CHILD!

I said OKAY.

Dear Diary,

It's Saturday afternoon and I just woke up. Mom must be letting me sleep in cuz of all my lost summer joy. She doesn't know I was out patrolling. If she did...Let's not think about that. That scares me more than vampires.

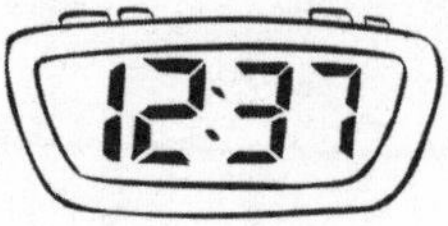
12:37

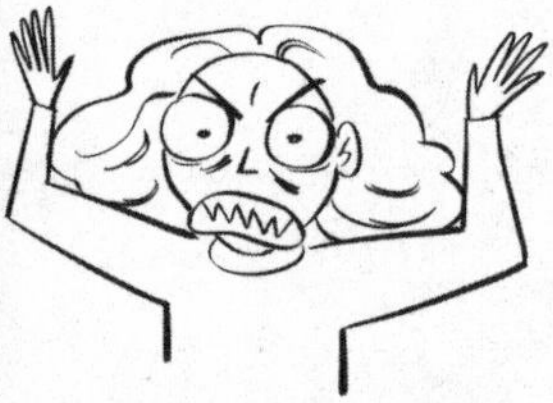

Anyway, last night Sparky and I had a long talk over our milk shakes—mine: banana birthday cake, hers: vanilla cappuccino. I thought about telling her about what the vampire was saying about the hot weather, but I figure it's not worth worrying about. It's probably nothing.

It really <u>IS</u> hot right now, and that guy was, like, wearing a leather jacket! I would leave, too, if I were him.

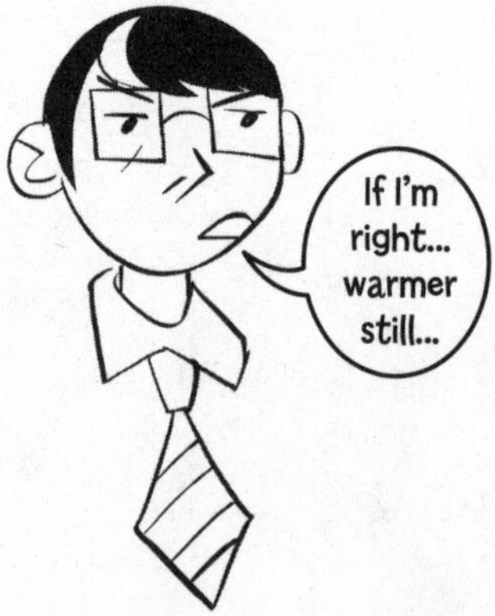
If I'm right... warmer still...

Speaking of warm weather, tomorrow is finally my first BEACH DAY OF THE YEAR! Okay, so it's not an ocean beach like in California—it's a Lake Erie beach—but a beach is a beach, so I'm not complaining. Especially since there'll be hot dogs, soda, and CAKE cuz it's Sarafina's birthday! I got her a bunch of different-colored candles after I googled "gifts for witches." They're apparently good for special spells and stuff.

Sarafina's
12 th
BIRTHDAY BASH
NORTHSHORE PARK
JUNE 15 3:00 PM

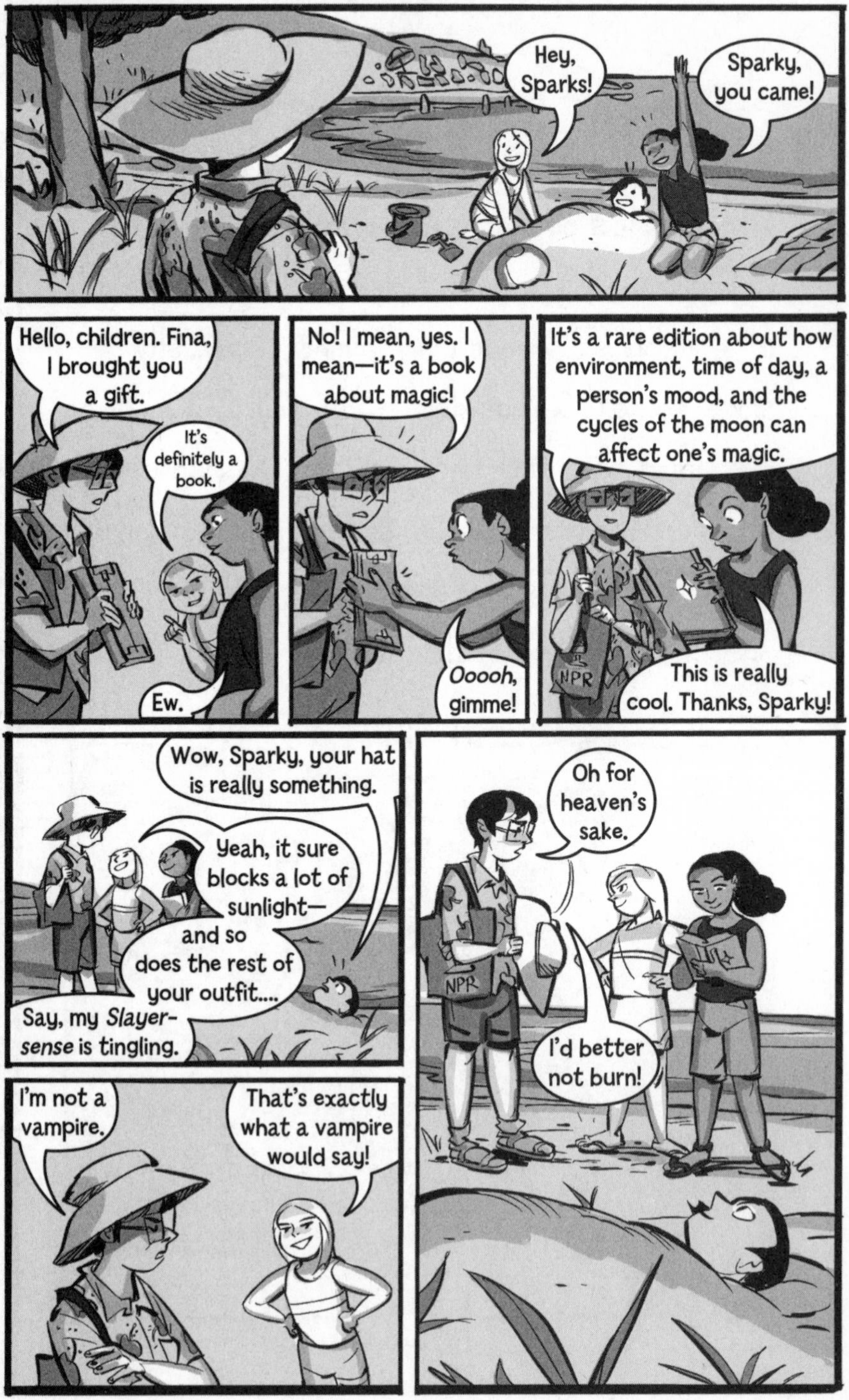
Hey, Sparks!
Sparky, you came!
Hello, children. Fina, I brought you a gift.
It's definitely a book.
Ew.
No! I mean, yes. I mean—it's a book about magic!
Ooooh, gimme!
It's a rare edition about how environment, time of day, a person's mood, and the cycles of the moon can affect one's magic.
NPR
This is really cool. Thanks, Sparky!
Wow, Sparky, your hat is really something.
Yeah, it sure blocks a lot of sunlight—
and so does the rest of your outfit....
Say, my Slayer-sense is tingling.
I'm not a vampire.
That's exactly what a vampire would say!
Oh for heaven's sake.
NPR
I'd better not burn!

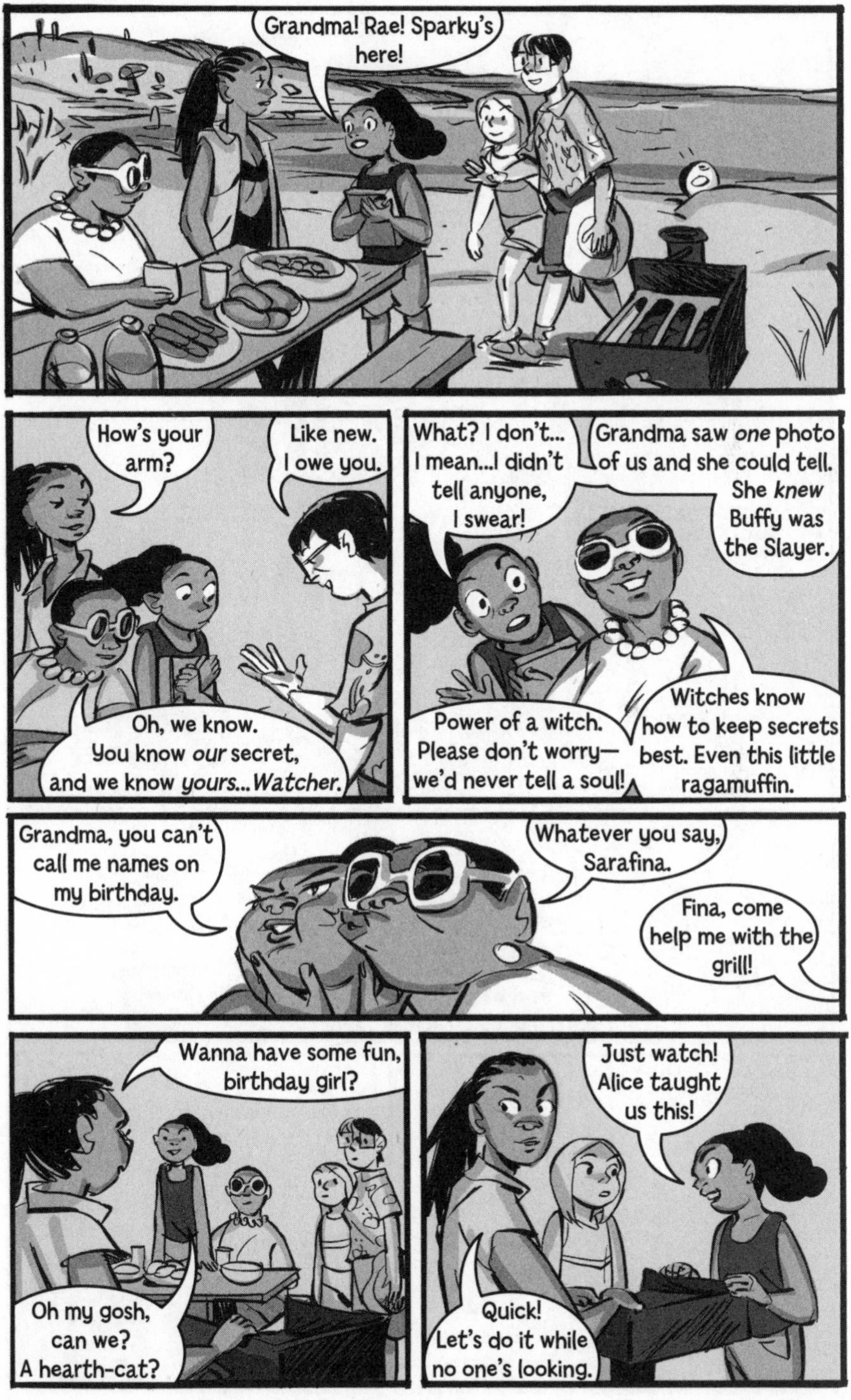
Grandma! Rae! Sparky's here!
How's your arm?
Like new. I owe you.
Oh, we know. You know *our* secret, and we know *yours*...*Watcher*.
What? I don't... I mean...I didn't tell anyone, I swear!
Grandma saw *one* photo of us and she could tell. She *knew* Buffy was the Slayer.
Power of a witch. Please don't worry—we'd never tell a soul!
Witches know how to keep secrets best. Even this little ragamuffin.
Grandma, you can't call me names on my birthday.
Whatever you say, Sarafina.
Fina, come help me with the grill!
Wanna have some fun, birthday girl?
Oh my gosh, can we? A hearth-cat?
Just watch! Alice taught us this!
Quick! Let's do it while no one's looking.

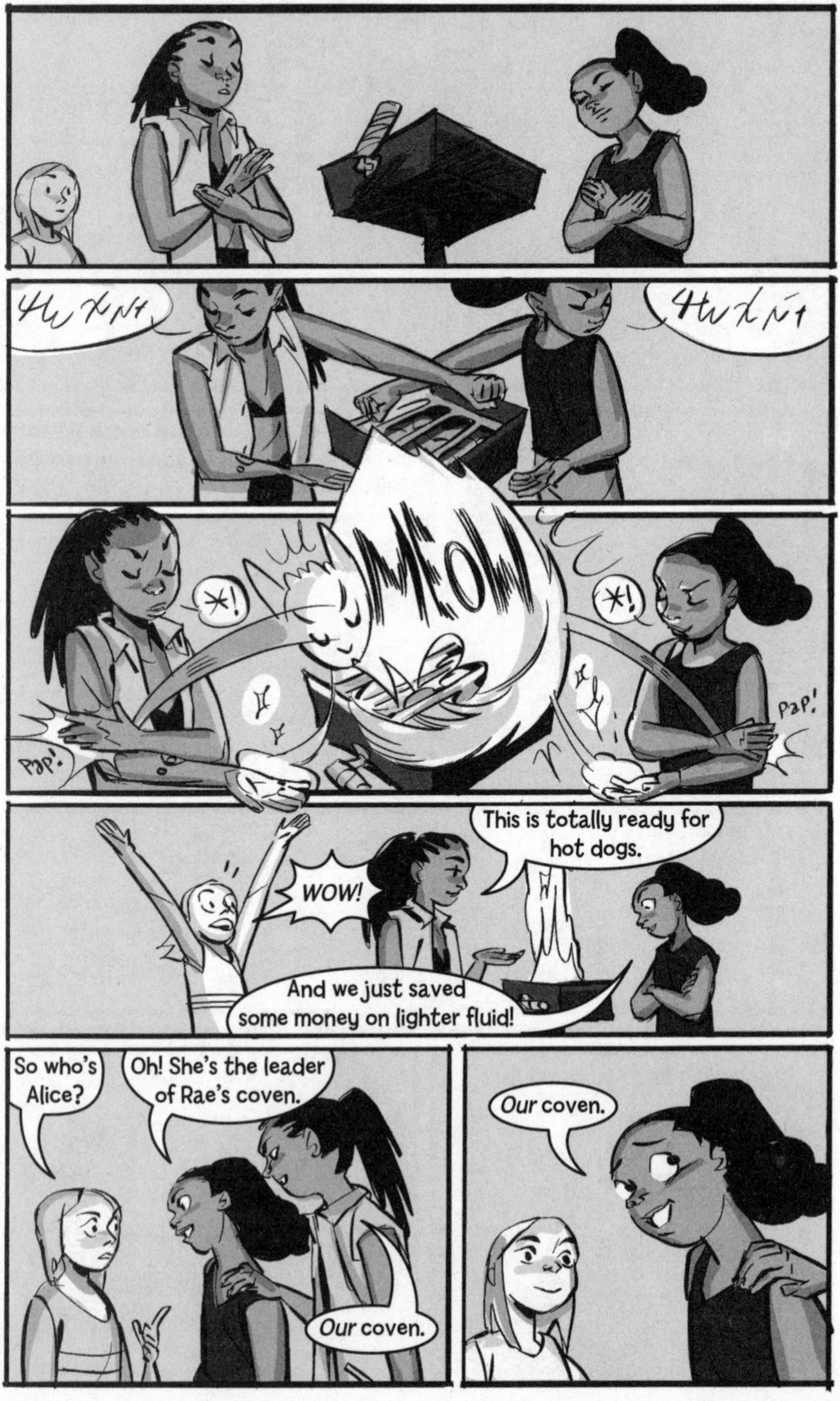
MEOW
PAP!
PAP!
WOW!
This is totally ready for hot dogs.
And we just saved some money on lighter fluid!
So who's Alice?
Oh! She's the leader of Rae's coven.
Our coven.
Our coven.

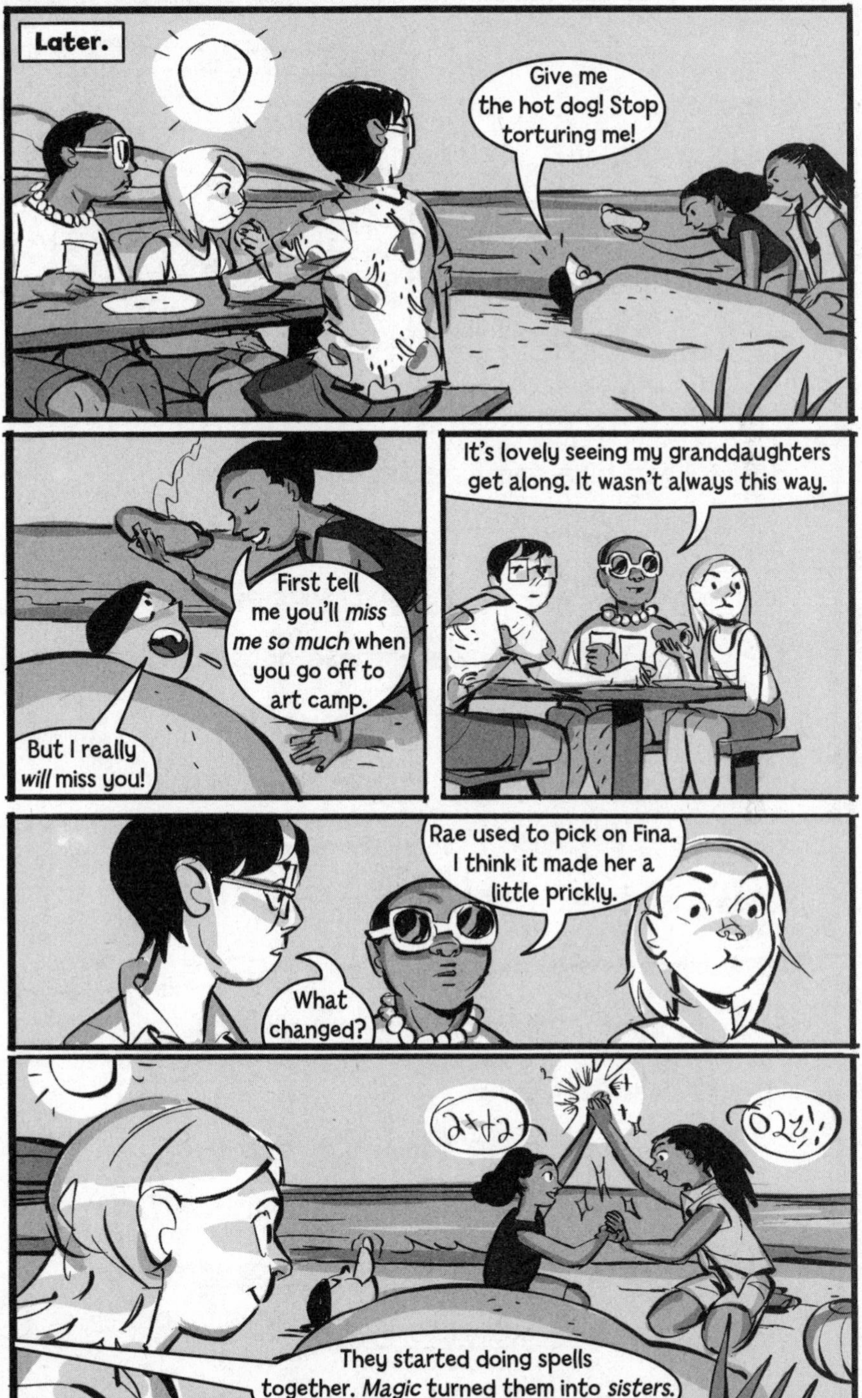
Later.
Give me the hot dog! Stop torturing me!
First tell me you'll *miss me so much* when you go off to art camp.
But I really *will* miss you!
It's lovely seeing my granddaughters get along. It wasn't always this way.
Rae used to pick on Fina. I think it made her a little prickly.
What changed?
They started doing spells together. *Magic* turned them into *sisters.*

Dear Diary,

I got a really nice taste of summer today at Fina's birthday party. We stayed on the beach till the sun went

down. Then Fina and Rae set off fireworks, except they weren't fireworks—they were more like magic swizzle sparks that shot out from their fingertips. They were these dots of light that zoomed through the air and pulsed and changed color based on everyone's feelings. It made me really wish I could do magic...and even kinda wish I had a sister. Of course, I barely have time for me—when would I have time for a sibling? Maybe I could take a few minutes around...I dunno. Dawn?

Anyway, today was fun while it lasted. Tomorrow the torture resumes because, after <u>school</u>, I have to go to my <u>archnemesis's</u> house to work on an <u>English assignment</u>. Yuck x4.

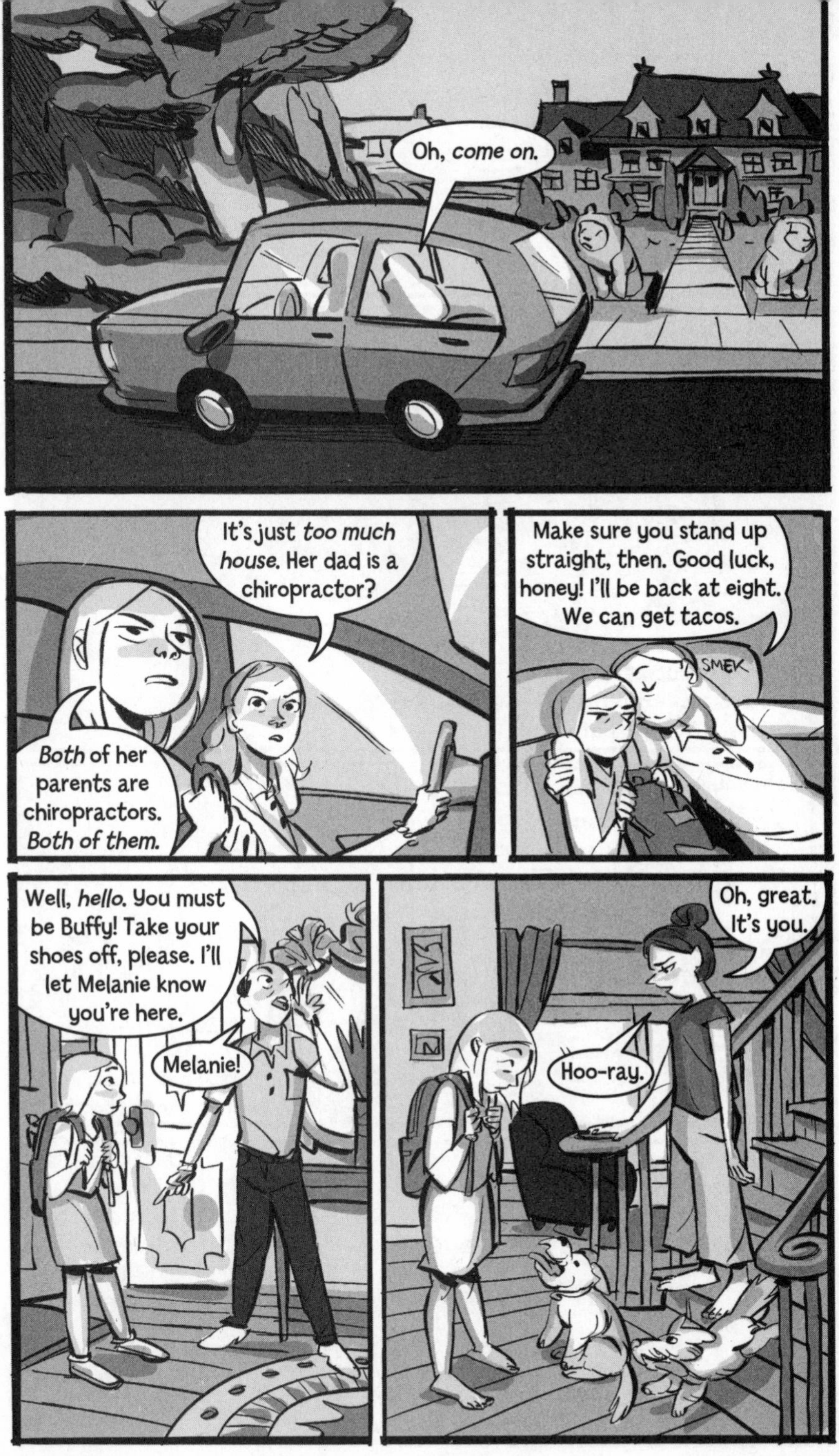
Oh, *come on.*
It's just *too much house*. Her dad is a chiropractor?
Both of her parents are chiropractors. *Both of them.*
Make sure you stand up straight, then. Good luck, honey! I'll be back at eight. We can get tacos.
SMEK
Well, *hello*. You must be Buffy! Take your shoes off, please. I'll let Melanie know you're here.
Melanie!
Oh, great. It's you.
Hoo-ray.

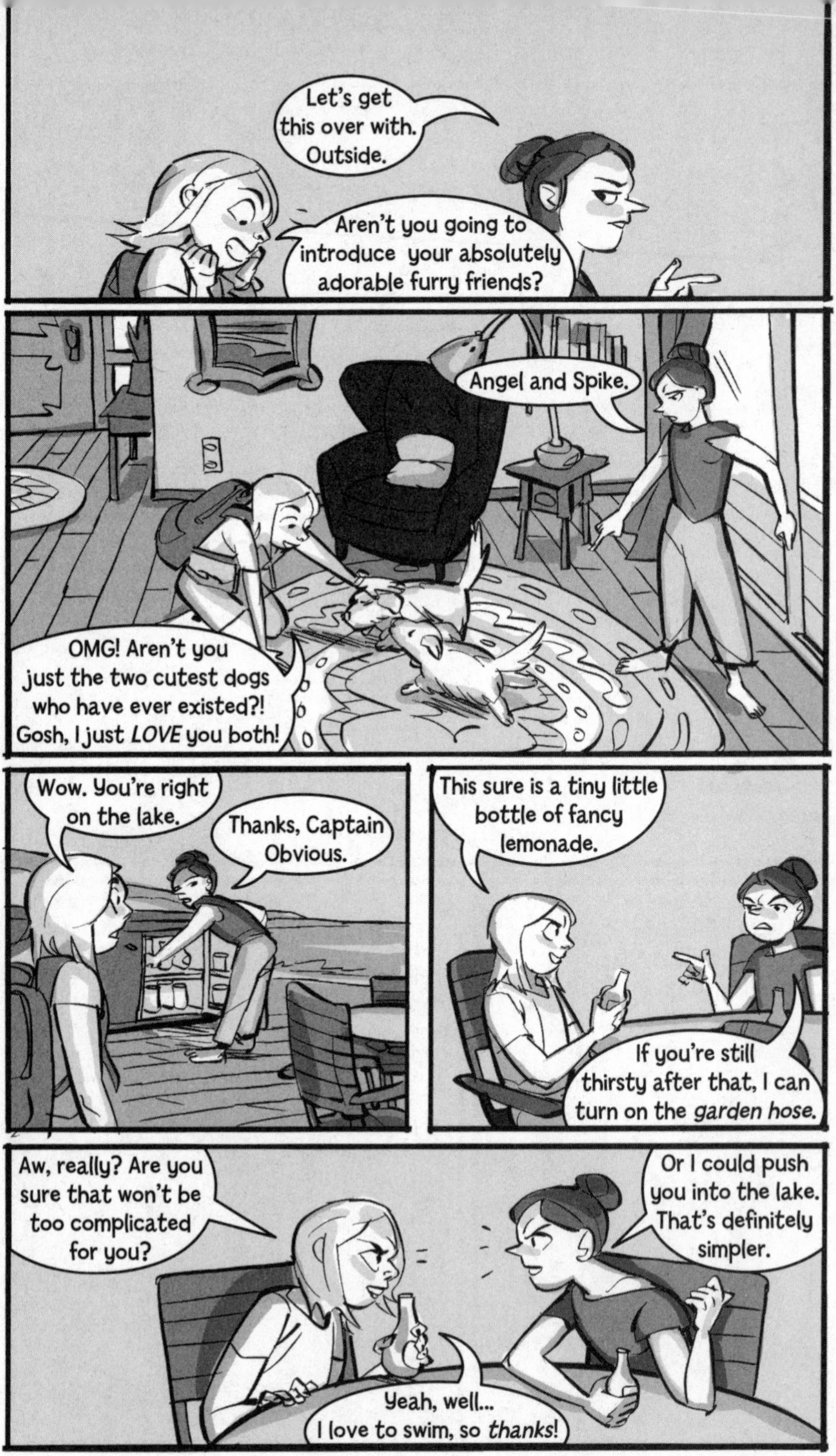
Let's get this over with. Outside.
Aren't you going to introduce your absolutely adorable furry friends?
Angel and Spike.
OMG! Aren't you just the two cutest dogs who have ever existed?! Gosh, I just *LOVE* you both!
Wow. You're right on the lake.
Thanks, Captain Obvious.
This sure is a tiny little bottle of fancy lemonade.
If you're still thirsty after that, I can turn on the *garden hose*.
Aw, really? Are you sure that won't be too complicated for you?
Or I could push you into the lake. That's definitely simpler.
Yeah, well... I love to swim, so *thanks*!

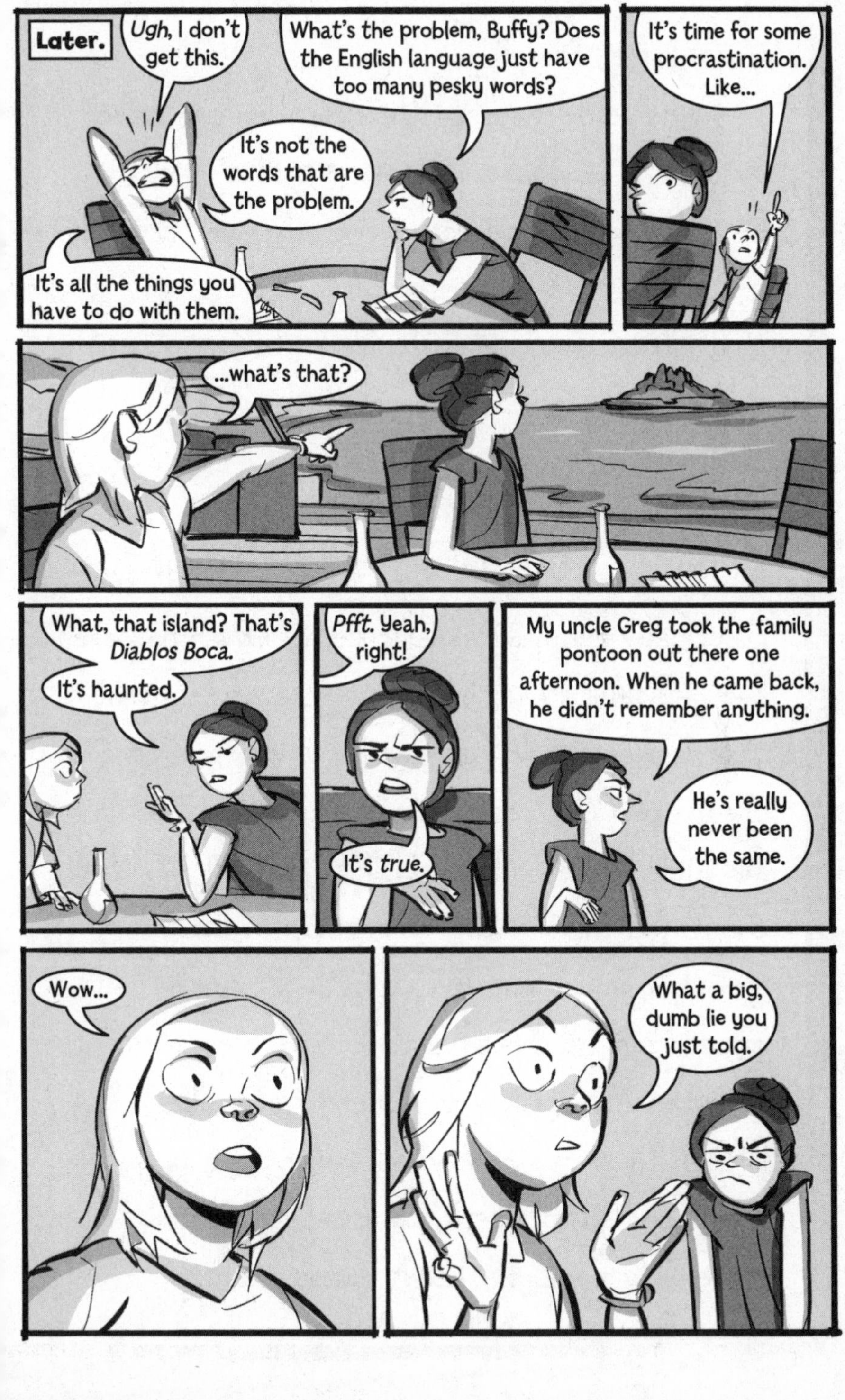

Later.
Ugh, I don't get this.
What's the problem, Buffy? Does the English language just have too many pesky words?
It's not the words that are the problem.
It's all the things you have to do with them.
It's time for some procrastination. Like...
...what's that?
What, that island? That's *Diablos Boca.*
It's haunted.
Pfft. Yeah, right!
It's *true.*
My uncle Greg took the family pontoon out there one afternoon. When he came back, he didn't remember anything.
He's really never been the same.
Wow...
What a big, dumb lie you just told.

Guess what, Diary?

I survived! I entered the lion's den and came out full of lemonade. Melanie is still a jerk, obviously, but her parents were nice and her dogs are super-duper cute. So cute that I honestly couldn't decide which was cuter. Who do _you_ think is cuter?

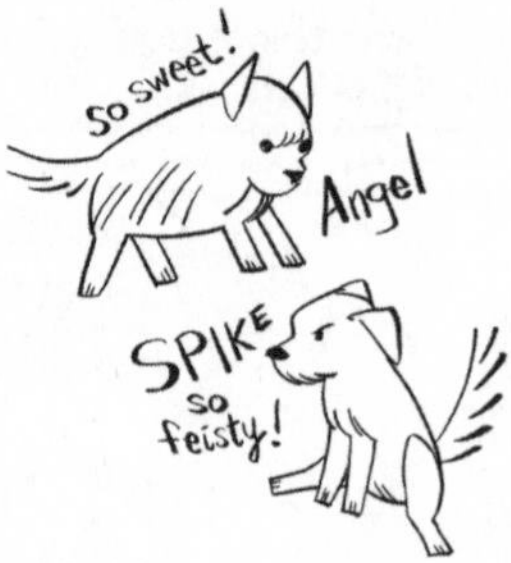
So sweet!
Angel
SPIKE
so feisty!

Anyhoo, Melanie's mom gave us fancy popcorn and chocolate from France. It was practically the best experience my mouth has ever had! Also, Mrs. Dutch used to be a professional cheerleader! I told her I wish I could have gone to cheer camp this year instead of summer school, and Melanie was all, "TELL ME ABOUT IT," and there was this moment we realized we had something in common, and we both got really grossed out at the same time.

Later, Mom picked me up and I ate, like, fifteen tacos. Now I'm gonna watch some puppy videos and go to sleep. Tomorrow = school + Slayer stuff = Buffy needs zzzzzzzzzzs.

http://www.clevelandcreepypasta.com

Cleveland Creepypasta

The Eerie Erie Report: Strange Happenings in Cleveland, USA

Xander Schippa is the latest teen to go MISSING in a series of strange disappearances that have scared the community. Schippa resembles the other victims in that he was also a really cool and good-looking teen boy.

Local legends about creepy island in Lake Erie

Please read these articles. - Inbox

Message

TO: Buffy Summers
FROM: Miss Sparks
SUBJECT: Please read these articles.

Buffy! Please read these articles. I realize they don't come from a reliable source, but I find the conclusions very compelling!

Buffy's Stuff

Library Science

DOGS WHO HATE BROCCOLI

Sparky

 Buffy, did you receive my email?

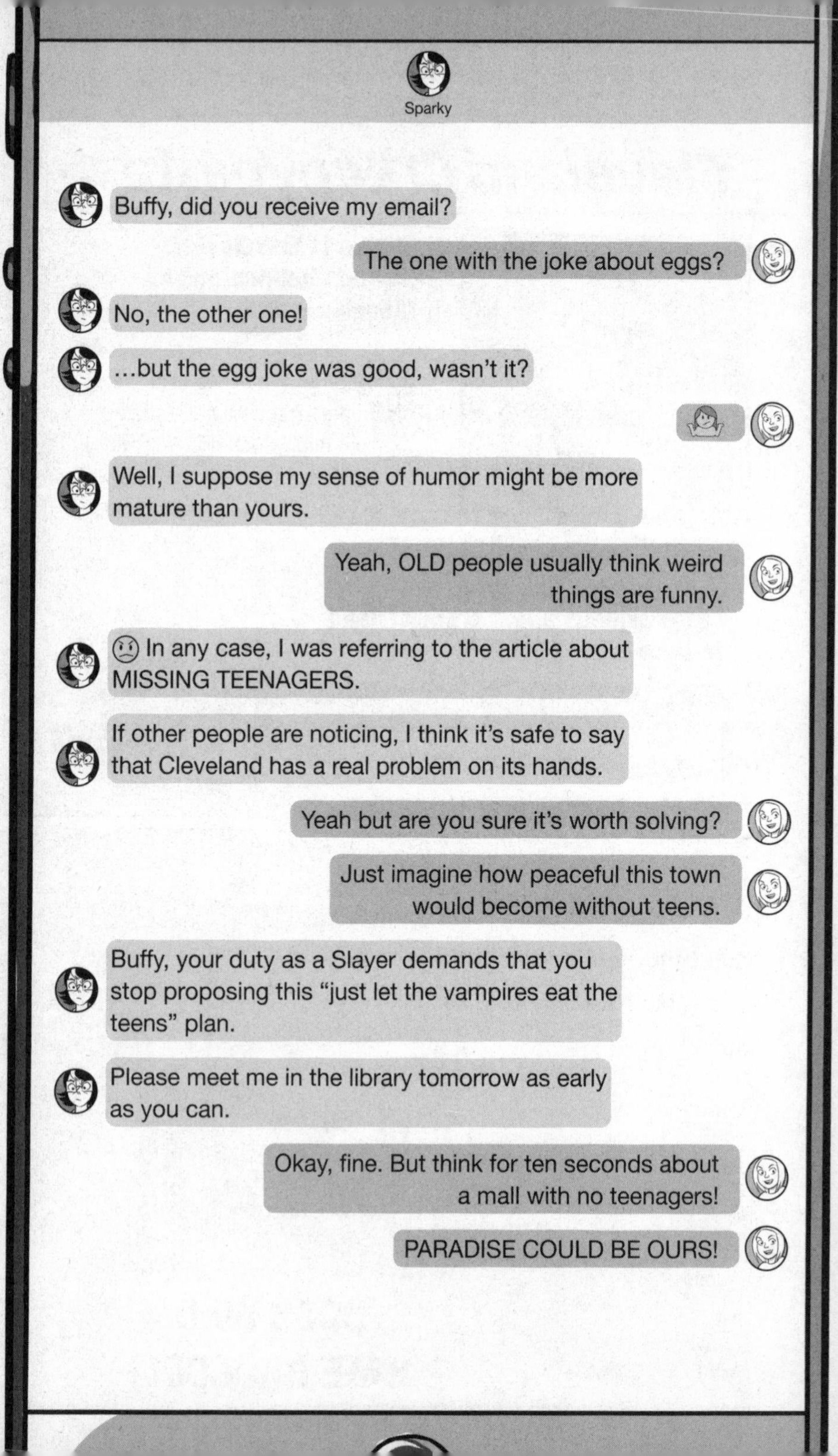

The one with the joke about eggs?

 No, the other one!

 ...but the egg joke was good, wasn't it?

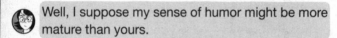

Well, I suppose my sense of humor might be more mature than yours.

Yeah, OLD people usually think weird things are funny.

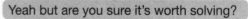

😠 In any case, I was referring to the article about MISSING TEENAGERS.

If other people are noticing, I think it's safe to say that Cleveland has a real problem on its hands.

Yeah but are you sure it's worth solving?

Just imagine how peaceful this town would become without teens.

 Buffy, your duty as a Slayer demands that you stop proposing this "just let the vampires eat the teens" plan.

 Please meet me in the library tomorrow as early as you can.

Okay, fine. But think for ten seconds about a mall with no teenagers!

PARADISE COULD BE OURS!

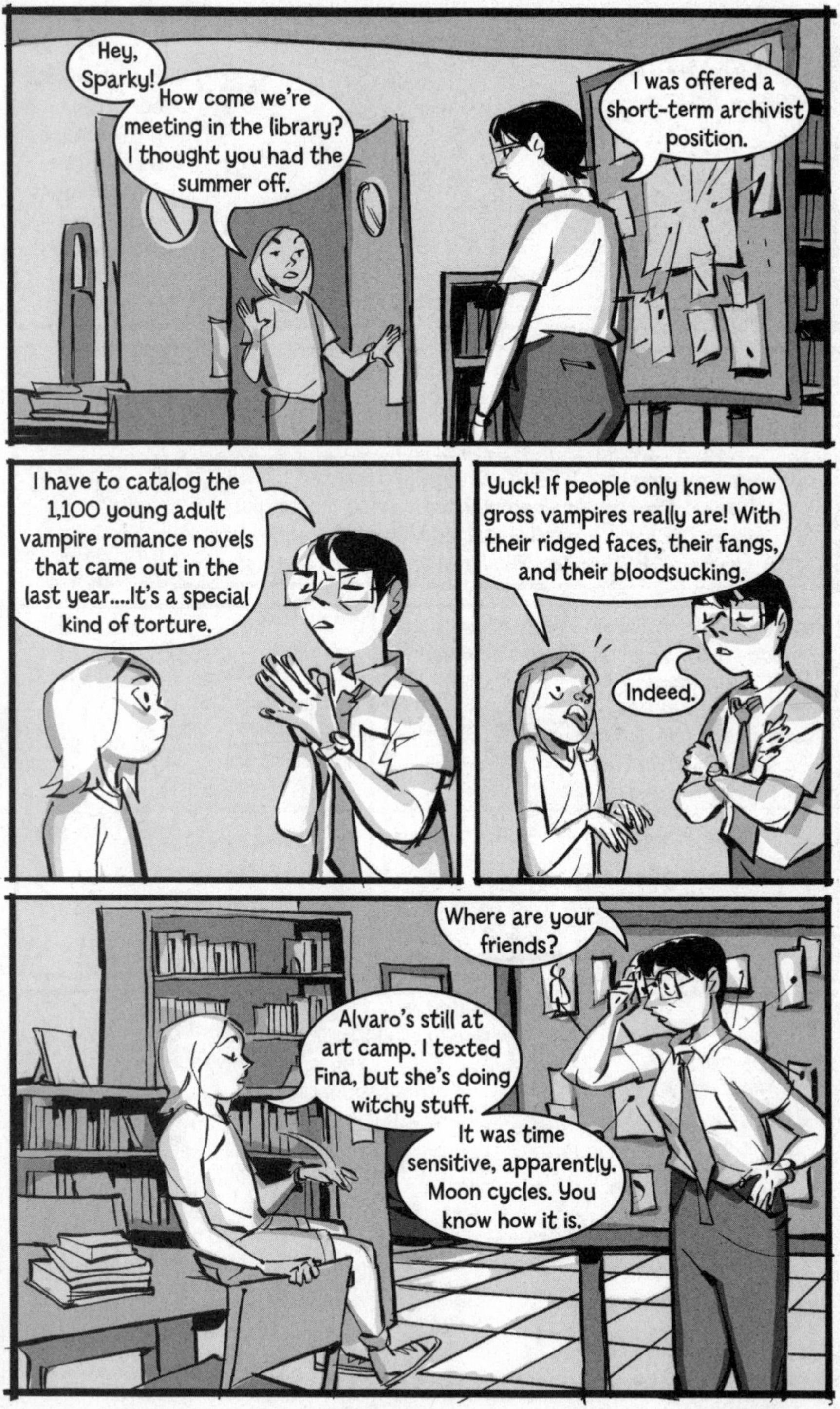
Hey, Sparky!
How come we're meeting in the library? I thought you had the summer off.
I was offered a short-term archivist position.
I have to catalog the 1,100 young adult vampire romance novels that came out in the last year....It's a special kind of torture.
Yuck! If people only knew how gross vampires really are! With their ridged faces, their fangs, and their bloodsucking.
Indeed.
Where are your friends?
Alvaro's still at art camp. I texted Fina, but she's doing witchy stuff.
It was time sensitive, apparently. Moon cycles. You know how it is.

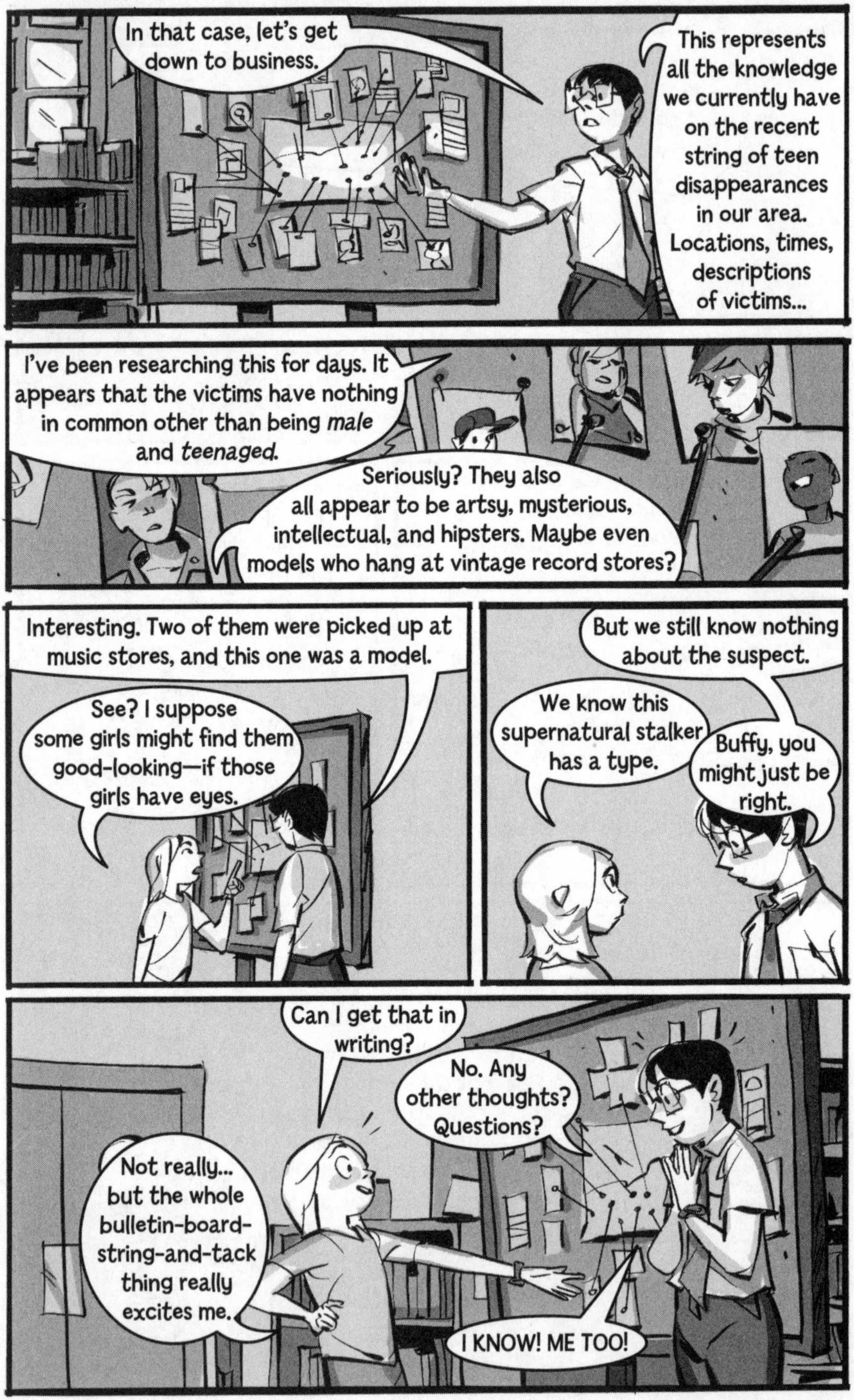

In that case, let's get down to business.
This represents all the knowledge we currently have on the recent string of teen disappearances in our area. Locations, times, descriptions of victims...
I've been researching this for days. It appears that the victims have nothing in common other than being *male* and *teenaged*.
Seriously? They also all appear to be artsy, mysterious, intellectual, and hipsters. Maybe even models who hang at vintage record stores?
Interesting. Two of them were picked up at music stores, and this one was a model.
See? I suppose some girls might find them good-looking—if those girls have eyes.
But we still know nothing about the suspect.
We know this supernatural stalker has a type.
Buffy, you might just be right.
Can I get that in writing?
No. Any other thoughts? Questions?
Not really... but the whole bulletin-board-string-and-tack thing really excites me.
I KNOW! ME TOO!

Dear Buff-ster,

Letter writing! So retro! I know you don't think it's as good as texting, but, hey, you get to keep my words on this physical paper <u>FOREVER</u>, and it even comes with a cute little sticker called a <u>stamp</u>. I think it's nice. Plus how often do you get a text hand-delivered? Almost never, probably.

Art camp is even better than I imagined! They have a real darkroom for students to use, but the chemicals smell like rotten eggs. My poor wolfy nose can't take it! Along with my photography classes, I'm also taking a free-drawing class that's pretty cool. But none of it is nearly as exciting as what us Scoobies do in Cleveland!

I heard teenagers are still going missing. That's really crazy. Have you solved the mystery yet? If not, I'll be back in a couple weeks to help out. But let's try to get it solved before my art opening! You're coming, right? You probably have to since it's at your mom's art gallery. Yay!

I miss you and Fina so much!! Happy slaying!!

Love,

Alvaro

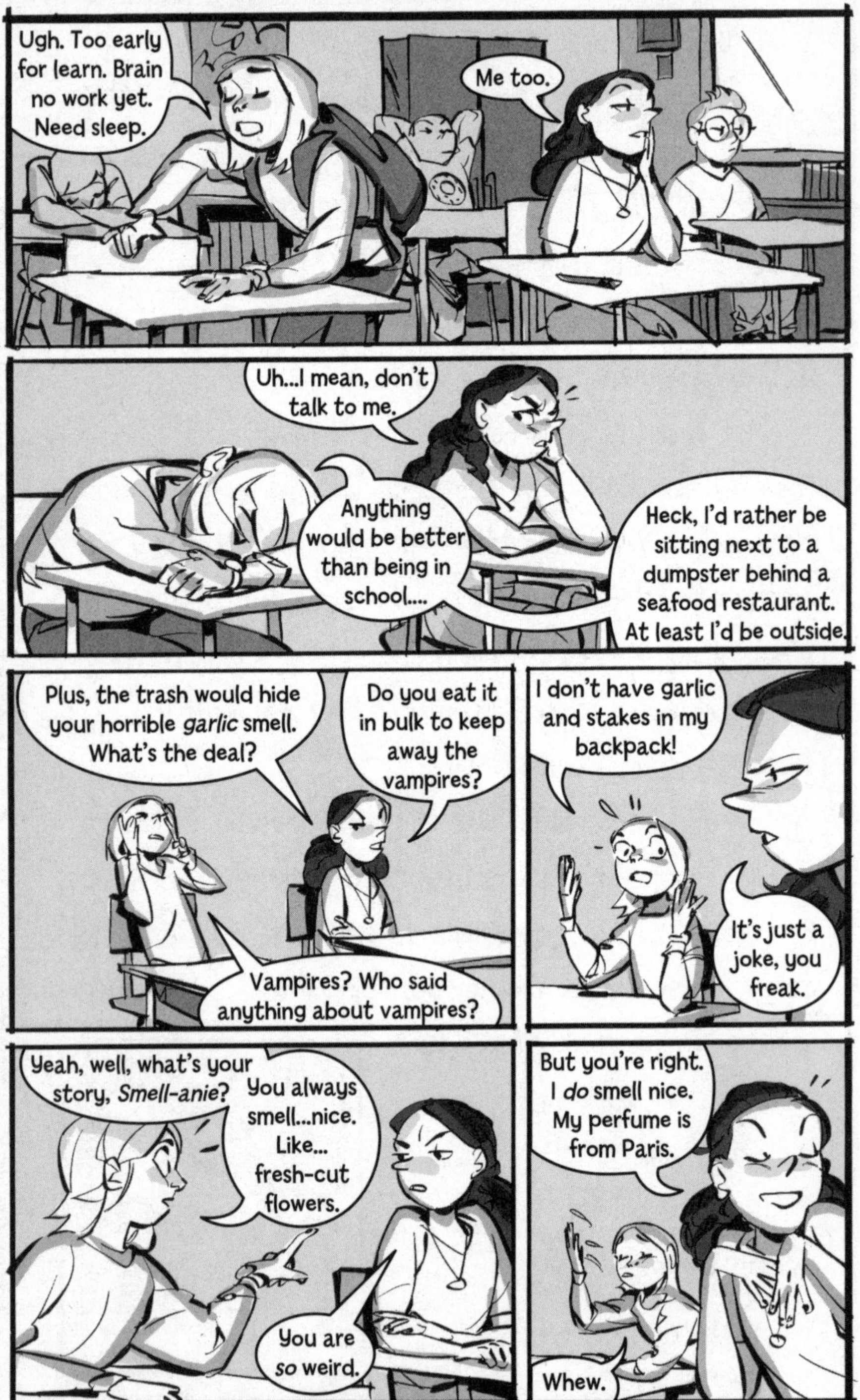

Ugh. Too early for learn. Brain no work yet. Need sleep.
Me too.
Uh...I mean, don't talk to me.
Anything would be better than being in school....
Heck, I'd rather be sitting next to a dumpster behind a seafood restaurant. At least I'd be outside.
Plus, the trash would hide your horrible *garlic* smell. What's the deal?
Do you eat it in bulk to keep away the vampires?
Vampires? Who said anything about vampires?
I don't have garlic and stakes in my backpack!
It's just a joke, you freak.
Yeah, well, what's your story, *Smell-anie*?
You always smell...nice. Like... fresh-cut flowers.
You are *so* weird.
But you're right. I *do* smell nice. My perfume is from Paris.
Whew.

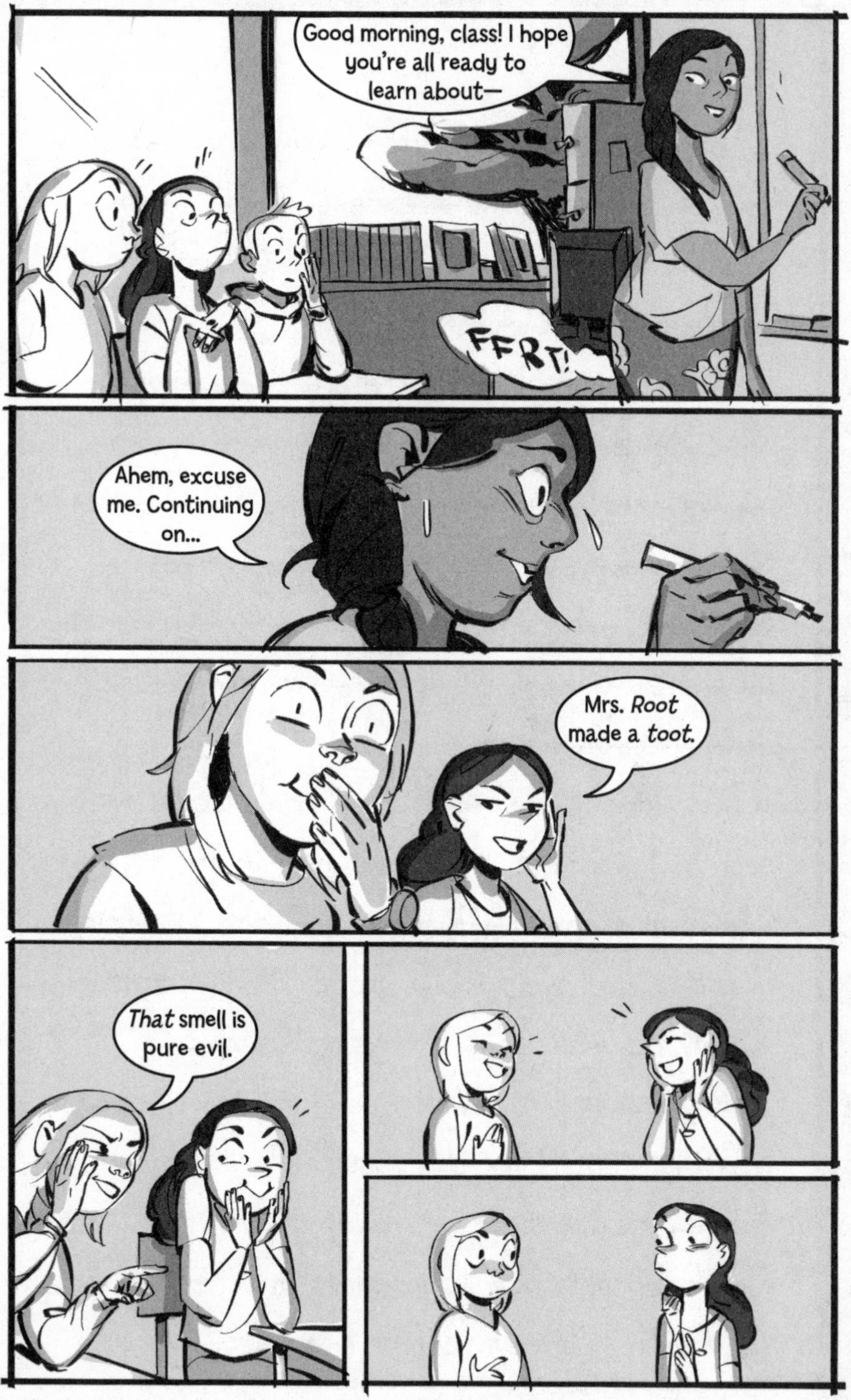
Good morning, class! I hope you're all ready to learn about—
FFRT!
Ahem, excuse me. Continuing on...
Mrs. *Root* made a *toot.*
That smell is pure evil.

Dear Diary,

~~Some really weird stuff is going on and I can't talk to anybody about it except YOU. Ya know, cuz you're a book, and books don't tell other people's secrets...right?~~

~~So I think I'm kinda sorta starting to...not hate...Melanie. Maybe it's because we're both in summer school, or maybe it's cuz my friends are MIA. Or maybe it's because we live over a Heckmouth where weird and crazy stuff happens all the time. Vampires, demons, and now Melanie and I becoming friends....~~

No. Nope! Never mind! That's ridiculous. As soon as I wrote it, I was like, <u>nuh-uh</u> and <u>no way</u>. I have an overactive imagination. We're just being nice cuz we have to. Our grades depend on it. Yup, that's what it is. Anyways. Moving on!

My best friends, Alvaro and Fina, have been... less than around for the past few days. Alvaro gets an excuse since he's away at art camp. But Fina has practically disappeared off the face of the Earth. I haven't seen or heard from her in ages! She's deep into magical stuff, which is really cool, but, like, isn't magic all about sisterhood? And aren't best girl friends like sisters? So shouldn't she and I be, like...closer? I mean, we saved the school together! That's a bond that shouldn't break just because her big sister is home from college.

Sigh. Before school ended, I dreamed of having an awesome summer with Alvaro and Fina, doing all normal-kid stuff—like riding bikes and laying out in the sun for too long. We'd eat slushies and stay up all night watching rom-coms....

Ya know what? No more talky-talky/writey-writey. It's time to go over to her house and see if she's there! Sure, it's old-fashioned and very creepy, but I can barely remember her face and she's my best friend in the whole world! Yup, that's what I'm gonna do. Fina is my best friend. ~~Not Melanie with her nice-smelling and perfect hair.~~ Why am I still writing?!

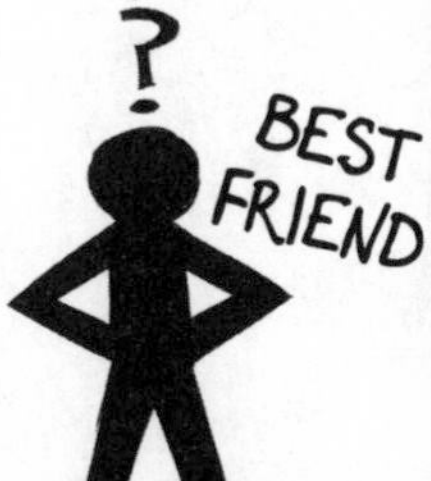
?
BEST FRIEND

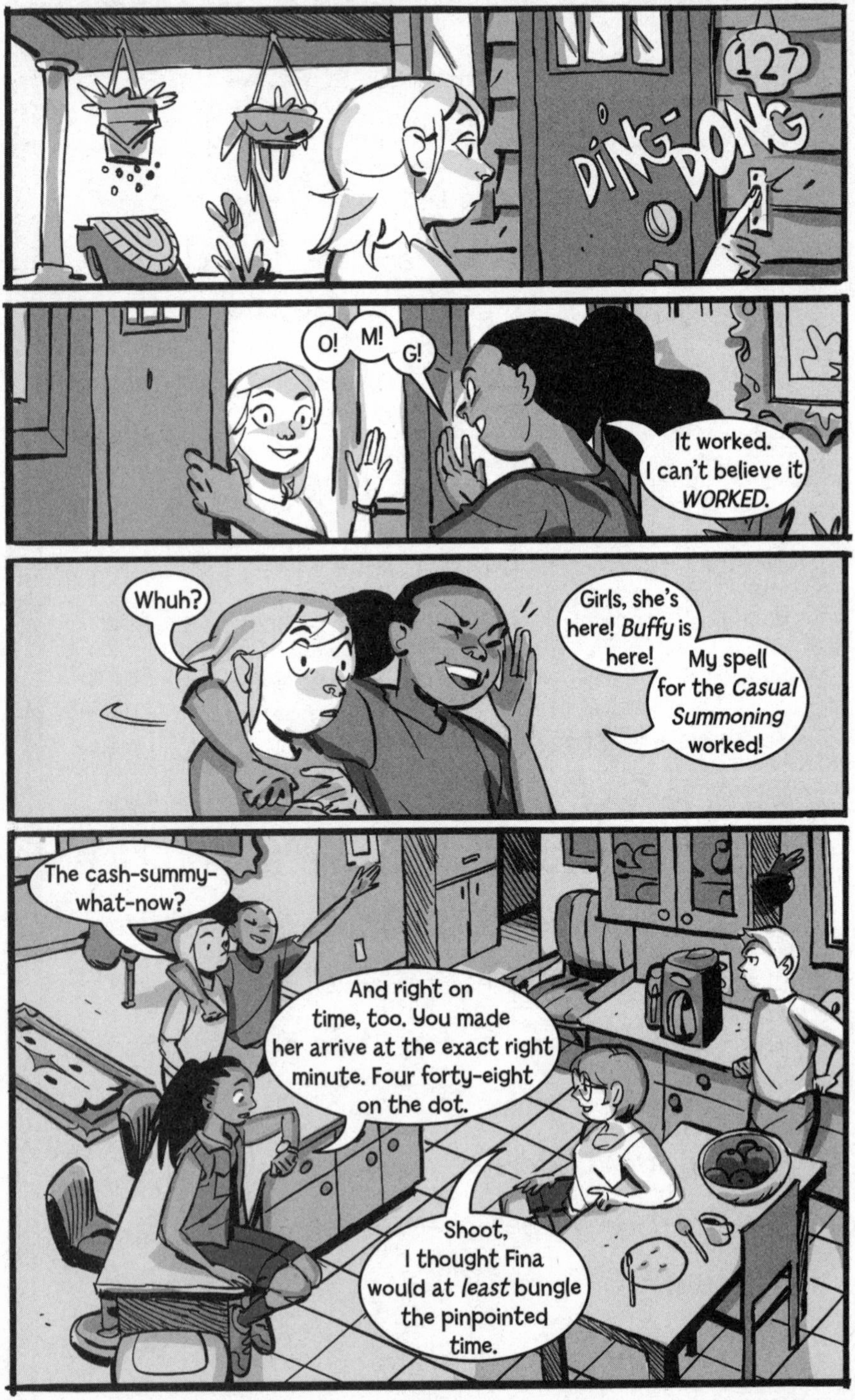
127
DING-DONG
O! M! G!
It worked. I can't believe it *WORKED.*
Whuh?
Girls, she's here! *Buffy* is here!
My spell for the *Casual Summoning* worked!
The cash-summy-what-now?
And right on time, too. You made her arrive at the exact right minute. Four forty-eight on the dot.
Shoot, I thought Fina would at *least* bungle the pinpointed time.

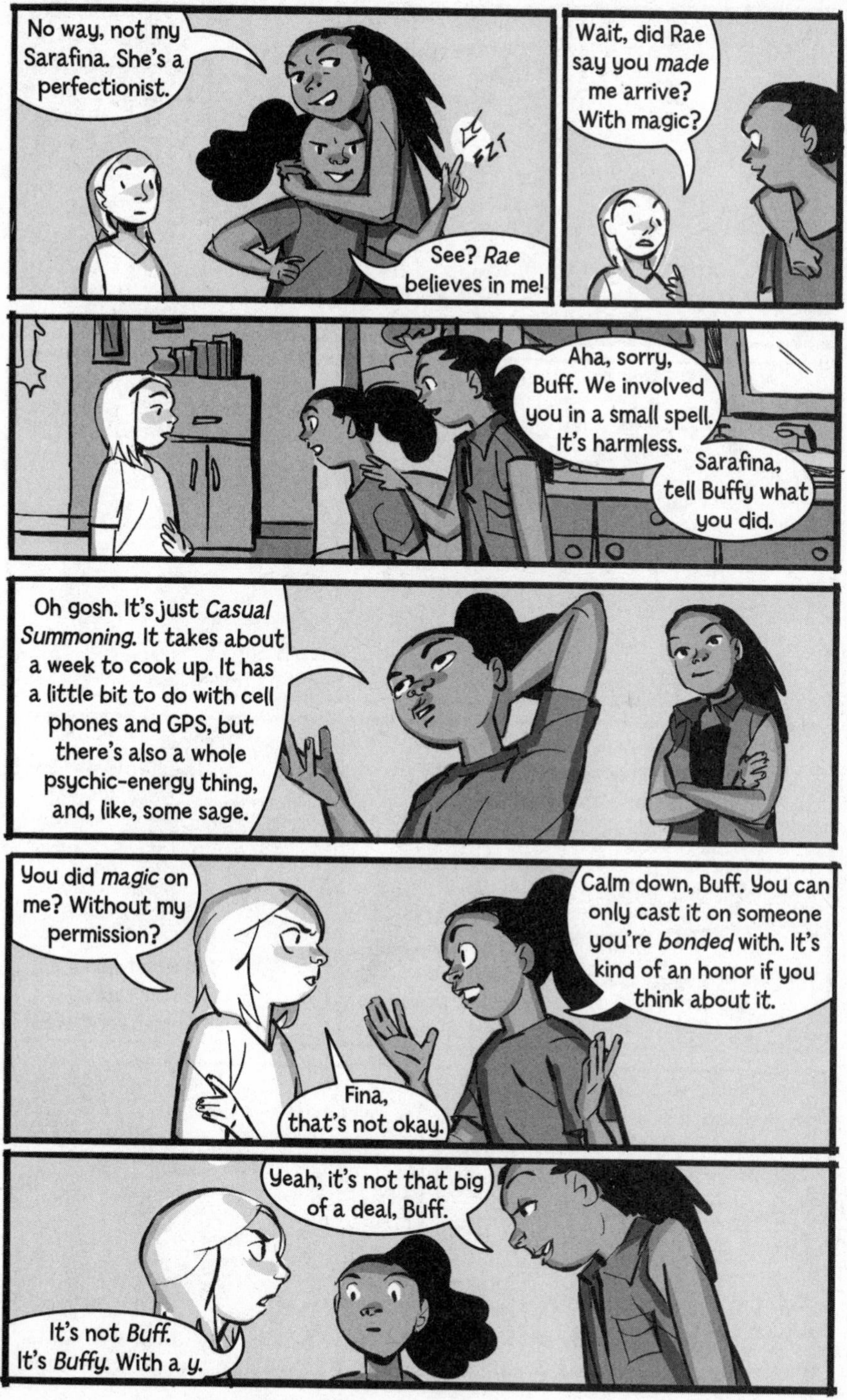
No way, not my Sarafina. She's a perfectionist.
FZT
See? *Rae* believes in me!
Wait, did Rae say you *made* me arrive? With magic?
Aha, sorry, Buff. We involved you in a small spell. It's harmless.
Sarafina, tell Buffy what you did.
Oh gosh. It's just *Casual Summoning*. It takes about a week to cook up. It has a little bit to do with cell phones and GPS, but there's also a whole psychic-energy thing, and, like, some sage.
You did *magic* on me? Without my permission?
Calm down, Buff. You can only cast it on someone you're *bonded* with. It's kind of an honor if you think about it.
Fina, that's not okay.
Yeah, it's not that big of a deal, Buff.
It's not *Buff*. It's *Buffy*. With a *y*.

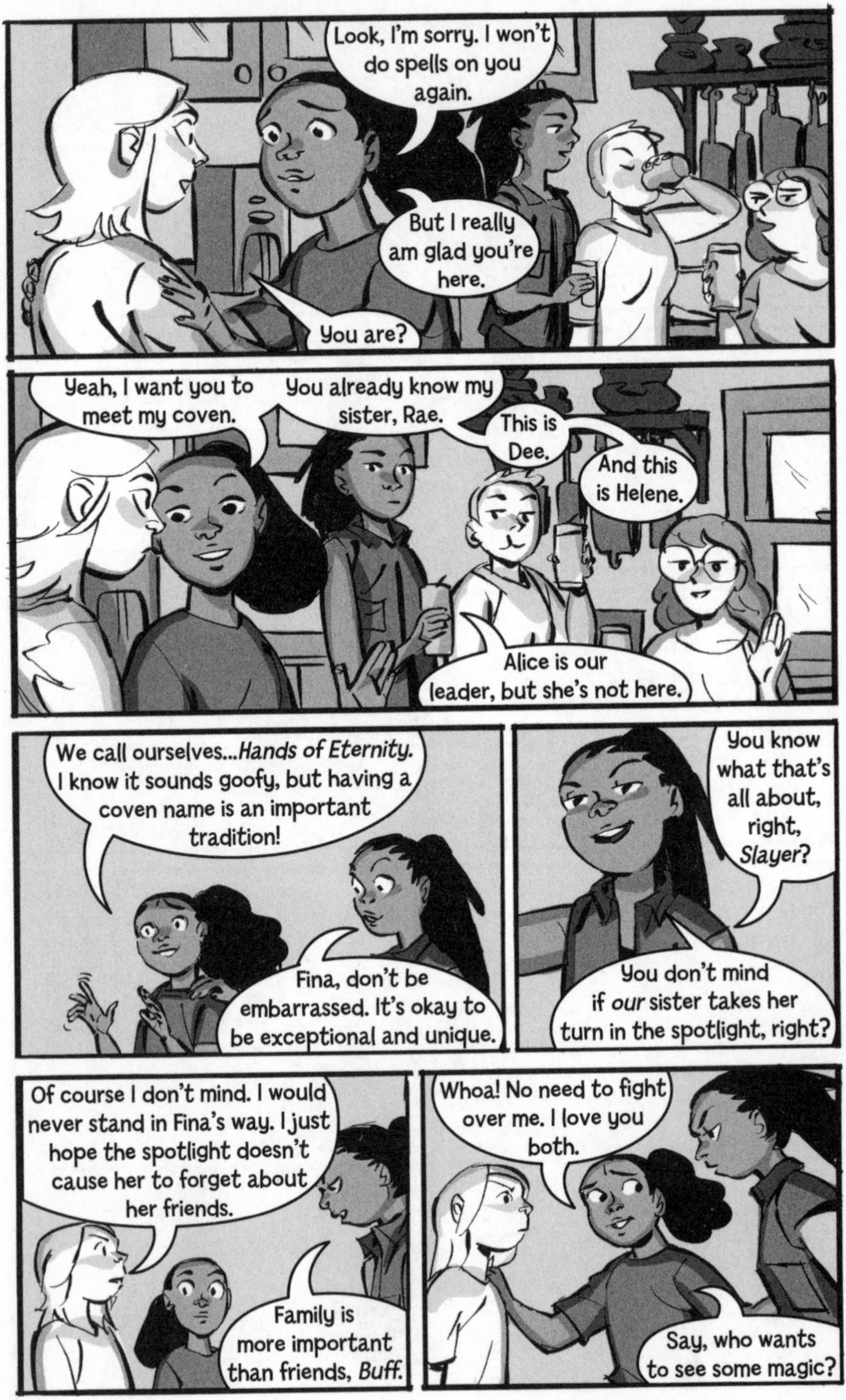
Look, I'm sorry. I won't do spells on you again.
But I really am glad you're here.
You are?
Yeah, I want you to meet my coven.
You already know my sister, Rae.
This is Dee.
And this is Helene.
Alice is our leader, but she's not here.
We call ourselves...*Hands of Eternity.* I know it sounds goofy, but having a coven name is an important tradition!
Fina, don't be embarrassed. It's okay to be exceptional and unique.
You know what that's all about, right, *Slayer*?
You don't mind if *our* sister takes her turn in the spotlight, right?
Of course I don't mind. I would never stand in Fina's way. I just hope the spotlight doesn't cause her to forget about her friends.
Family is more important than friends, *Buff*.
Whoa! No need to fight over me. I love you both.
Say, who wants to see some magic?

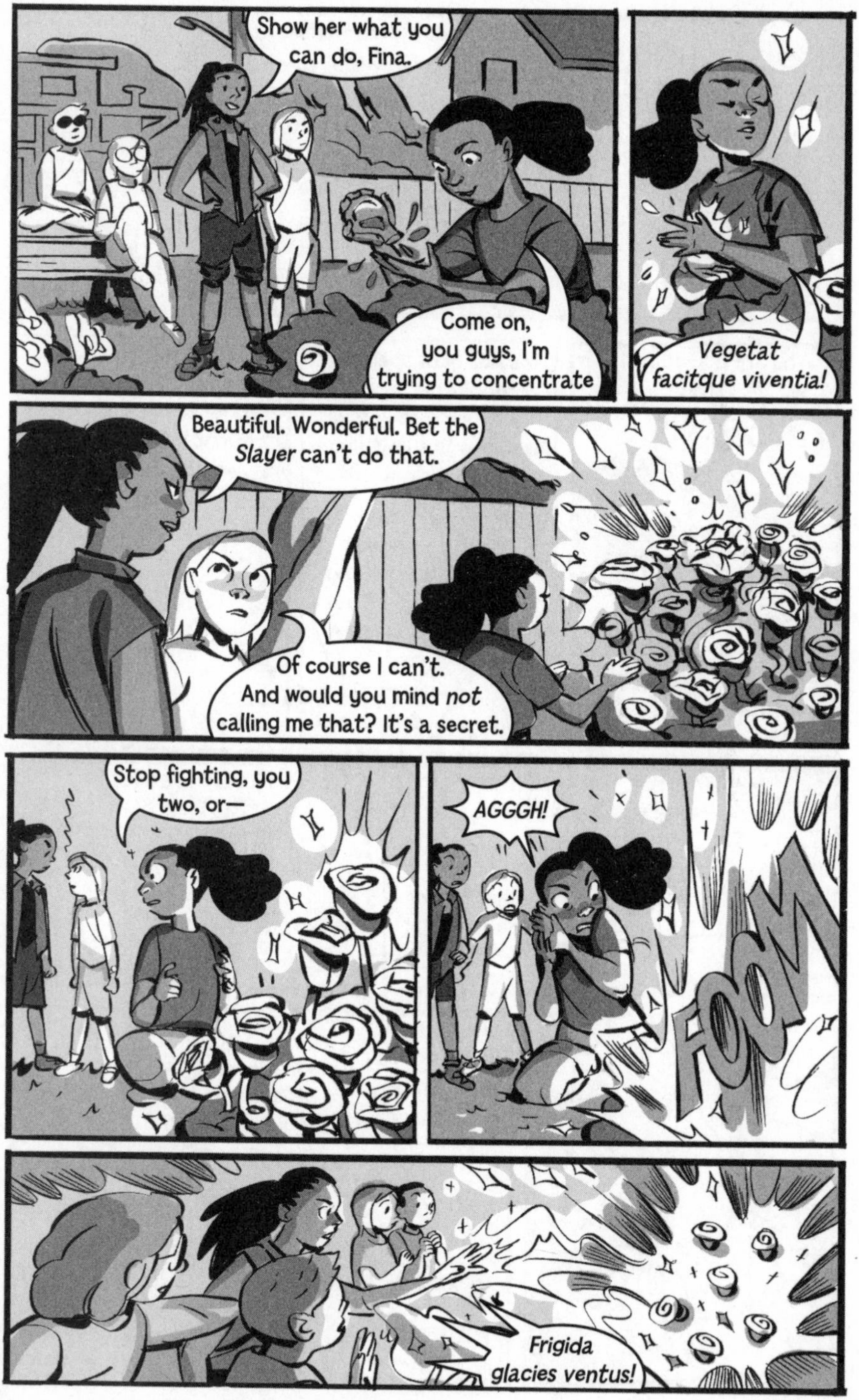
Show her what you can do, Fina.
Come on, you guys, I'm trying to concentrate
Vegetat facitque viventia!
Beautiful. Wonderful. Bet the *Slayer* can't do that.
Of course I can't. And would you mind *not* calling me that? It's a secret.
Stop fighting, you two, or—
AGGGH!
FOOM
Frigida glacies ventus!

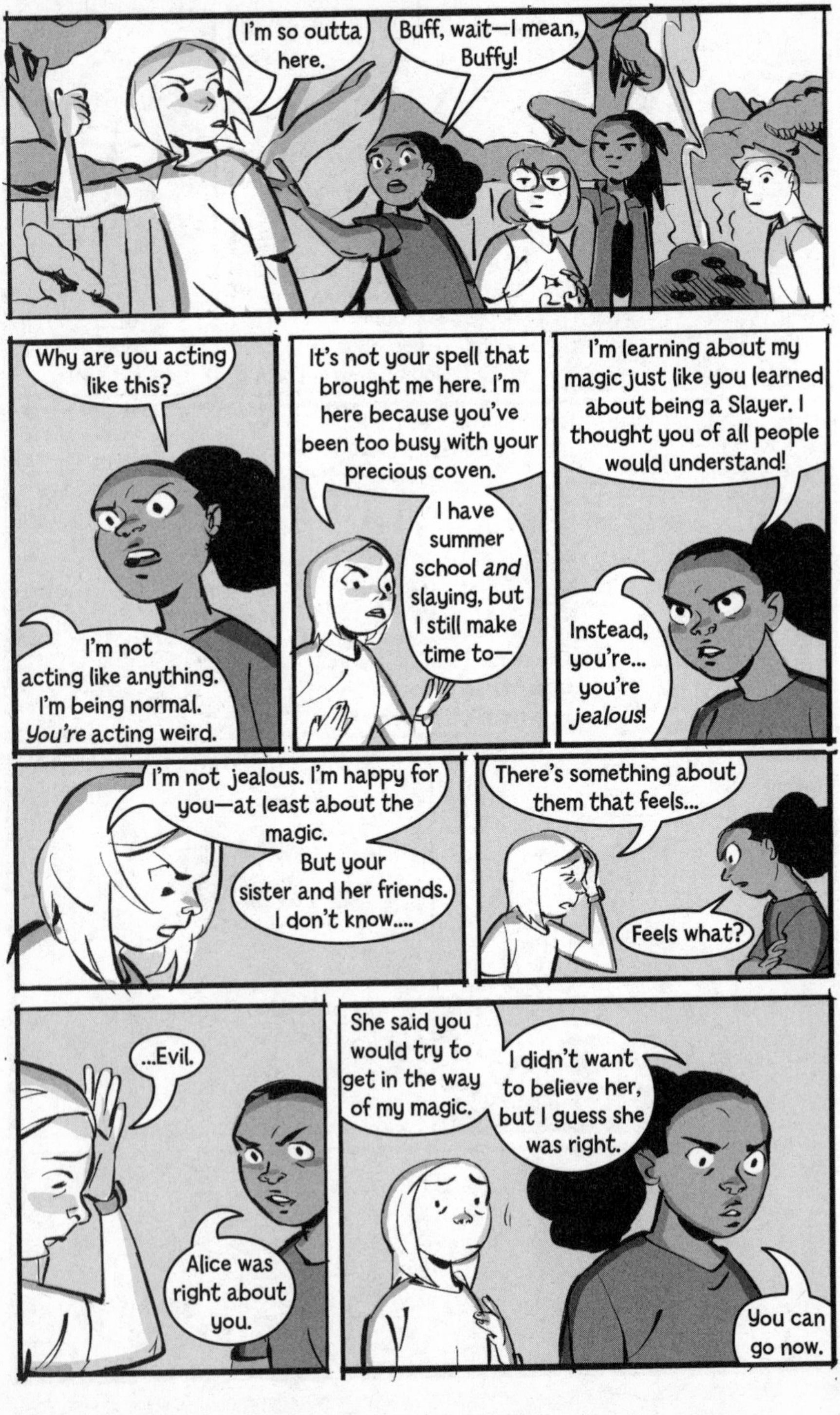
I'm so outta here.
Buff, wait—I mean, Buffy!
Why are you acting like this?
I'm not acting like anything. I'm being normal. *You're* acting weird.
It's not your spell that brought me here. I'm here because you've been too busy with your precious coven.
I have summer school *and* slaying, but I still make time to—
I'm learning about my magic just like you learned about being a Slayer. I thought you of all people would understand!
Instead, you're... you're *jealous*!
I'm not jealous. I'm happy for you—at least about the magic.
But your sister and her friends. I don't know....
There's something about them that feels...
Feels what?
...Evil.
Alice was right about you.
She said you would try to get in the way of my magic.
I didn't want to believe her, but I guess she was right.
You can go now.

Dear Diary,

Everything is falling apart. Summer is supposed to be a vacation, full of fun and friends. So far, mine is just full of sad faces and succubus-es. Succubus-ses? Succubi? I dunno. A succubus is a scary, screamy demon lady. I fought two of them last night. I slayed them, but not before they busted Sparky's and my eardrums.  Ouchie. I couldn't hear anything Mrs. Root said in school today. Luckily, Melanie shared her notes with me.

But who cares about all that stuff? Fina and I are in our first fight. I said some stuff, and she said some stuff, and now she's really mad at me. I want to be mad at her, but really I just want my friend back. Why did her dumb sister and her dumb coven friends have to come back from college? Ugh. And who is this dumb Alice who warned Fina about me? I don't even know her, so she definitely doesn't know me! And I'm not jealous. I'm just...worried. I joke about my tingly Slayer-sense, but for real...when I was around Rae and her friends, they felt... wrong.

Hmm. Maybe I am jealous and just don't know it. Feelings are tricky. Like vampires. One minute, they look normal, but the next minute, they're all fangs and scary. I mean, Fina's like a sister to me, but Rae is her real sister. And they all have magic powers, but I am just strong.

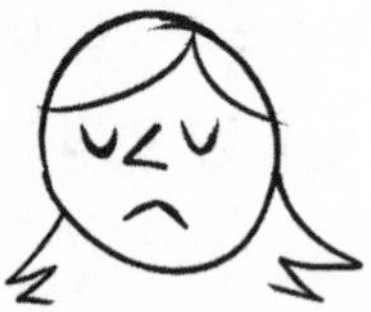

I'm a lonely Slayer.

In other news: My mom is dropping me off at the mall next Saturday so I can spend my lawn-mowing money. That's right: DROPPING ME OFF—ALONE!! As in, she's going to drive me there, then I'm going to get out of the car, then she's going to LEAVE. I get to buy whatever I want—candy, clothes, junk!—with zero parental input!! At the end of school year, I maybe saved everyone in my school from certain death by defeating an ancient vampire—but really, what's that compared to the potential of finding a truly perfect outfit without my mom insisting that jeans should never cost more than twenty-five dollars?

You know what? The mall is a magical place. And Fina and I need some magic healing. I'm gonna text Fina to see if she wants to come!! Then with chocolate shakes and curly fries, I'll have a good talk with her. Once more—with feeling! We'll have a clean slate, then we'll be besties and everything will be great again!

Hey Fina.
I'm really sorry about the other day. I was thinking, we should talk (this time with no raised voices). You're my best friend, and I really miss you. Want to go to the mall?

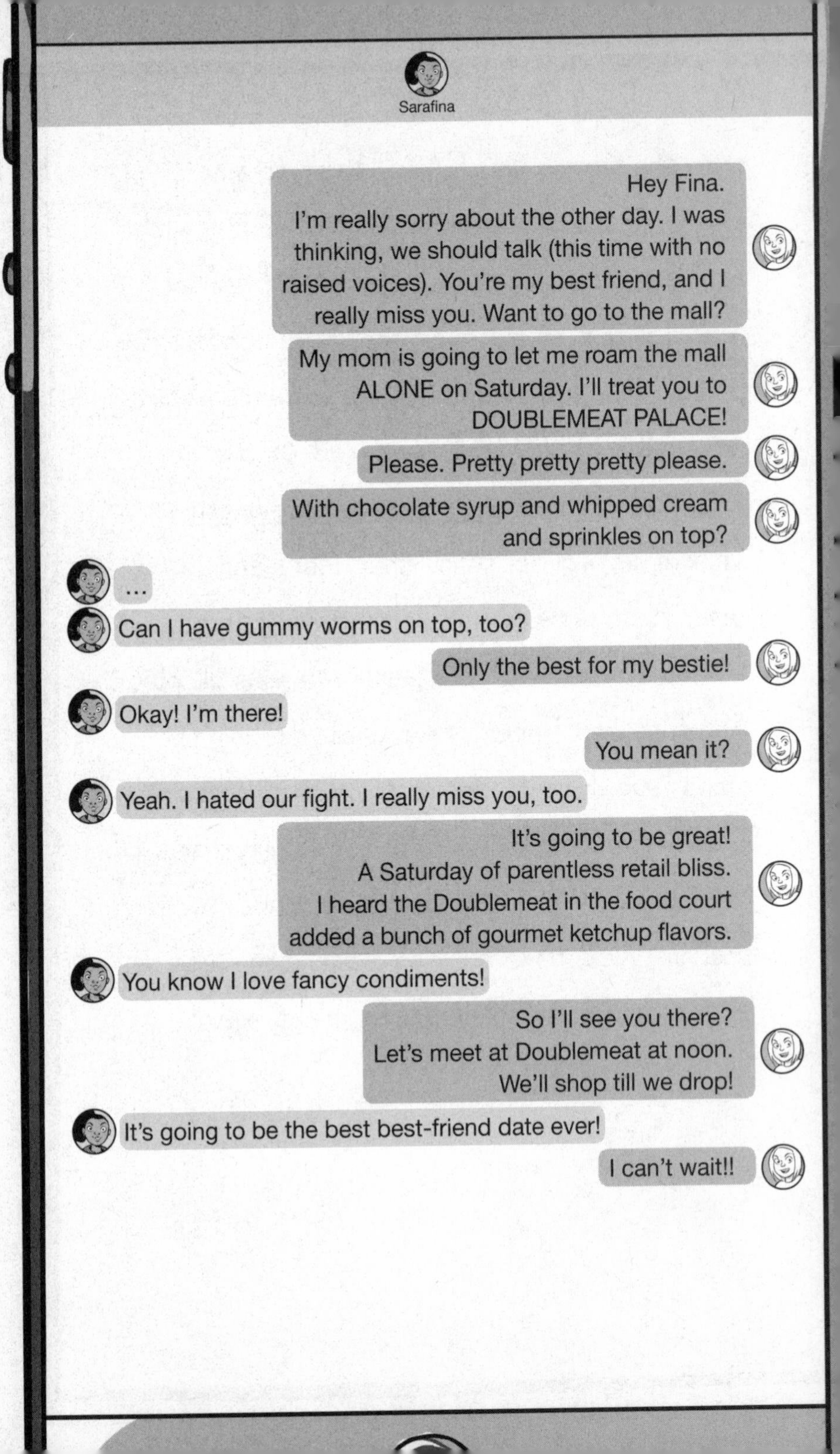

My mom is going to let me roam the mall ALONE on Saturday. I'll treat you to DOUBLEMEAT PALACE!

Please. Pretty pretty pretty please.

With chocolate syrup and whipped cream and sprinkles on top?

 ...

 Can I have gummy worms on top, too?

Only the best for my bestie!

 Okay! I'm there!

You mean it?

 Yeah. I hated our fight. I really miss you, too.

It's going to be great!
A Saturday of parentless retail bliss.
I heard the Doublemeat in the food court added a bunch of gourmet ketchup flavors.

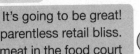 You know I love fancy condiments!

So I'll see you there?
Let's meet at Doublemeat at noon.
We'll shop till we drop!

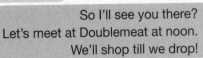 It's going to be the best best-friend date ever!

I can't wait!!

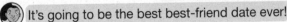

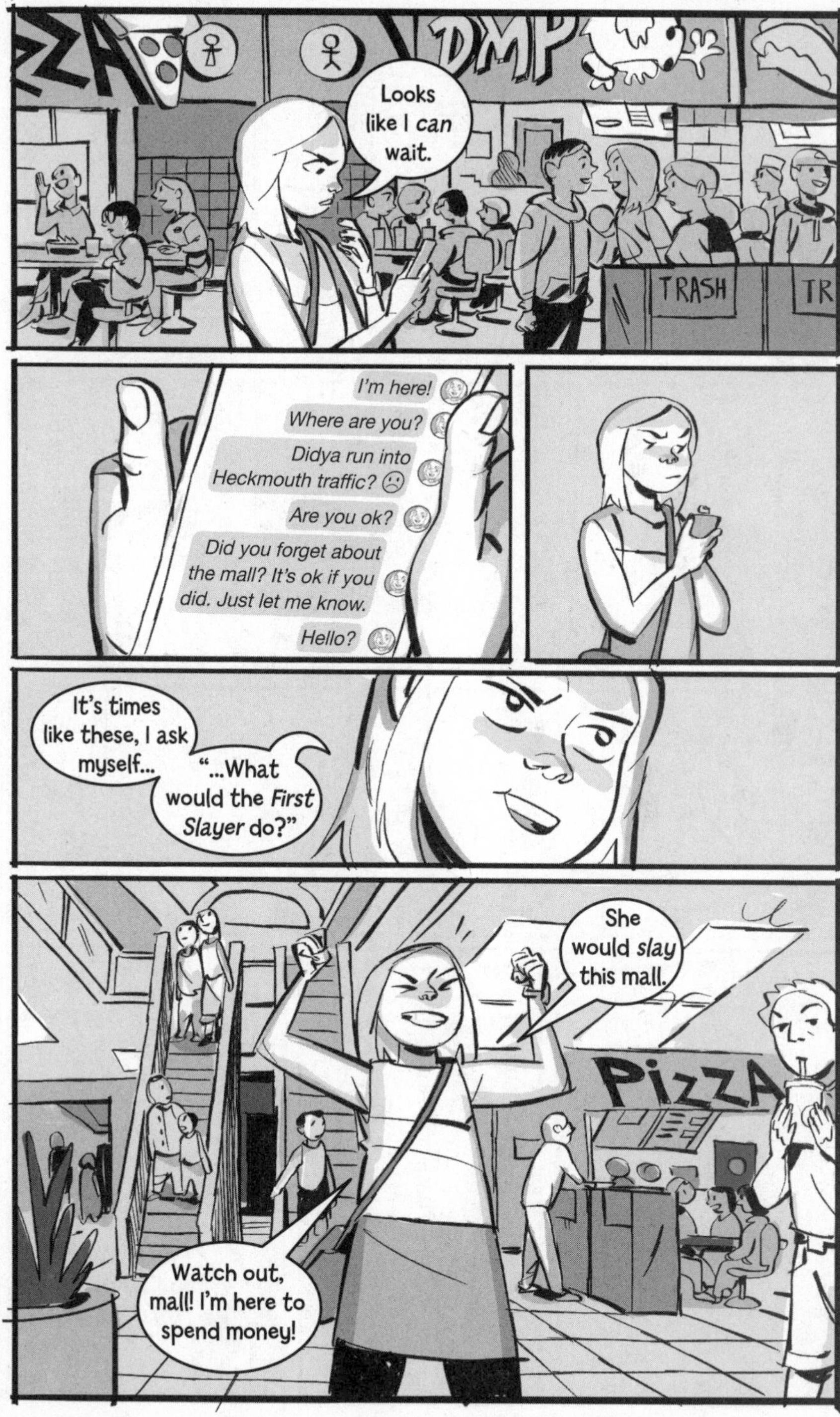
ZZA
DMP
Looks like I *can* wait.
TRASH
TR
I'm here!
Where are you?
Didya run into Heckmouth traffic? ☹
Are you ok?
Did you forget about the mall? It's ok if you did. Just let me know.
Hello?
It's times like these, I ask myself...
"...What would the *First Slayer* do?"
She would *slay* this mall.
PIZZA
Watch out, mall! I'm here to spend money!

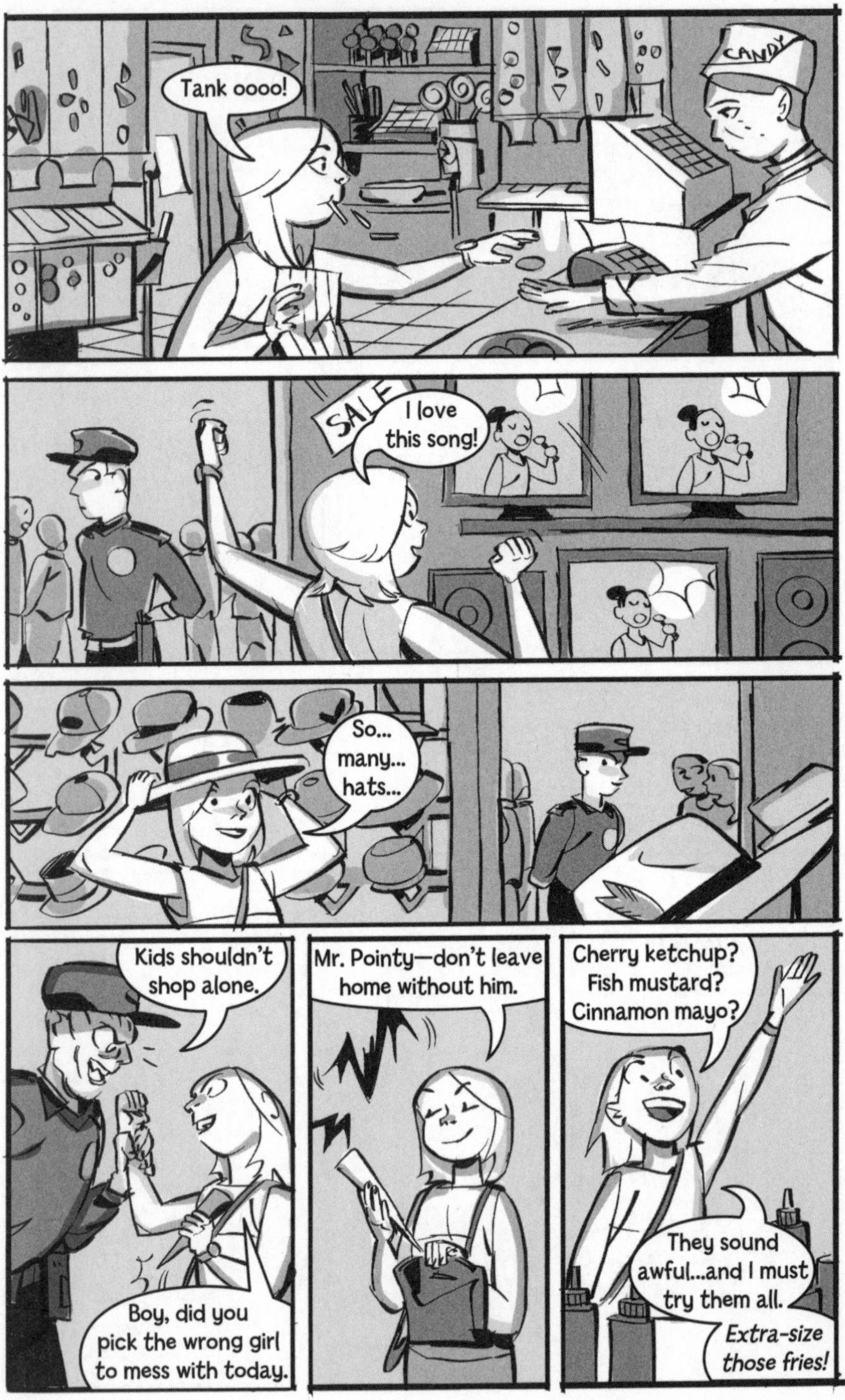
Tank oooo!
CANDY
SALE
I love this song!
So... many... hats...
Kids shouldn't shop alone.
Boy, did you pick the wrong girl to mess with today.
Mr. Pointy—don't leave home without him.
Cherry ketchup? Fish mustard? Cinnamon mayo?
They sound awful...and I must try them all.
Extra-size those fries!

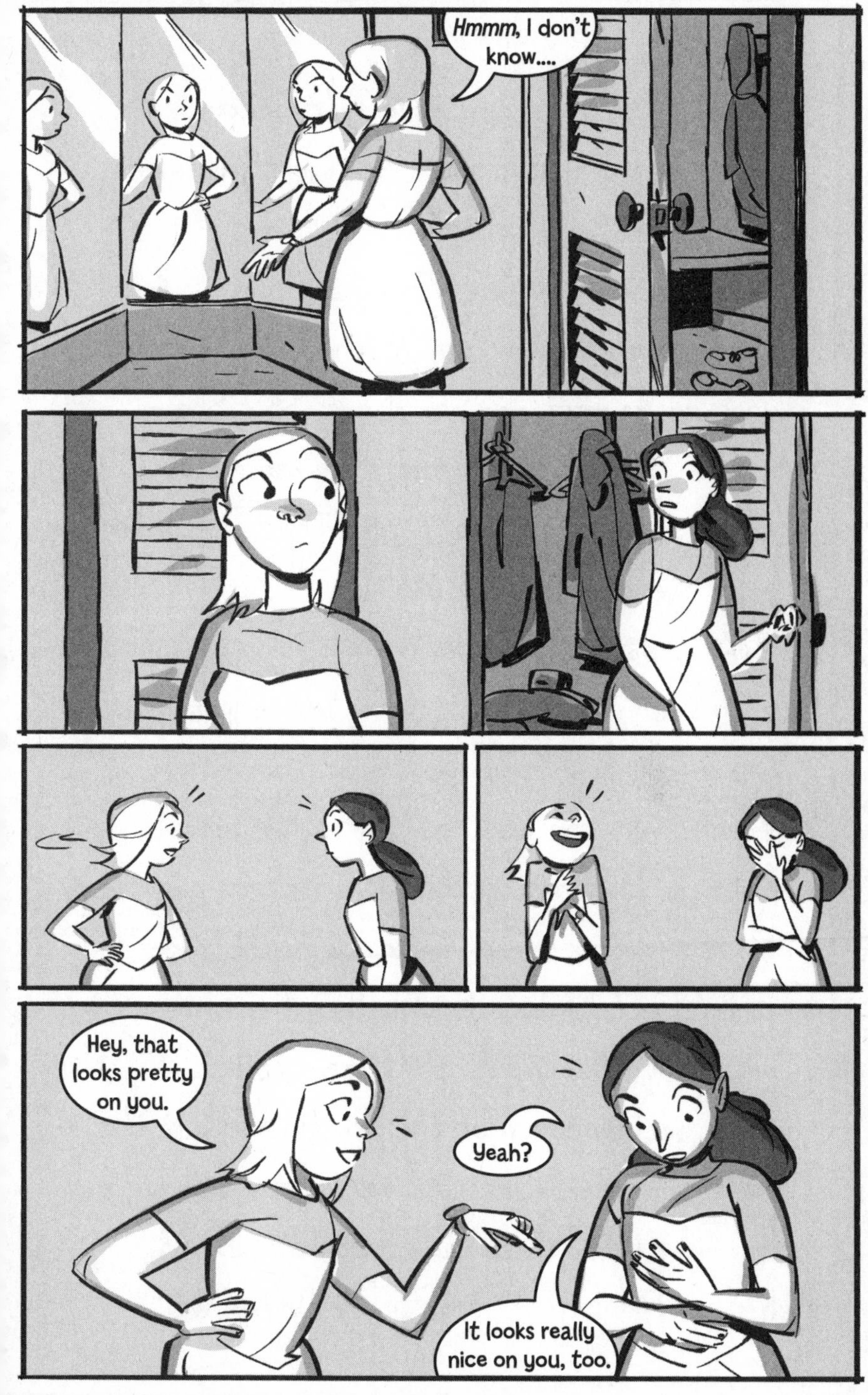
Hmmm, I don't know....
Hey, that looks pretty on you.
Yeah?
It looks really nice on you, too.

Diary, I slay vampires and fight demons and live on a Heckmouth, but today might have been the strangest day of my life.

As you know, today was my big, cool grown-up independent day at the mall. Fina was supposed to meet me. She didn't show. She didn't even text, which really bummed me out. So I decided to <u>Carpool Diaz</u>. (That's Latin for "seize the day.")

(At least I think it is.)

So yeah, there I was, having my very own shopping montage, and guess who I run into—Melanie. And she was really nice. We kinda wound up sticking together. It wasn't on purpose at first—we just kept ending up in the same stores! First Bimbots Books, then the Shoe Shack, then the Impuzzible Puzzle Palace. Finally, we ended up at the Frosty Swirl at the exact same time! She told me to stop following her, and I told her to stop following me, and then we fell into a fit of giggles. When we ordered our Frostys, we both got the triple mocha peppermint with extra whipped cream and cherries. It was like, WHOA. After that, we just...hung out. We had a really fun time.

Crazy, right? Do I have a head injury from some Slayer battle? Because I feel crazy. Melanie is supposed to be my archnemesis. And the person I thought was my best friend, Fina, texted me, like, six hours later and said: "Oops. Forgot. Busy with Alice and the coven. Hope you had fun." That's an exact quote from her text to me, by the way. She didn't even apologize.

I don't know what to do about Fina. I guess, for now, I'm going to try not to think about it. After all, I had a really good day. Guess I'll try to just focus on that.

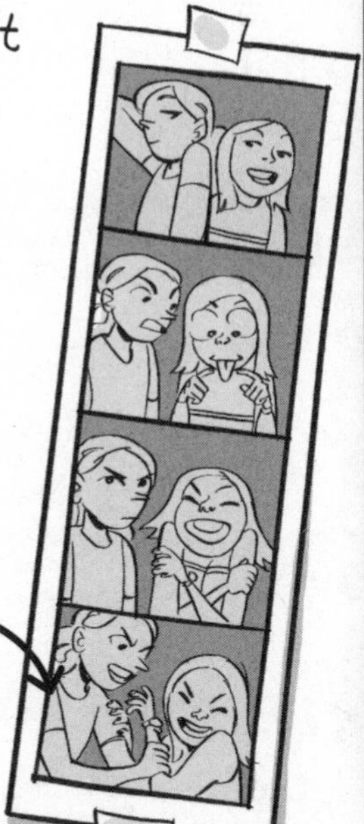

Uncontrollable laughter
+ abnormal behavior
= best time ever!

Buffy. Are you ready to patrol tonight?

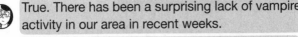 Can we skip? I have homework. AND we've patrolled the last 6 nights in a row and haven't had a single vamp sighting.

 True. There has been a surprising lack of vampire activity in our area in recent weeks.

 I find it somewhat disconcerting. I worry they are fleeing from some greater, more terrifying force.

OR they know there's a super-strong and fashionable new Slayer in town and they've all decided to hit the road!

 Interesting theory. Here's another: Having an "inflated ego" is a side effect of a Slayer's destiny.

Oh ha-ha, Sparks. Good one.

 I know patrol isn't your favorite pastime.

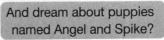 No, it's not. But sleep is. Remember sleep? Where you close your eyes in bed for the nighttime?

 But you are the Slayer, and I am your Watcher, and it is our duty.

And dream about puppies named Angel and Spike?

 We protect innocence from the forces of darkness.

 We may not be seeing a lot of vampires, but we still need to find the missing teenagers.

Sigh. I guess you're right.

 Am I reading this correctly? Did you just say that?

Shush. Before I take it back.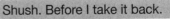

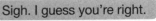

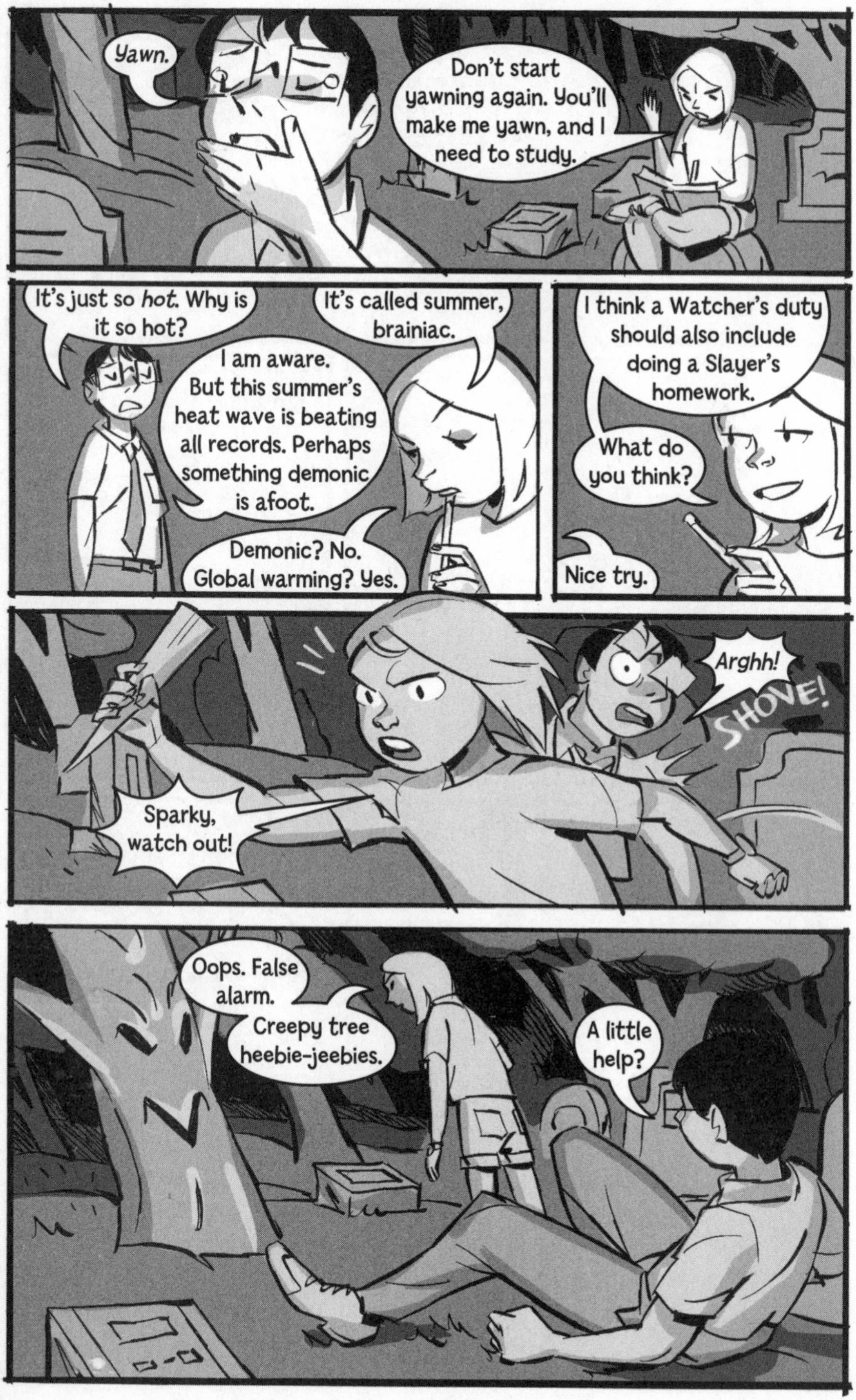
Yawn.
Don't start yawning again. You'll make me yawn, and I need to study.
It's just so *hot*. Why is it so hot?
It's called summer, brainiac.
I am aware. But this summer's heat wave is beating all records. Perhaps something demonic is afoot.
Demonic? No. Global warming? Yes.
I think a Watcher's duty should also include doing a Slayer's homework.
What do you think?
Nice try.
Arghh!
SHOVE!
Sparky, watch out!
Oops. False alarm.
Creepy tree heebie-jeebies.
A little help?

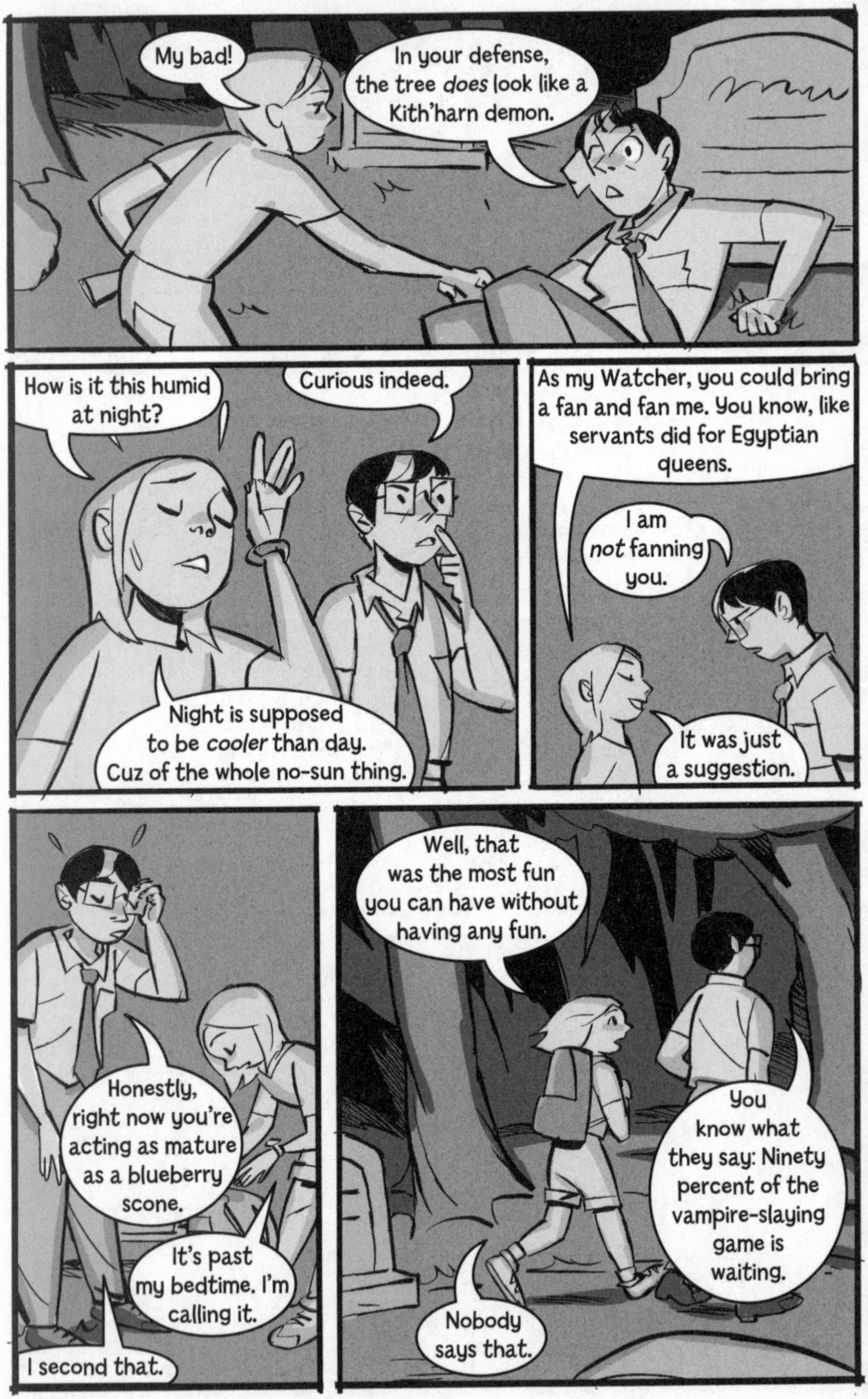
My bad!
In your defense, the tree *does* look like a Kith'harn demon.
How is it this humid at night?
Curious indeed.
Night is supposed to be *cooler* than day. Cuz of the whole no-sun thing.
As my Watcher, you could bring a fan and fan me. You know, like servants did for Egyptian queens.
I am *not* fanning you.
It was just a suggestion.
Honestly, right now you're acting as mature as a blueberry scone.
It's past my bedtime. I'm calling it.
I second that.
Well, that was the most fun you can have without having any fun.
You know what they say: Ninety percent of the vampire-slaying game is waiting.
Nobody says that.

Hello, Diary,

I worry for your safety. It is getting very hot in Cleveland. Not summer-hot, but, like, surface-of-the-sun-hot. You might burst into flames, and then who would I tell all my secrets to? It's crazy. Every time I walk outside, I sweat right through my clothes. Mom says it's the humidity, but I think Sparky might be right. It's evil-demon-hot. I wonder if there's a demon that makes things hot. If so, maybe there's a good demon that makes it snow. Where's he (or she)?

Oh yeah, GREAT NEWS: <u>Alvaro is coming home from art camp on Friday!</u> I've missed him so much! Between Fina spending all her time with her coven (lame) and Alvaro being away (sad-face), it's no wonder Melanie was able to trick me into being her friend! Just kidding. As I get to know Melanie, she's actually pretty fun. I mean, she's definitely funny. She makes fun of me and I make fun of her, but in a really friendly kind of way. I don't know if that makes sense. Like the other day, her mom brought me home after school, and Melanie was like, "Your house is so small," and I was like, "Like your brain." Then her mom said, "Girls, be nice!" but we were laughing so hard we didn't care.

I like hanging out with Melanie, but if I'm being honest, I really miss Fina. I wonder if she'll be going to Alvaro's art show. I hope so. It's at Mom's gallery, so she knows I'll be there. Maybe with Alvaro here, everything will go back to normal....

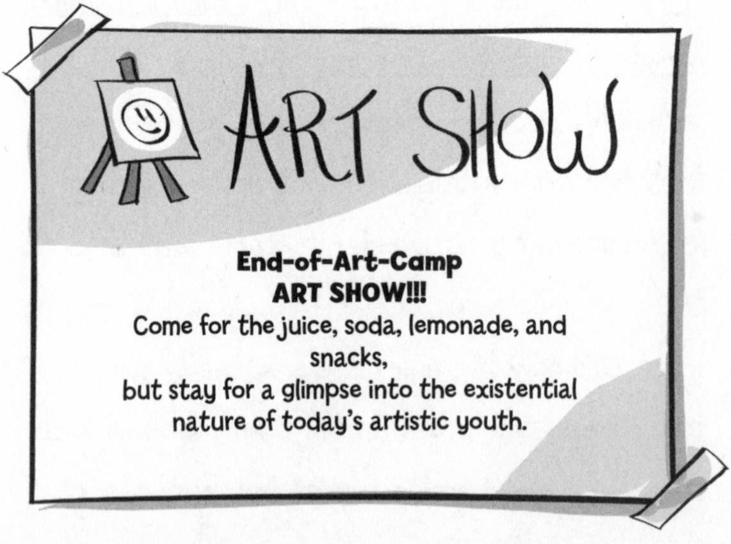
ART SHOW
End-of-Art-Camp
ART SHOW!!!
Come for the juice, soda, lemonade, and snacks,
but stay for a glimpse into the existential nature of today's artistic youth.

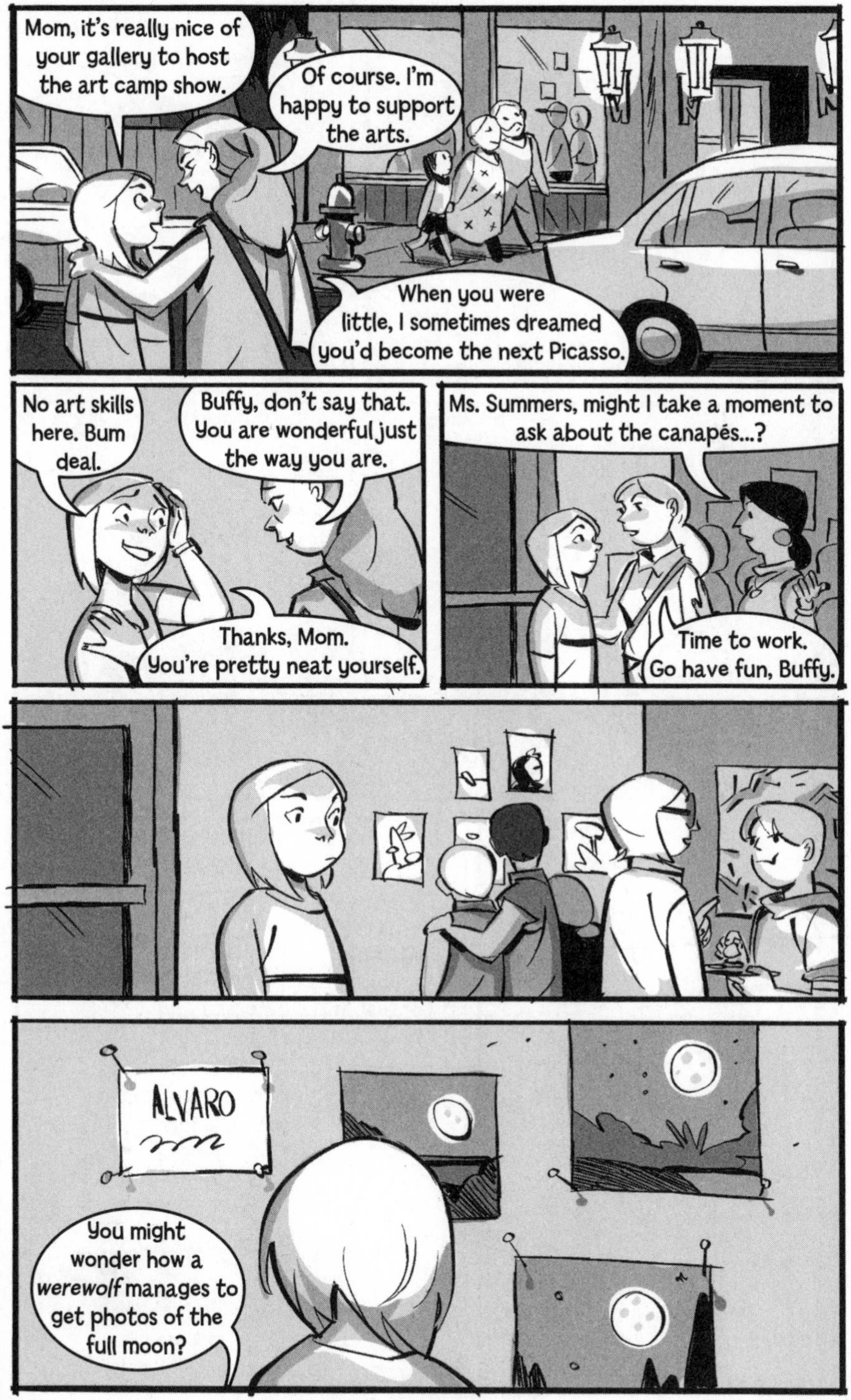
Mom, it's really nice of your gallery to host the art camp show.
Of course. I'm happy to support the arts.
When you were little, I sometimes dreamed you'd become the next Picasso.
No art skills here. Bum deal.
Buffy, don't say that. You are wonderful just the way you are.
Thanks, Mom. You're pretty neat yourself.
Ms. Summers, might I take a moment to ask about the canapés...?
Time to work. Go have fun, Buffy.
ALVARO
You might wonder how a *werewolf* manages to get photos of the full moon?

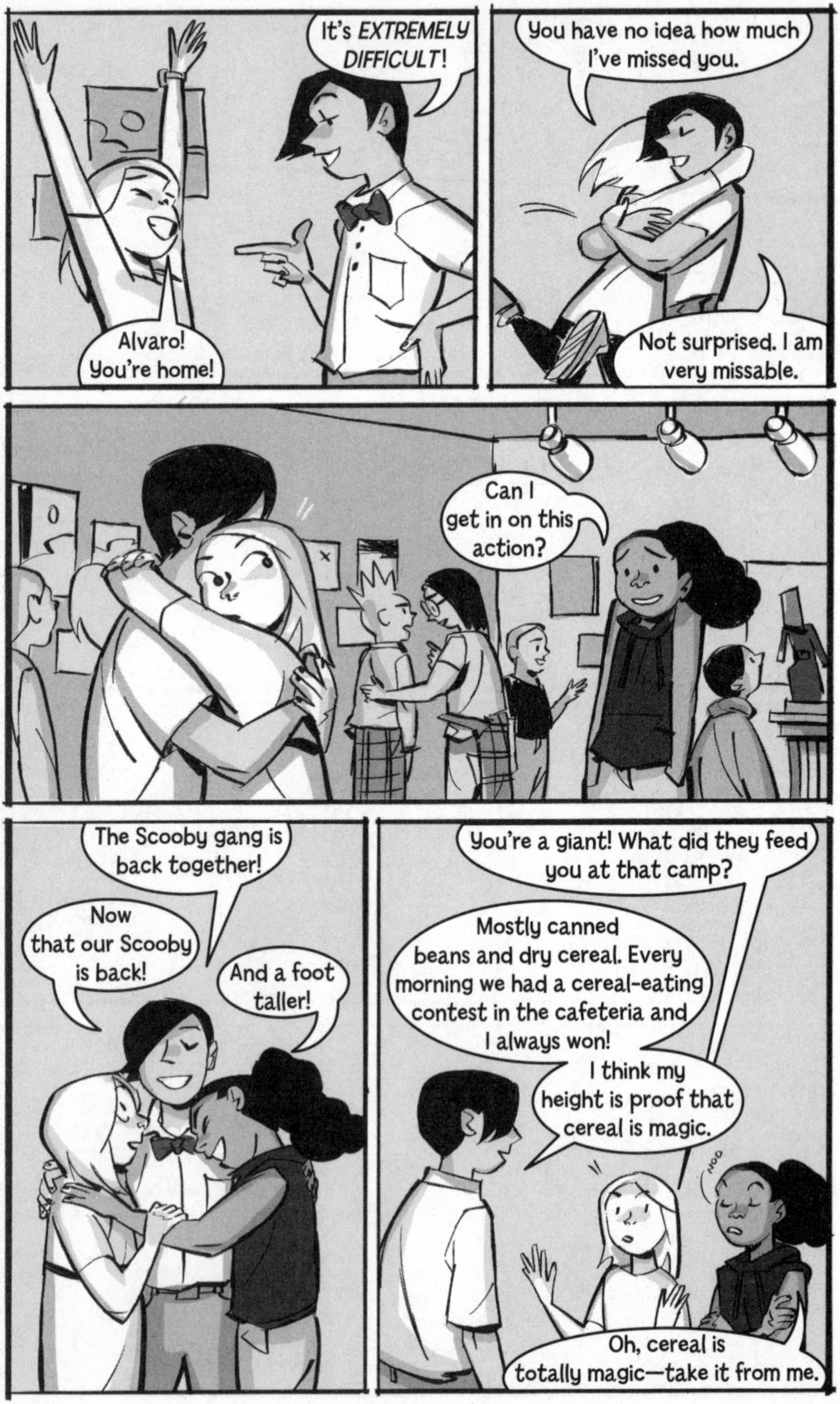
Alvaro! You're home!
It's *EXTREMELY DIFFICULT*!
You have no idea how much I've missed you.
Not surprised. I am very missable.
Can I get in on this action?
The Scooby gang is back together!
Now that our Scooby is back!
And a foot taller!
You're a giant! What did they feed you at that camp?
Mostly canned beans and dry cereal. Every morning we had a cereal-eating contest in the cafeteria and I always won!
I think my height is proof that cereal is magic.
NOD
Oh, cereal is totally magic—take it from me.

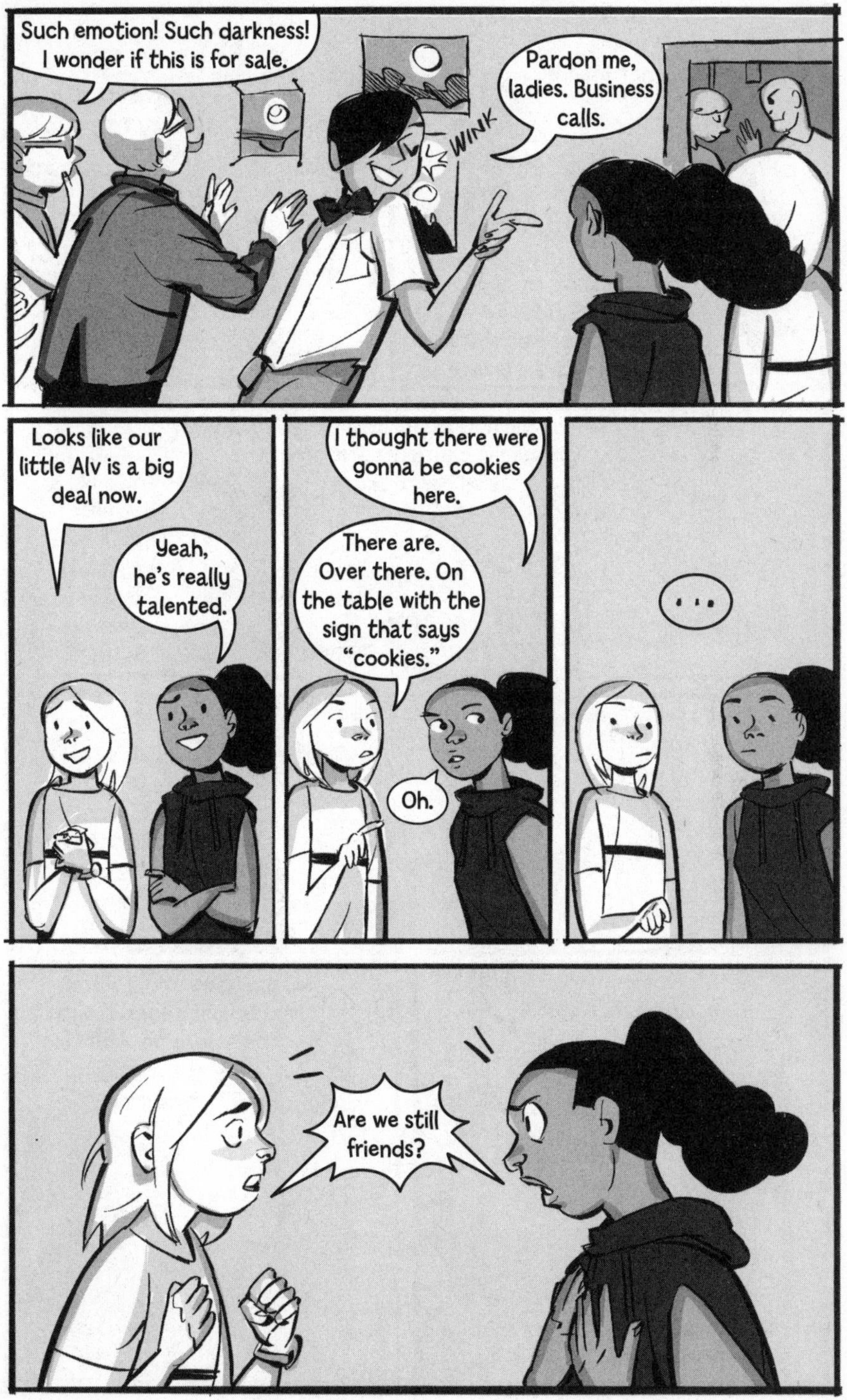
Such emotion! Such darkness! I wonder if this is for sale.
WINK
Pardon me, ladies. Business calls.
Looks like our little Alv is a big deal now.
Yeah, he's really talented.
I thought there were gonna be cookies here.
There are. Over there. On the table with the sign that says "cookies."
Oh.
...
Are we still friends?

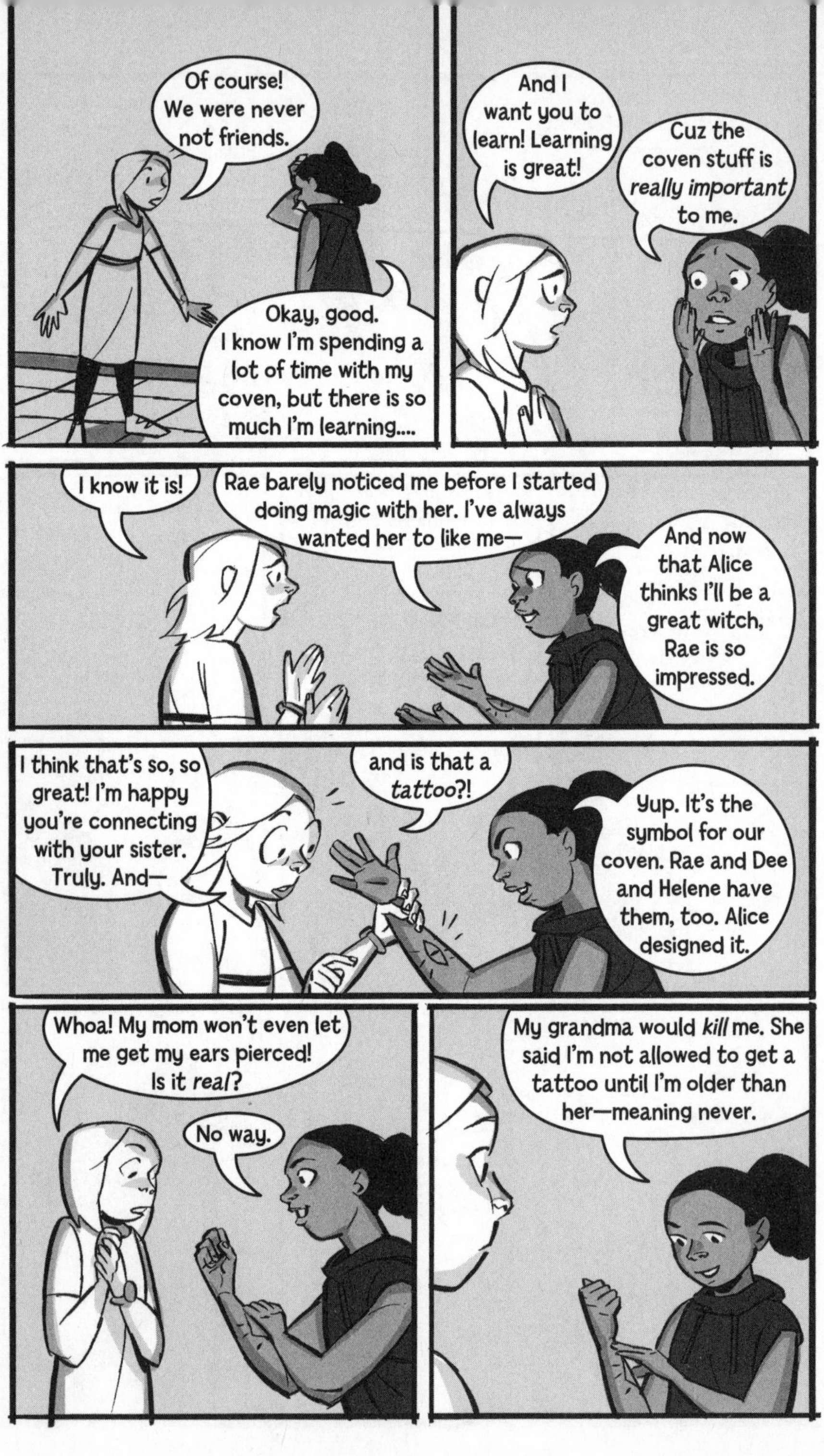
Of course! We were never not friends.
Okay, good. I know I'm spending a lot of time with my coven, but there is so much I'm learning....
And I want you to learn! Learning is great!
Cuz the coven stuff is *really important* to me.
I know it is!
Rae barely noticed me before I started doing magic with her. I've always wanted her to like me—
And now that Alice thinks I'll be a great witch, Rae is so impressed.
I think that's so, so great! I'm happy you're connecting with your sister. Truly. And—
and is that a *tattoo*?!
Yup. It's the symbol for our coven. Rae and Dee and Helene have them, too. Alice designed it.
Whoa! My mom won't even let me get my ears pierced! Is it *real*?
No way.
My grandma would *kill* me. She said I'm not allowed to get a tattoo until I'm older than her—meaning never.

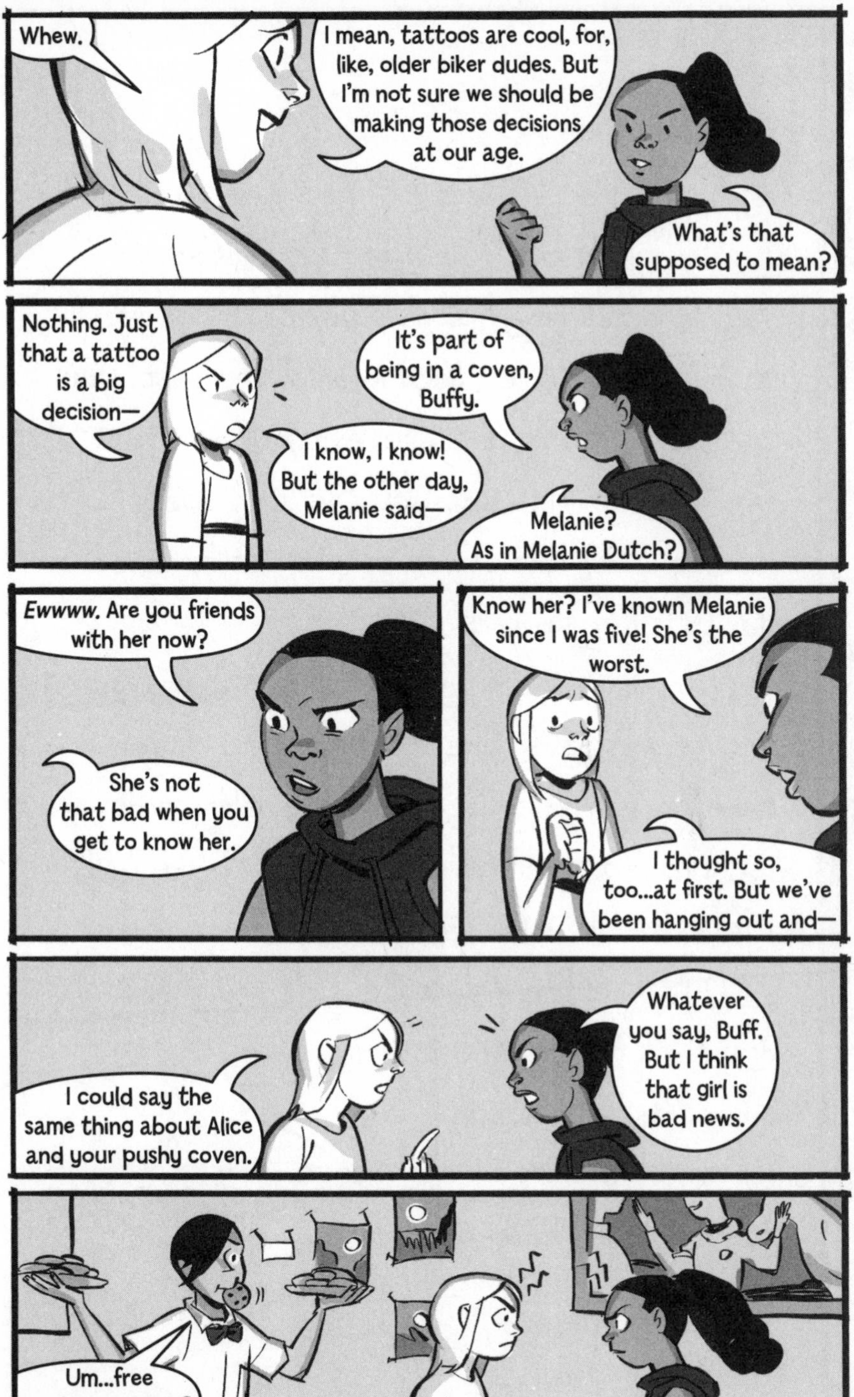
Whew.
I mean, tattoos are cool, for, like, older biker dudes. But I'm not sure we should be making those decisions at our age.
What's that supposed to mean?
Nothing. Just that a tattoo is a big decision—
It's part of being in a coven, Buffy.
I know, I know! But the other day, Melanie said—
Melanie? As in Melanie Dutch?
Ewwww. Are you friends with her now?
She's not that bad when you get to know her.
Know her? I've known Melanie since I was five! She's the worst.
I thought so, too...at first. But we've been hanging out and—
Whatever you say, Buff. But I think that girl is bad news.
I could say the same thing about Alice and your pushy coven.
Um...free cookies, anyone?

Hey Diary,

Fina is mad at me again. This time cuz I told her I'm friends with Melanie. But that's not fair. Fina has new friends—why can't I? I get it, I guess. Melanie's been mean in the past. But so have I. And so has, like, everyone who has ever gone to middle school. But that doesn't mean anything. Sometimes people just have bad days. Or bad summers!

Why do Fina and I keep fighting? I don't get it! She was never like this before her sister came home from college. And everything ends up being about her coven now. I'm a Slayer AND I have friends. Why can't Fina have her coven AND still be friendly, too? I don't know. And now she's drawing this symbol on her arm cuz her sister and the other witches have the tattoo.

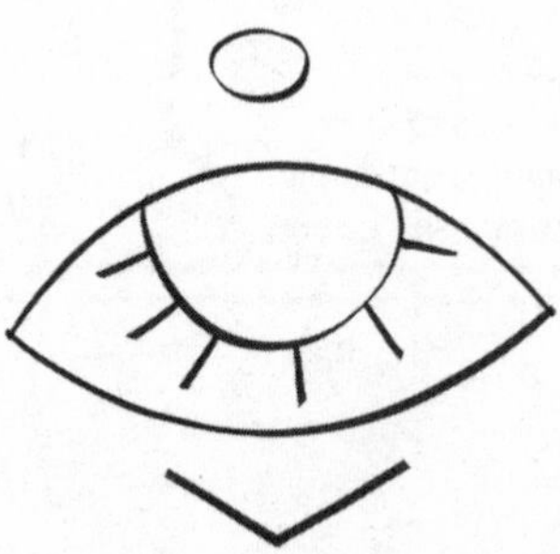

The weird thing? Every time I look at the symbol I get a weird, gross feeling in my tummy. Like it's __not__ good. I wish I could say that to Fina, but she'd probably never speak to me again. I feel far away from Fina right now, and I super-super don't like it!

At least Alvaro is back, which makes things feel a little more normal. Tomorrow we're having our first Scooby meet-up of the summer with all of us together again. Alvaro always brings the best snacks.

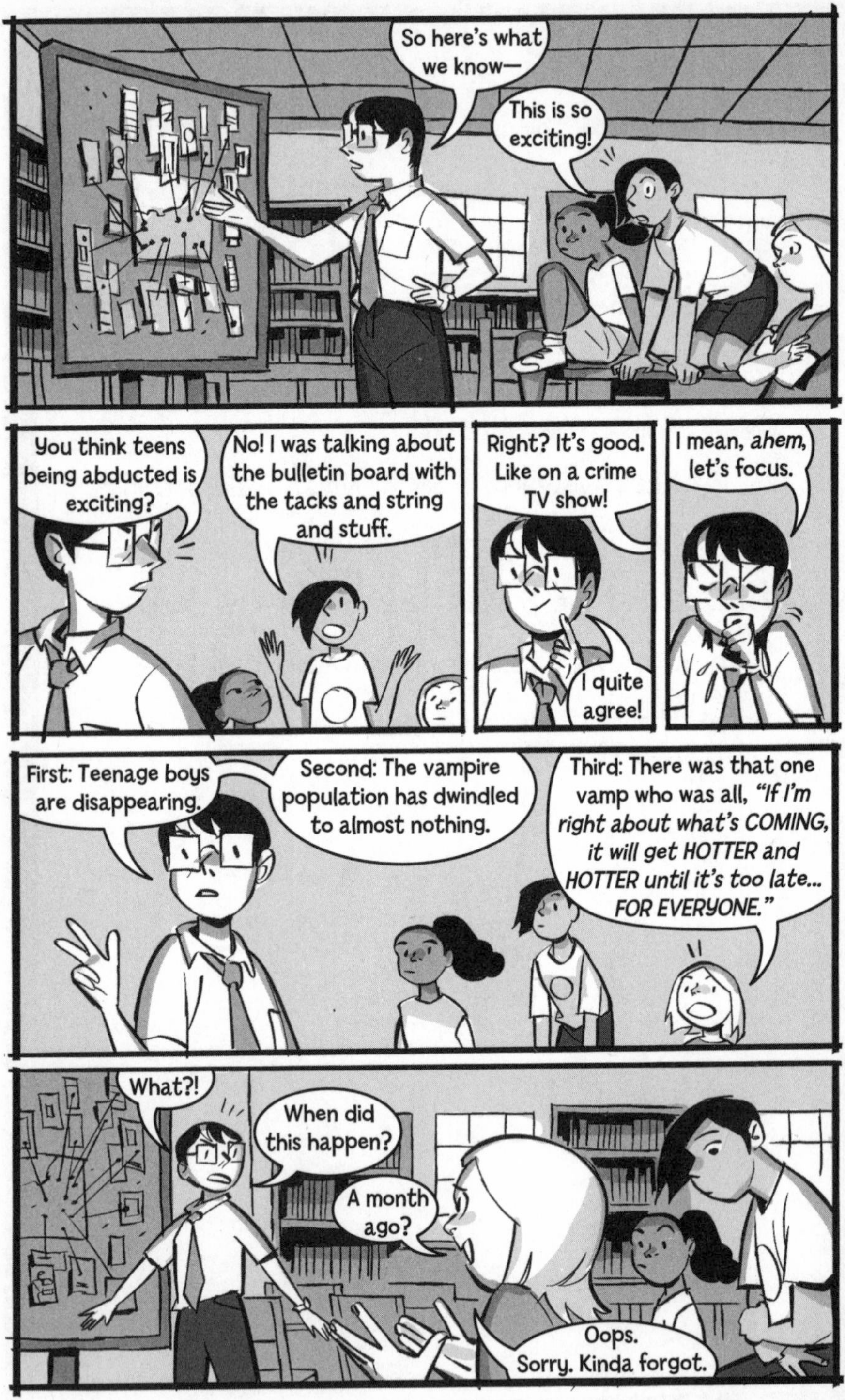
So here's what we know—
This is so exciting!
You think teens being abducted is exciting?
No! I was talking about the bulletin board with the tacks and string and stuff.
Right? It's good. Like on a crime TV show!
I quite agree!
I mean, *ahem*, let's focus.
First: Teenage boys are disappearing.
Second: The vampire population has dwindled to almost nothing.
Third: There was that one vamp who was all, *"If I'm right about what's COMING, it will get HOTTER and HOTTER until it's too late... FOR EVERYONE."*
What?!
When did this happen?
A month ago?
Oops. Sorry. Kinda forgot.

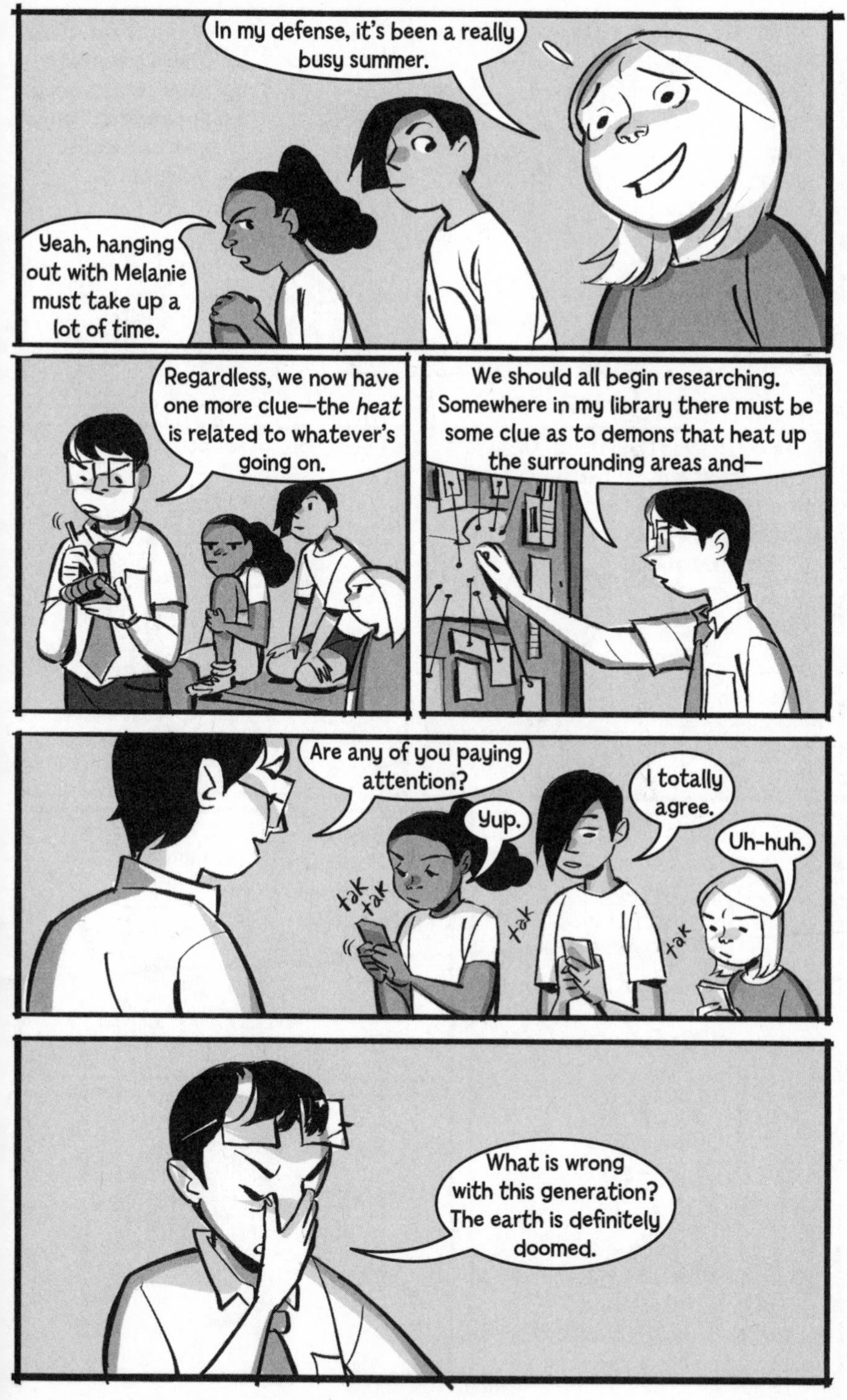
In my defense, it's been a really busy summer.
Yeah, hanging out with Melanie must take up a lot of time.
Regardless, we now have one more clue—the *heat* is related to whatever's going on.
We should all begin researching. Somewhere in my library there must be some clue as to demons that heat up the surrounding areas and—
Are any of you paying attention?
Yup.
tak tak
I totally agree.
tak
Uh-huh.
tak
What is wrong with this generation? The earth is definitely doomed.

Actually, I was just looking at weather patterns in the Farmers' Almanac over the decades. The heat right now is off the charts.

I was just googling "heat monsters in mythology." There're tons of them.

And I was just searching local news reports for any more teenage-boy disappearances. Turns out we had a near-abduction....

Some guy named Liam Davis says he almost got nabbed by an incredibly strong teenage girl with a weird face. Sounds like a vamp to me.

Check your phone. I just forwarded you the article.

tak tak

You...you...were actually helping?

I'm so *proud*.

Okay, let's get to work. Fina, Alvaro, you research the monsters.

Buffy, you're with me. We'll track down this Liam and we'll question him ourselves—

Tonight's the Fourth of July, remember? I'm having a barbecue.

Yeah. Fireworks before fire monsters. Sorry, Sparky.

No can do!

Sigh.

Dear Diary,

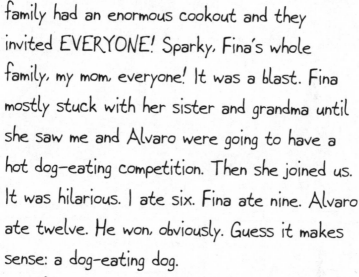

<u>Happy Fourth of July!</u>
What a fun day! Alvaro's family had an enormous cookout and they invited EVERYONE! Sparky, Fina's whole family, my mom, everyone! It was a blast. Fina mostly stuck with her sister and grandma until she saw me and Alvaro were going to have a hot dog–eating competition. Then she joined us. It was hilarious. I ate six. Fina ate nine. Alvaro ate twelve. He won, obviously. Guess it makes sense: a dog-eating dog.

Afterward, we had a humongous water-gun battle and Sparky got soaked. Then we made tie-dye shirts, ate barbecue and red-white-and-blue cupcakes, and then the best part: We watched the fireworks!! Summer's <u>finally</u> looking up.

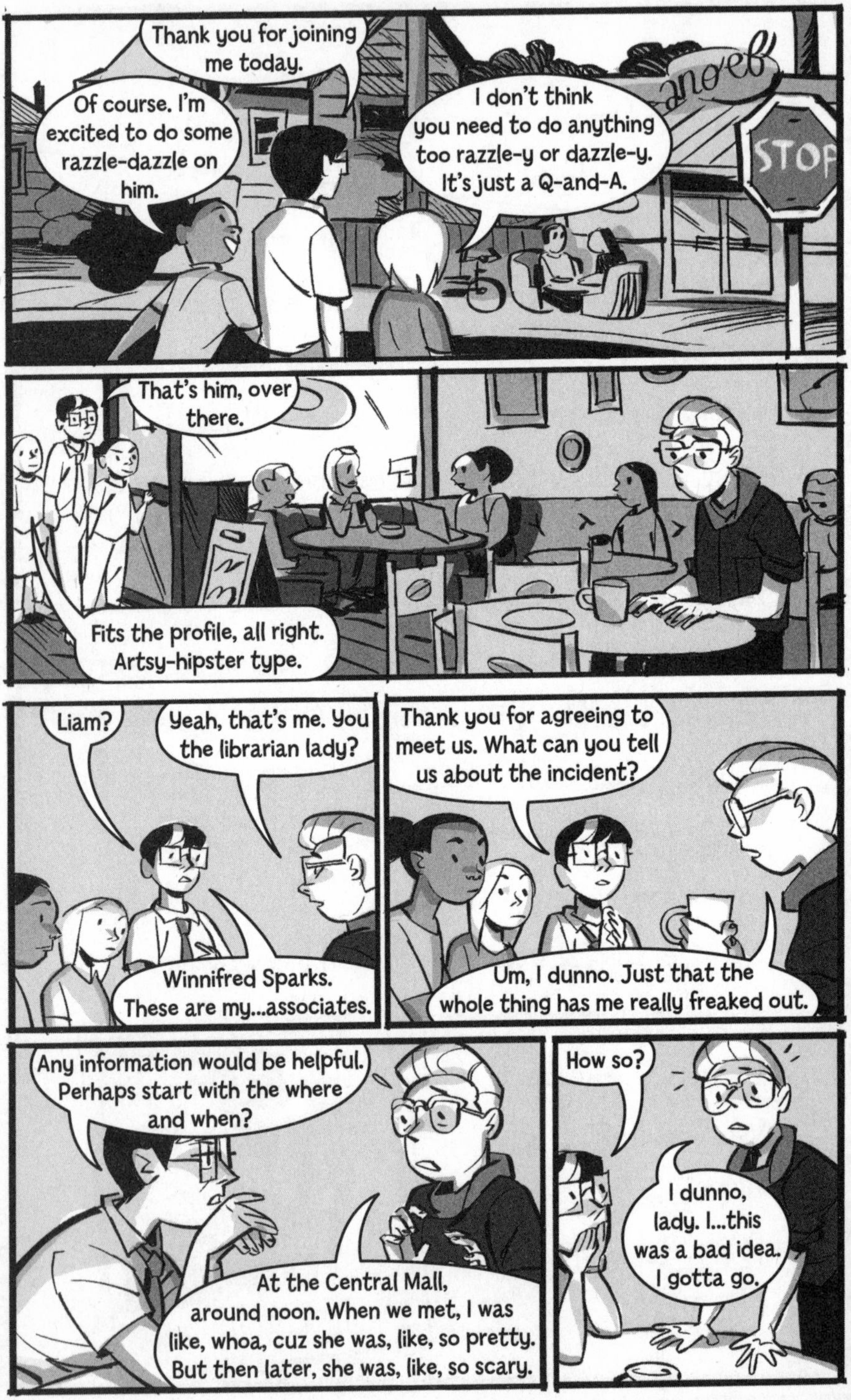
Thank you for joining me today.
Of course. I'm excited to do some razzle-dazzle on him.
I don't think you need to do anything too razzle-y or dazzle-y. It's just a Q-and-A.
STOP
That's him, over there.
Fits the profile, all right. Artsy-hipster type.
Liam?
Yeah, that's me. You the librarian lady?
Winnifred Sparks. These are my...associates.
Thank you for agreeing to meet us. What can you tell us about the incident?
Um, I dunno. Just that the whole thing has me really freaked out.
Any information would be helpful. Perhaps start with the where and when?
At the Central Mall, around noon. When we met, I was like, whoa, cuz she was, like, so pretty. But then later, she was, like, so scary.
How so?
I dunno, lady. I...this was a bad idea. I gotta go.

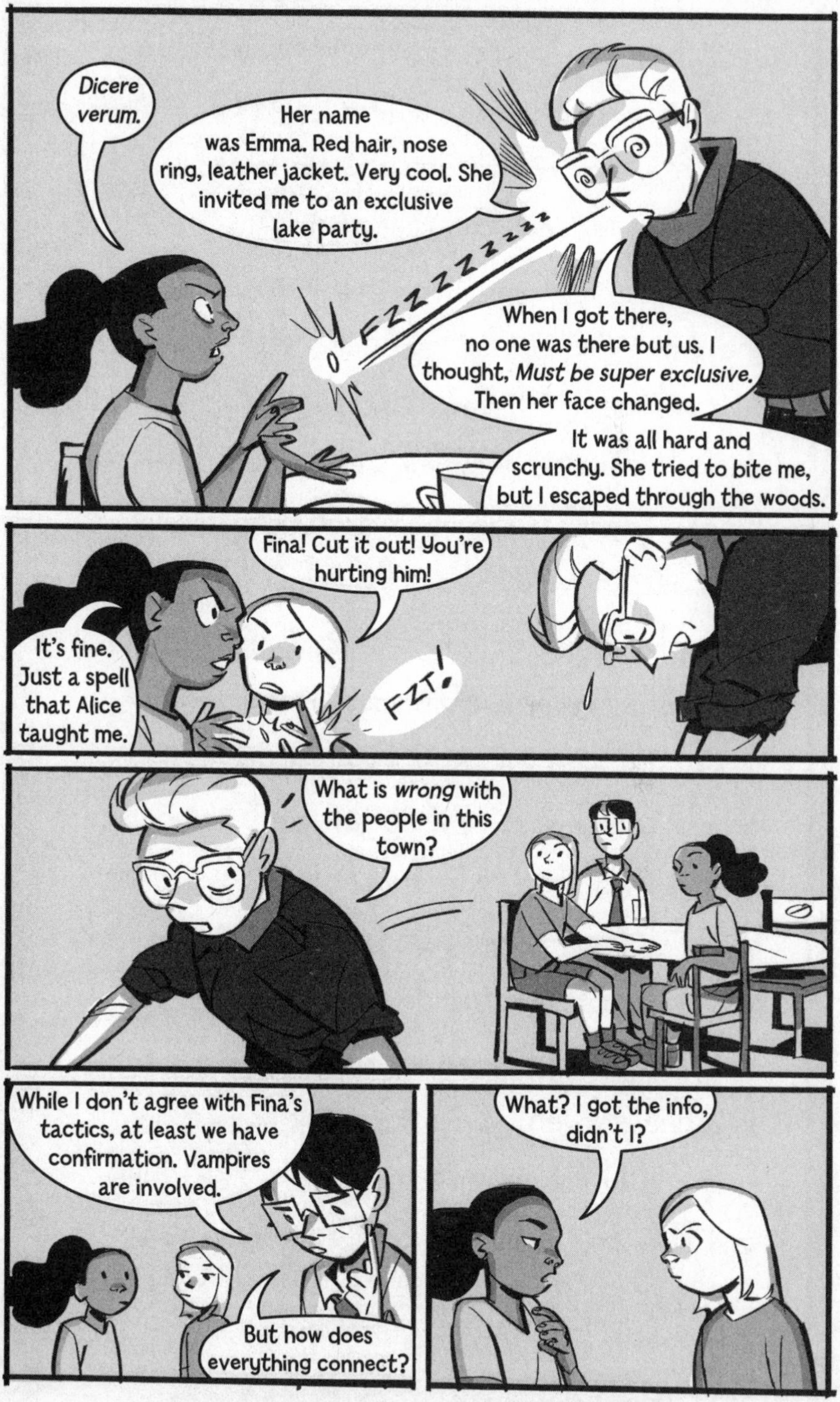
Dicere verum.
Her name was Emma. Red hair, nose ring, leather jacket. Very cool. She invited me to an exclusive lake party.
FZZZZZZzzz
When I got there, no one was there but us. I thought, *Must be super exclusive.* Then her face changed.
It was all hard and scrunchy. She tried to bite me, but I escaped through the woods.
Fina! Cut it out! You're hurting him!
It's fine. Just a spell that Alice taught me.
FZT!
What is *wrong* with the people in this town?
While I don't agree with Fina's tactics, at least we have confirmation. Vampires are involved.
But how does everything connect?
What? I got the info, didn't I?

Well, Diary, Sparky is pretty sure the Big Bad is a vamp, which explains the missing teenagers...but not the rising heat.

Liam says he saw the vamp in the mall during the day. Which seems odd cuz, hello? Vamps and daytime are not friends. Sparky's drawing a blank. It can't be the Gem of Amara again—Sparky keeps it in a vault that only she knows the code to. Now she's going crazy with her big old books, trying to find artifacts and curses and spells, anything that could give us a clue.

I'm still worried about Fina, though. She totally used magic on that guy. He looked so scared. And that scared me. She said she got the spell from <u>Alice</u>, just like she got that dumb fake tattoo from Alice. I feel like everything with Fina started going bad as soon as Alice showed up. I asked why I'd met everyone in the coven except Alice, and Fina said they only meet her on special occasions. I don't like it. But what can I do?

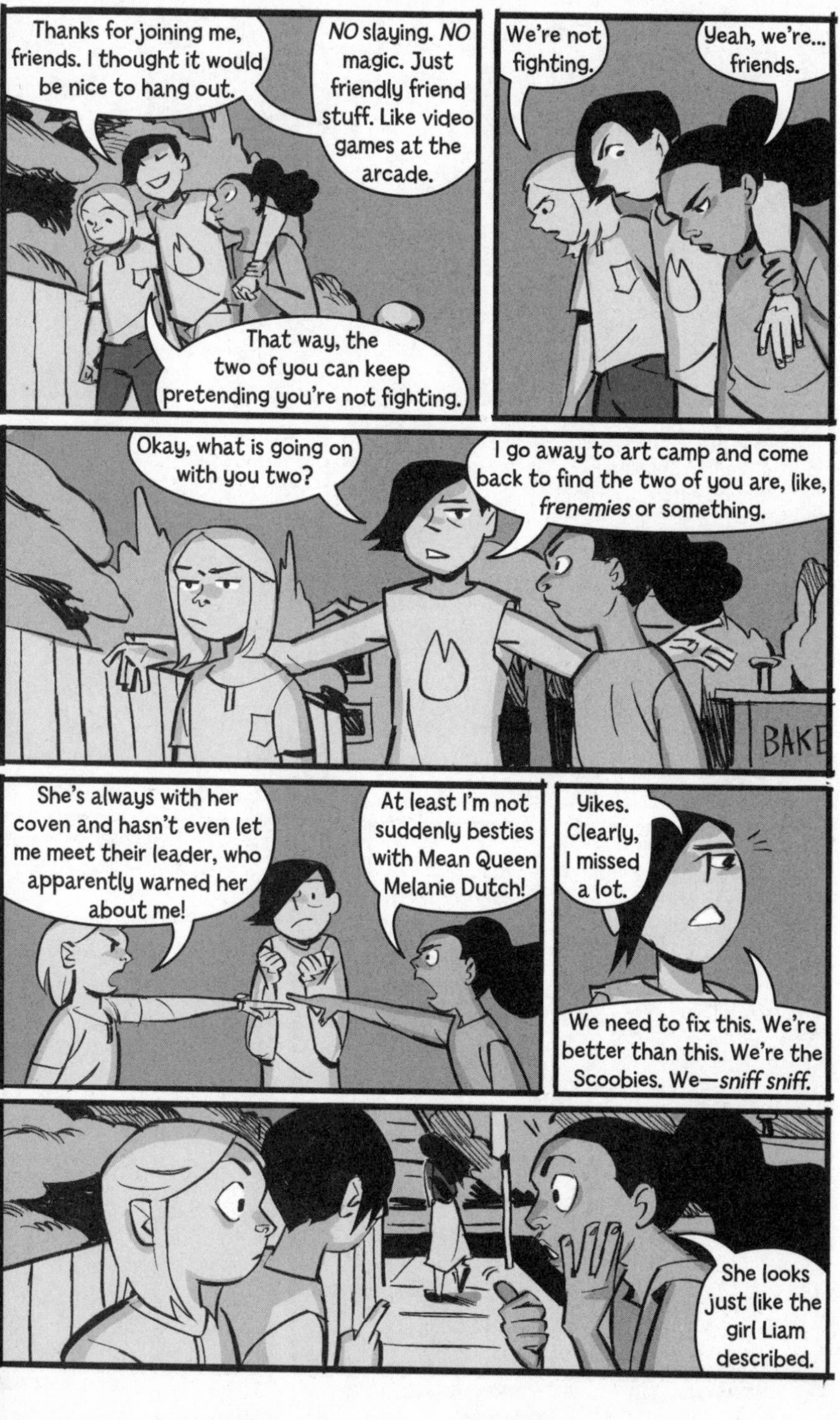
Thanks for joining me, friends. I thought it would be nice to hang out.
NO slaying. *NO* magic. Just friendly friend stuff. Like video games at the arcade.
That way, the two of you can keep pretending you're not fighting.
We're not fighting.
Yeah, we're... friends.
Okay, what is going on with you two?
I go away to art camp and come back to find the two of you are, like, *frenemies* or something.
BAKE
She's always with her coven and hasn't even let me meet their leader, who apparently warned her about me!
At least I'm not suddenly besties with Mean Queen Melanie Dutch!
Yikes. Clearly, I missed a lot.
We need to fix this. We're better than this. We're the Scoobies. We—*sniff sniff.*
She looks just like the girl Liam described.

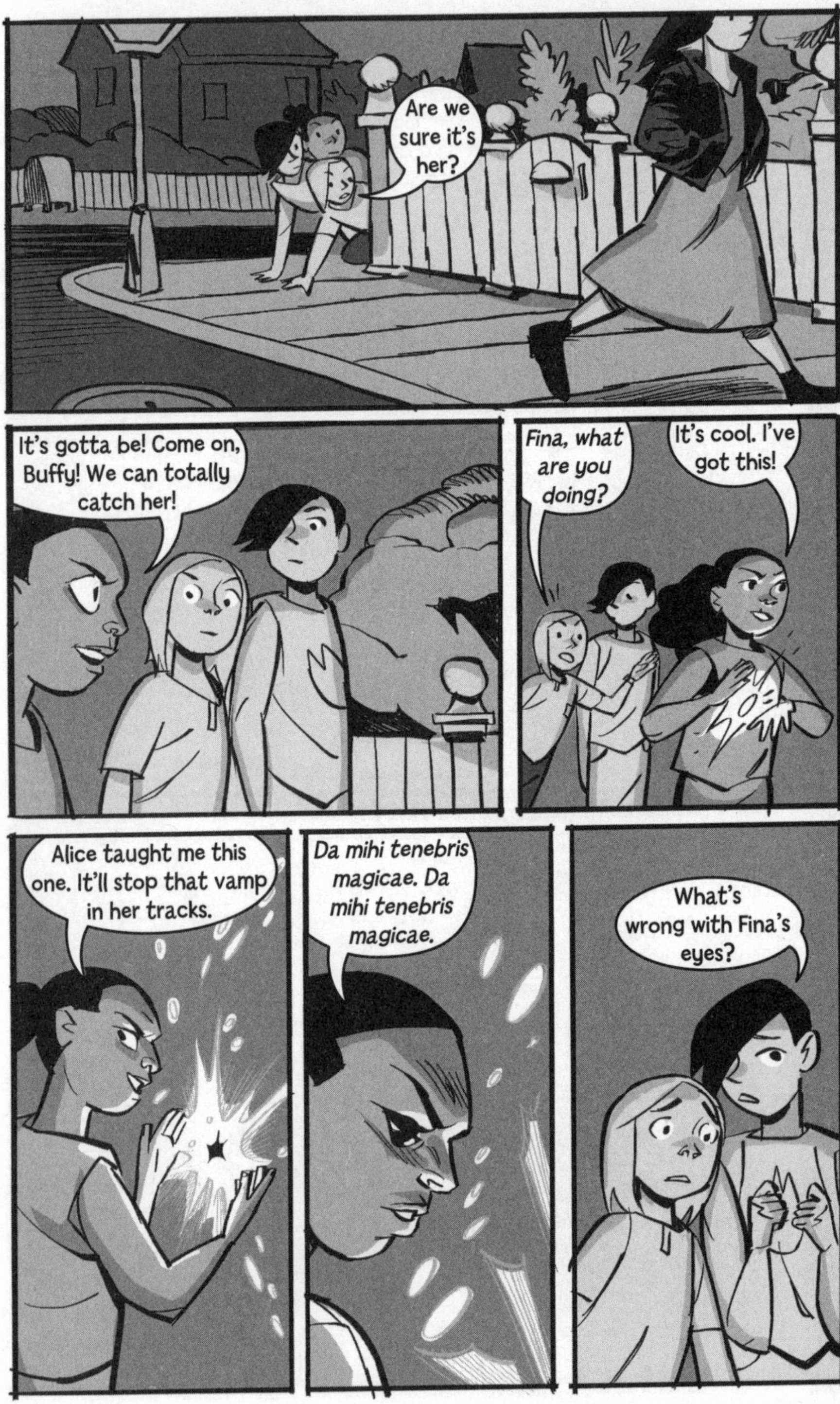
Are we sure it's her?
It's gotta be! Come on, Buffy! We can totally catch her!
Fina, what are you doing?
It's cool. I've got this!
Alice taught me this one. It'll stop that vamp in her tracks.
Da mihi tenebris magicae. Da mihi tenebris magicae.
What's wrong with Fina's eyes?

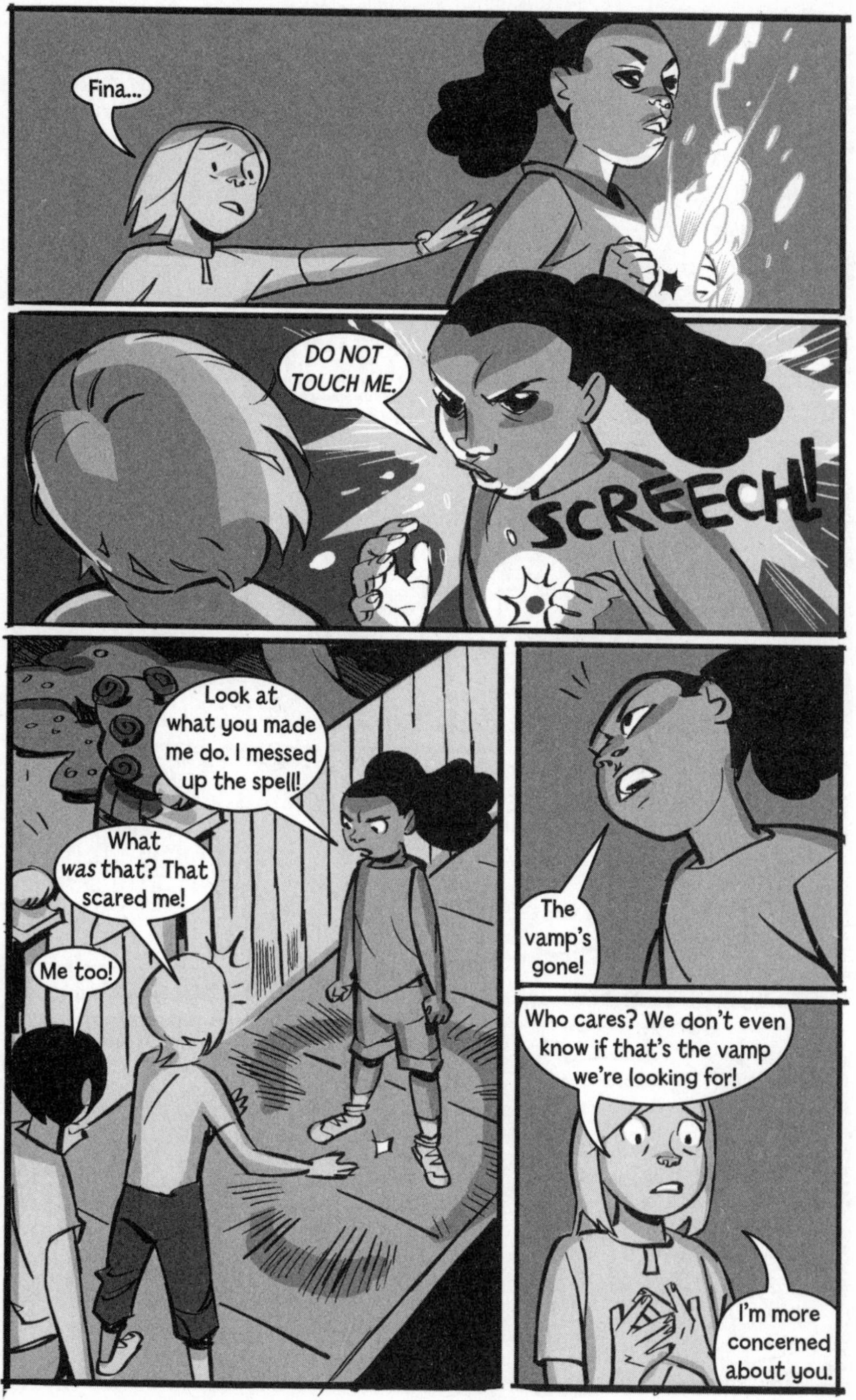
Fina...
DO NOT TOUCH ME.
SCREECH!
Look at what you made me do. I messed up the spell!
What *was* that? That scared me!
Me too!
The vamp's gone!
Who cares? We don't even know if that's the vamp we're looking for!
I'm more concerned about you.

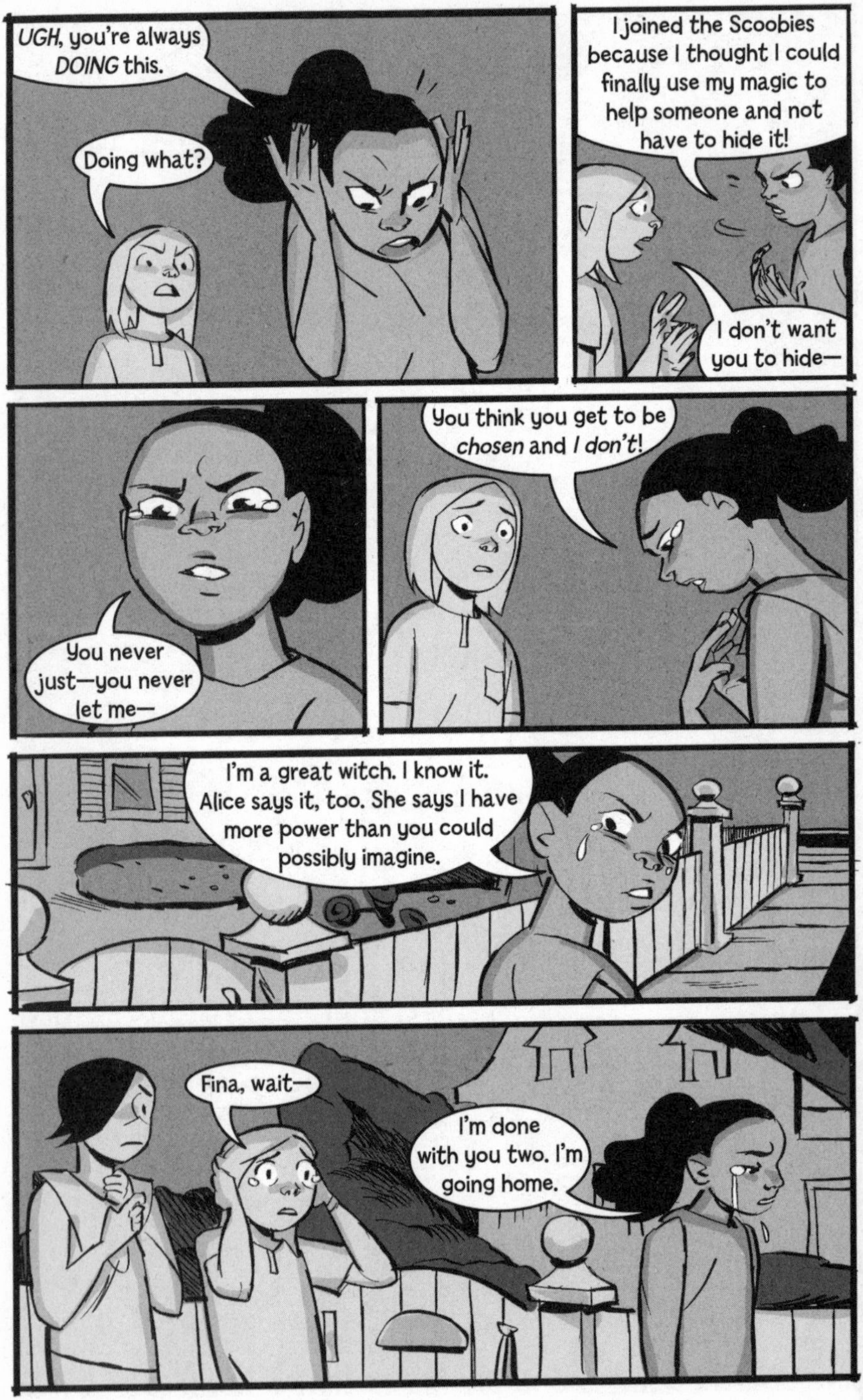
UGH, you're always DOING this.
Doing what?
I joined the Scoobies because I thought I could finally use my magic to help someone and not have to hide it!
I don't want you to hide—
You never just—you never let me—
You think you get to be chosen and I don't!
I'm a great witch. I know it. Alice says it, too. She says I have more power than you could possibly imagine.
Fina, wait—
I'm done with you two. I'm going home.

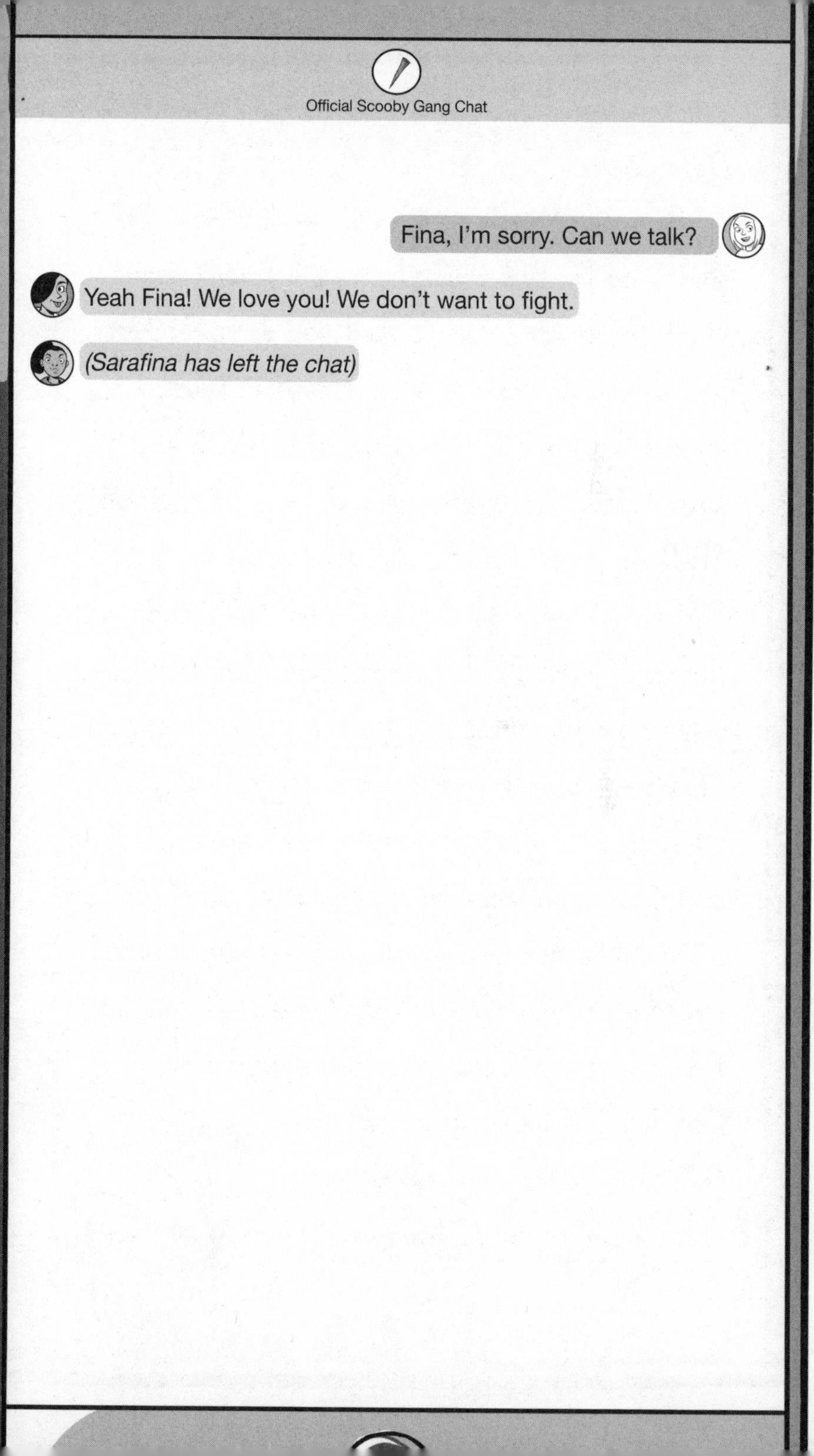
Official Scooby Gang Chat
Fina, I'm sorry. Can we talk?
Yeah Fina! We love you! We don't want to fight.
(Sarafina has left the chat)

Dear Diary,

Fina won't talk to me OR Alvaro now. She's mad. And I'm sad that she's mad. I don't know what to do here, Diary. And you don't, either, because you're just a book. Maybe if I just keep my pen moving, I'll have some realization about what friendship is or means or how to have one. She's my best friend and I don't want to fight.

I think Sarafina thinks I think she's the Slayer's sidekick. But that's not even true! I may be kinda strong and have a piece of paper telling me that I'm destined to fight, but she's so much better at so many other things! She's smart and can make anything out of yarn! She's a witch—a really awesome and powerful witch who can do stuff that I can't even imagine. Ugh. I hope she stops being mad because I already miss her. I've missed her all summer.

I'm really super sad and now...

...I have to go do homework.

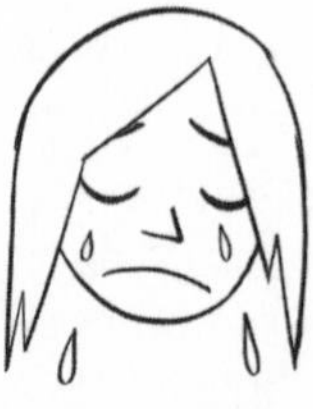

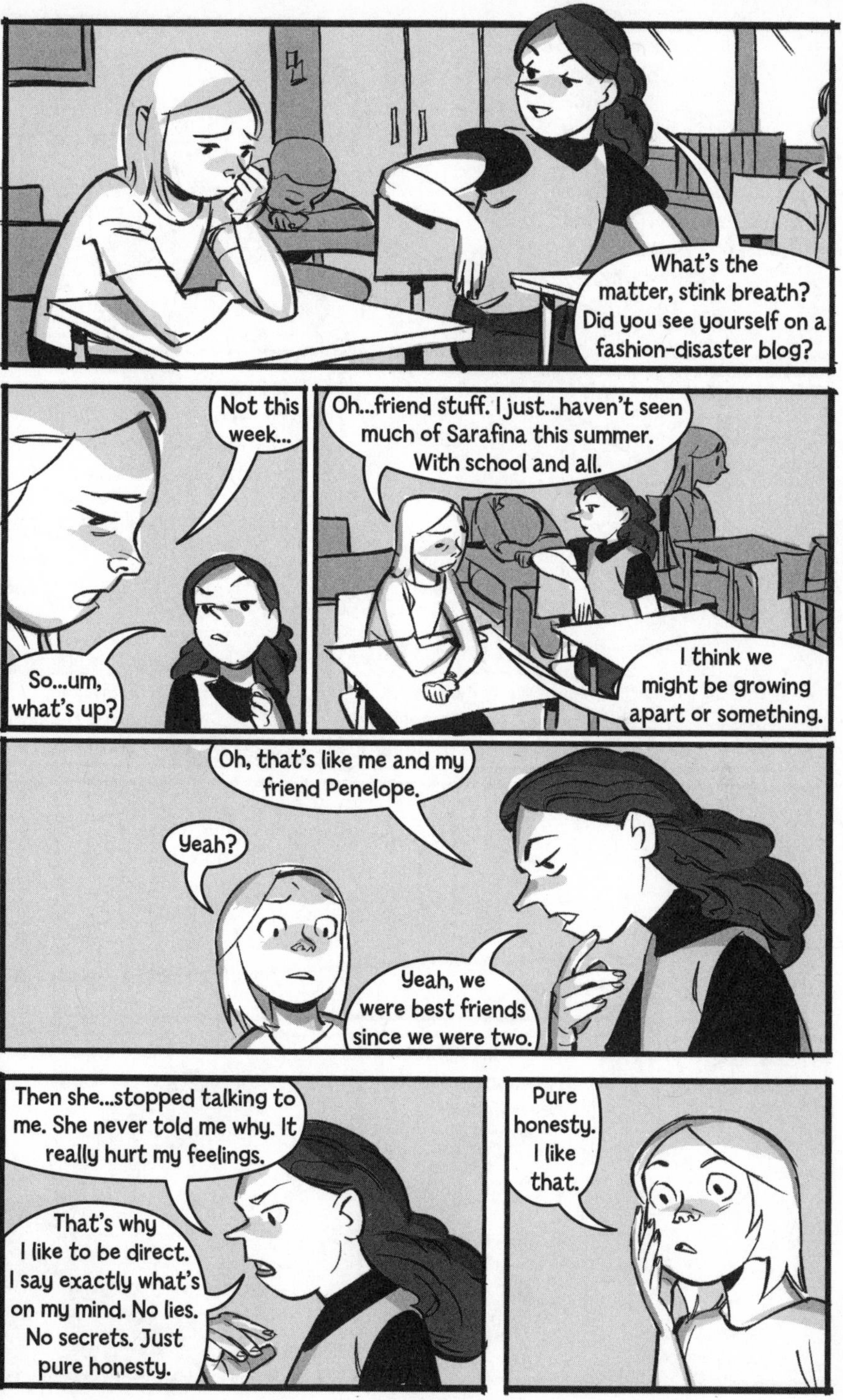
What's the matter, stink breath? Did you see yourself on a fashion-disaster blog?
Not this week...
So...um, what's up?
Oh...friend stuff. I just...haven't seen much of Sarafina this summer. With school and all.
I think we might be growing apart or something.
Oh, that's like me and my friend Penelope.
Yeah?
Yeah, we were best friends since we were two.
Then she...stopped talking to me. She never told me why. It really hurt my feelings.
That's why I like to be direct. I say exactly what's on my mind. No lies. No secrets. Just pure honesty.
Pure honesty. I like that.

Honesty can be a double-edged sword, though.

Like the other day: My mom was like, "Do you like my dress?" and I was like, "NO! Burn it with fire!" I don't think she liked hearing that.

What if telling the truth starts a fight?

Pff. I fight with my friends all the time.

Really?

Yeah! We tell each other what we're *really* thinking. It's healthy. Then we get over it.

But Fina won't even answer my texts!

Well, you could go totally Stone Age and just show up at her house.

She can always tell you to get lost.

But at least she'd know you still want to be friends.

That's, like...really good advice.

Yeah, well, my mom lets me hang out with her spin class....

Those ladies have *real* problems.

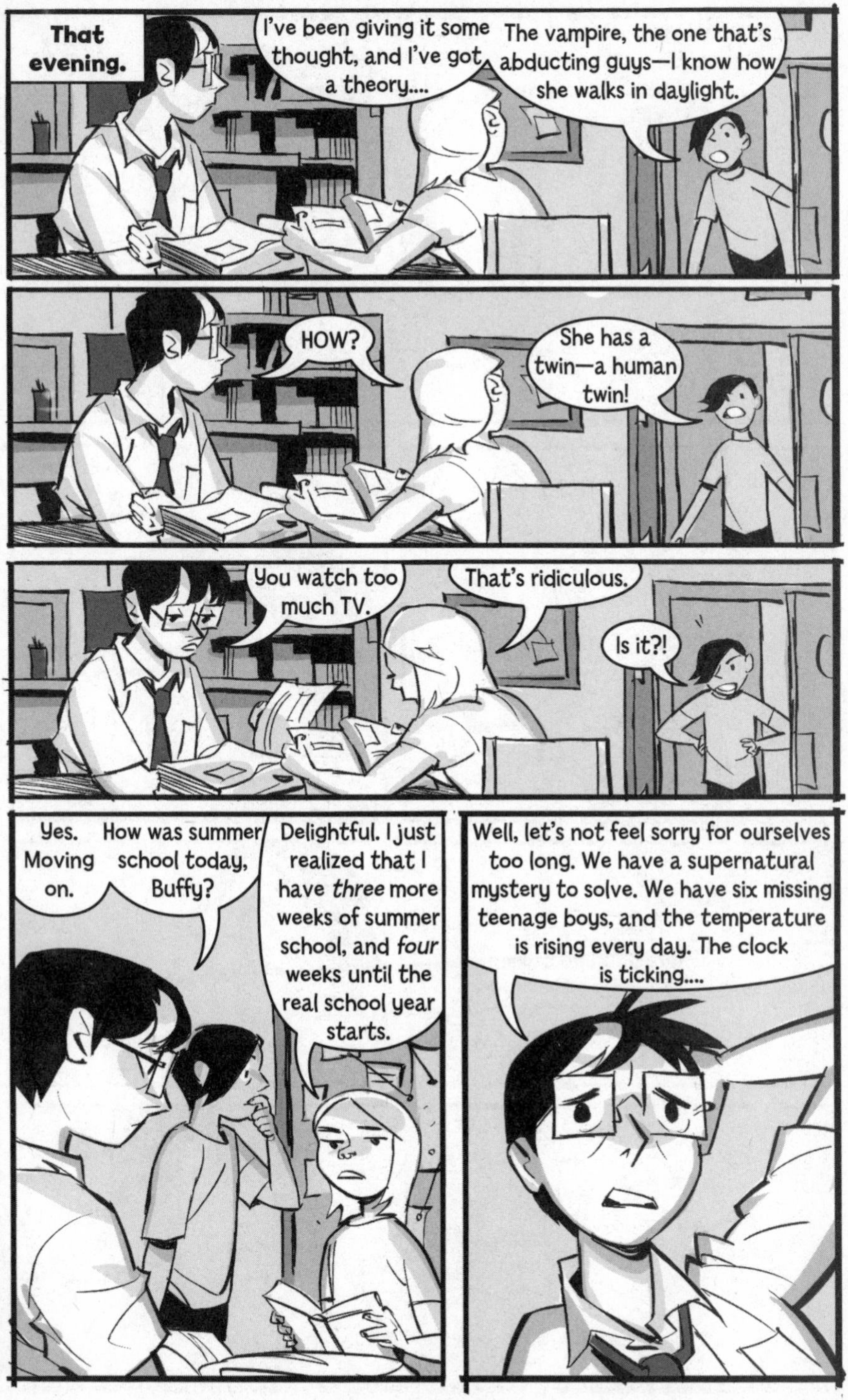

That evening.
I've been giving it some thought, and I've got a theory....
The vampire, the one that's abducting guys—I know how she walks in daylight.
HOW?
She has a twin—a human twin!
You watch too much TV.
That's ridiculous.
Is it?!
Yes. Moving on.
How was summer school today, Buffy?
Delightful. I just realized that I have *three* more weeks of summer school, and *four* weeks until the real school year starts.
Well, let's not feel sorry for ourselves too long. We have a supernatural mystery to solve. We have six missing teenage boys, and the temperature is rising every day. The clock is ticking....

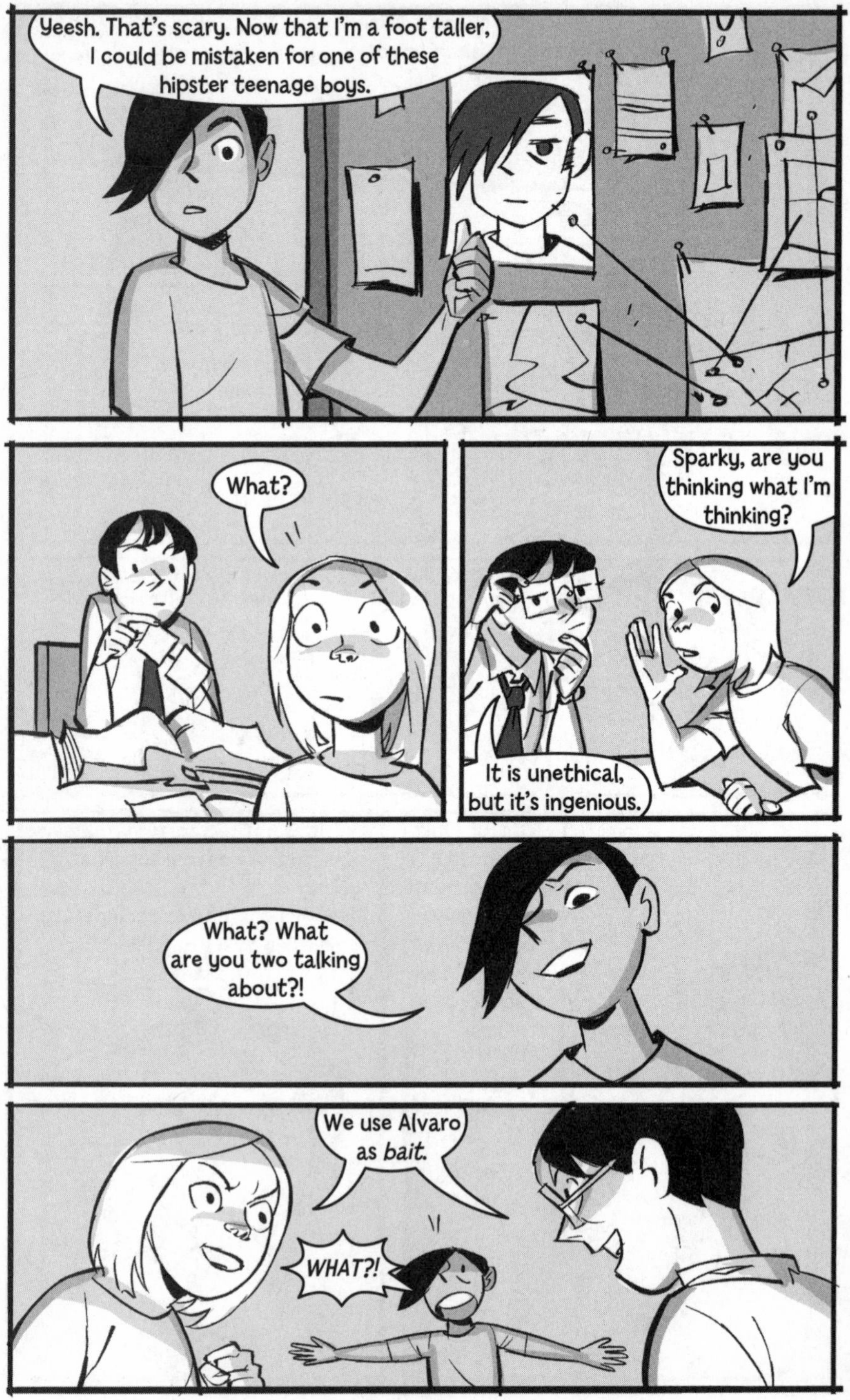
Yeesh. That's scary. Now that I'm a foot taller, I could be mistaken for one of these hipster teenage boys.
What?
Sparky, are you thinking what I'm thinking?
It is unethical, but it's ingenious.
What? What are you two talking about?!
We use Alvaro as *bait*.
WHAT?!

Dear Diary,

Today was great. I had two big breakthroughs!

Melanie gave me some awesome advice today and I think I might take it! Fina still won't answer her texts, so I'm just gonna bike to her house and say hi. Is this, like, a flowers situation? Nah, probably not. That's grown-up stuff for dates and funerals. I feel like I should bring <u>something</u>, though, as a peace offering. What's a good gift for a witch? A broom? A cat? Ugh.

Sparky and I want to take Alvaro to the mall and use him as bait for the redheaded vamp teen-napper. I know that sounds a little scary, but Sparky and I are going to be, like, ten feet away the whole time. As soon as someone tries to invite him to an exclusive party at the lake, I'm gonna introduce them to Mr. Pointy. Well... <u>after</u> Sparky questions them. She thinks I'm too quick to poof vamps. Which seems silly, cuz that's kinda my job.

Well, wish me luck. Twice!

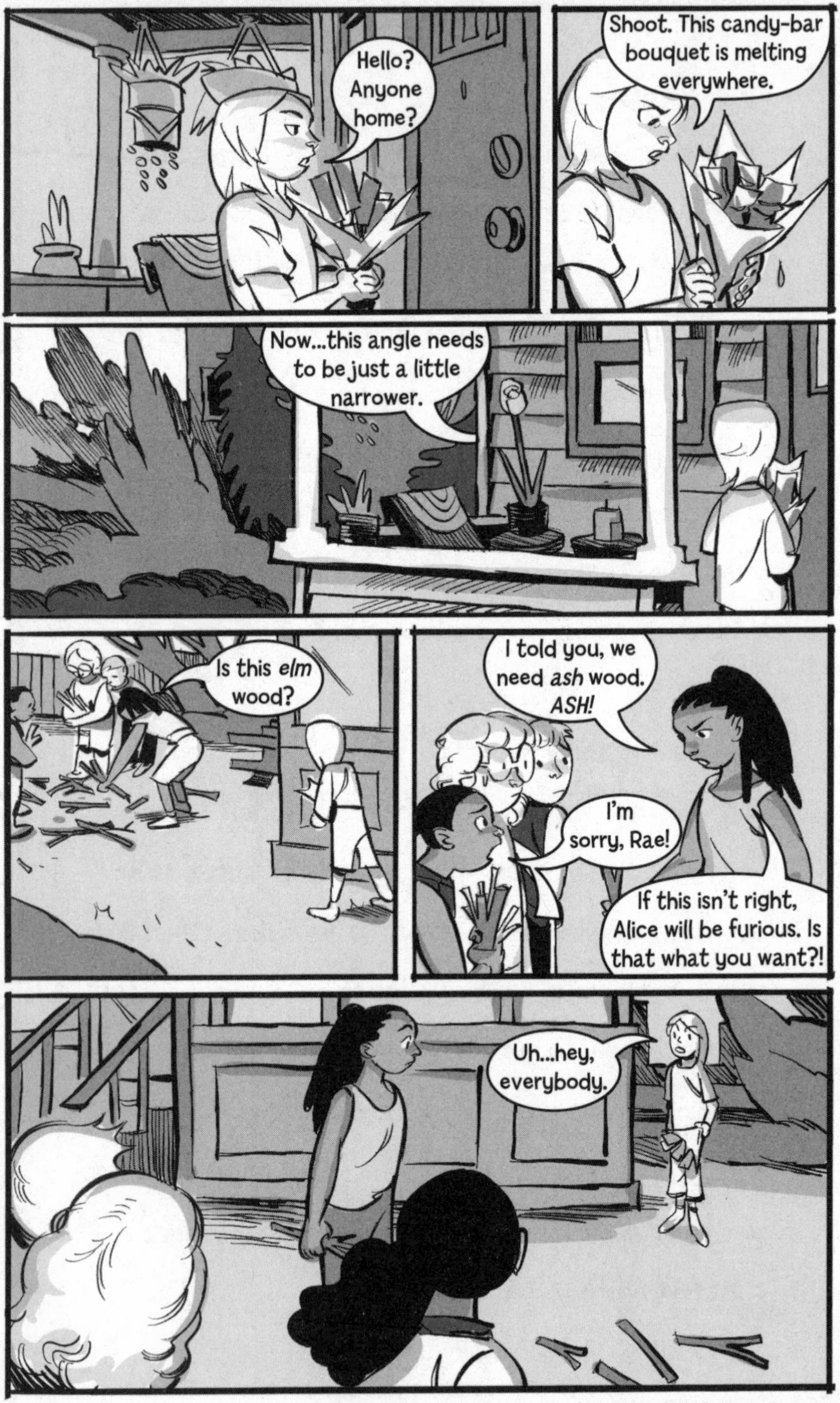
Hello? Anyone home?
Shoot. This candy-bar bouquet is melting everywhere.
Now...this angle needs to be just a little narrower.
Is this *elm* wood?
I told you, we need *ash* wood. *ASH!*
I'm sorry, Rae!
If this isn't right, Alice will be furious. Is that what you want?!
Uh...hey, everybody.

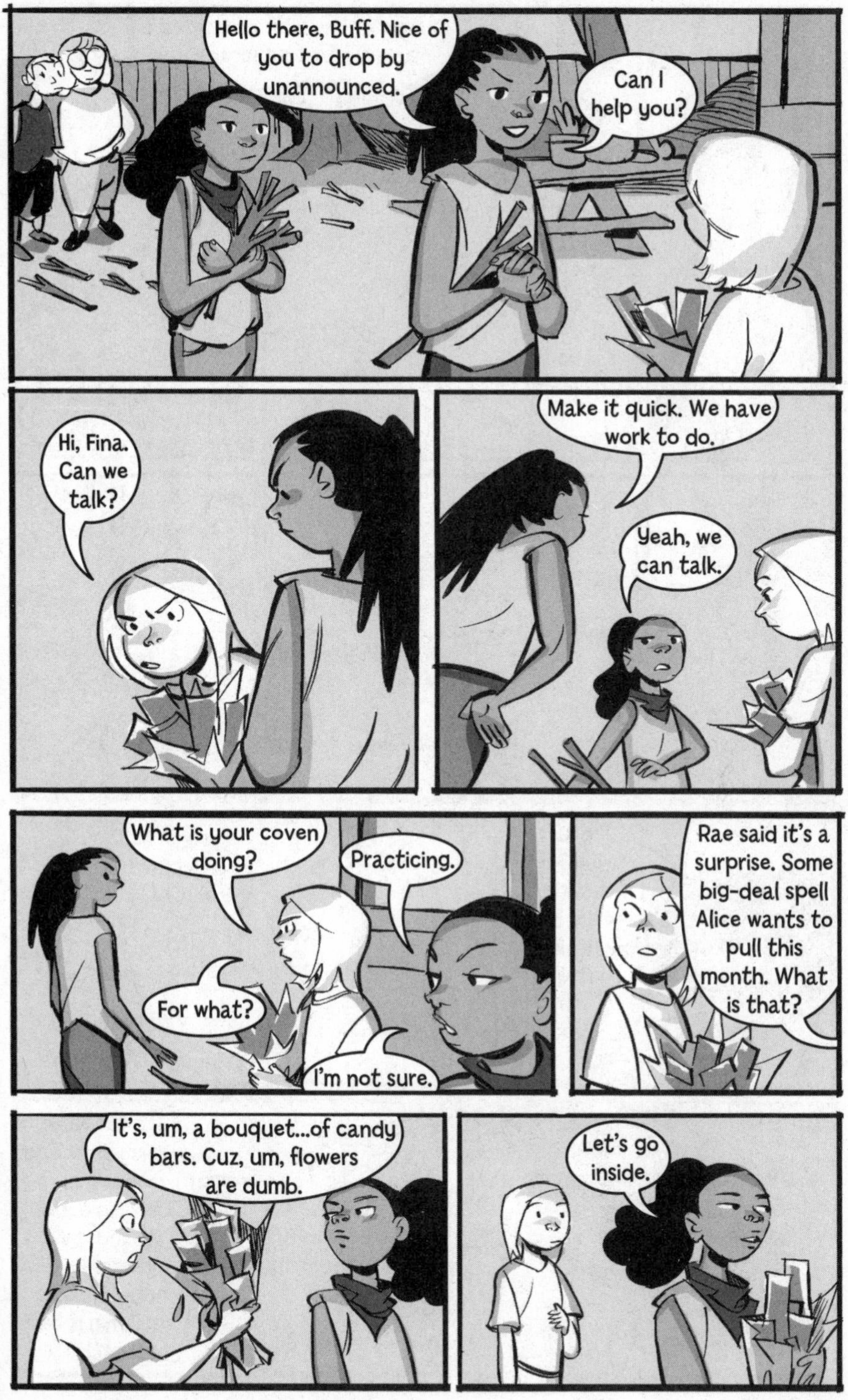
Hello there, Buff. Nice of you to drop by unannounced.
Can I help you?
Hi, Fina. Can we talk?
Make it quick. We have work to do.
Yeah, we can talk.
What is your coven doing?
Practicing.
For what?
I'm not sure.
Rae said it's a surprise. Some big-deal spell Alice wants to pull this month. What is that?
It's, um, a bouquet...of candy bars. Cuz, um, flowers are dumb.
Let's go inside.

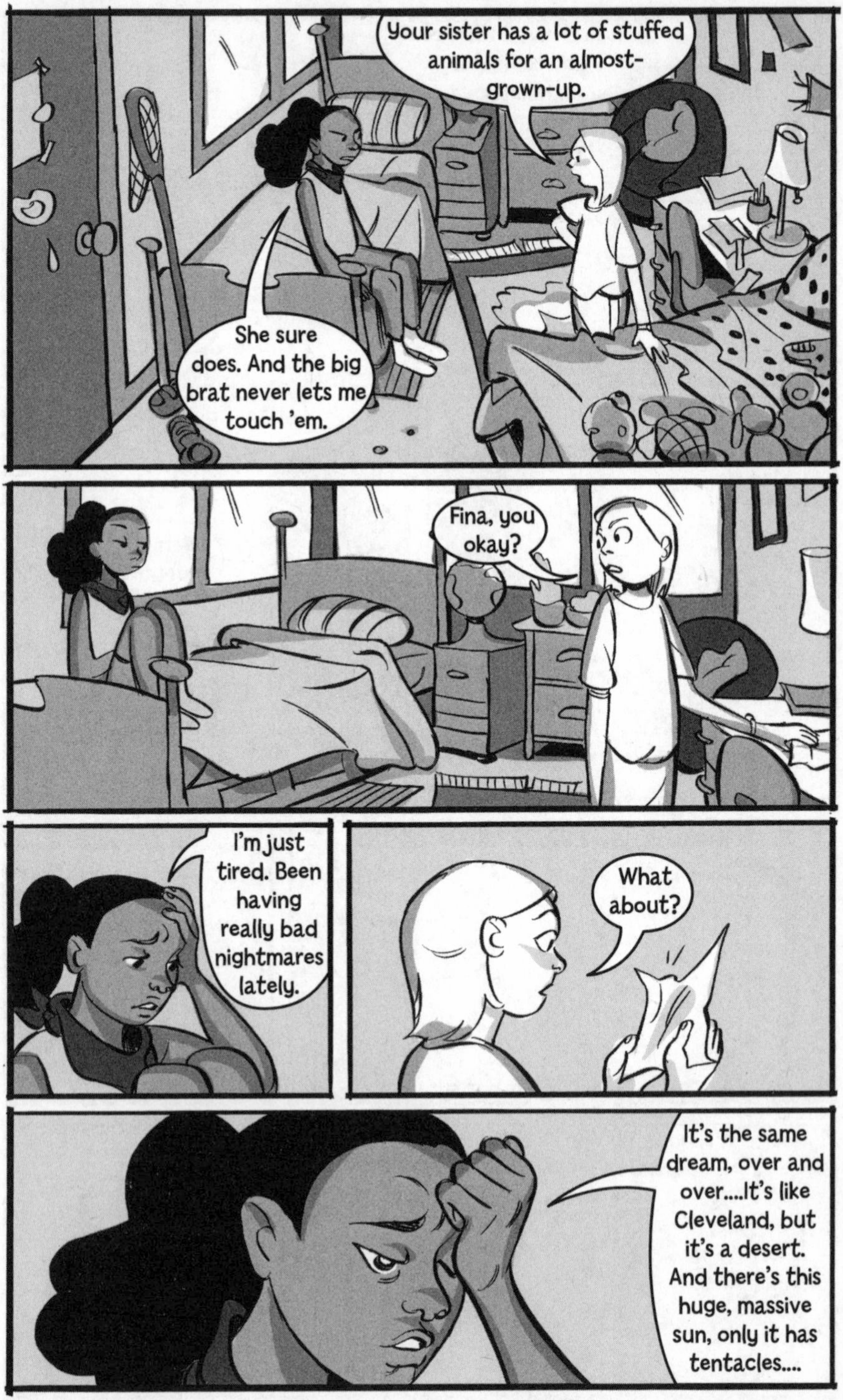
Your sister has a lot of stuffed animals for an almost-grown-up.
She sure does. And the big brat never lets me touch 'em.
Fina, you okay?
I'm just tired. Been having really bad nightmares lately.
What about?
It's the same dream, over and over....It's like Cleveland, but it's a desert. And there's this huge, massive sun, only it has tentacles....

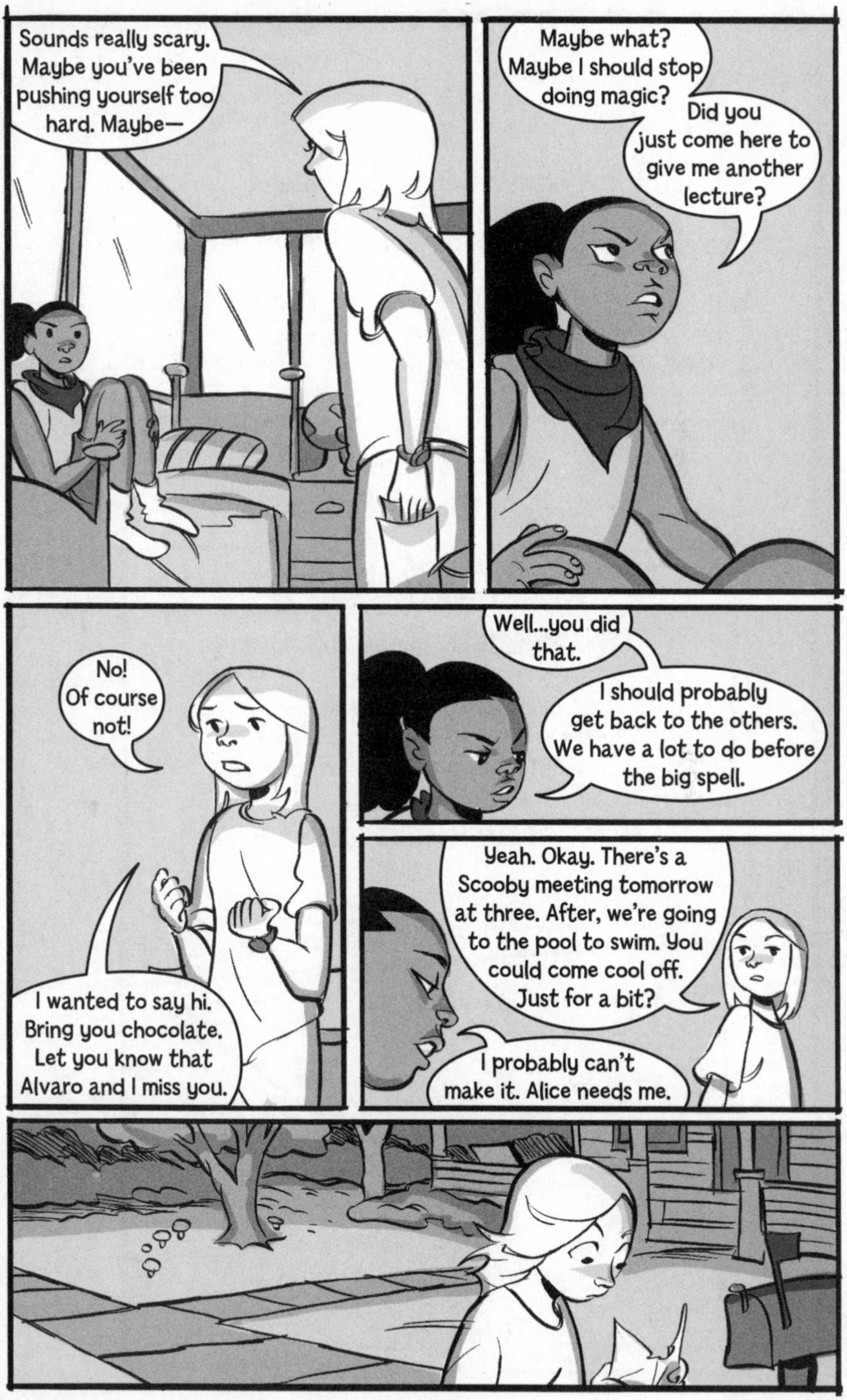
Sounds really scary. Maybe you've been pushing yourself too hard. Maybe—
Maybe what? Maybe I should stop doing magic?
Did you just come here to give me another lecture?
No! Of course not!
I wanted to say hi. Bring you chocolate. Let you know that Alvaro and I miss you.
Well...you did that.
I should probably get back to the others. We have a lot to do before the big spell.
Yeah. Okay. There's a Scooby meeting tomorrow at three. After, we're going to the pool to swim. You could come cool off. Just for a bit?
I probably can't make it. Alice needs me.

Dear Diary,

The plot thickens. I think I found something in Rae's room. A map of some kind. I have to show Sparky ASAP. But right now I'm late to the mall stakeout. Time to use Alvaro as bait.

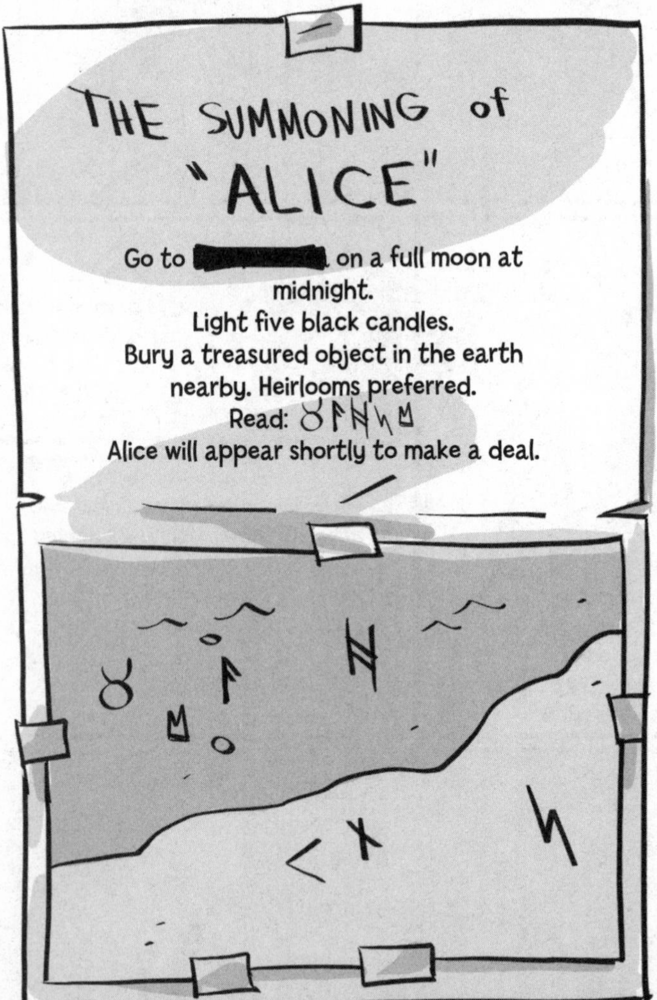
THE SUMMONING of
"ALICE"
Go to [redacted] on a full moon at midnight.
Light five black candles.
Bury a treasured object in the earth nearby. Heirlooms preferred.
Read:
Alice will appear shortly to make a deal.

Alvaro! Sparky! I'm sorry I'm running late. Mom's driving me to the mall right now! Almost there! Don't start the vampire trap without me!

And, Alvaro, I got your texts. There is NOTHING to worry about. Sparky and I will be like two steps away from you at all times.

I'm the Slayer, I'm not gonna let anybody bite my werewolf buddy.

 And just when I thought you couldn't get any weirder.

Melanie?

Oh no...

 Oh yes.

You have officially mastered the power of TEXTING THE WRONG PERSON.

So what's all this about vampires and werewolves?

UHHHHHHHH....

BRB

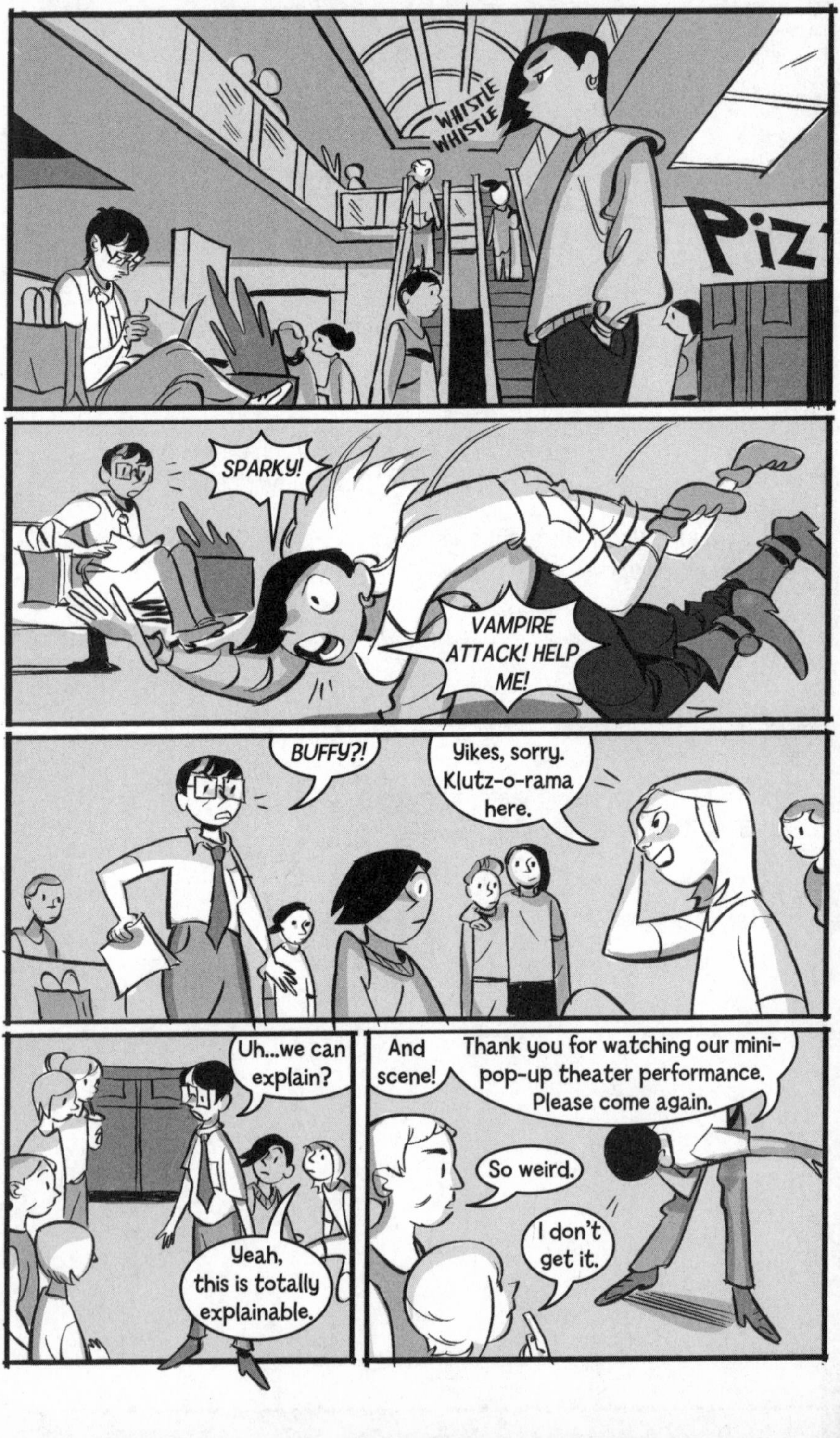
WHISTLE WHISTLE
Piz
SPARKY!
VAMPIRE ATTACK! HELP ME!
BUFFY?!
Yikes, sorry. Klutz-o-rama here.
Uh...we can explain?
Yeah, this is totally explainable.
And scene!
Thank you for watching our mini-pop-up theater performance. Please come again.
So weird.
I don't get it.

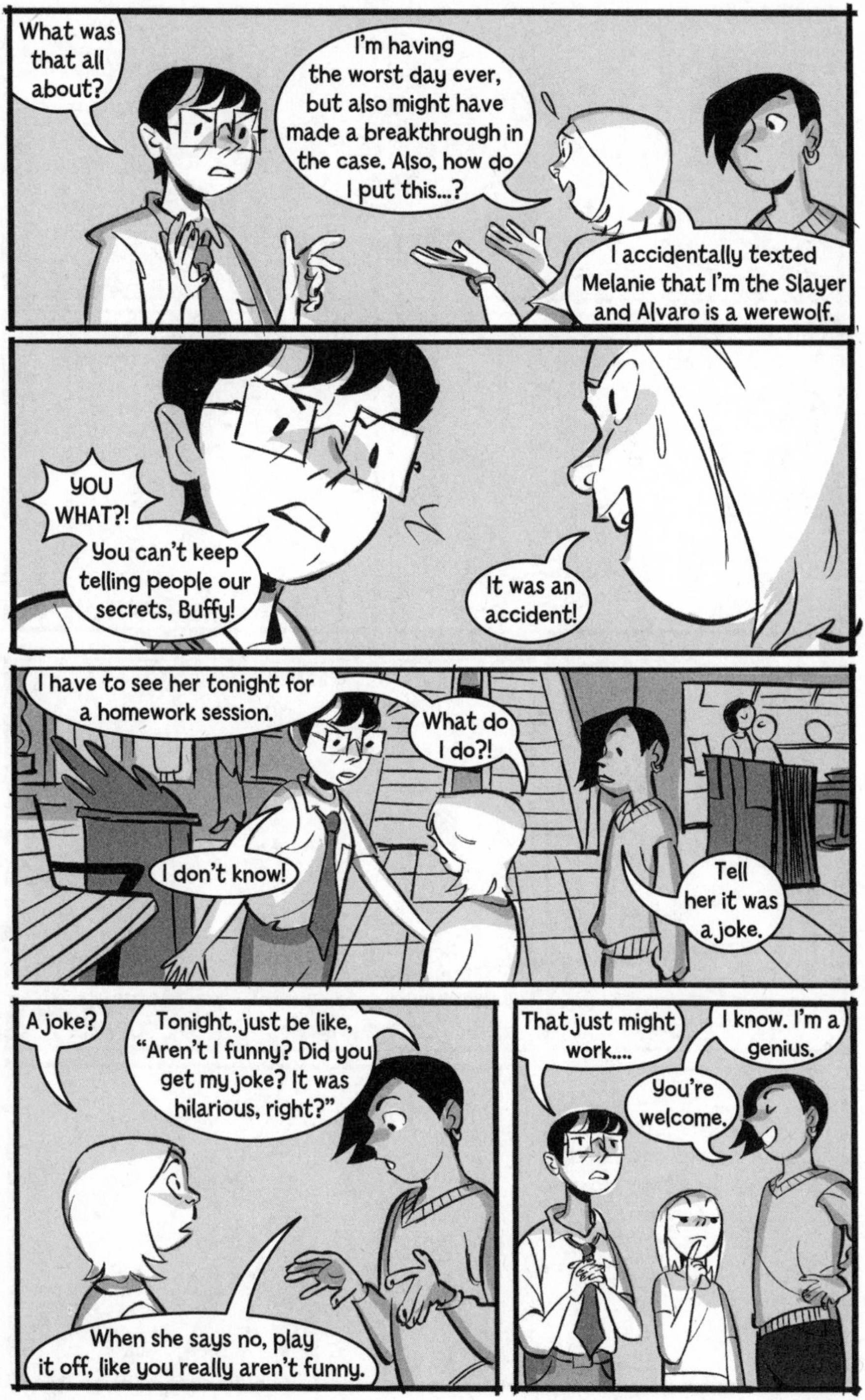
What was that all about?
I'm having the worst day ever, but also might have made a breakthrough in the case. Also, how do I put this...?
I accidentally texted Melanie that I'm the Slayer and Alvaro is a werewolf.
YOU WHAT?!
You can't keep telling people our secrets, Buffy!
It was an accident!
I have to see her tonight for a homework session.
What do I do?!
I don't know!
Tell her it was a joke.
A joke?
Tonight, just be like, "Aren't I funny? Did you get my joke? It was hilarious, right?"
When she says no, play it off, like you really aren't funny.
That just might work....
I know. I'm a genius.
You're welcome.

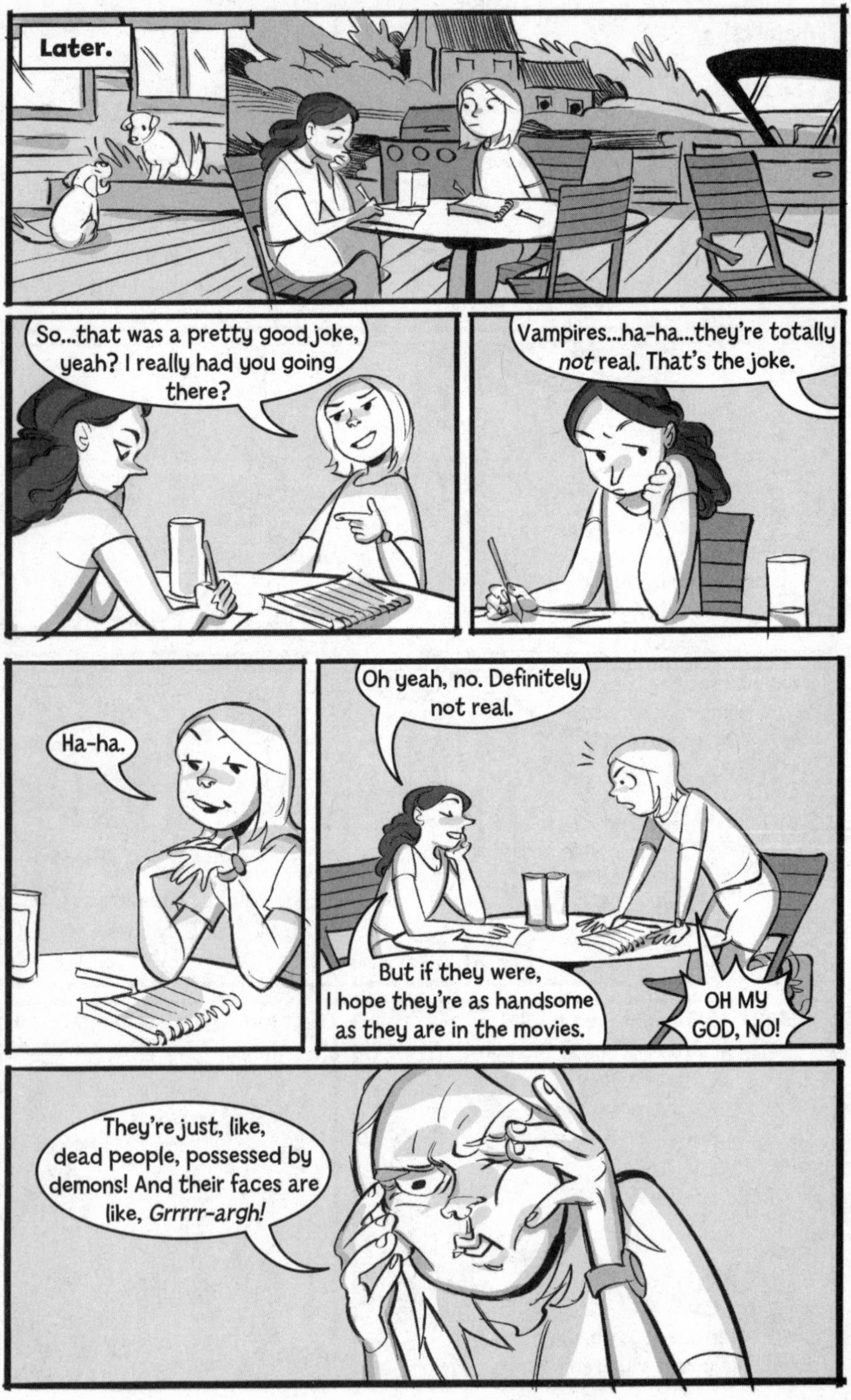
Later.
So...that was a pretty good joke, yeah? I really had you going there?
Vampires...ha-ha...they're totally *not* real. That's the joke.
Ha-ha.
Oh yeah, no. Definitely not real.
But if they were, I hope they're as handsome as they are in the movies.
OH MY GOD, NO!
They're just, like, dead people, possessed by demons! And their faces are like, *Grrrrr-argh!*

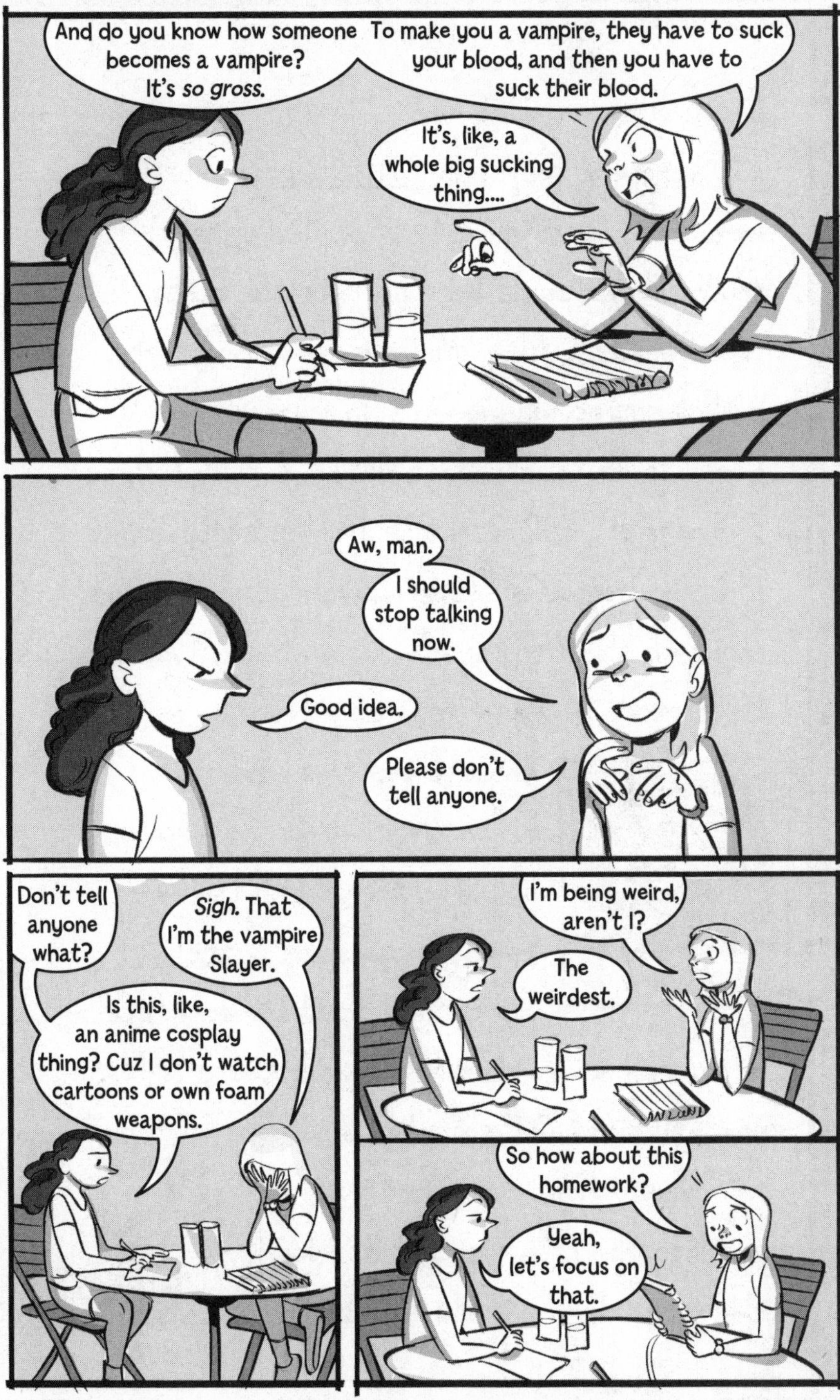
And do you know how someone becomes a vampire? It's *so gross.*
To make you a vampire, they have to suck your blood, and then you have to suck their blood.
It's, like, a whole big sucking thing....
Aw, man.
I should stop talking now.
Good idea.
Please don't tell anyone.
Don't tell anyone what?
Sigh. That I'm the vampire Slayer.
Is this, like, an anime cosplay thing? Cuz I don't watch cartoons or own foam weapons.
I'm being weird, aren't I?
The weirdest.
So how about this homework?
Yeah, let's focus on that.

Dear Diary,

Being the Slayer is STRESSFUL! This week, the beans almost got spilled by yours truly. They woulda been all over the place, those beans. Luckily, Melanie (and the general public) has no idea what a vampire Slayer is or does. So now she just thinks I'm totally bizarre. I wonder if she'll wanna be friends still. Oh no. Is losing friends a Slayer power no one told me about or something?

In other news, we've used Alvaro as bait three times this week, and so far...nothing. Tomorrow morning is gonna be the fourth time we take our fake artsy teen hipster boy to the mall. I hope it gets us somewhere this time because being at the mall and NOT shopping is no fun. Plus, Alvaro is getting WAY too into the role. He told Sparky the other day he could see the

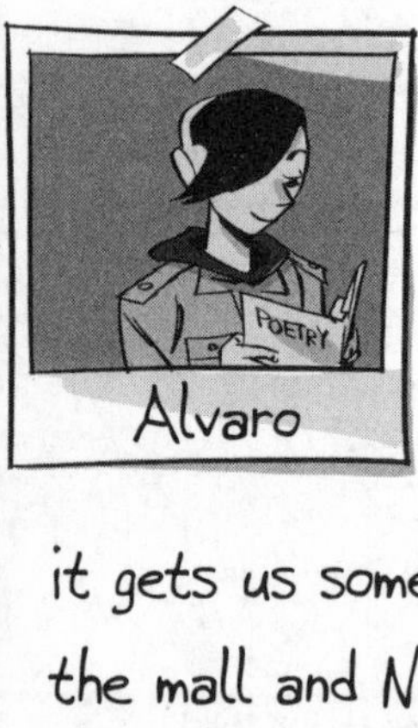
POETRY
Alvaro

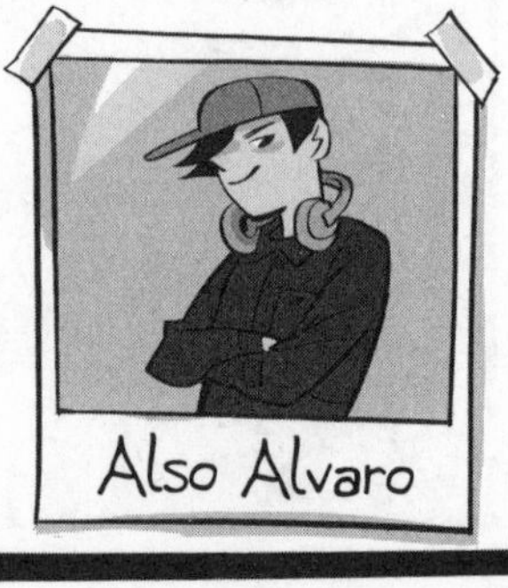
Also Alvaro

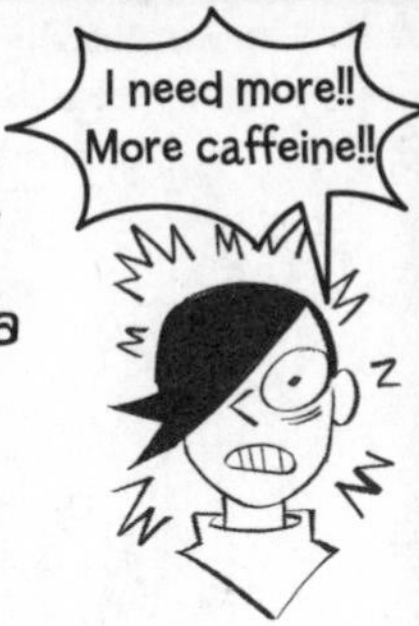
I need more!!
More caffeine!!

"poetry of sadness" in her eyes. And every time we go out, he insists on a new "edgier" look. Oh, and he's, like, addicted to coffee now.

Oh, and UPDATE! So I gave Sparky the map, and she was all, "This is really badly drawn." And I was like, "Focus!" and she was like, "This is definitely a clue—but to what?" I guess the spell was in ancient Draconian-Atlantean-Proto-Phoenician or something, so Sparky has to learn how to translate it to see what it says. I wish I could tell Fina now that it looks like bad news, but without anything concrete, she'd just get more mad at me. And I don't want that.

Tomorrow, we're going back to the mall to keep trying to lure out the vampire (who Alvaro still insists is twins). Hopefully we can wrap up the "Missing Teen" case so we can focus on Fina and getting her out of whatever trouble she's in.

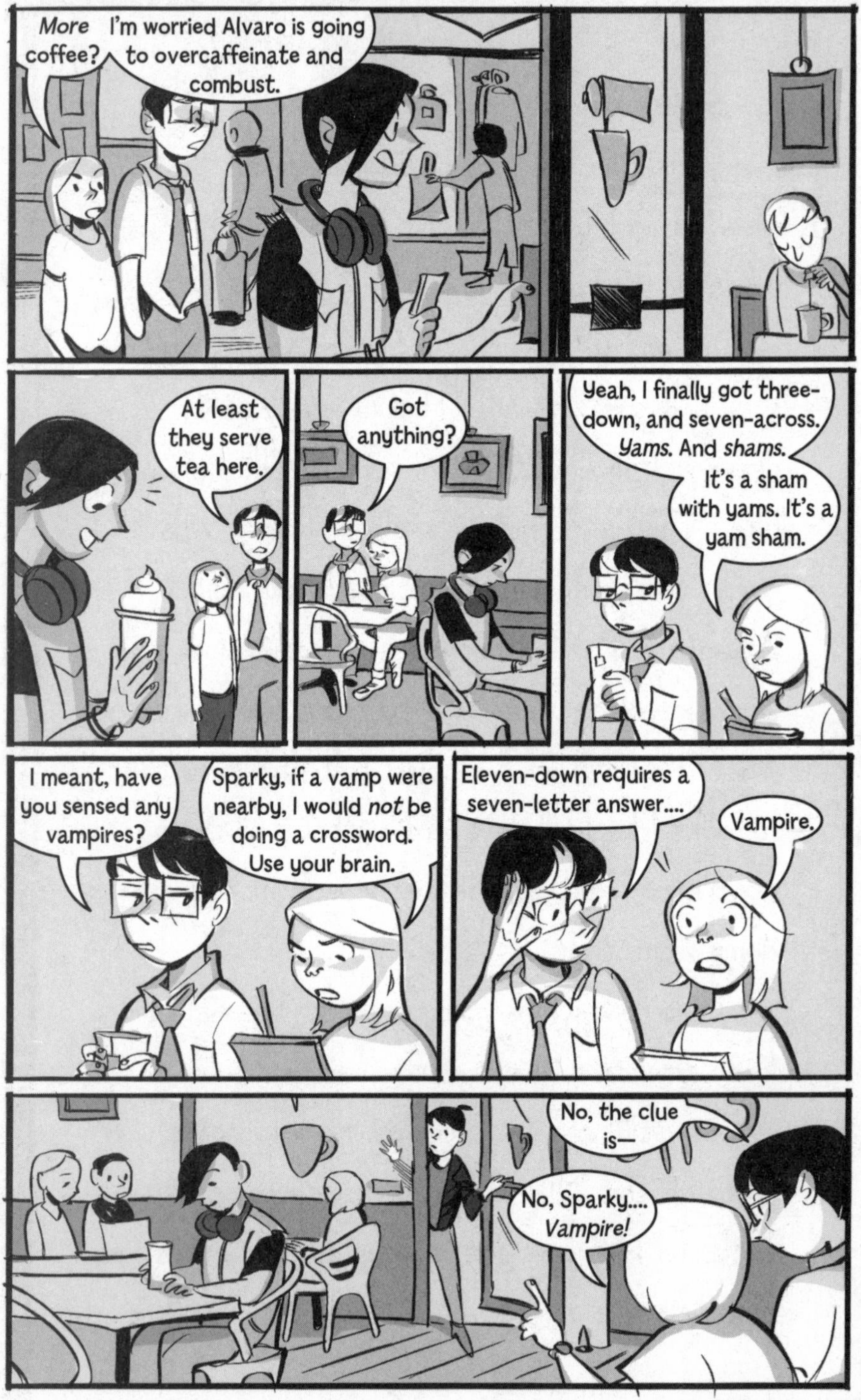

More coffee?
I'm worried Alvaro is going to overcaffeinate and combust.
At least they serve tea here.
Got anything?
Yeah, I finally got three-down, and seven-across. *Yams.* And *shams.*
It's a sham with yams. It's a yam sham.
I meant, have you sensed any vampires?
Sparky, if a vamp were nearby, I would *not* be doing a crossword. Use your brain.
Eleven-down requires a seven-letter answer....
Vampire.
No, the clue is—
No, Sparky.... *Vampire!*

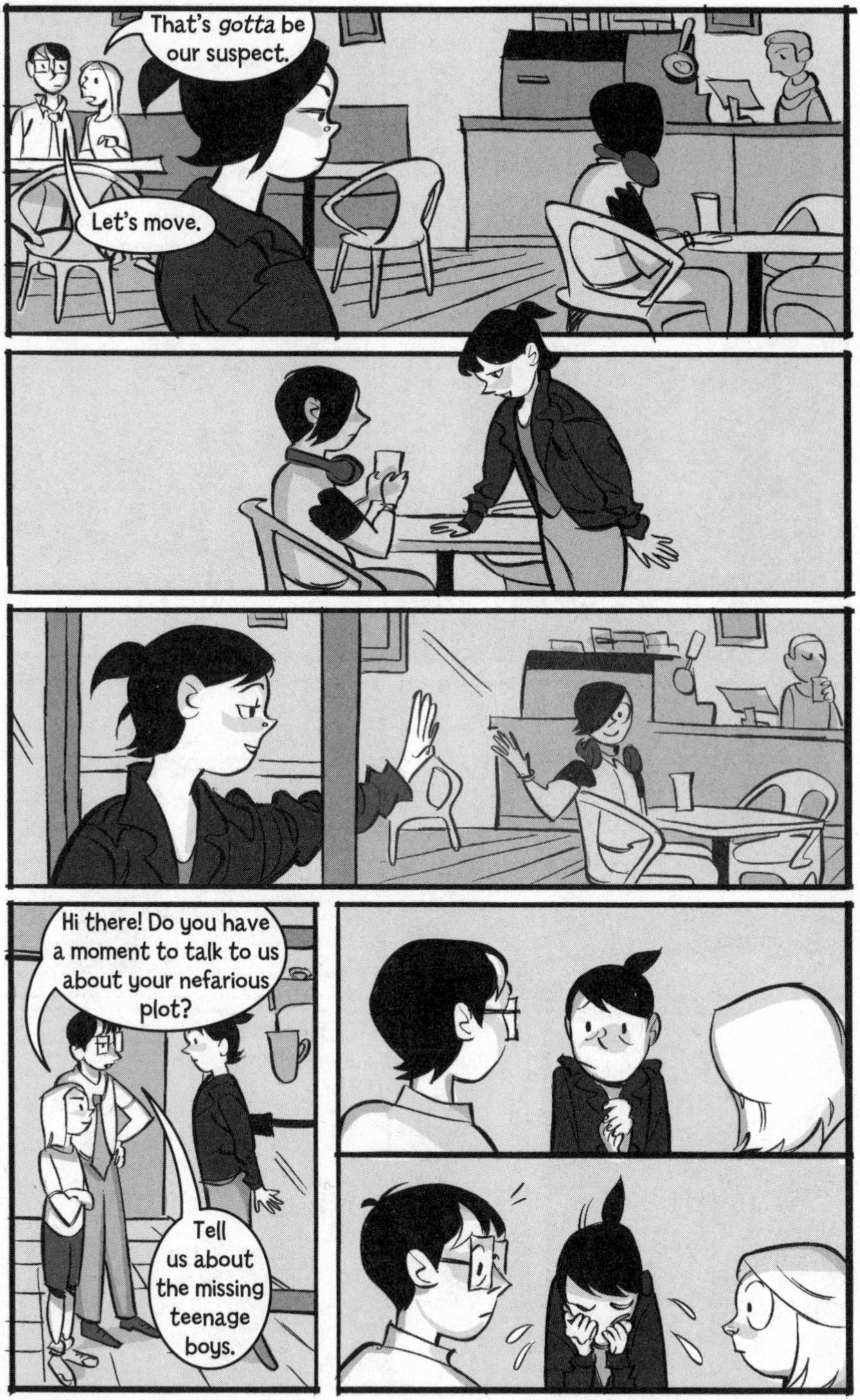
That's *gotta* be our suspect.
Let's move.
Hi there! Do you have a moment to talk to us about your nefarious plot?
Tell us about the missing teenage boys.

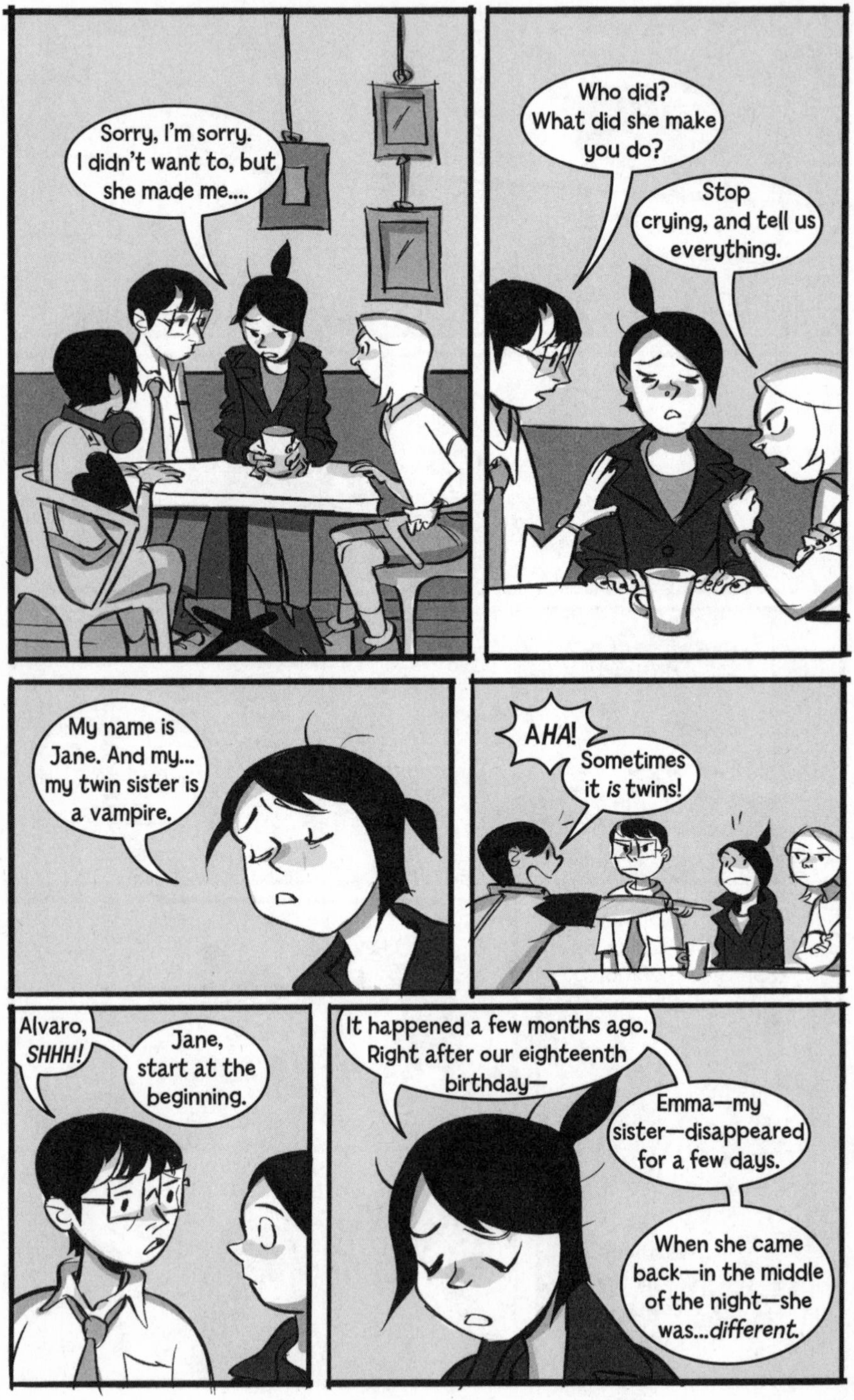

Sorry, I'm sorry. I didn't want to, but she made me....
Who did? What did she make you do?
Stop crying, and tell us everything.
My name is Jane. And my... my twin sister is a vampire.
AHA!
Sometimes it *is* twins!
Alvaro, *SHHH!*
Jane, start at the beginning.
It happened a few months ago. Right after our eighteenth birthday—
Emma—my sister—disappeared for a few days.
When she came back—in the middle of the night—she was...*different*.

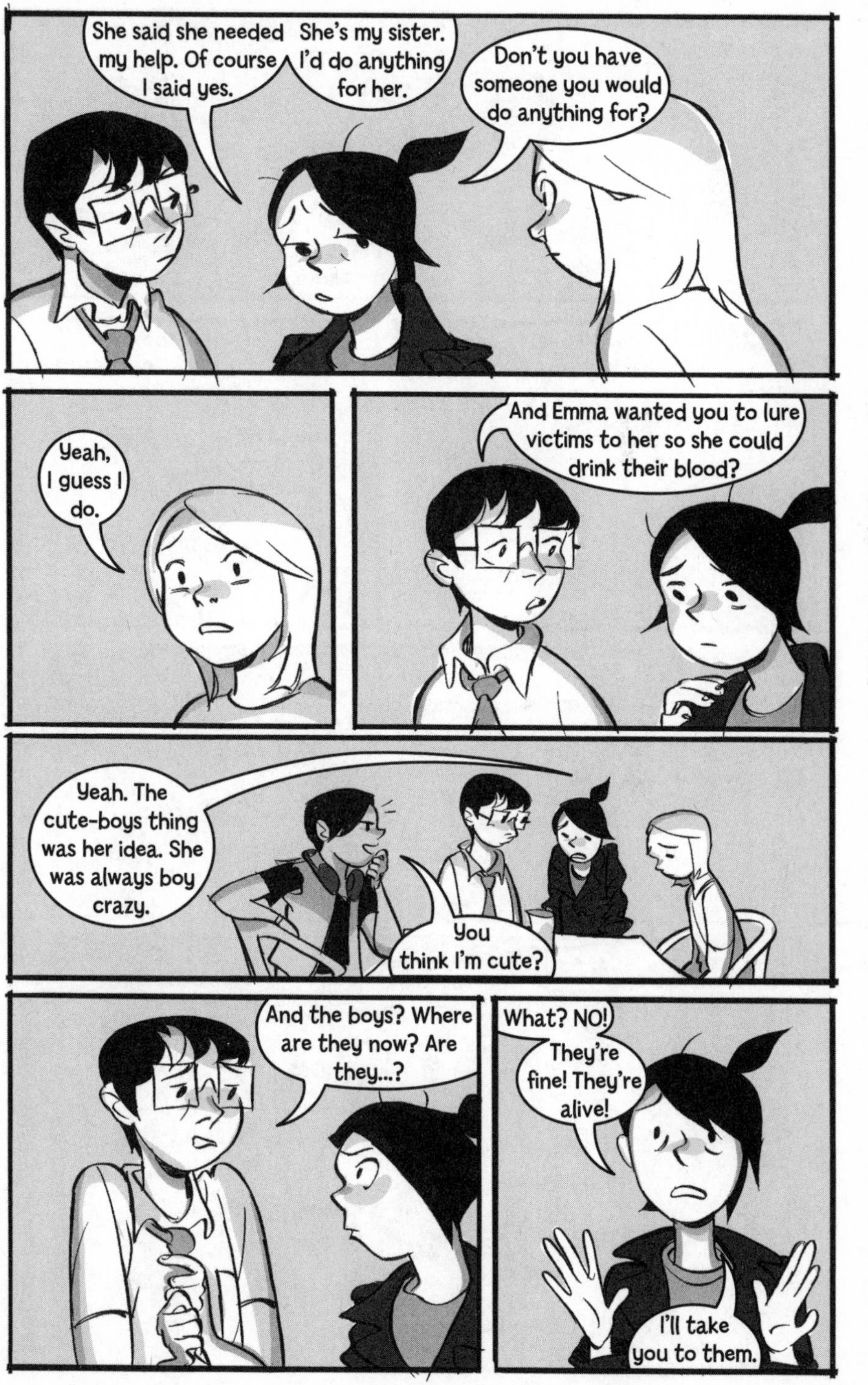
She said she needed my help. Of course I said yes.
She's my sister. I'd do anything for her.
Don't you have someone you would do anything for?
Yeah, I guess I do.
And Emma wanted you to lure victims to her so she could drink their blood?
Yeah. The cute-boys thing was her idea. She was always boy crazy.
You think I'm cute?
And the boys? Where are they now? Are they...?
What? NO!
They're fine! They're alive!
I'll take you to them.

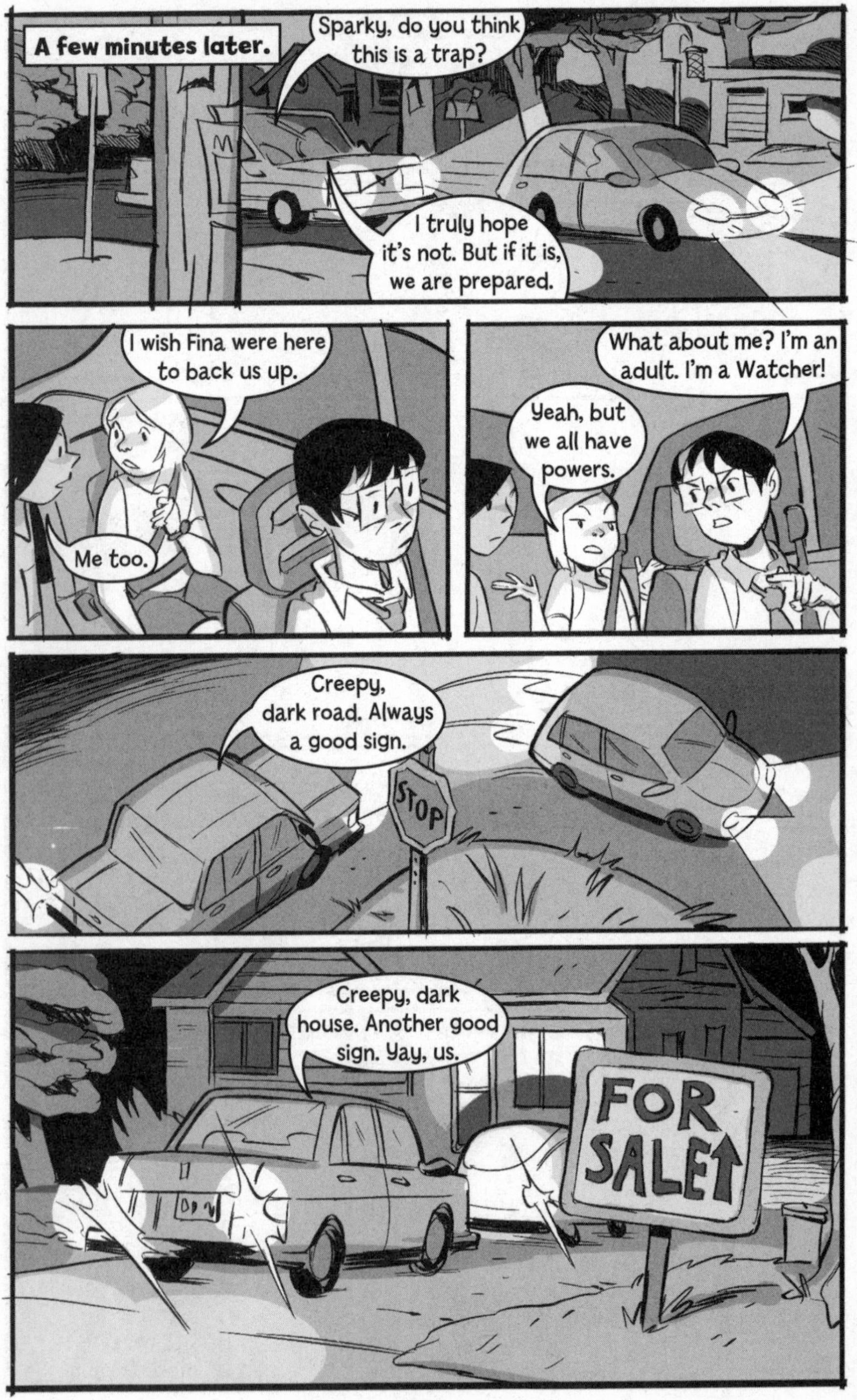
A few minutes later.
Sparky, do you think this is a trap?
I truly hope it's not. But if it is, we are prepared.
I wish Fina were here to back us up.
Me too.
What about me? I'm an adult. I'm a Watcher!
Yeah, but we all have powers.
Creepy, dark road. Always a good sign.
STOP
Creepy, dark house. Another good sign. Yay, us.
FOR SALE

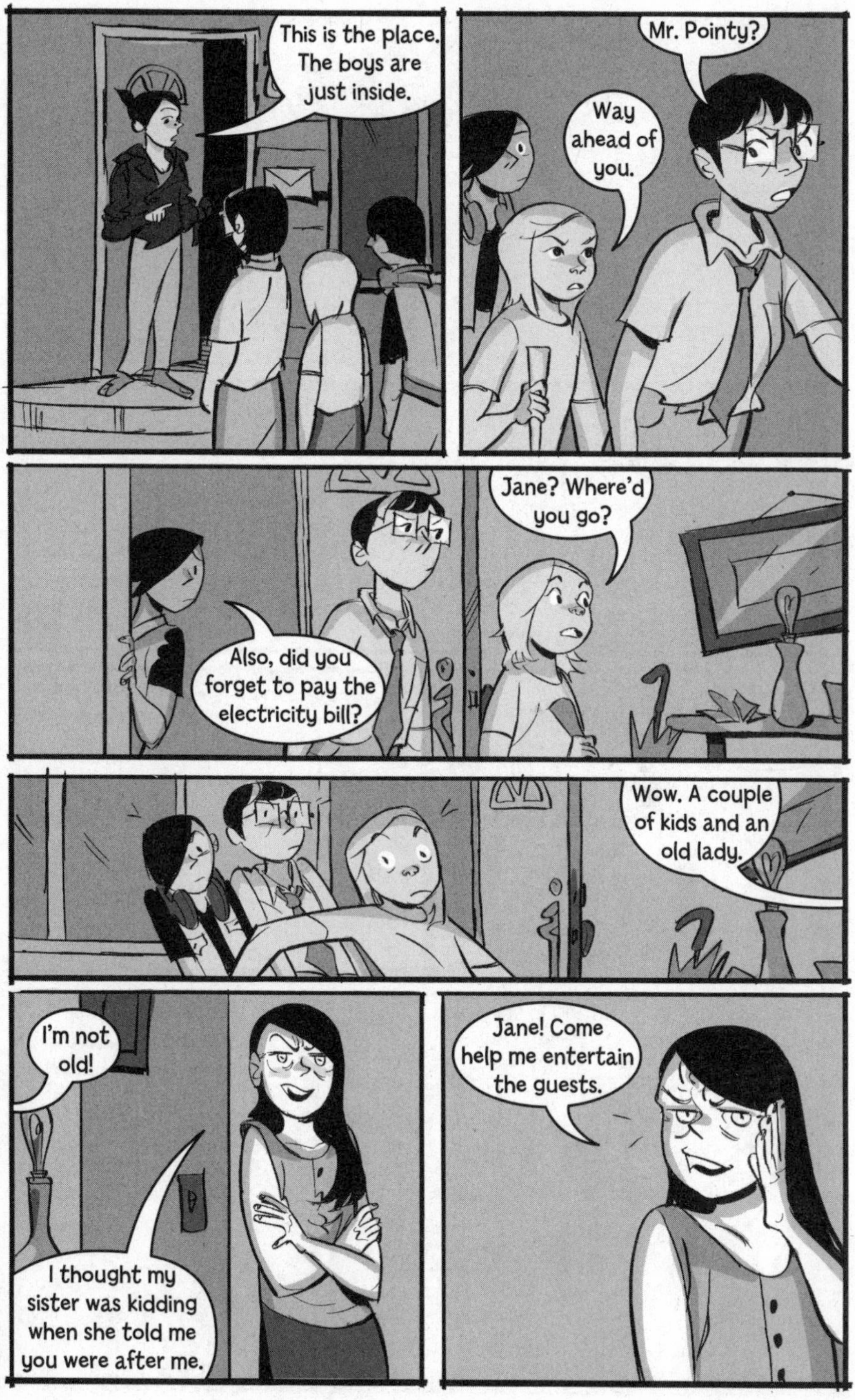
This is the place. The boys are just inside.
Mr. Pointy?
Way ahead of you.
Jane? Where'd you go?
Also, did you forget to pay the electricity bill?
Wow. A couple of kids and an old lady.
I'm not old!
I thought my sister was kidding when she told me you were after me.
Jane! Come help me entertain the guests.

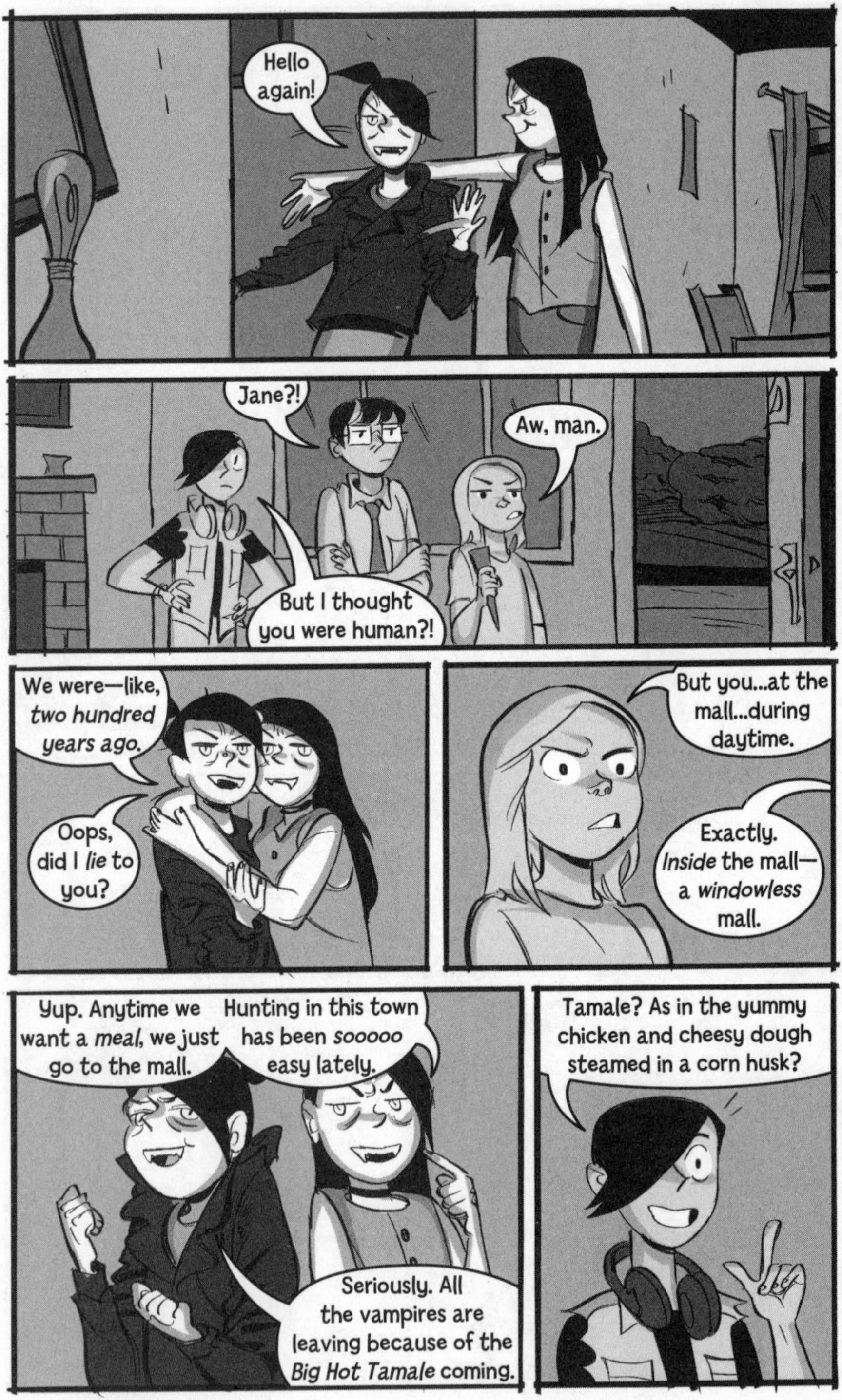
Hello again!
Jane?!
Aw, man.
But I thought you were human?!
We were—like, *two hundred years ago.*
Oops, did I *lie* to you?
But you...at the mall...during daytime.
Exactly. *Inside* the mall—a *windowless* mall.
Yup. Anytime we want a *meal*, we just go to the mall.
Hunting in this town has been *sooooo* easy lately.
Seriously. All the vampires are leaving because of the *Big Hot Tamale* coming.
Tamale? As in the yummy chicken and cheesy dough steamed in a corn husk?

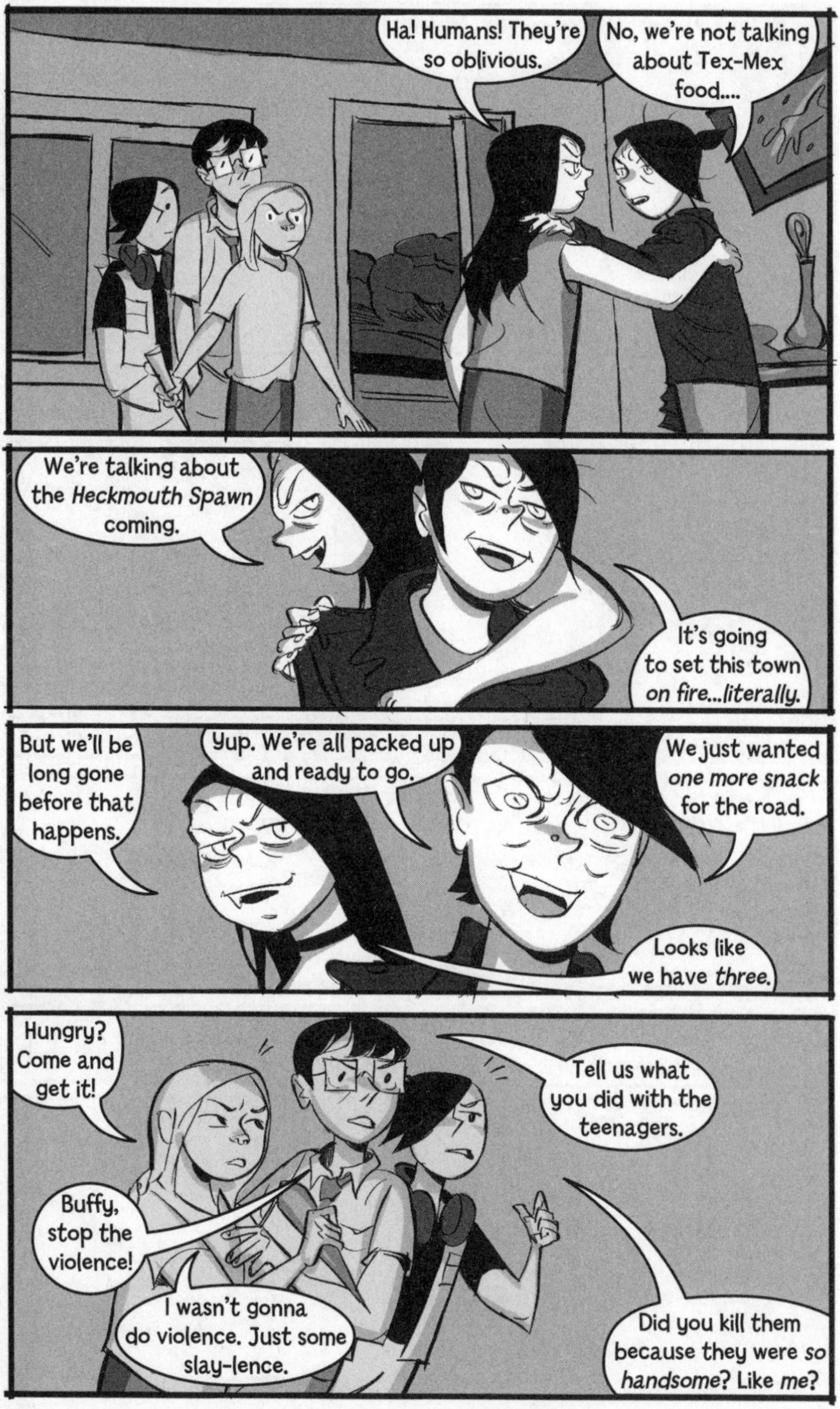
Ha! Humans! They're so oblivious.
No, we're not talking about Tex-Mex food....
We're talking about the *Heckmouth Spawn* coming.
It's going to set this town *on fire...literally.*
But we'll be long gone before that happens.
Yup. We're all packed up and ready to go.
We just wanted *one more snack* for the road.
Looks like we have *three.*
Hungry? Come and get it!
Tell us what you did with the teenagers.
Buffy, stop the violence!
I wasn't gonna do violence. Just some slay-lence.
Did you kill them because they were *so handsome*? Like *me*?

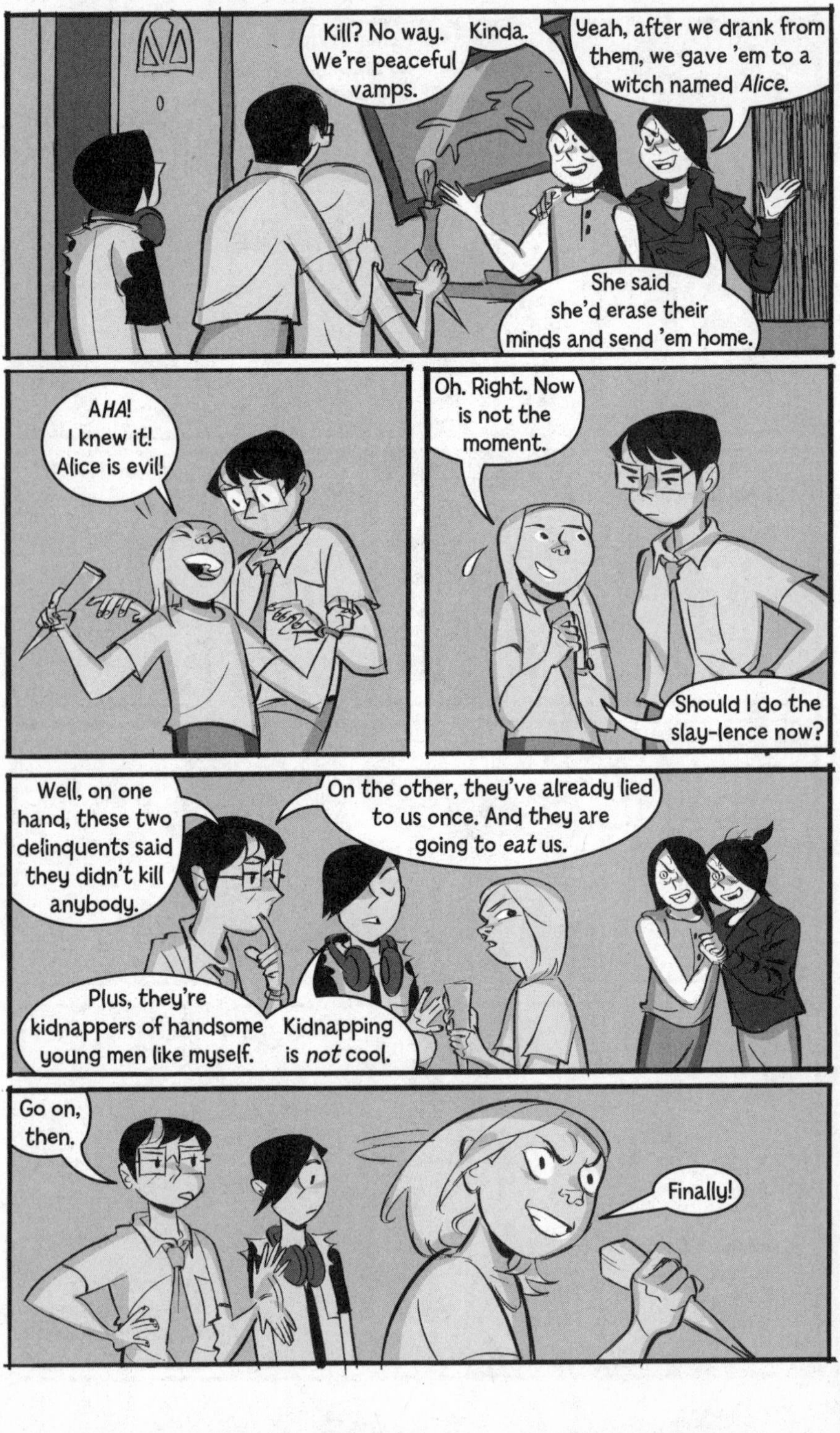
Kill? No way. We're peaceful vamps.
Kinda.
Yeah, after we drank from them, we gave 'em to a witch named *Alice*.
She said she'd erase their minds and send 'em home.
A*HA*! I knew it! Alice is evil!
Oh. Right. Now is not the moment.
Should I do the slay-lence now?
Well, on one hand, these two delinquents said they didn't kill anybody.
On the other, they've already lied to us once. And they are going to *eat* us.
Plus, they're kidnappers of handsome young men like myself.
Kidnapping is *not* cool.
Go on, then.
Finally!

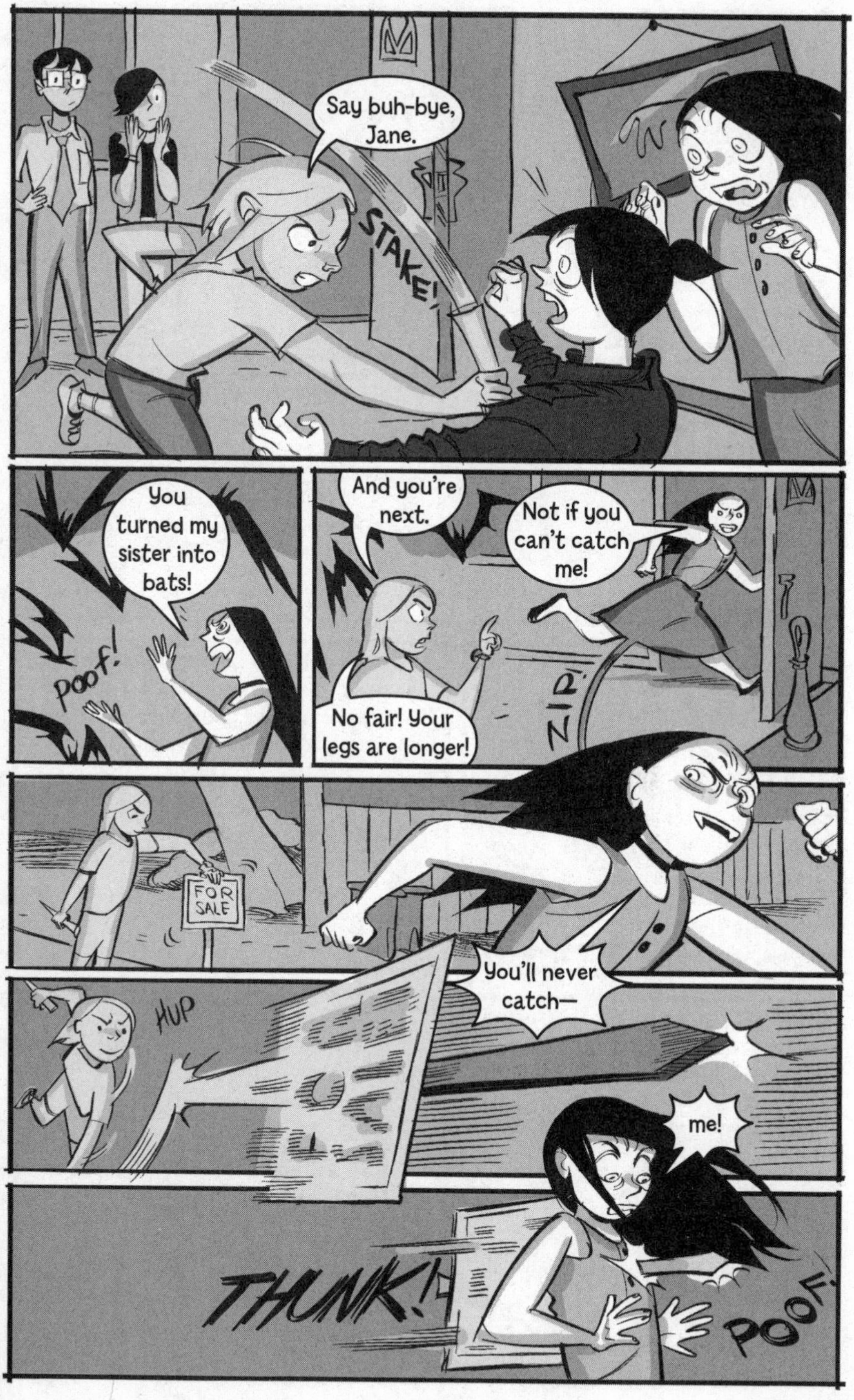
Say buh-bye, Jane.
STAKE!
You turned my sister into bats!
poof!
And you're next.
Not if you can't catch me!
No fair! Your legs are longer!
ZIP
FOR SALE
You'll never catch—
HUP
me!
THUNK!
POOF!

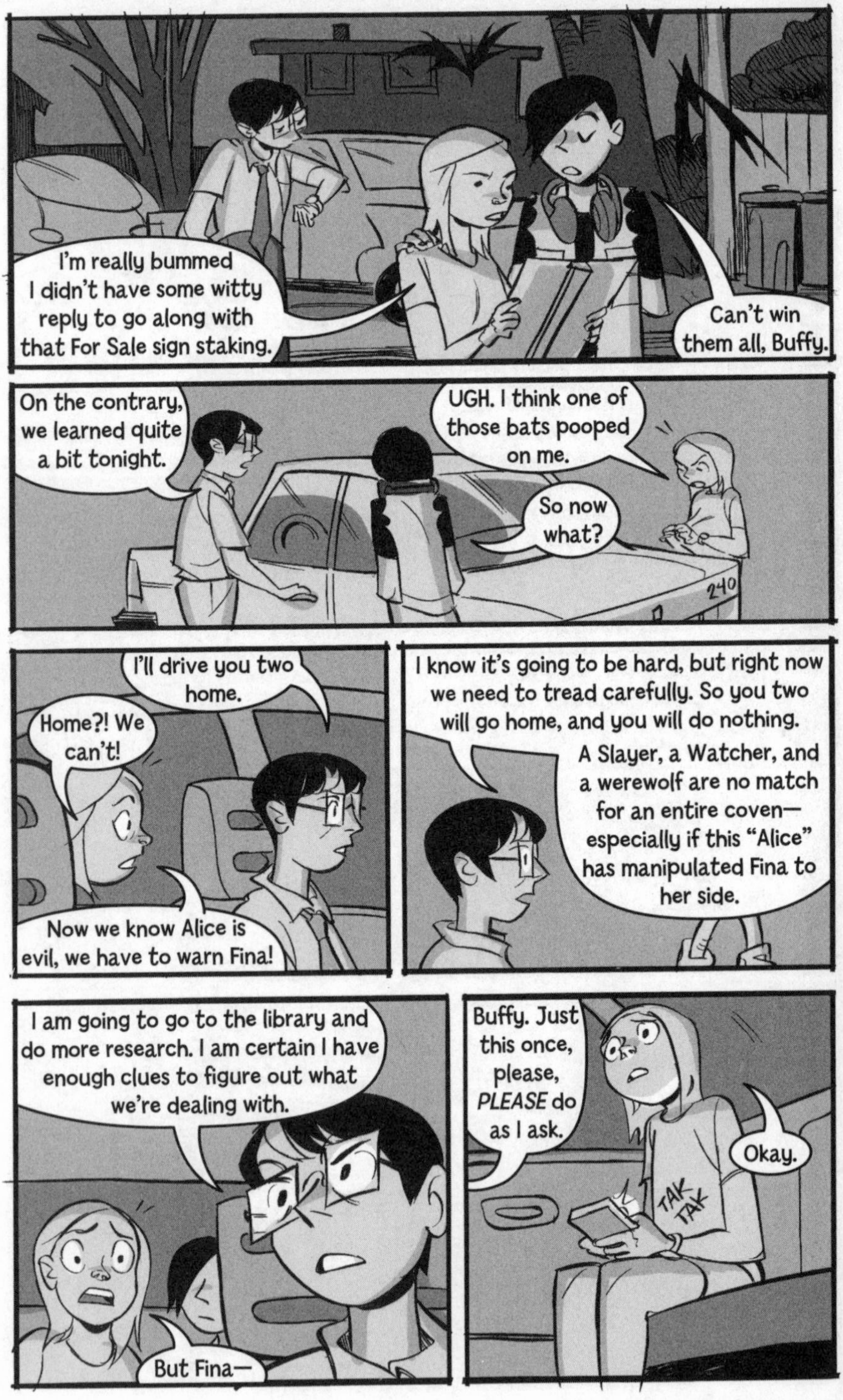
I'm really bummed I didn't have some witty reply to go along with that For Sale sign staking.
Can't win them all, Buffy.
On the contrary, we learned quite a bit tonight.
UGH. I think one of those bats pooped on me.
So now what?
240
I'll drive you two home.
Home?! We can't!
Now we know Alice is evil, we have to warn Fina!
I know it's going to be hard, but right now we need to tread carefully. So you two will go home, and you will do nothing.
A Slayer, a Watcher, and a werewolf are no match for an entire coven— especially if this "Alice" has manipulated Fina to her side.
I am going to go to the library and do more research. I am certain I have enough clues to figure out what we're dealing with.
But Fina—
Buffy. Just this once, please, *PLEASE* do as I ask.
TAK TAK
Okay.

Sarafina

10:23 PM

Fina! We have to talk. Call me ASAP.

10:48 PM

This is a 911 situation, Fina. Please call me.

11:37 PM

Well you should at least know the mystery of the vanishing teenage boys has been solved. We used Alvaro as bait. Don't worry, he's safe. But we learned something else. Please call me.

12:02 AM

Okay, I'm going to bed, cuz I have summer school in the morning. But I'll leave my phone on. Call me.

Please?

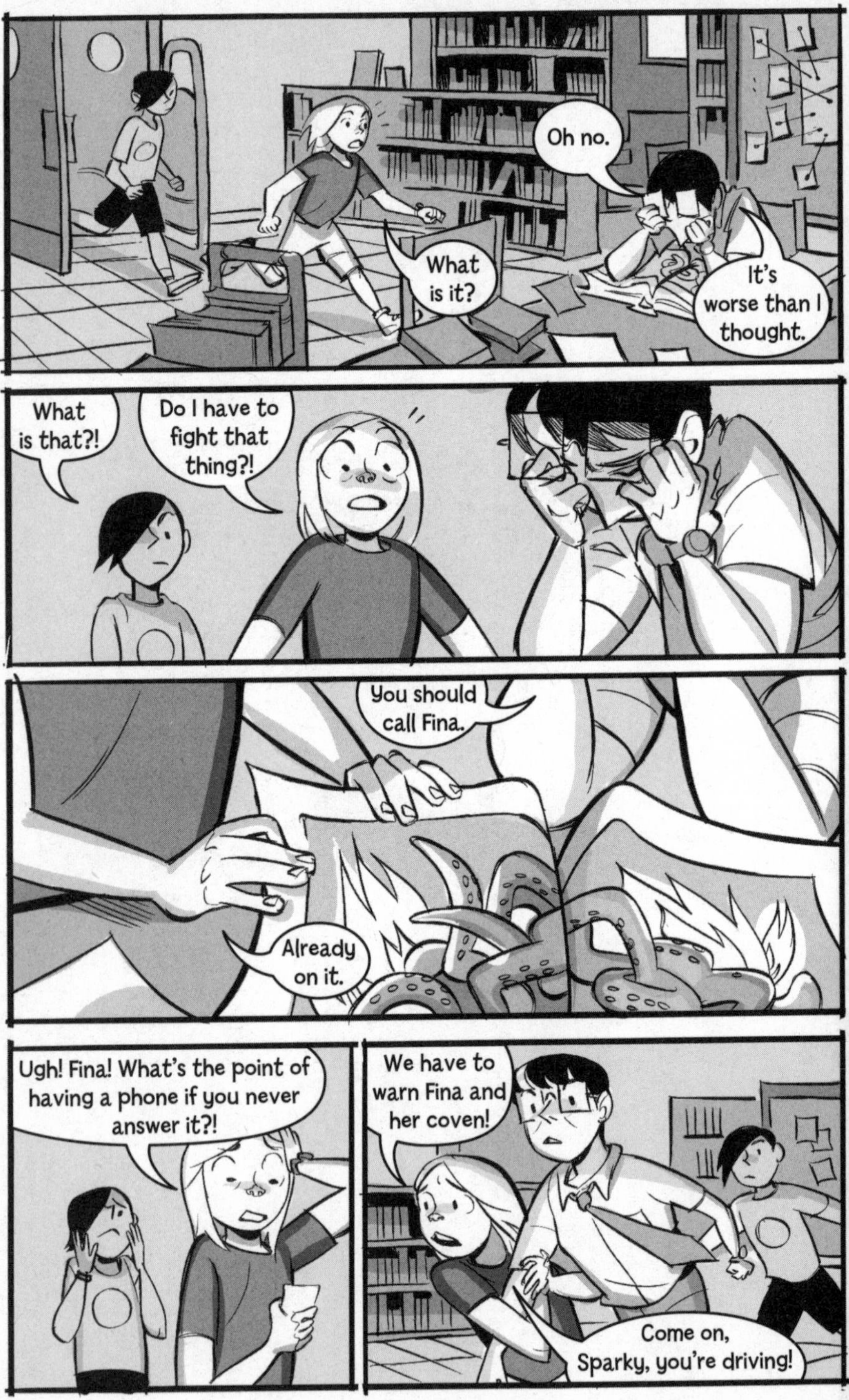
Oh no.
What is it?
It's worse than I thought.
What is that?!
Do I have to fight that thing?!
You should call Fina.
Already on it.
Ugh! Fina! What's the point of having a phone if you never answer it?!
We have to warn Fina and her coven!
Come on, Sparky, you're driving!

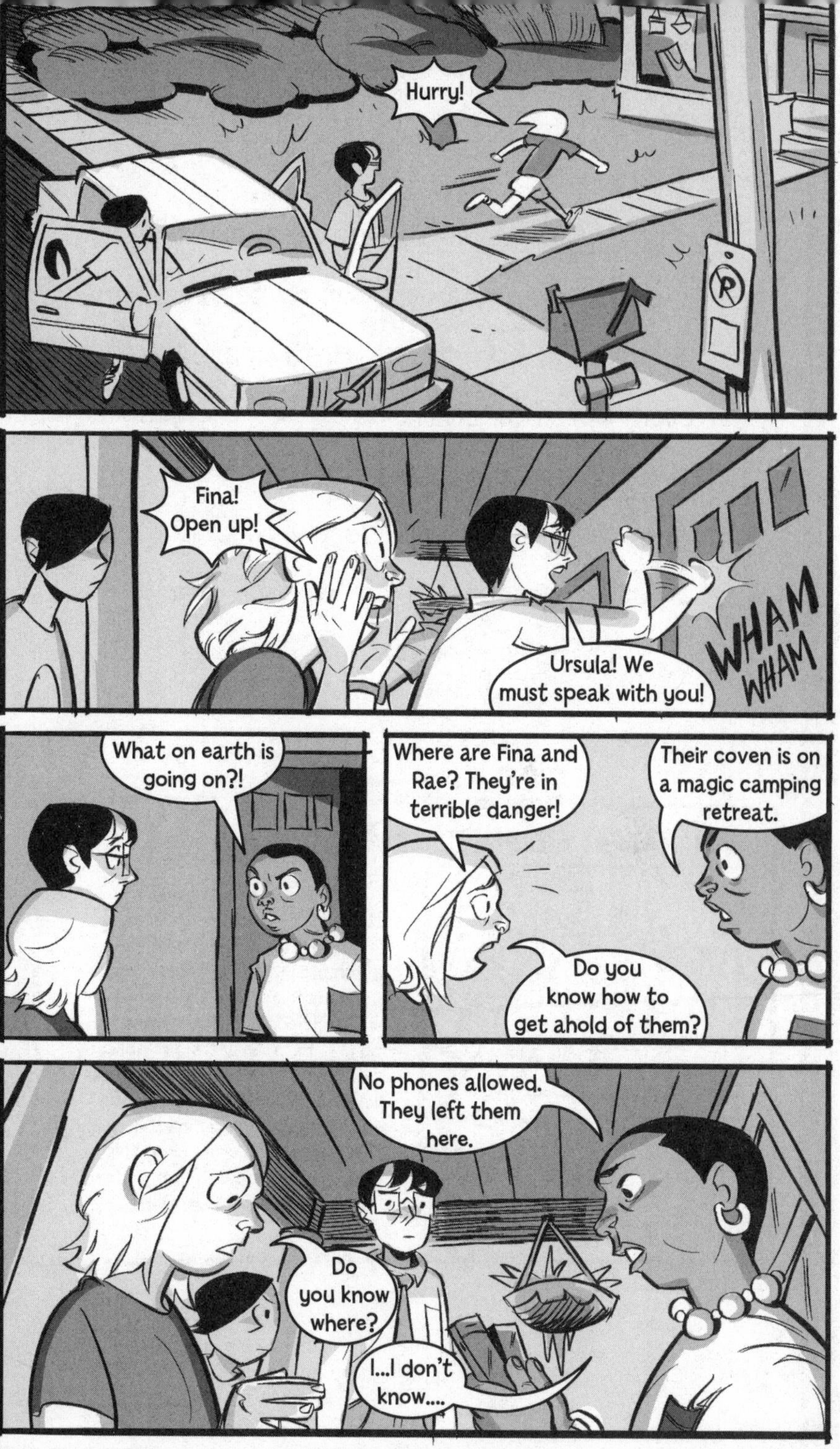
Hurry!
Fina! Open up!
Ursula! We must speak with you!
WHAM WHAM
What on earth is going on?!
Where are Fina and Rae? They're in terrible danger!
Do you know how to get ahold of them?
Their coven is on a magic camping retreat.
No phones allowed. They left them here.
Do you know where?
I...I don't know....

Dear Diary,

Worst! Week! Ever!! First we found the teen-napping vampire twins, but no teens. Then some bats pooped on one of my favorite shirts. And then, worst of all, it turns out the leader of my best friend's coven is a demon intent on destroying the whole city! Seriously. Check out what Sparky photocopied for me from one of her big, scary demon books....

SOL ZAMALE TRINITY DEMON

A demon intent on breaking through the Heckmouth from its world into ours. Signs of its attempts include excessive heat and manipulation of local covens. This demon has three forms. The first form: An astral projection as a friendly ghost or witch offering power to witches in exchange for aid in obtaining materials that will allow it to fully cross over. This demon usually tricks young witches into performing the spell.

The second form: Once the spell is finished, the demon becomes solid and can pass through the Heckmouth. This form is, essentially, a beast with a hundred tentacles. This is also when it is at its strongest.

The third form: The final body is granted after it has eaten the coven and a dozen male teenagers. This hearty meal allows the Sol Zamale to become a monster of pure heat and fire that can destroy an entire city.

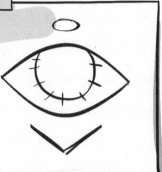

(Recognize the symbol?)

So, that's the bad news. The good news is... gotcha! There is <u>NO</u> good news. Of all the Heckmouths in the world, I had to move to this one. (Why couldn't Mom have moved us to Sunnydale, California? Sparky mentioned a Heckmouth is there. I'm sure no crazy tentacle demon is attacking it right now, and I bet the weather is a lot nicer, too.)

So, it looks like Rae and Fina's coven was tricked by a crazy demon-lady-ghost that's really a tentacle-monster who wants to cross into our world and eat teenagers to become a mini-sun so it can destroy the whole city. The worst part is, we don't even know where to find Fina and her coven, or the demon. And tomorrow night is the full moon. Sparky says that's probably when they're gonna do the spell. So we have less than a day to come up with a plan, figure out where the coven and the demon are, GET to wherever they are, and save the day.

Oh, and did I mention this is the last week of summer school? Yeah, I have final exams on Friday. If I don't pass, I'll get held back a year. And Mom will kill me. Looks like this is the end of Buffy Summers one way or another.

Hope we get to chat again, Diary. Fingers crossed for good luck.

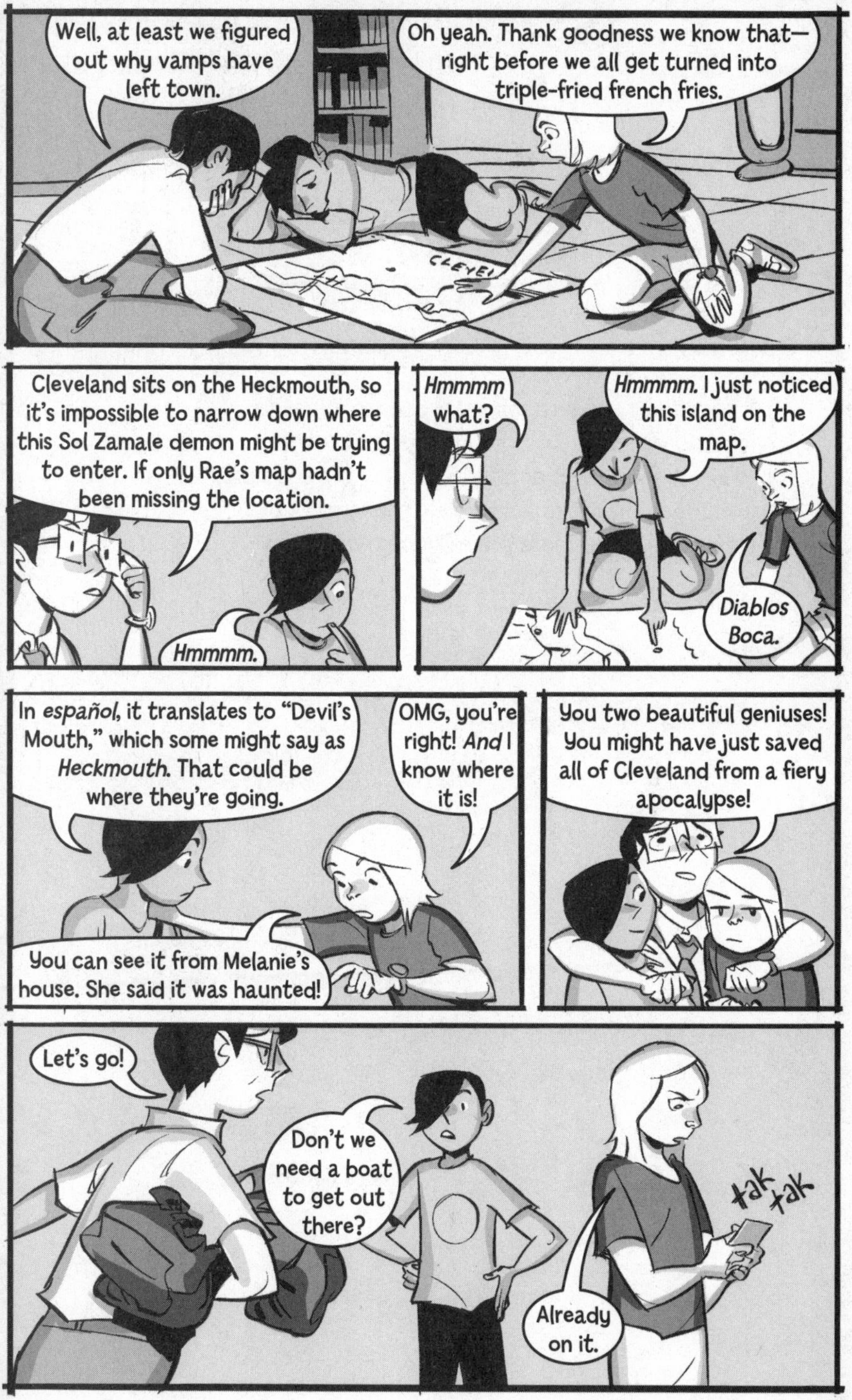
Well, at least we figured out why vamps have left town.
Oh yeah. Thank goodness we know that—right before we all get turned into triple-fried french fries.
CLEVEL
Cleveland sits on the Heckmouth, so it's impossible to narrow down where this Sol Zamale demon might be trying to enter. If only Rae's map hadn't been missing the location.
Hmmmm.
Hmmmm what?
Hmmmm. I just noticed this island on the map.
Diablos Boca.
In *español*, it translates to "Devil's Mouth," which some might say as *Heckmouth*. That could be where they're going.
OMG, you're right! *And* I know where it is!
You can see it from Melanie's house. She said it was haunted!
You two beautiful geniuses! You might have just saved all of Cleveland from a fiery apocalypse!
Let's go!
Don't we need a boat to get out there?
tak tak
Already on it.

Melanie

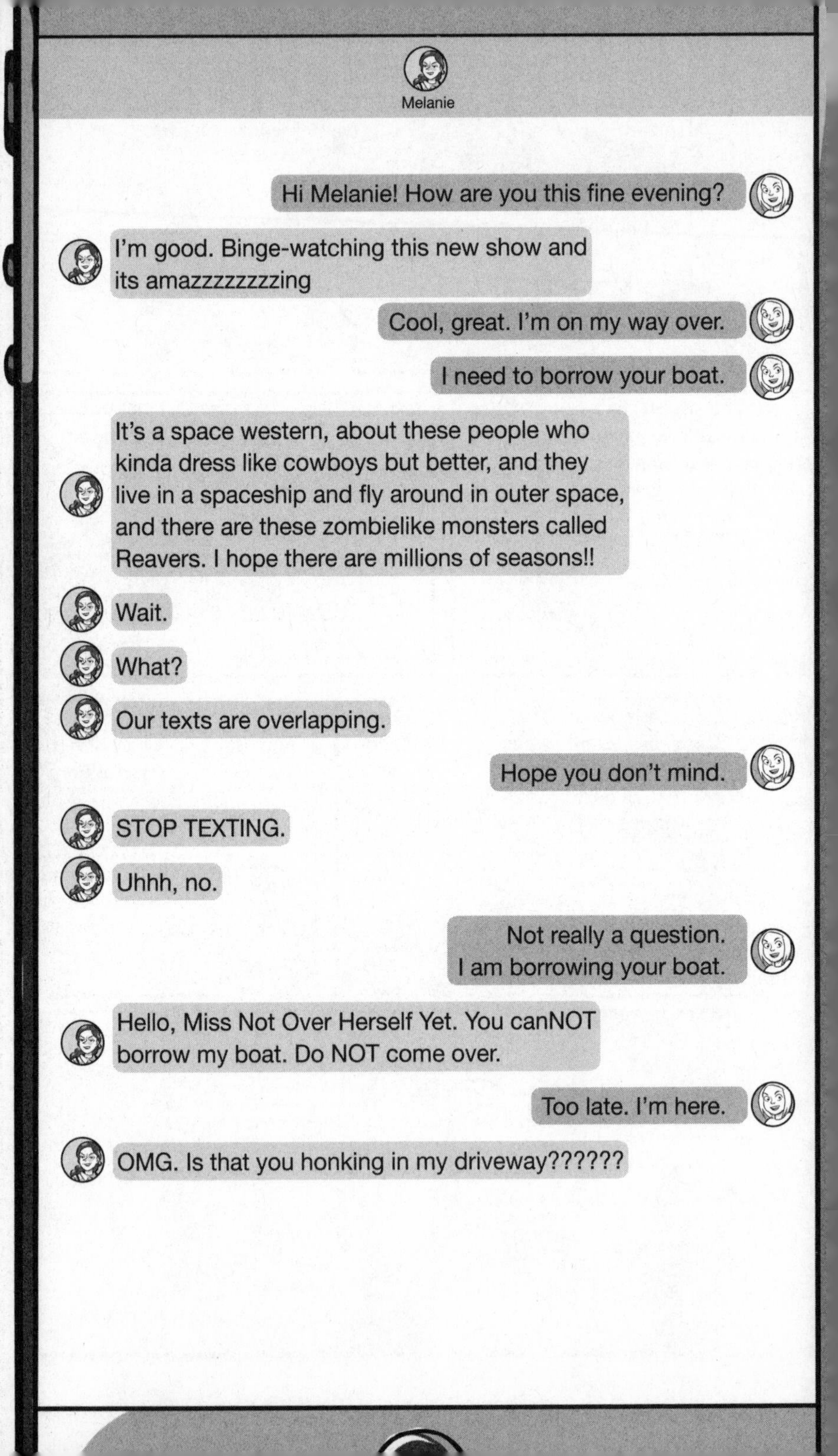

Hi Melanie! How are you this fine evening?

 I'm good. Binge-watching this new show and its amazzzzzzzzing

Cool, great. I'm on my way over.

I need to borrow your boat.

 It's a space western, about these people who kinda dress like cowboys but better, and they live in a spaceship and fly around in outer space, and there are these zombielike monsters called Reavers. I hope there are millions of seasons!!

 Wait.

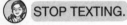 What?

 Our texts are overlapping.

Hope you don't mind.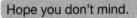

 STOP TEXTING.

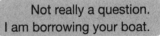 Uhhh, no.

Not really a question.
I am borrowing your boat.

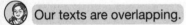 Hello, Miss Not Over Herself Yet. You canNOT borrow my boat. Do NOT come over.

Too late. I'm here.

OMG. Is that you honking in my driveway??????

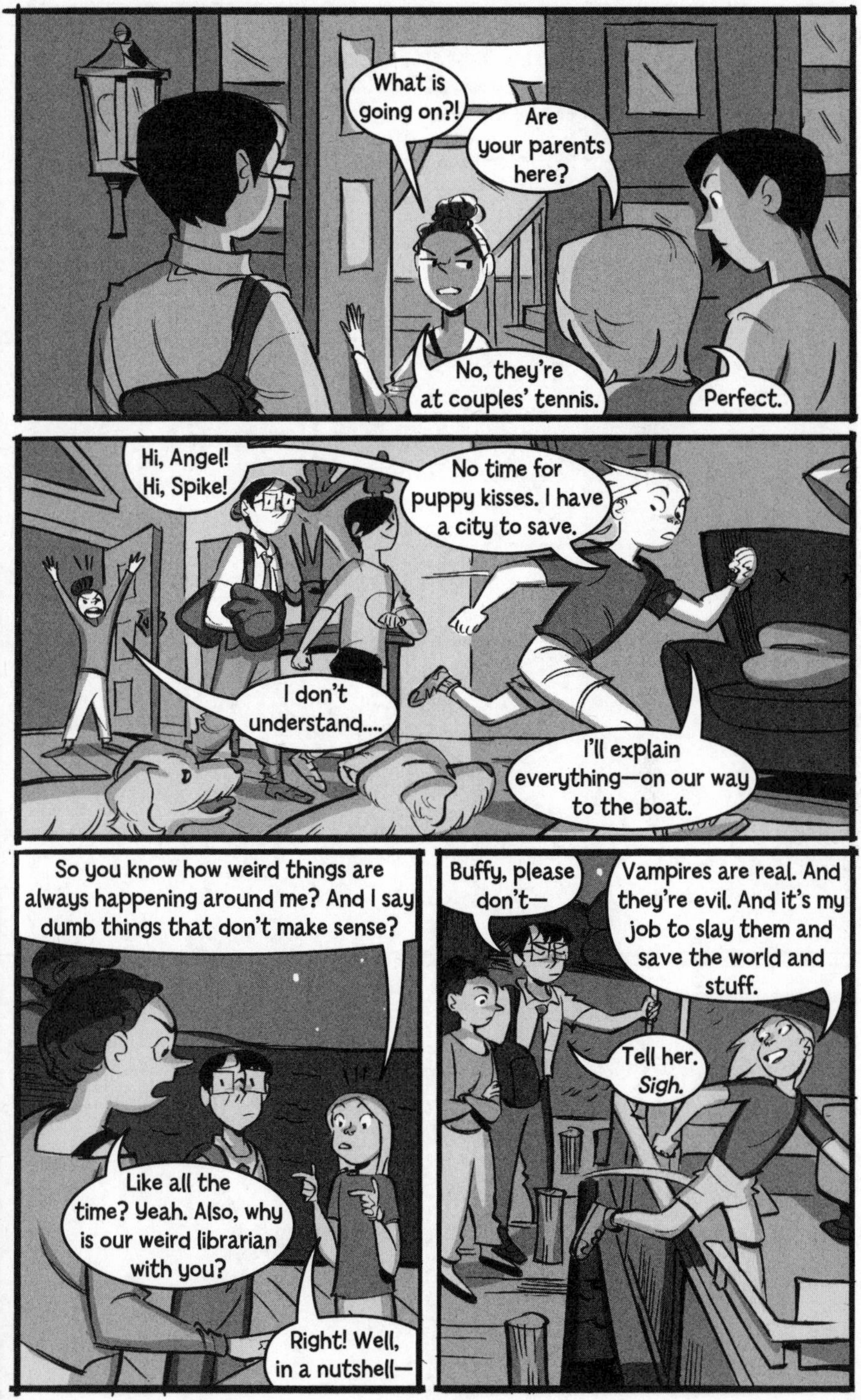
What is going on?!
Are your parents here?
No, they're at couples' tennis.
Perfect.
Hi, Angel! Hi, Spike!
No time for puppy kisses. I have a city to save.
I don't understand....
I'll explain everything—on our way to the boat.
So you know how weird things are always happening around me? And I say dumb things that don't make sense?
Like all the time? Yeah. Also, why is our weird librarian with you?
Right! Well, in a nutshell—
Buffy, please don't—
Vampires are real. And they're evil. And it's my job to slay them and save the world and stuff.
Tell her. *Sigh.*

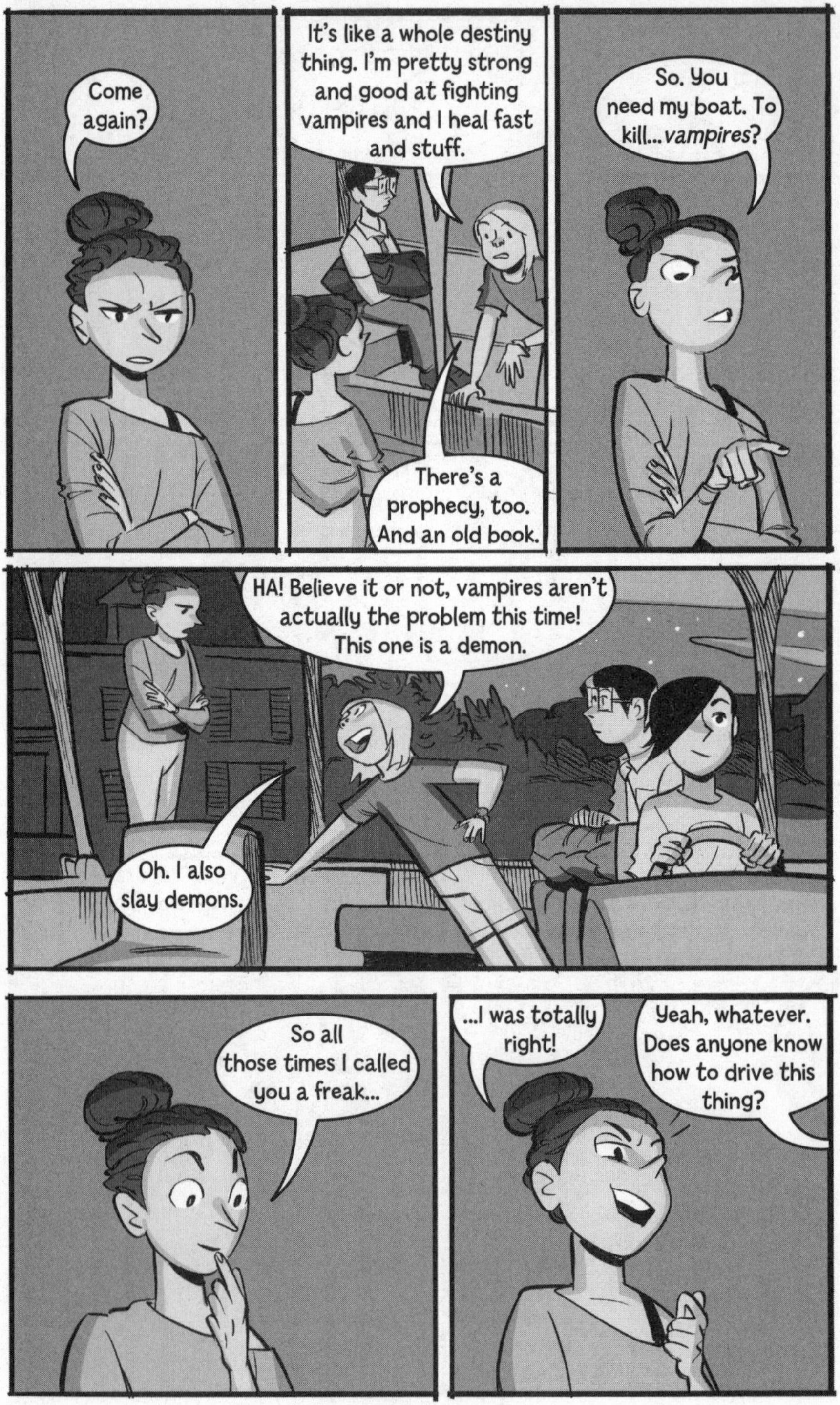
Come again?
It's like a whole destiny thing. I'm pretty strong and good at fighting vampires and I heal fast and stuff.
There's a prophecy, too. And an old book.
So. You need my boat. To kill...*vampires*?
HA! Believe it or not, vampires aren't actually the problem this time! This one is a demon.
Oh. I also slay demons.
So all those times I called you a freak...
...I was totally right!
Yeah, whatever. Does anyone know how to drive this thing?

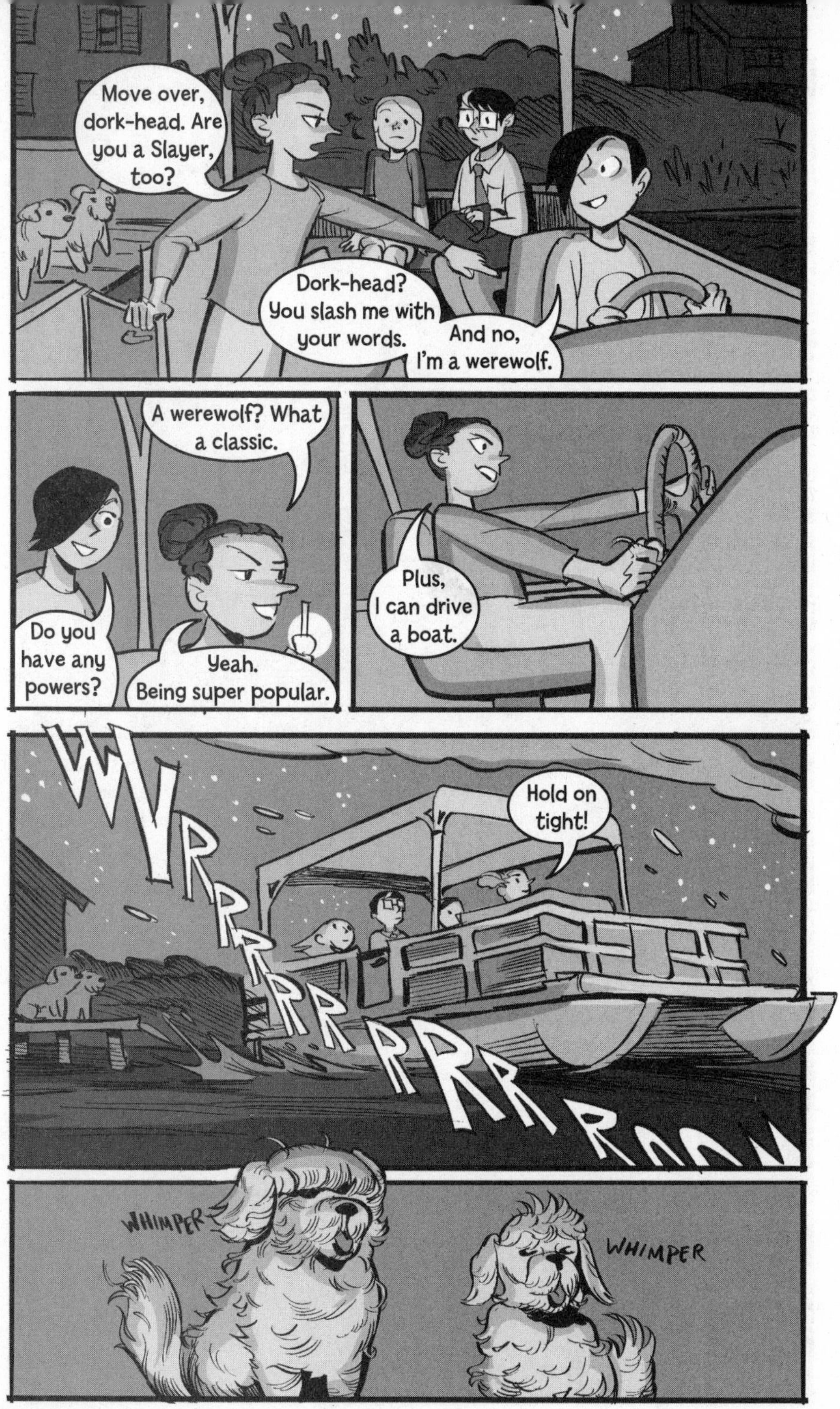
Move over, dork-head. Are you a Slayer, too?
Dork-head? You slash me with your words.
And no, I'm a werewolf.
A werewolf? What a classic.
Do you have any powers?
Yeah. Being super popular.
Plus, I can drive a boat.
Hold on tight!
WVRRRRRRRRRRRRROOO
WHIMPER
WHIMPER

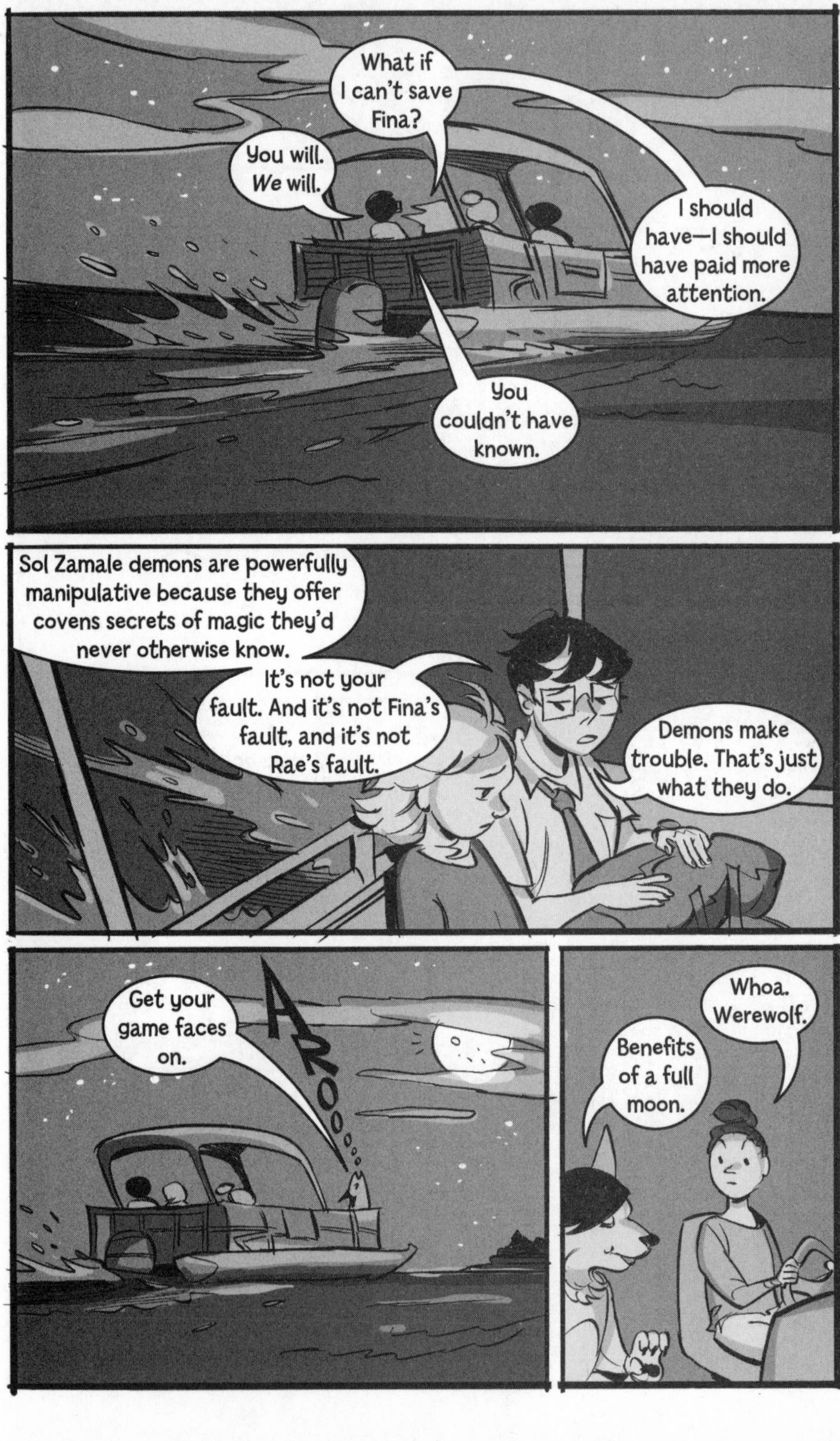
What if I can't save Fina?
You will. *We* will.
I should have—I should have paid more attention.
You couldn't have known.
Sol Zamale demons are powerfully manipulative because they offer covens secrets of magic they'd never otherwise know.
It's not your fault. And it's not Fina's fault, and it's not Rae's fault.
Demons make trouble. That's just what they do.
Get your game faces on.
AROOOOOO
Whoa. Werewolf.
Benefits of a full moon.

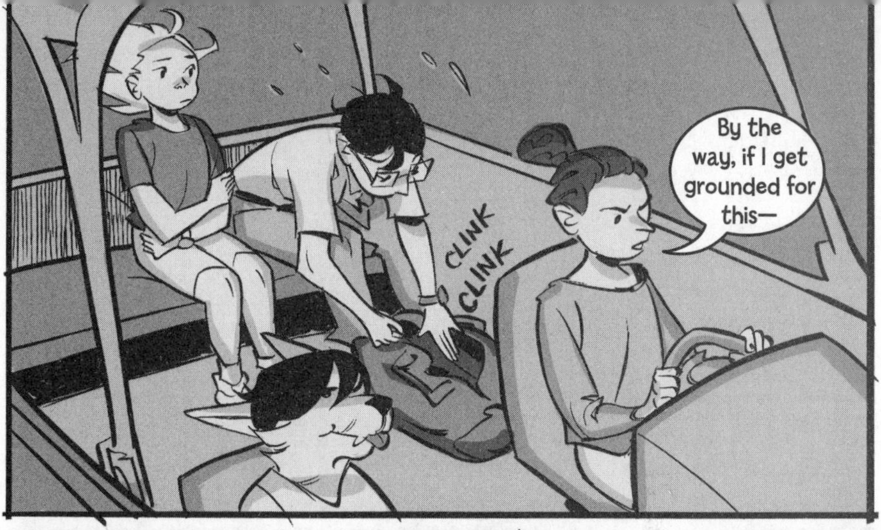
CLINK
CLINK
By the way, if I get grounded for this—

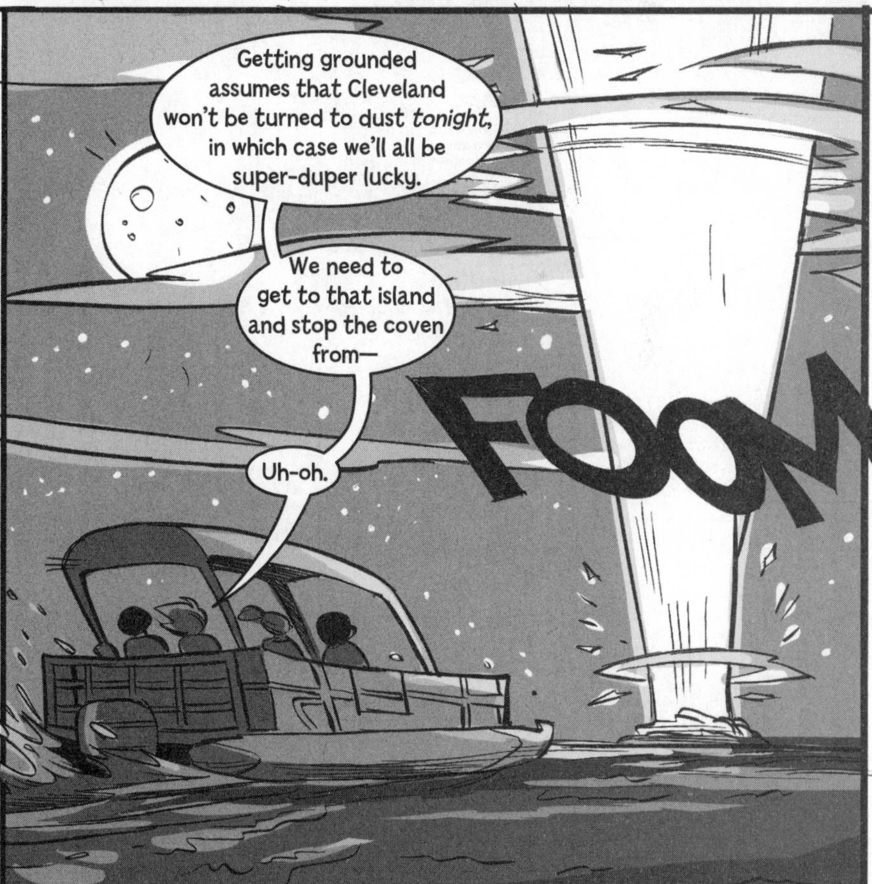
Getting grounded assumes that Cleveland won't be turned to dust *tonight*, in which case we'll all be super-duper lucky.
We need to get to that island and stop the coven from—
FOOM
Uh-oh.

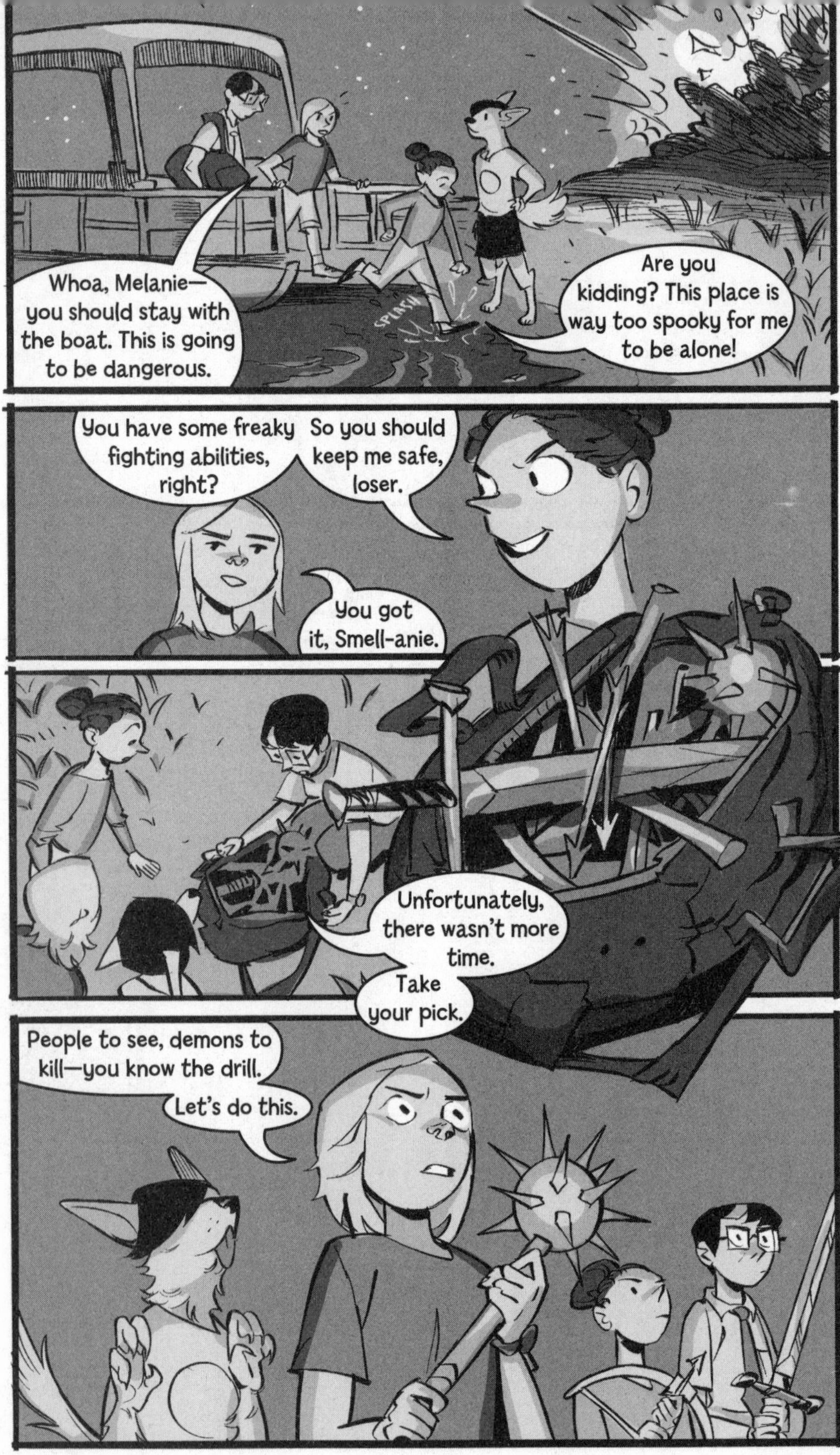
Whoa, Melanie—you should stay with the boat. This is going to be dangerous.
SPLASH
Are you kidding? This place is way too spooky for me to be alone!
You have some freaky fighting abilities, right?
So you should keep me safe, loser.
You got it, Smell-anie.
Unfortunately, there wasn't more time.
Take your pick.
People to see, demons to kill—you know the drill.
Let's do this.

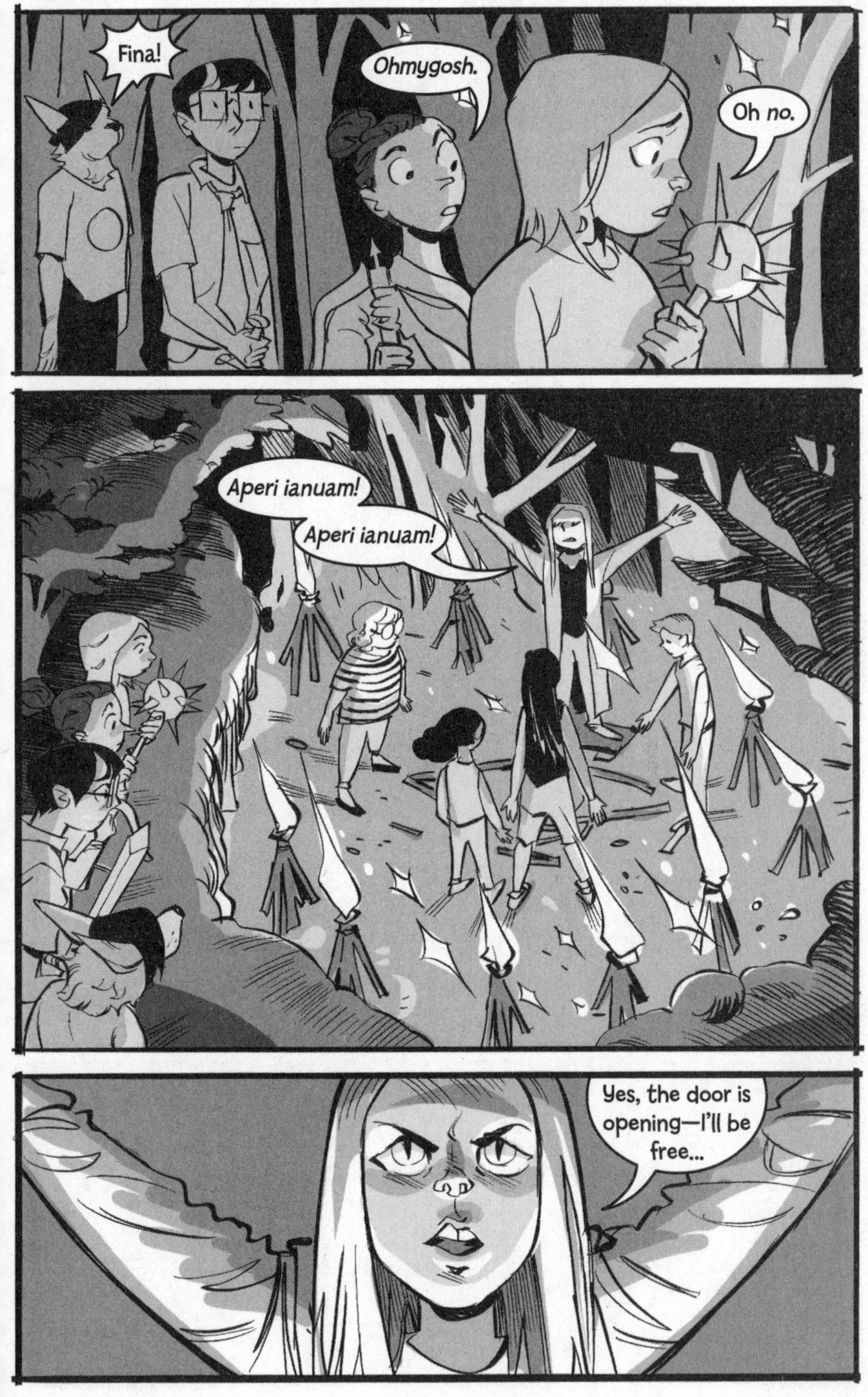
Fina!
Ohmygosh.
Oh no.
Aperi ianuam!
Aperi ianuam!
Yes, the door is opening—I'll be free...

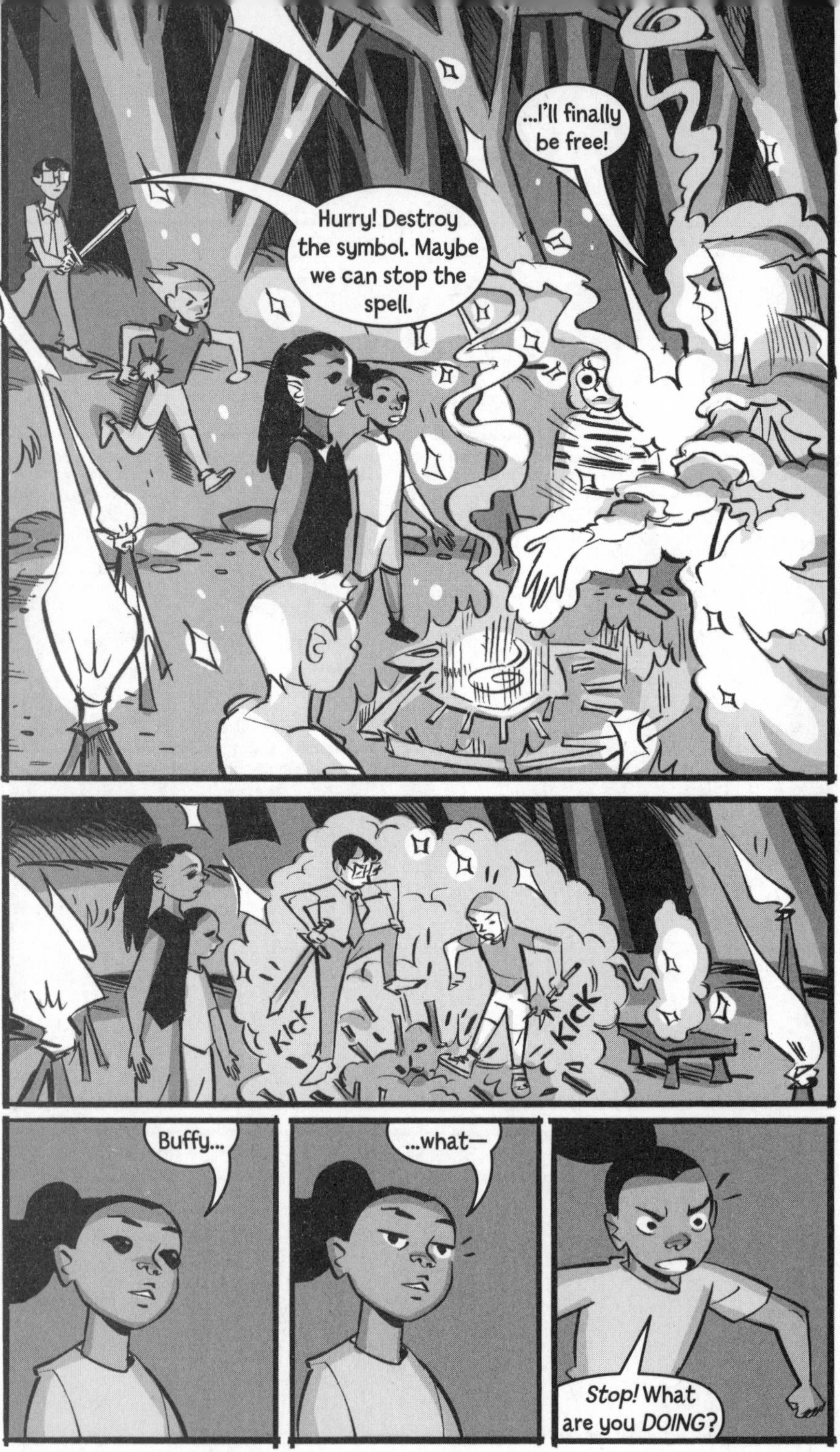
Hurry! Destroy the symbol. Maybe we can stop the spell.
...I'll finally be free!
KICK
KICK
Buffy...
...what—
Stop! What are you *DOING*?

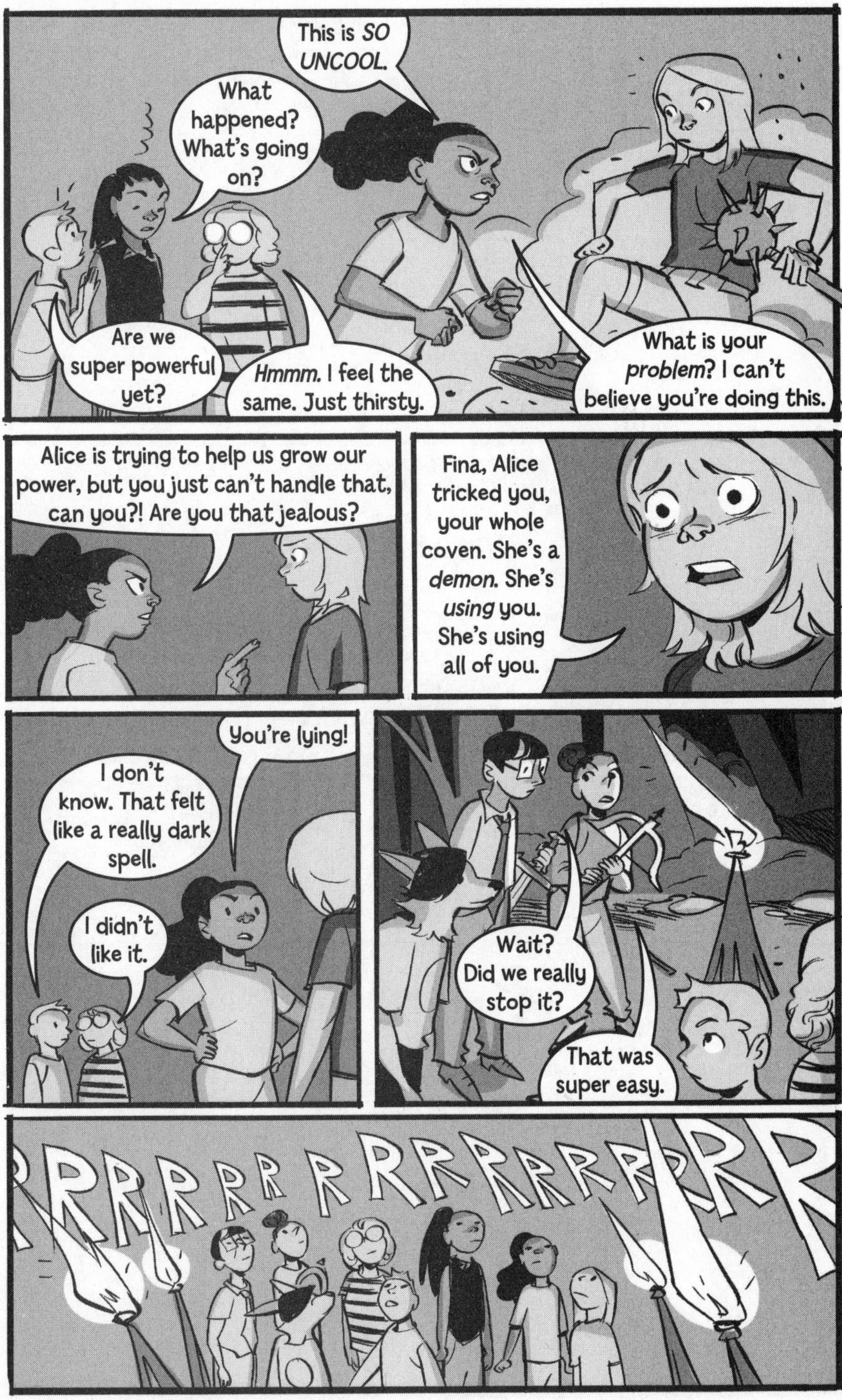
What happened? What's going on?
This is *SO UNCOOL.*
Are we super powerful yet?
Hmmm. I feel the same. Just thirsty.
What is your *problem*? I can't believe you're doing this.
Alice is trying to help us grow our power, but you just can't handle that, can you?! Are you that jealous?
Fina, Alice tricked you, your whole coven. She's a *demon.* She's *using* you. She's using all of you.
You're lying!
I don't know. That felt like a really dark spell.
I didn't like it.
Wait? Did we really stop it?
That was super easy.
RRRRRRRRRRRRRRRRR

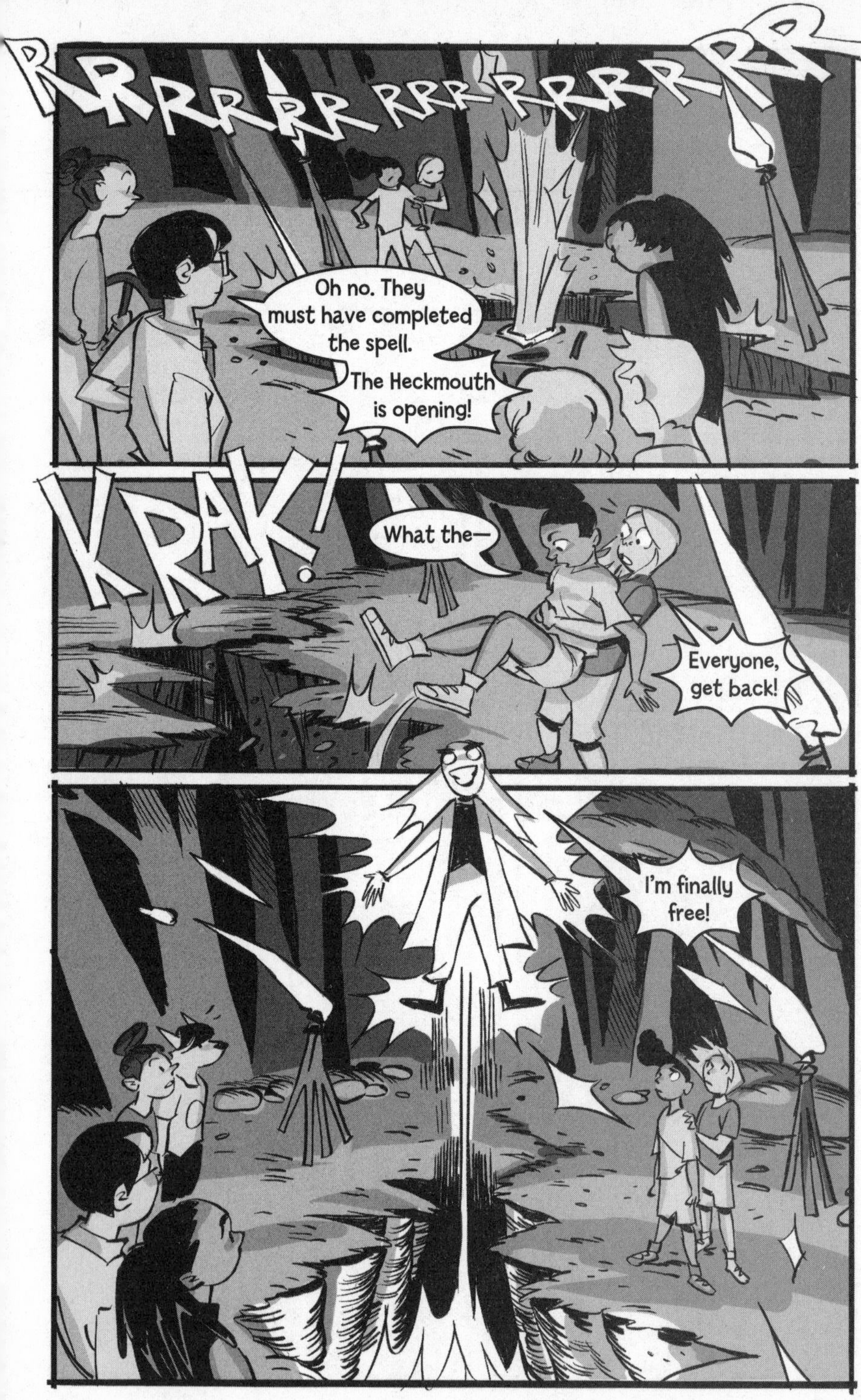
RRRRRRR RRRRRRRRRRR
Oh no. They must have completed the spell.
The Heckmouth is opening!
KRAK!
What the—
Everyone, get back!
I'm finally free!

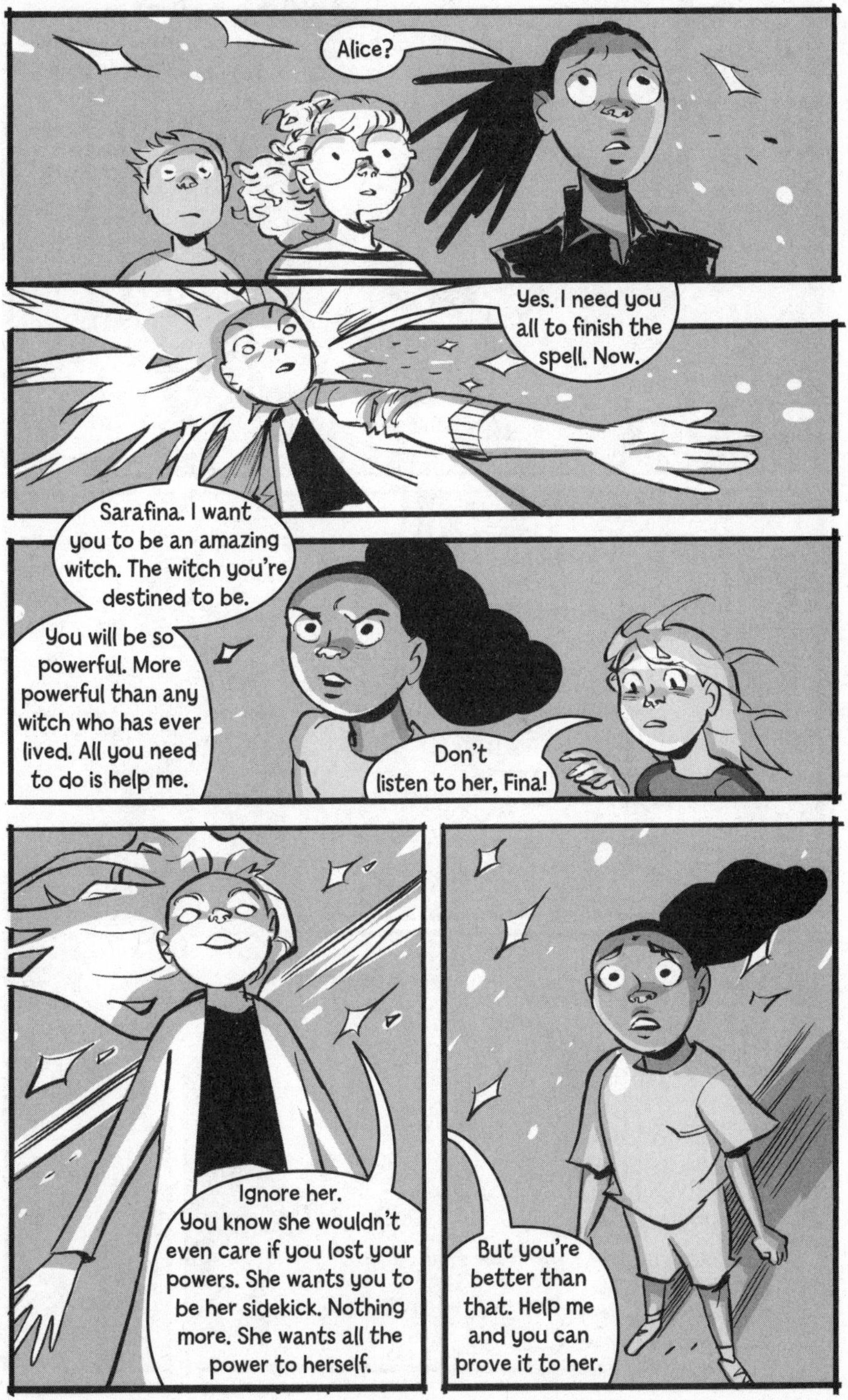
Alice?
Yes. I need you all to finish the spell. Now.
Sarafina. I want you to be an amazing witch. The witch you're destined to be.
You will be so powerful. More powerful than any witch who has ever lived. All you need to do is help me.
Don't listen to her, Fina!
Ignore her. You know she wouldn't even care if you lost your powers. She wants you to be her sidekick. Nothing more. She wants all the power to herself.
But you're better than that. Help me and you can prove it to her.

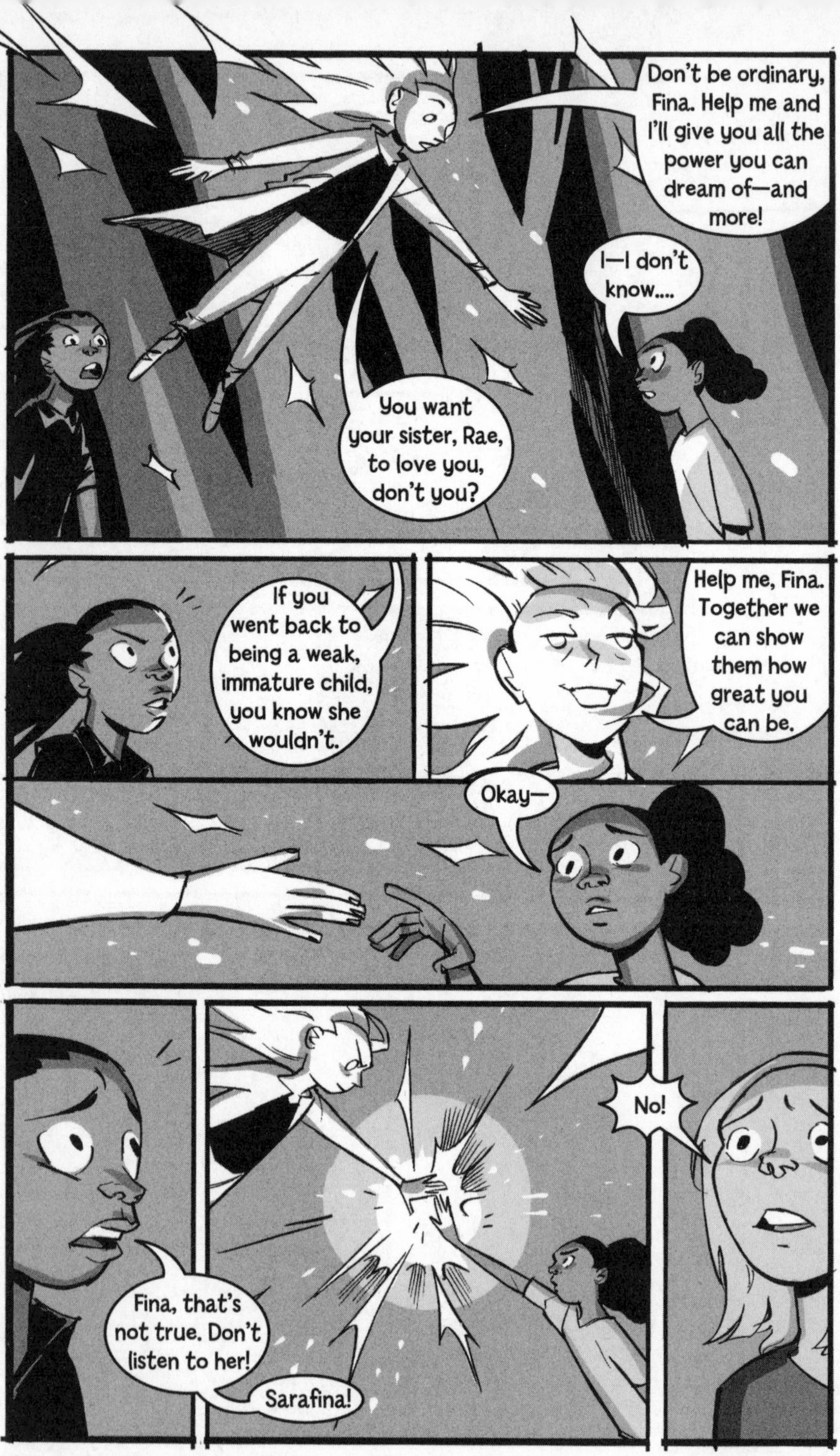
Don't be ordinary, Fina. Help me and I'll give you all the power you can dream of—and more!
I—I don't know....
You want your sister, Rae, to love you, don't you?
If you went back to being a weak, immature child, you know she wouldn't.
Help me, Fina. Together we can show them how great you can be.
Okay—
Fina, that's not true. Don't listen to her!
Sarafina!
No!

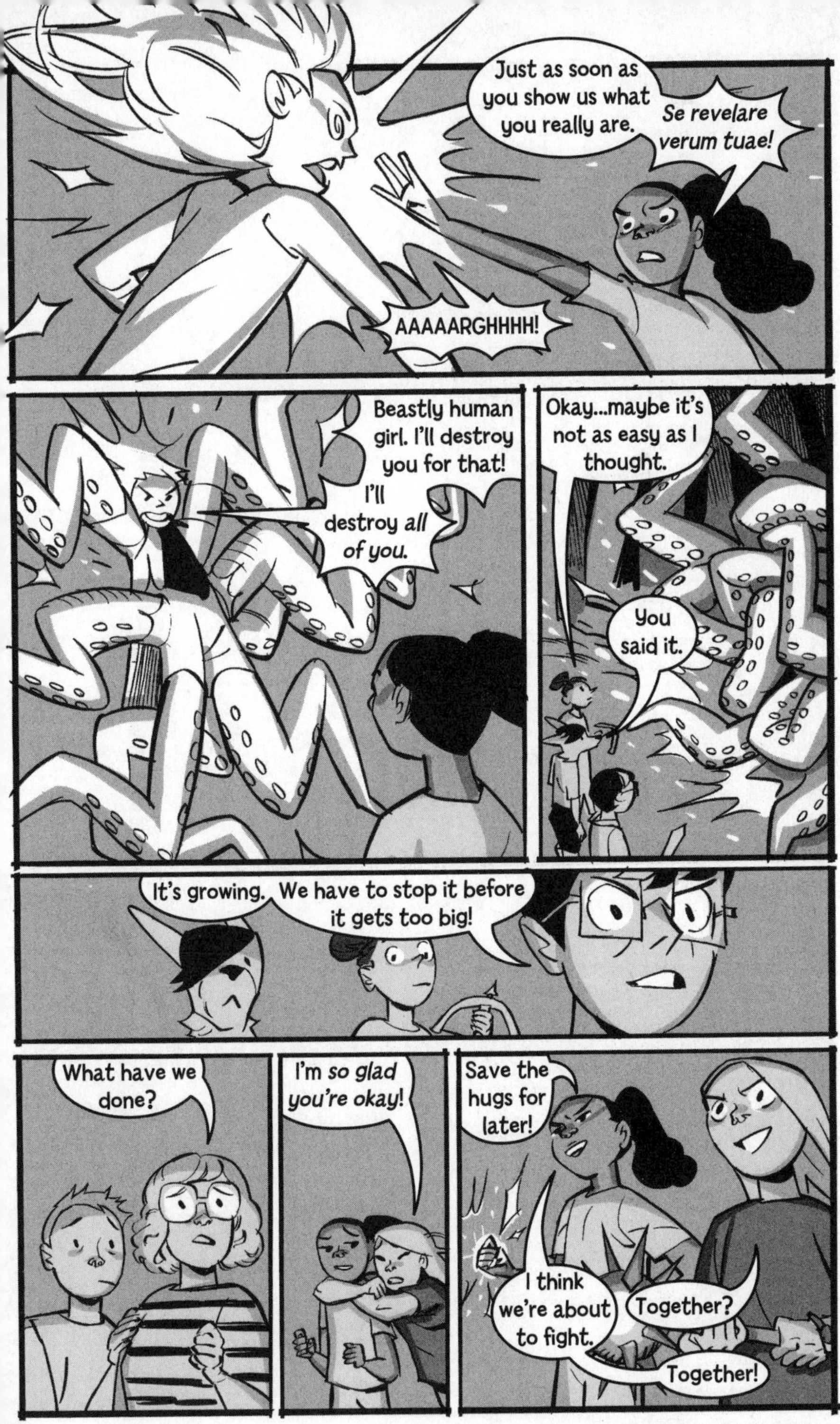
Just as soon as you show us what you really are.
Se revelare verum tuae!
AAAAARGHHHH!
Beastly human girl. I'll destroy you for that!
I'll destroy *all* of you.
Okay...maybe it's not as easy as I thought.
You said it.
It's growing.
We have to stop it before it gets too big!
What have we done?
I'm so *glad you're okay*!
Save the hugs for later!
I think we're about to fight.
Together?
Together!

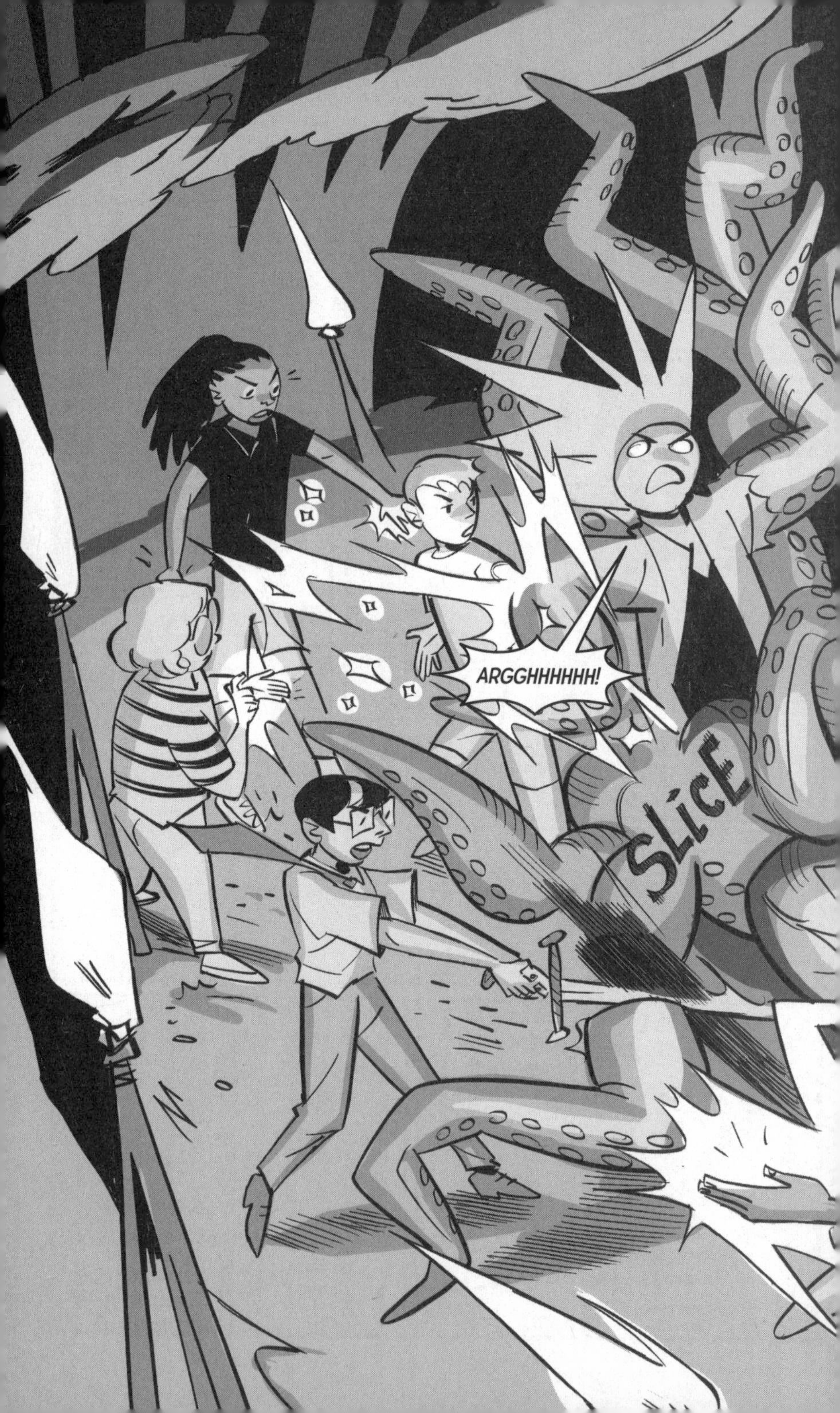
ARGGHHHHHH!
SLICE

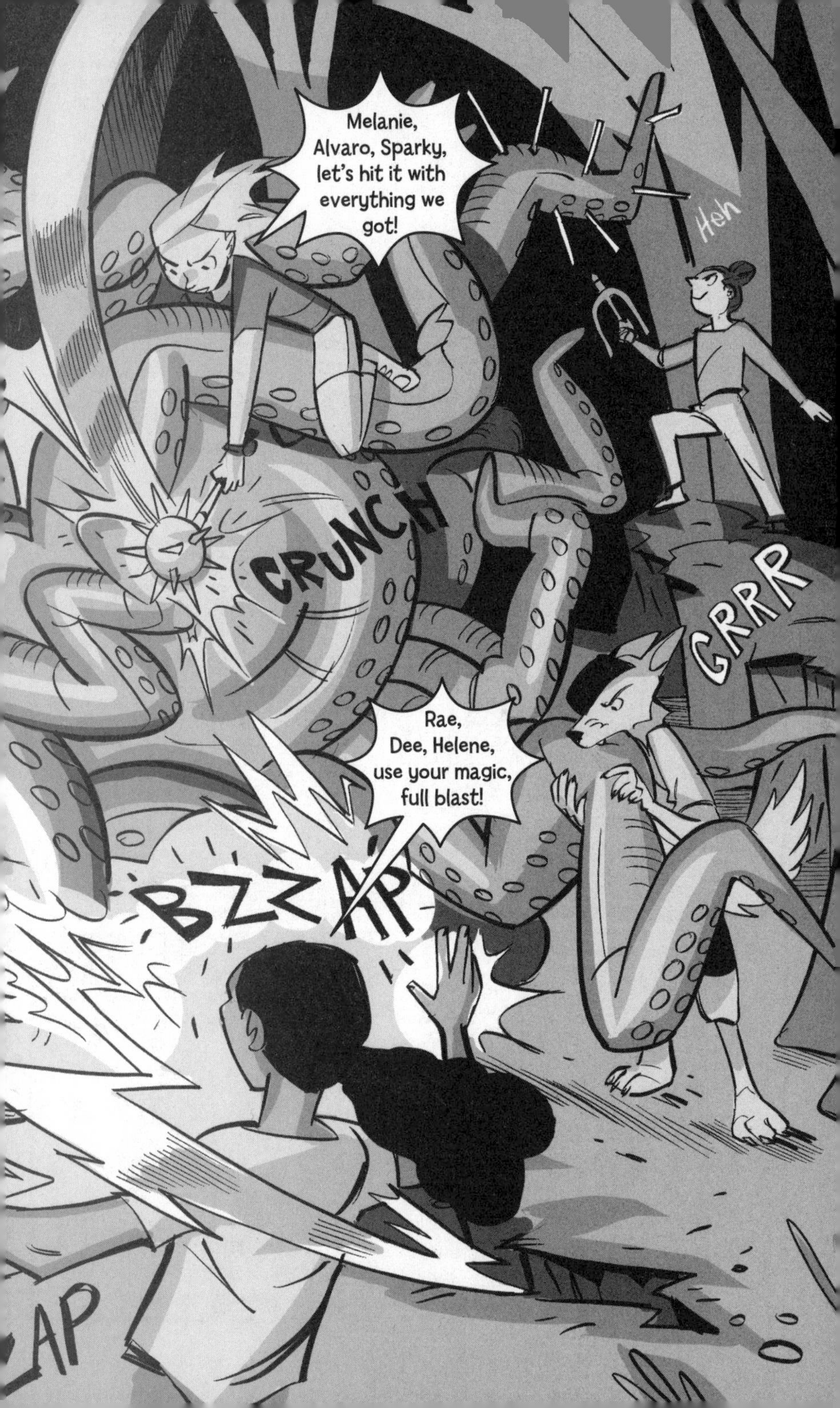

Melanie, Alvaro, Sparky, let's hit it with everything we got!
Heh
CRUNCH
GRRR
Rae, Dee, Helene, use your magic, full blast!
BZZAP
AP

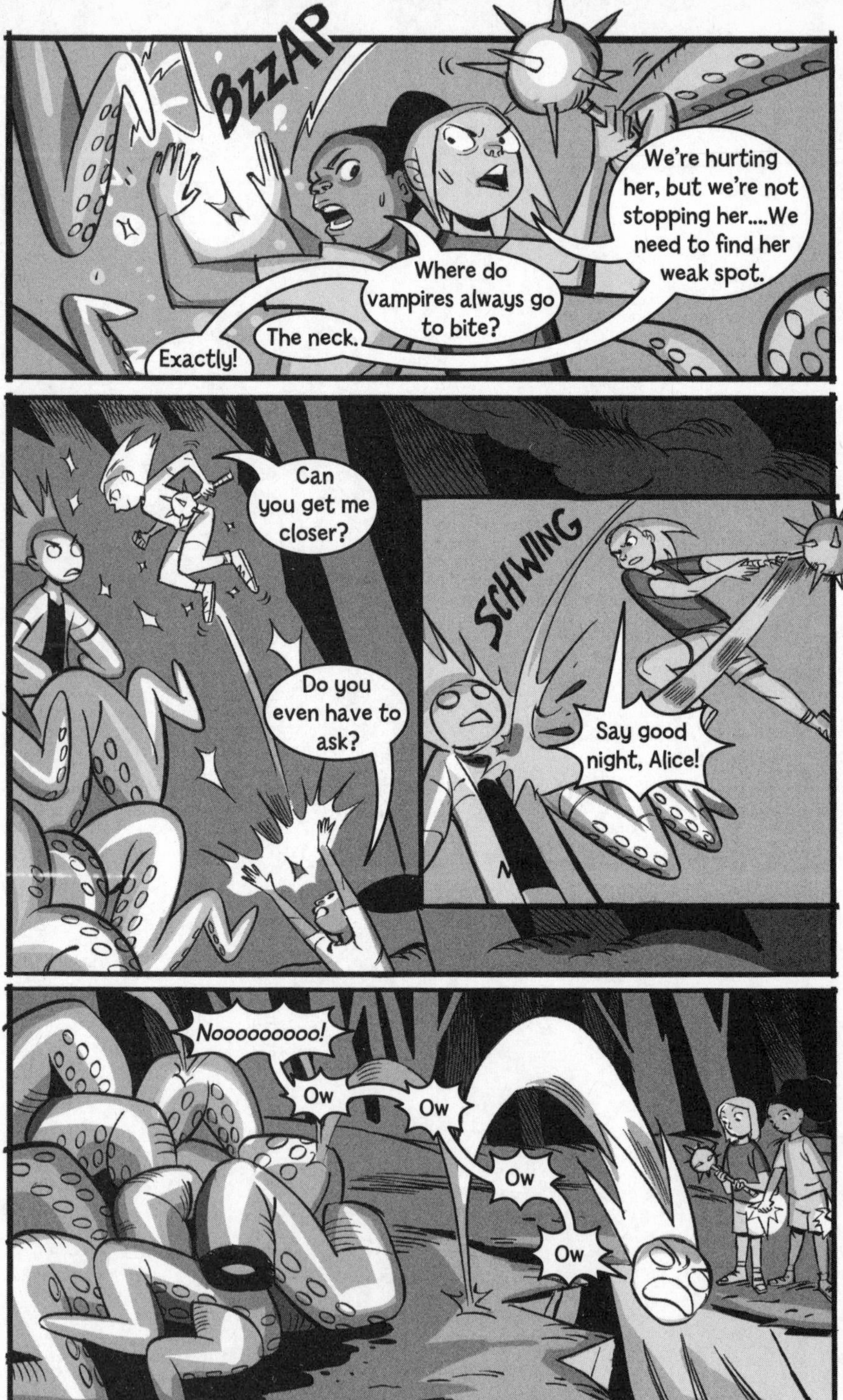
BZZAP
We're hurting her, but we're not stopping her....We need to find her weak spot.
Where do vampires always go to bite?
The neck.
Exactly!
Can you get me closer?
Do you even have to ask?
SCHWING
Say good night, Alice!
Nooooooooo!
Ow
Ow
Ow
Ow

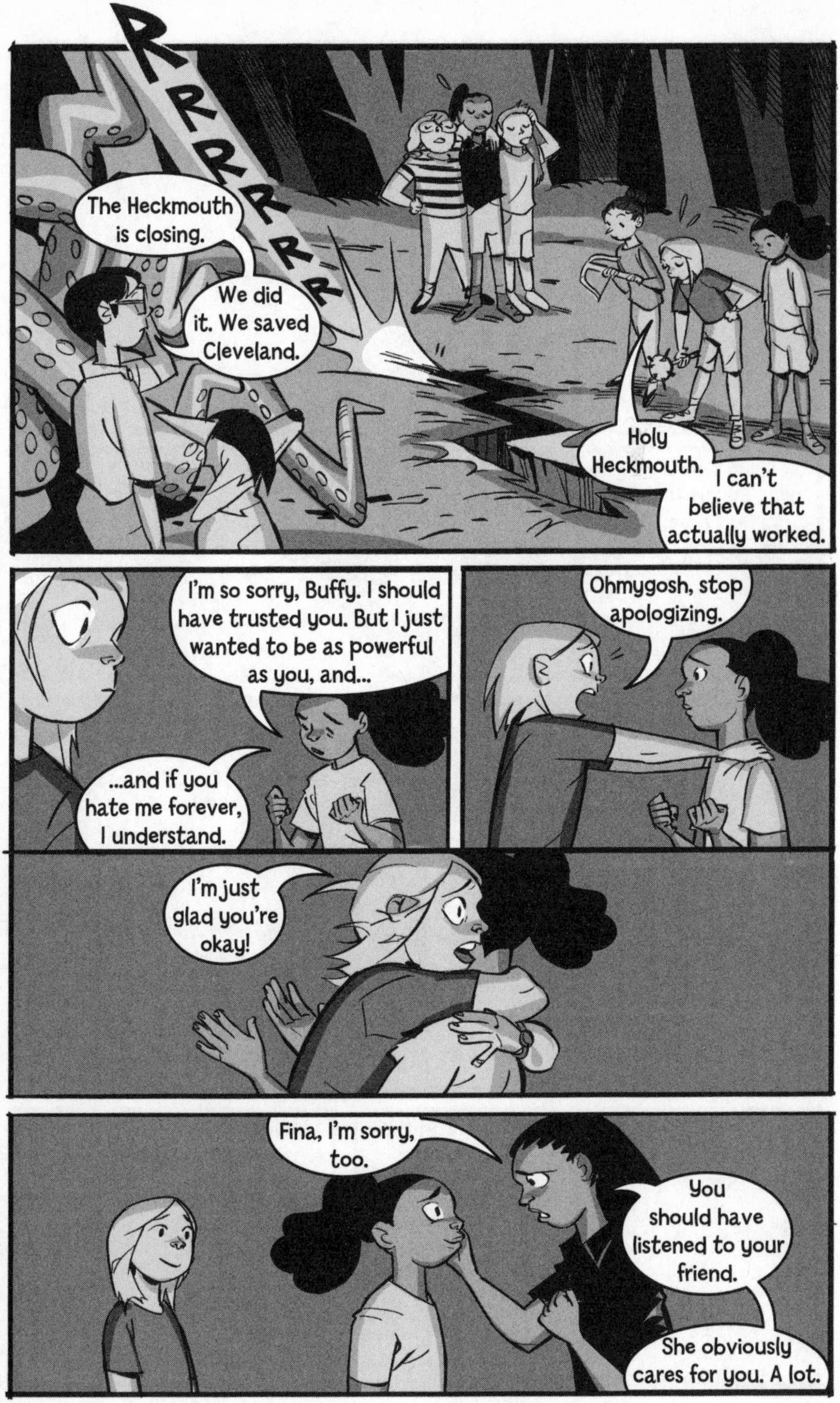
RRRRRRR
The Heckmouth is closing.
We did it. We saved Cleveland.
Holy Heckmouth.
I can't believe that actually worked.
I'm so sorry, Buffy. I should have trusted you. But I just wanted to be as powerful as you, and...
...and if you hate me forever, I understand.
Ohmygosh, stop apologizing.
I'm just glad you're okay!
Fina, I'm sorry, too.
You should have listened to your friend.
She obviously cares for you. A lot.

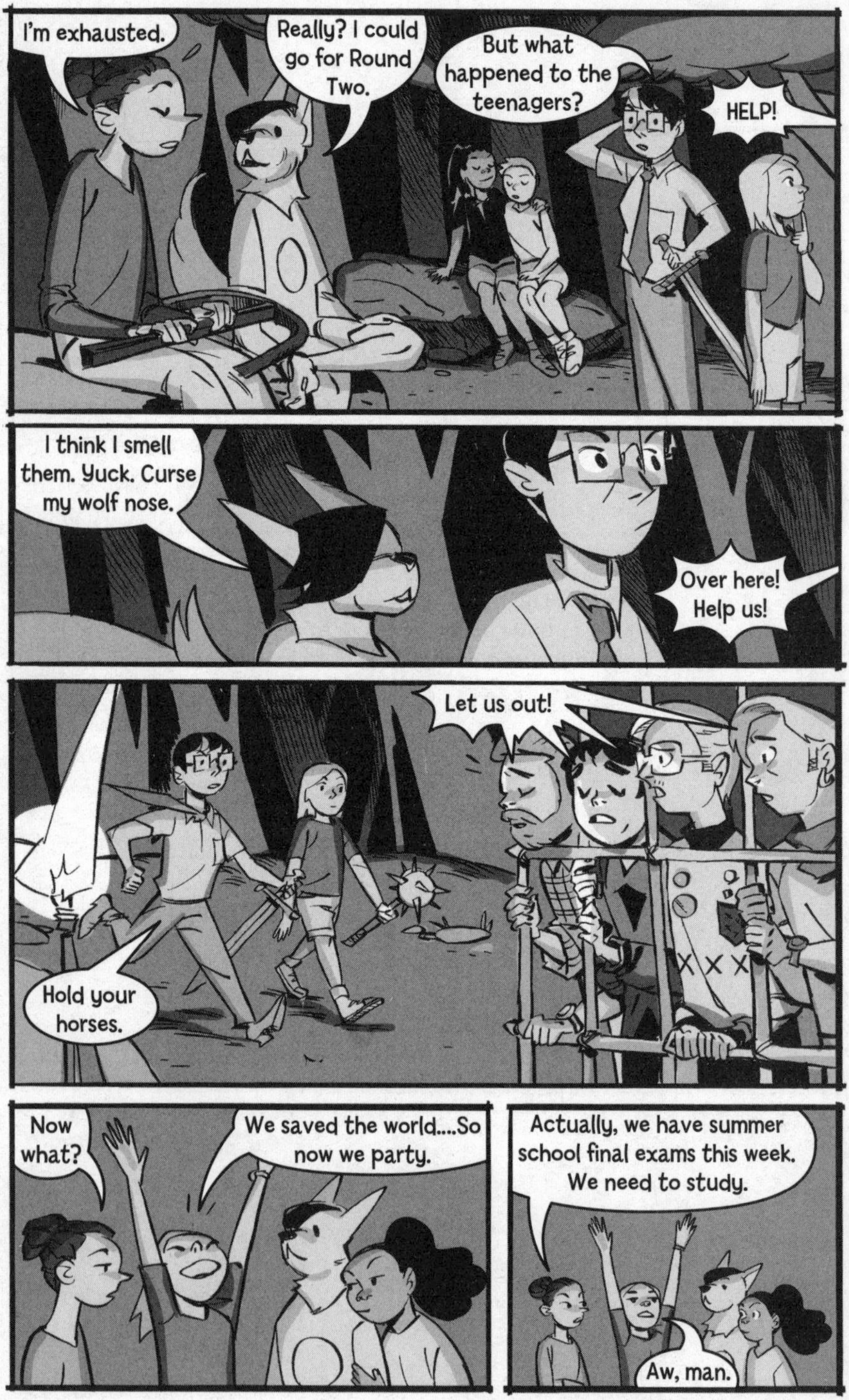
I'm exhausted.
Really? I could go for Round Two.
But what happened to the teenagers?
HELP!
I think I smell them. Yuck. Curse my wolf nose.
Over here! Help us!
Let us out!
Hold your horses.
Now what?
We saved the world....So now we party.
Actually, we have summer school final exams this week. We need to study.
Aw, man.

Dear Diary,

I am <u>soooooooooooooooooooooooooooooooooooooooooooooooooooooooooooooooooooooooooooooooo</u> tired that I don't think I can write a whole page. I just wanted to say that we did it. We saved Fina and her coven and all of Cleveland, and we even found all those missing teenagers.

Sure, when I got home, Mom grounded me because I was out way past curfew, but hey, still saved the day. And being grounded is good, I guess. Now I have nothing to do this week but study. Which I'm going to need to do if I want to pass summer school.

Also, Fina isn't mad at me anymore. She apologized, like, a thousand times, and I was like, "Stop! We're okay!" And we <u>are</u> okay. Everything is okay. As long as I pass summer school. If I don't, it really will be the end of the world, cuz Mom will go <u>BALLISTIC</u>.

Yawn. Funny how killing monsters and saving the day makes me so sleepy.

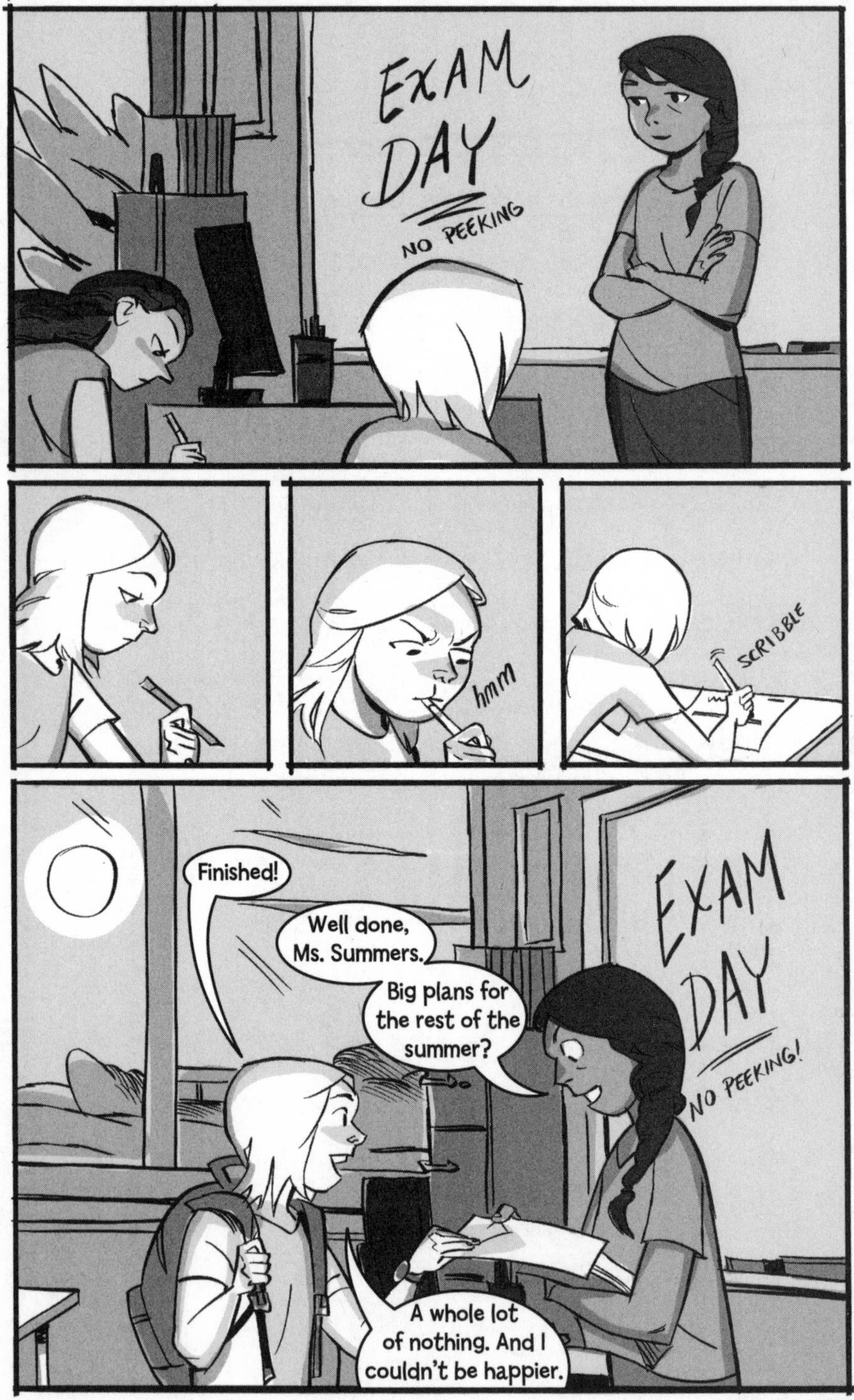
EXAM DAY
NO PEEKING
hmm
SCRIBBLE
Finished!
Well done, Ms. Summers.
Big plans for the rest of the summer?
EXAM DAY
NO PEEKING!
A whole lot of nothing. And I couldn't be happier.

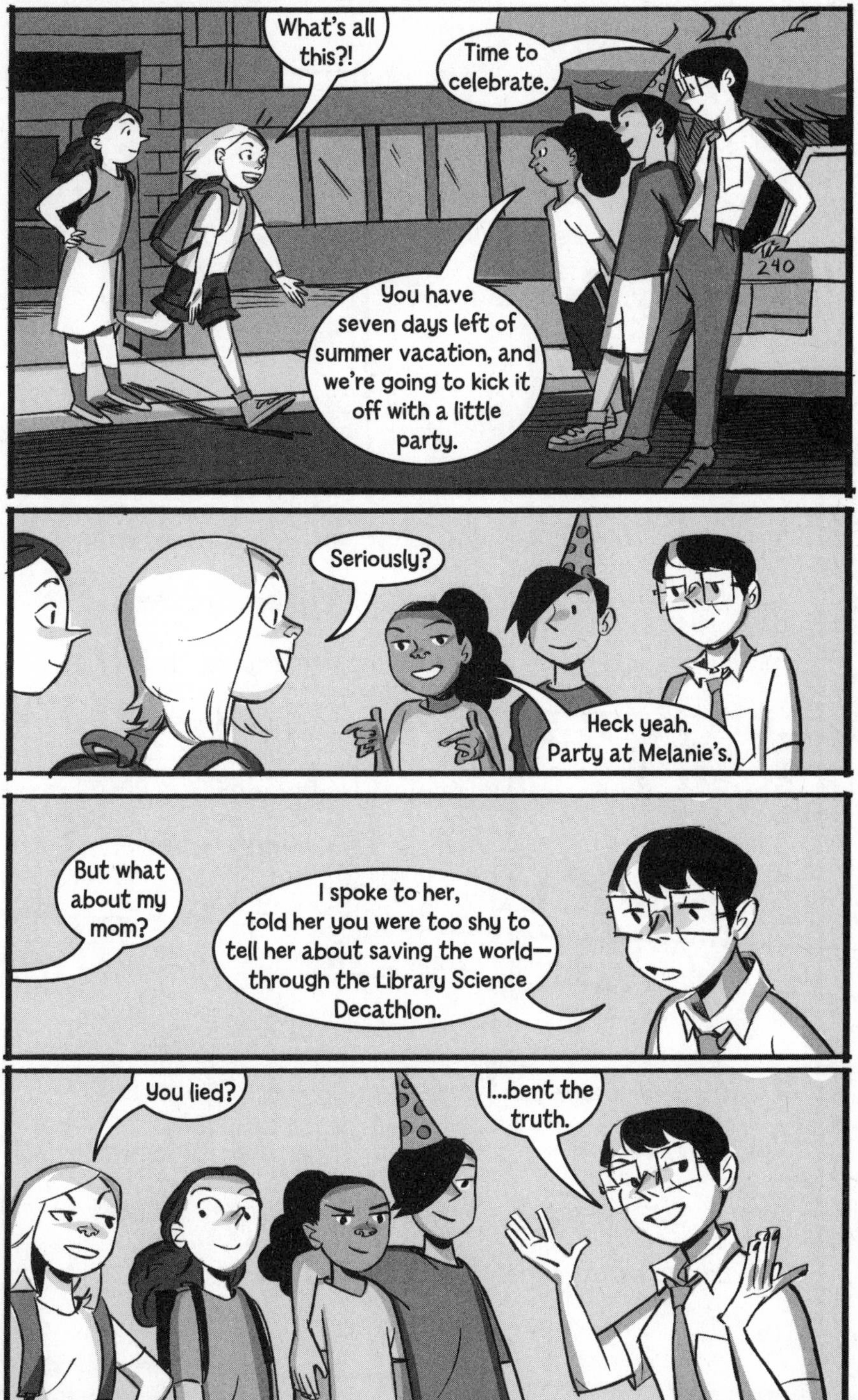

What's all this?!
Time to celebrate.
You have seven days left of summer vacation, and we're going to kick it off with a little party.
240
Seriously?
Heck yeah. Party at Melanie's.
But what about my mom?
I spoke to her, told her you were too shy to tell her about saving the world—through the Library Science Decathlon.
You lied?
I...bent the truth.

My dearest Diary,

You're alive because my friends and I saved the whole city of Cleveland from certain fiery destruction. And after a victorious battle (and a

terrifying test), we did what any band of heroes would do—we went back to Melanie's house and pool-partied. There were root-beer floats,

hamburgers, hot dogs, all kinds of chips, more fancy little lemonades, water-gun fights, and even a dance-off.

I tell ya, not being dead puts me in such a good mood. Oh my gosh, even Fina and Melanie were getting along. Do we have another Scooby to add to our gang? I mean, she's not a

werewolf and she can't do magic and she doesn't have any prophecies written about her, but she <u>does</u> have a boat and a pool. I guess when you save the world together, it kinda bonds you, which is pretty neat.

As far as Alice goes, Sparky and Rae's coven have checked out the Heckmouth door a few times, and it's sealed shut. Turns out Helene used the wrong kind of wood in the spell, so the

door was never gonna stay open anyway. Funny how things work out, huh?

What else? Oh, Fina asked me to come over before Rae went back to college. Rae felt really bad about the whole inviting-a-demon-into-their-coven thing. But Fina was really nice to her and said it bonded them. Rae may be in college, but I swear that Fina is the mature one in that relationship.

Anyway, tomorrow I get my grades. Cross your fingers. Oh yeah, you're a book. Cross your pages, I guess?

HUGS,
Buffy

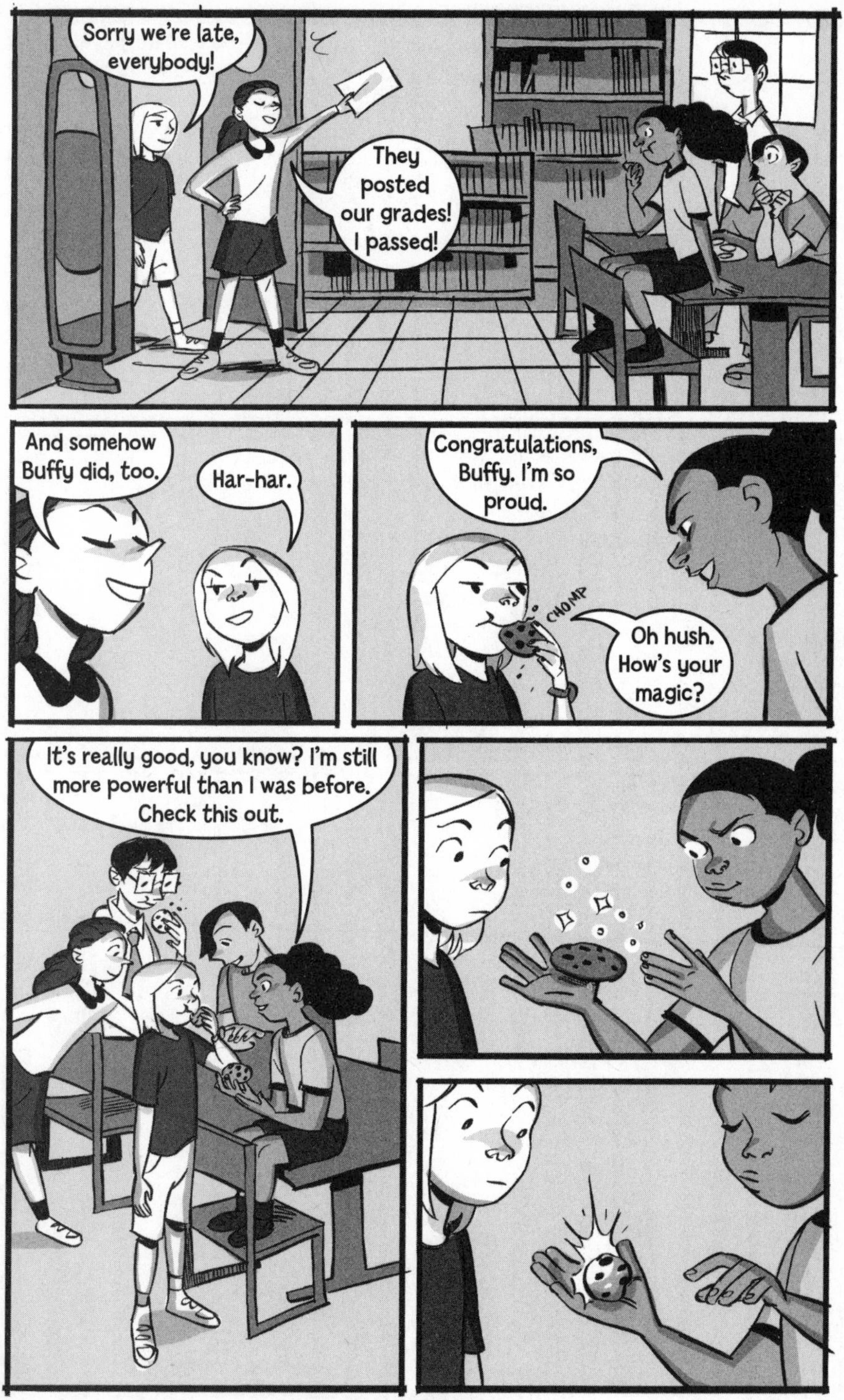

Sorry we're late, everybody!
They posted our grades! I passed!
And somehow Buffy did, too.
Har-har.
Congratulations, Buffy. I'm so proud.
CHOMP
Oh hush. How's your magic?
It's really good, you know? I'm still more powerful than I was before. Check this out.

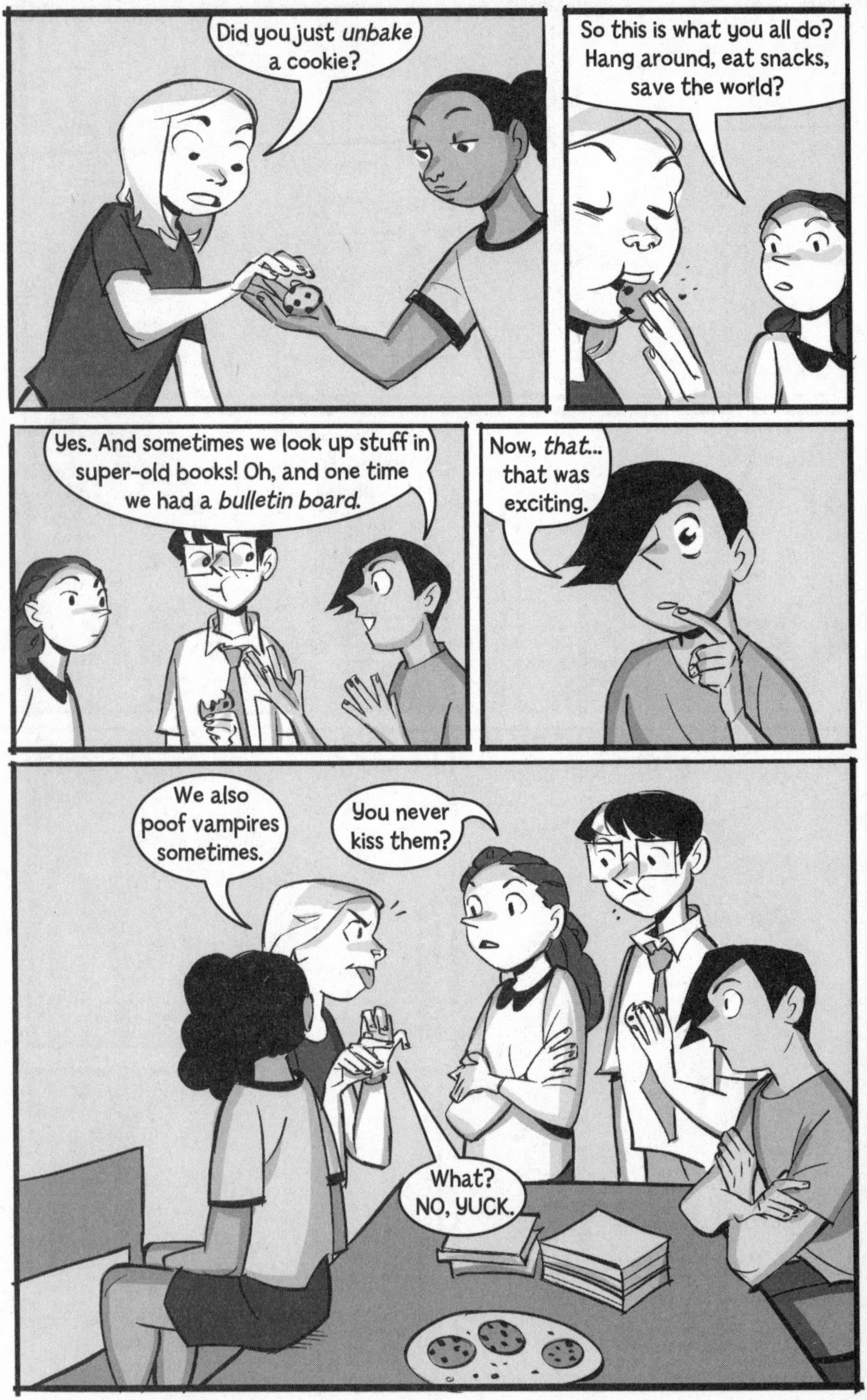
Did you just *unbake* a cookie?
So this is what you all do? Hang around, eat snacks, save the world?
Yes. And sometimes we look up stuff in super-old books! Oh, and one time we had a *bulletin board*.
Now, *that*... that was exciting.
We also poof vampires sometimes.
You never kiss them?
What? NO, YUCK.

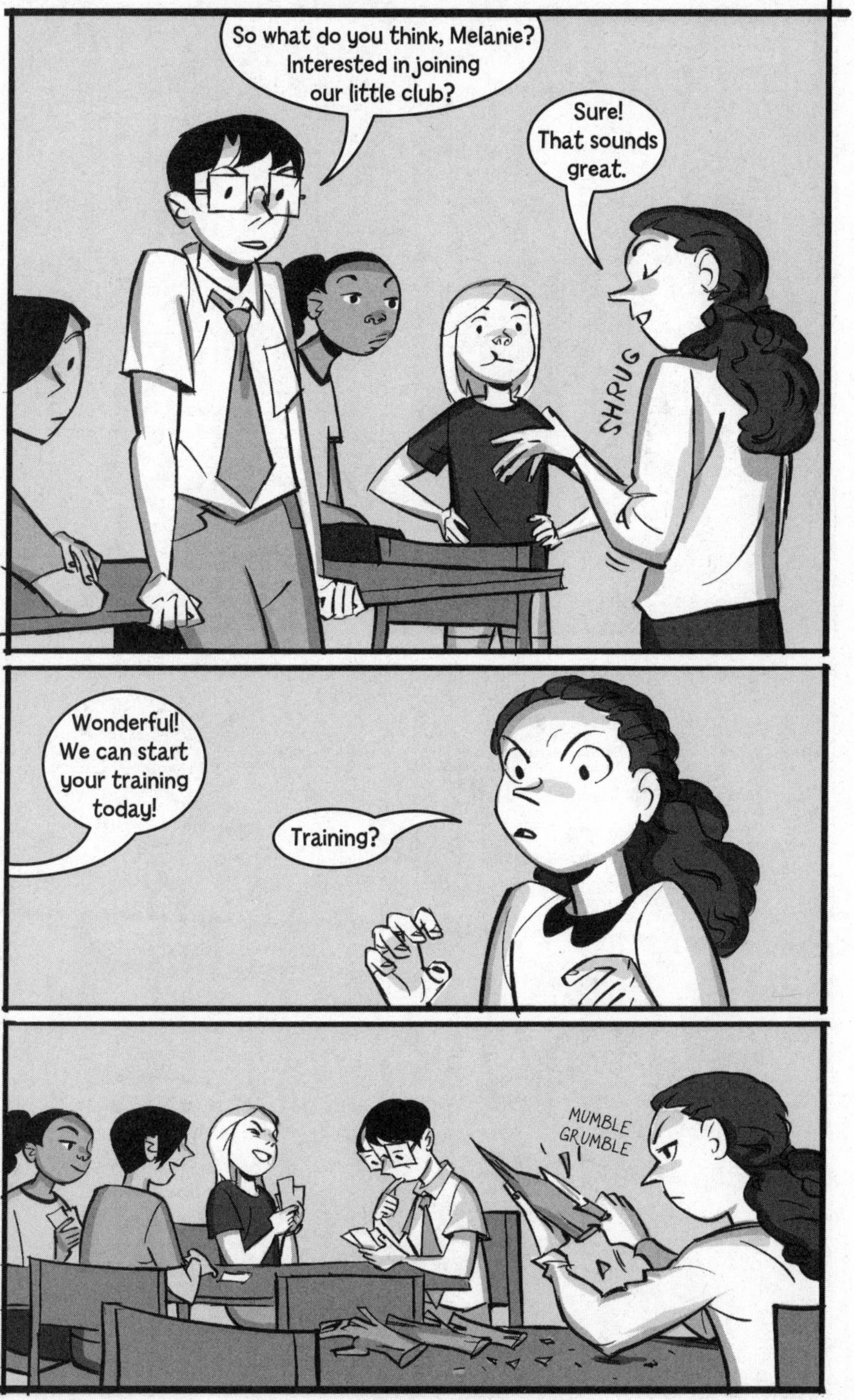
So what do you think, Melanie? Interested in joining our little club?
Sure! That sounds great.
SHRUG
Wonderful! We can start your training today!
Training?
MUMBLE GRUMBLE

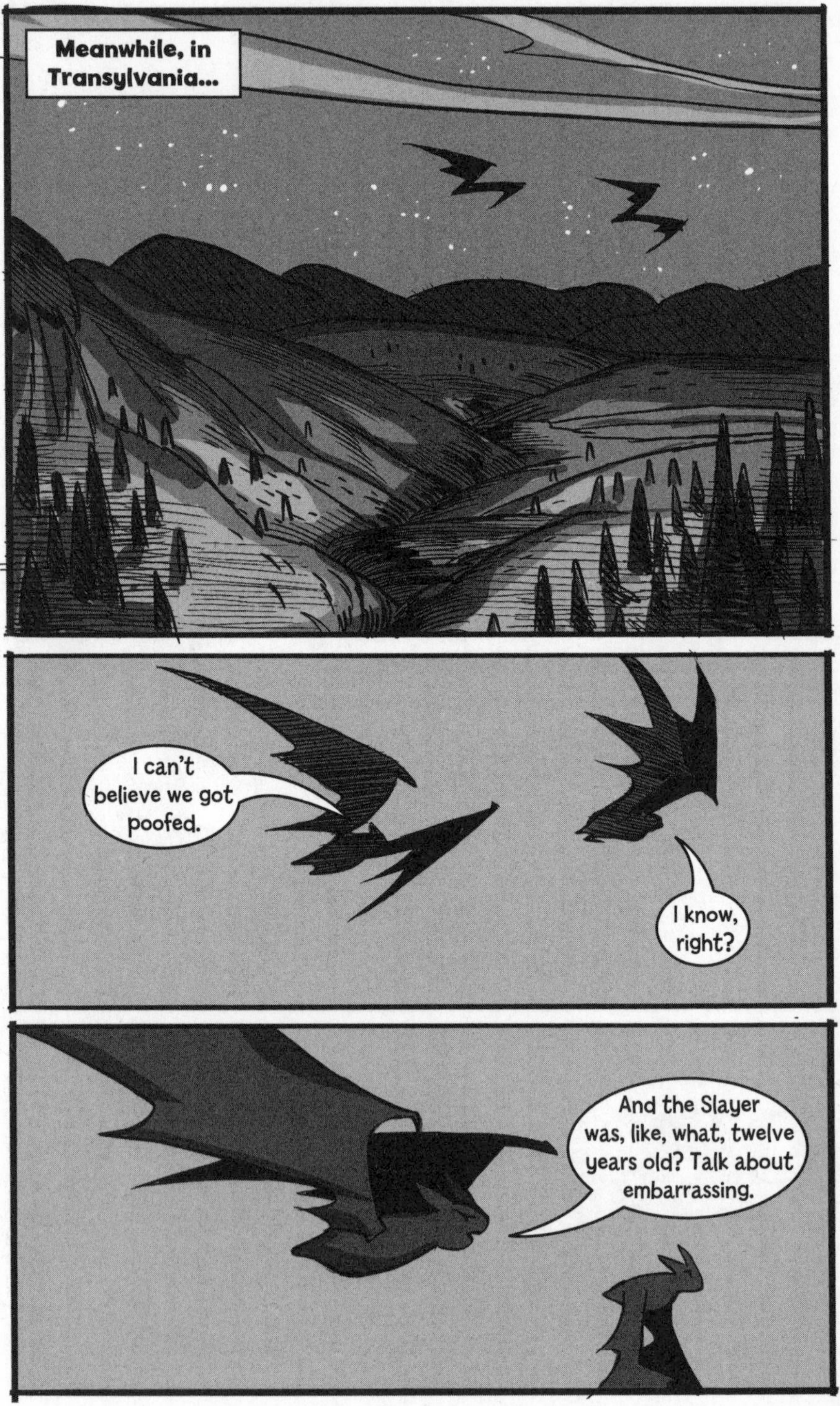
Meanwhile, in Transylvania...
I can't believe we got poofed.
I know, right?
And the Slayer was, like, what, twelve years old? Talk about embarrassing.

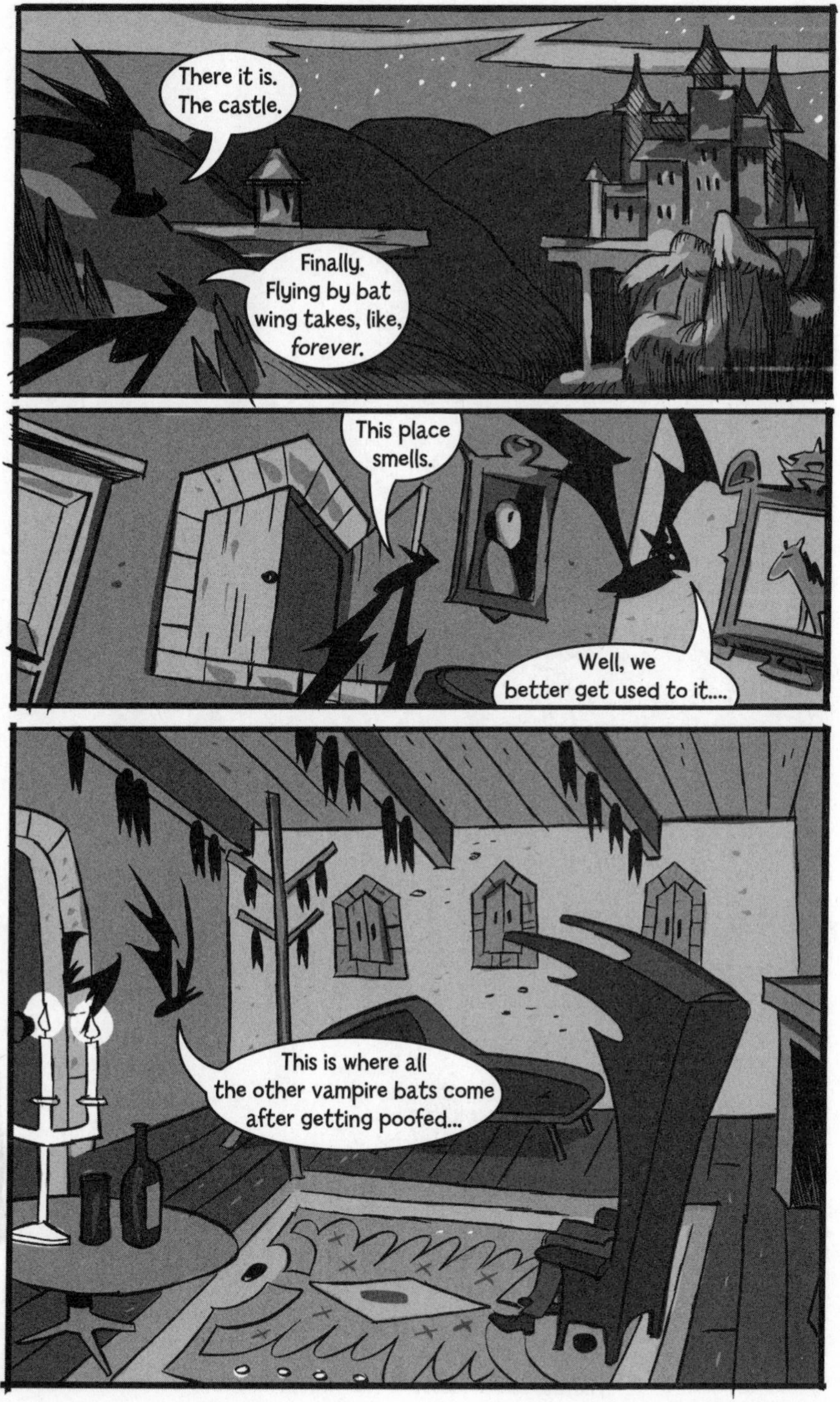
There it is. The castle.
Finally. Flying by bat wing takes, like, *forever.*
This place smells.
Well, we better get used to it....
This is where all the other vampire bats come after getting poofed...

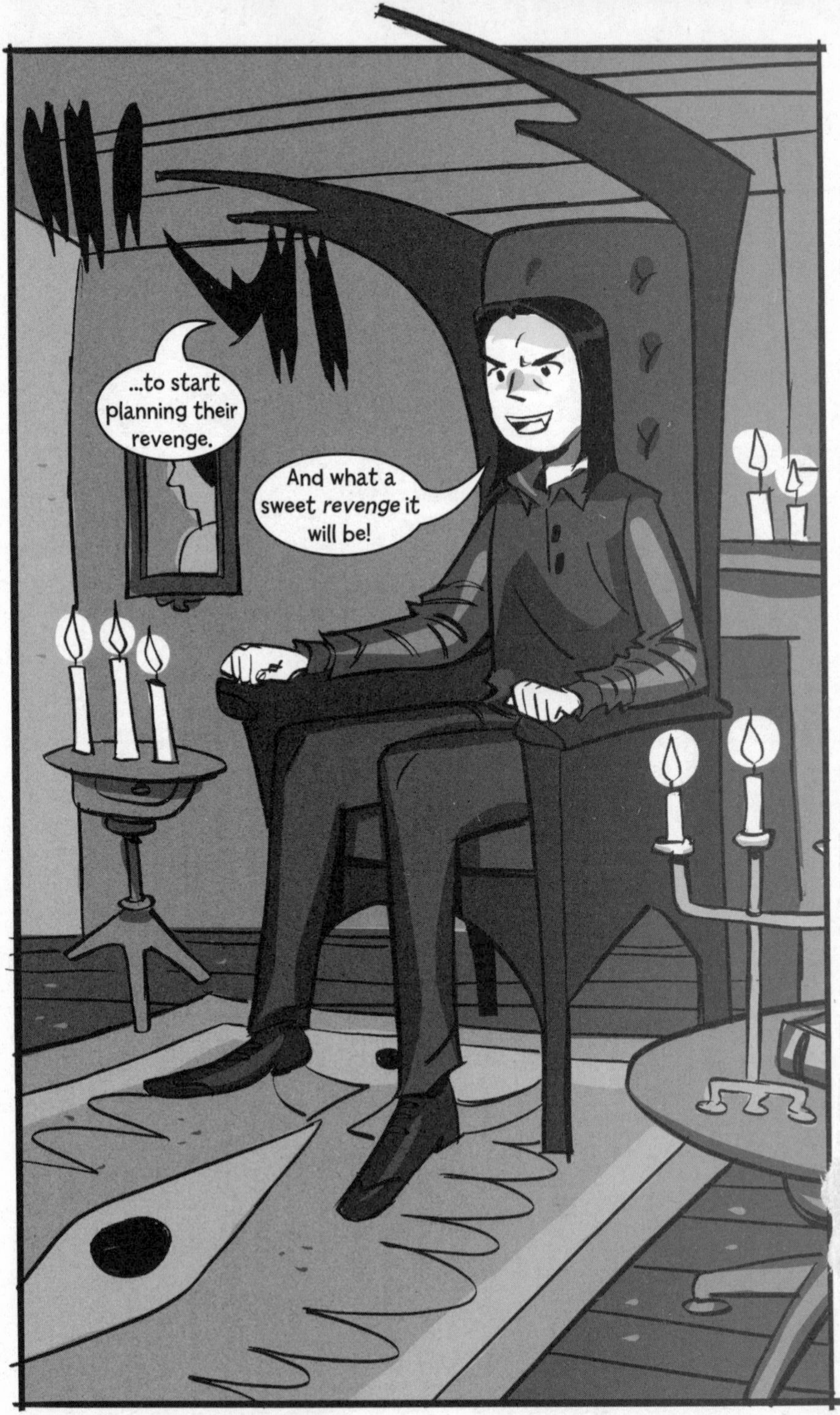

...to start planning their revenge.
And what a sweet *revenge* it will be!